‖‖‖‖‖‖‖‖‖‖‖‖‖‖‖‖‖‖‖‖‖‖‖

◁ **P9-AZX-644**

Family Reunion

The sight of it both sickened and mesmerized her. A creature huddled in the far corner, its legs drawn up against its massive chest, its head dropped down as it stared out at the world through burning eyes that glinted from beneath a jutting brow. From the depths of its throat an unending series of low moans was rising and falling, as if it were in some kind of unutterable pain. . . .

A scream rose in her throat but was choked off by the sudden realization that she was staring at her own son.

Bantam Books by John Saul
Ask your bookseller for the books you have missed

BRAINCHILD
CREATURE
THE GOD PROJECT
HELLFIRE
NATHANIEL
THE UNLOVED
THE UNWANTED

JOHN SAUL

CREATURE

BANTAM BOOKS
NEW YORK • TORONTO • LONDON • SYDNEY • AUCKLAND

CREATURE

A Bantam Book
Bantam hardcover edition / June 1989
Bantam paperback edition / June 1990

All rights reserved.
Copyright © 1989 by John Saul.
Cover art copyright © 1990 by Don Brautigam.
No part of this book may be reproduced or transmitted
in any form or by any means, electronic or mechanical,
including photocopying, recording, or by any information
storage and retrieval system, without permission in
writing from the publisher.
For information address: Bantam Books.

Library of Congress Cataloging-in-Publication Data

Saul, John.
  Creature.

  I. Title.
PS3569.A787C74   1989   813'.54   88-7770
ISBN 0-553-28411-8

Published simultaneously in the United States and Canada

Bantam Books are published by Bantam Books, a division of Bantam Doubleday Dell
Publishing Group, Inc. Its trademark, consisting of the words ''Bantam Books'' and the
portrayal of a rooster, is Registered in U.S. Patent and Trademark Office and in other
countries. Marca Registrada. Bantam Books, 666 Fifth Avenue, New York, New York 10103.

PRINTED IN THE UNITED STATES OF AMERICA

RAI   0 9 8 7 6 5 4 3 2 1

For Lynn Henderson,
who persevered
through all of this,
and, of course,
for Michael

1

The alarm went off with a soft buzz, and Mark Tanner lazily reached over to turn it off. He wasn't asleep—hadn't been for at least ten minutes. Rather, he'd been lying awake in bed, gazing out his window at the gulls wheeling slowly over San Francisco Bay. Now, as the alarm fell silent but Mark still made no move to get up, the big golden retriever that lay next to the bed stretched, got to his feet, nuzzled gently at the boy's neck, lapped at his cheek. Finally, Mark threw the covers back and sat up.

"Okay, Chivas," he said softly, taking the dog's big head in his hands and scratching him roughly behind the ears. "I know what time it is, and I know I have to get up, and I know I have to go to school. But just because I know it doesn't mean I have to like it!"

Chivas's lips seemed to twist into an almost human grin and his tail thumped heavily on the floor. As Mark stood up, he heard his mother calling from the hall.

"Breakfast in ten minutes. And no bathrobes at the table!"

Mark rolled his eyes at Chivas, who once more wagged his tail. Then the boy stripped off his pajamas, tossed them into the corner of his room, and pulled on a clean pair of underwear. He went to his closet and, ignoring the clothes his mother had purchased for him only two days earlier, fished a pair of worn jeans out of the pile of dirty clothes that covered the closet floor. He pulled them on, and as he did almost every morning, glumly surveyed his image in the mirror inside the closet door.

And, as always, he told himself that it wasn't his fault he was so much smaller than everyone else. The rheumatic fever that had kept him in bed for almost a year when he was seven seemed to have stopped his growth at the five-foot mark.

Sixteen years old, and barely over five feet tall.

And not only that, but with a narrow chest and thin arms. *Wiry.*

That's what his mother always told him he was, but he knew it wasn't true—he wasn't wiry at all, he was just plain skinny.

Skinny, and short.

His mother always told him it didn't matter, but Mark knew it did—he could see it in his father's eyes every time Blake Tanner looked at him.

Or looked down on him, which was not only the way Mark always felt, but was the absolute physical truth as well, for his father was six-feet-four and had been that tall since he was Mark's age. In case his father forgot to mention it—and it seemed to Mark he never did—the proof was all over the house, especially in the den, where the walls were covered with pictures of Blake Tanner in his football uniforms—first in high school, then in college—and well-polished trophies gleamed in a glass display case.

Most Valuable Player three years in high school and two in college.

All-Conference Quarterback his senior year in high school, again repeated in college.

As Mark pulled on a long-sleeved denim shirt and shoved his feet into his sneakers, he could picture the trophies lined up in the case and see the empty shelf at the top, which his father always said was being saved for Mark's own trophies.

Except, as both he and his father very well knew, he wasn't going to win any silver cups.

The deep secret—the secret he'd never told his father but suspected his mother knew—was that he didn't care. Though he'd done his best to get interested in football, had even spent all the preceding summer dutifully practicing his kicking—a skill his father insisted didn't require size, but only coordination —he'd somehow never managed to figure out what the big deal was. So what if a bunch of oversize jerks went charging down a field at each other? What did it mean?

Nothing, as far as he could tell.

He glanced once more at himself in the mirror and swung the closet door shut. With Chivas trailing after him, he left his bedroom, went down the hall to the family room, then slid the glass door open and stepped out into the backyard. He paused for a moment, breathing in fresh morning air that wasn't yet made acrid by the smog that sometimes threatened completely to choke the area around San Jose. The wind was coming off the bay this morning, and there was a tang to the air that seemed to cut right through Mark's dark mood. Suddenly he grinned, and Chivas, knowing the morning routine, trotted ahead and disappeared around the corner of the garage. When Mark caught up with him a moment later, the big dog was already sniffing at the cage full of Angora rabbits. Mark had been caring for them ever since he was twelve. It was another bone of contention between him and his father.

"If it wasn't for those damned rabbits," he'd heard his father telling his mother several months before, "maybe he'd start getting some exercise and build himself up a little."

"He gets plenty of exercise," Sharon Tanner had replied mildly. "And you know perfectly well his size doesn't have anything to do with how much exercise he gets. He's never going to be as big as you, and he's never going to be a jock. So stop worrying about it."

"Oh com'on!" his father had groused. *"Rabbits?"*

"Maybe he'll be a vet," his mother had suggested. "There's nothing wrong with that."

And maybe he would be a vet, Mark thought now as he opened the big plastic trash barrel that held the rabbit food and scooped out enough to fill the dish inside the hutch. He hadn't really thought much about it before, but since he'd overheard that conversation, he'd been thinking about it a lot. And the more he considered it, the more he liked the idea. It wasn't just the rabbits, and Chivas. It was the birds out in the flats by the bay, too. As long as he could remember, he'd liked to go out there by himself, to wander around the marsh and watch the birds. Every year he'd waited patiently for the migrations, then watched as some of the flocks passed by while others came down to nest in the marshes and tidal flats, raising their young during the summer, then moving on again.

A couple of years ago his mother had given him a camera for Christmas, and soon he'd begun photographing the birds. Once, while he'd been stalking the birds, searching for a perfect shot, he'd come across one that was injured and rescued it, bringing it home to nurse it back to health before taking it back to the marshes and releasing it once more. To watch the small creature take flight had been one of the most satisfying moments of his life. The more he thought about it, the more his mother's suggestion to his father seemed to make sense to him.

He opened the rabbit hutch and Chivas tensed, his eyes fixed on the little animals within. As Mark bent down and reached in to pour the food into the feeding dish, one of the rabbits saw its chance and slipped out of the hutch, hopping madly across the lawn toward the fence that separated the Tanners' house from the house next door.

"Bring him back, Chivas," Mark called out, though his words were unnecessary since the big dog was already bounding across the yard after the fleeing rabbit.

With the scoop of rabbit food still in his hand, Mark stood up to watch. The chase was over in less than a minute. As always, the rabbit reached the fence a few yards ahead of the dog, froze for a moment, then began frantically running along the fence, searching for a way to get through. Chivas caught up and, reaching out with one of his large forepaws, pinned the rabbit to the ground. The rabbit squealed in protest, but the retriever ignored the squeak, picked the wriggling creature up by the scruff of its neck, then proudly carried it back to the hutch. His tail wagging furiously, Chivas waited while Mark opened the cage door and dropped the rabbit inside. The white-furred animal, unharmed as always, scuttled away, then turned and stared dumbly at the dog, almost as if it couldn't understand why it was still alive.

"Good dog," Mark murmured. He patted Chivas's flanks, then filled the rabbits' bowl with food. He changed their water, slid the tray that caught their droppings out from under the hutch, hosed it out and replaced it. Just as he was finishing the job, he heard his mother calling out to him from the back door.

"Come and get it, or I'll throw it away!"

Smiling fondly at the half-dozen rabbits who were now gathered around their dish, Mark lingered for a moment, then reluctantly turned and started toward the house. Sensing his master's change of mood, Chivas paced beside him, his tail curving downward.

As soon as he came into the kitchen and seated himself at the table, Mark felt his father staring at him with silent disapprobation.

"Is that the way you dress for school on the first day?" Blake Tanner asked, his low voice edged with sarcasm.

Mark tried to ignore the tone. "Everybody wears jeans," he countered, and shot a warning look at his nine-year-old sister, who was grinning wickedly at him, obviously hoping he was going to get into trouble.

"If everybody wears jeans," Blake replied, leaning back in his chair, and folding his arms across the massive expanse of his chest in a gesture that invariably presaged his intention to demolish Mark's arguments with cool logic, "then why did your mother spend nearly two hundred dollars to buy you new clothes?"

Mark shrugged, and concentrated on cutting the segments

loose from the half grapefruit that sat on the table. He could feel his father's eyes still on him. Even before Blake spoke, he knew what was coming next.

"Joe Melendez likes the guys on the team to look good," Blake said, as if on cue. "He thinks the team should set a good example for everyone else."

Mark took a deep breath and met his father's eyes. "I'm not on the team," he said.

"You might be after this afternoon," Blake reminded him. "You're a better place kicker than I was."

"*I* was a better place kicker than you were," Sharon Tanner interrupted, sliding her husband's invariable stack of pancakes in front of him and wondering yet again why they never seemed to affect his athletic figure. "And Mark's right—everybody wears jeans to school. I knew that perfectly well when I bought him those clothes." She winked at her son, and Mark felt himself blush, embarrassed that his mother thought she had to defend him.

"It doesn't matter how good you say I am, Dad. I'm not any good, and even if I were, it wouldn't make any difference. I'm too small for the team."

"Kickers don't have to be big," Blake began, but Mark shook his head.

"We don't have kickers, Dad," he said. "This isn't a pro team—it's only San Marcos High School. And Mr. Melendez is only going to take the big guys who can do a lot more than kick. Besides, I can't be on the team and take pictures at the same time," he added, the idea that had been forming in the back of his mind surfacing before he'd fully thought it out.

His father looked at him in confusion. "Take pictures?" he echoed. "What are you talking about?"

"For the school paper," Mark said, his words coming faster now that he'd broached the idea. "I'm good with a camera—Mr. Hemmerling said I was better than almost anyone else last year. If I shoot the games for the paper, how can I be on the team? Anyway, isn't it better if I'm at least on the field doing something instead of just sitting on the bench?"

Blake's eyes narrowed darkly, but before he could say anything, Sharon spoke again. "Before you get into an argument, you might want to look at the clock."

Seizing his opportunity, Mark finished off the grapefruit, gulped down his cup of cocoa, and scuttled out of the kitchen. Only when Kelly, too, had gone, her face falling when the fight she'd been looking forward to didn't develop, did Blake turn his attention to his wife.

"We already decided," he said. "He was going out for the team this year. We talked about it all summer."

Sharon shook her head. "*You* talked about it all summer," she corrected him. "You've been talking about it ever since he was born. But it isn't going to happen, Blake." Her voice turned gentle. "I know how much it meant to you, darling. But Mark isn't you, and he never will be. Maybe if he hadn't gotten sick . . ." She fell silent, her eyes clouding at the memory of the illness that had nearly killed her son and destroyed all Blake's dreams that Mark would repeat his own glory on the football field. Then she took a deep breath, and finished the thought. "Maybe if he hadn't gotten sick, things would have been different. But they might not have been. Mark just isn't cut out for football. It's not just his size—it's his temperament, too. Can't you see it?"

Blake Tanner's face darkened as he lumbered to his feet. "I can see a lot, Sharon. I can see that I've got a son that's a wimp and a misfit, who has a mother who lets him get away with it. Christ! Spending all his time with a camera and a bunch of rabbits and half-dead birds! If I'd been that way when I was his age—"

"—your father would have whipped you!" Sharon made no attempt to keep the anger out of her voice as she finished the familiar litany. "And your father was a drunk who whipped you and your mother for anything he could think of, and a lot of things he couldn't! Is that what you want for Mark? To take out all his anger on the football field, like you did?"

"That wasn't it at all," Blake protested. But of course that was exactly it, and he knew it as well as Sharon did.

Indeed, it had been Sharon who understood it from the very beginning, when they'd first met in high school, and he'd fallen in love with her. And from then on, whenever things got too bad with his father, she'd always encouraged him not to fight back, not to make things any worse at home than they already were.

"There's the field," she'd told him over and over again. "Go put on your uniform and get out there and keep at it till you're not mad anymore. Because if you don't do something about it now, you'll turn out just like your dad, and I'll never marry a man like that." And so he'd done what she'd told him, and it had worked. All the fury he'd felt toward his father had been directed to the game instead, and in the end the skills he'd gained on the field had paid his way through college.

He wasn't like his father and never would be.

Except . . . Except that deep inside he still nurtured the hope that his son would be just like him; that through Mark he could relive the days of his youth, when he'd heard the crowds cheering him from the grandstand, felt the thrill of completing a sixty-yard pass, felt the flush of exultation that came with every touchdown he'd scored. It didn't matter that Sharon was certain it would never happen, for deep in his heart he was certain that it would.

Mark, after all, was only a sophomore this year. He'd lost a year when he was sick, so now he was the oldest in his class. He could still begin to grow—the doctors had said when he was sick that though he'd probably never grow as large as Blake himself, there was no reason to think he'd be less than average. So this year—or next summer—he could still begin shooting up the way Blake had the year he was fifteen. And when he did . . .

But Blake said nothing of his hopes, for Sharon, who read his mind so perfectly after all their years together, knew his thoughts almost as well as he did himself. Instead, he simply gave her a hug and a kiss, then left the kitchen to pick up his briefcase. Before he got to the door, however, she stopped him.

"He's a good boy, Blake," she said. "He's not you, and he might never be. But he's still our son, and we could have done a lot worse."

Blake flashed a grin back over his shoulder. "Didn't say he wasn't," he agreed. "All I want for him is the best. And there isn't any reason why he shouldn't have it."

Then he left for the office and Sharon was alone in the house. She began doing the breakfast dishes. With Mark gone for the day, Chivas shifted his attention to her, nuzzling at her hand until she reached down and scratched his ears.

"Well, that wasn't so bad, was it, Chivas? Bet you thought there was going to be a big fight and you were going to have to protect Mark from his dad, didn't you? Well, you were wrong. Blake loves Mark just as much as you do." She smiled sadly. "He just doesn't understand him quite as well, that's all."

Almost as if he understood her words, Chivas trotted out of the kitchen and curled up on the floor at Mark's bedroom door, where he would wait patiently for the rest of the day.

It was nearly four o'clock that afternoon when Blake's secretary, Rosalie Adams, appeared in the doorway of his office. "All set for the big meeting?"

Blake shrugged. He and Rosalie had been trying to figure out what was going on all day, but so far neither of them had come up with an answer as to why Ted Thornton might want to talk to Blake. Thornton, after all, was the CEO of TarrenTech, and though Blake's own position as Marketing Manager of the Digital Division was hardly low on the totem pole, everything at TarrenTech was done according to the chain of command. If John Ripley, who was Blake's immediate superior, was in trouble, it would have been Ripley's boss—the Executive Vice President of the division—who would have summoned Blake to tell him he was replacing John. But as far as both Blake and Rosalie could determine (and Rosalie had spent most of the morning on the secretaries' network, gathering gossip), John Ripley was in no trouble at all. Besides, since it was Thornton himself who wanted to see Blake, the "poor old Ripley's out" scenario had never really made much sense. There were a lot of other people Thornton would have informed long before getting down the chain as far as Blake Tanner.

"No late bulletins?" Blake asked Rosalie as he got up and straightened his tie. He almost reached for his briefcase, but stopped himself in time, remembering that there had been no instructions for him to bring any files with him.

That, too, seemed unusual.

"Nothing," Rosalie replied. "Nobody seems to be in trouble, and if you've been a bad boy, either what you did was so awful no one's telling me, or you covered your tracks so well you haven't been caught. So go on in, and take good notes—I want to hear every detail of what the great man has to say."

And "great man," Blake reflected as he walked toward the large suite of offices at the far end of the corridor that housed Ted Thornton and his staff, was precisely the phrase that applied to TarrenTech's Chief Executive Officer. For it was Thornton who had begun the company a little more than a decade ago, and built it from a minor supplier of computer software into the giant high-tech conglomerate it had become. Though software was still one of TarrenTech's major product lines, Thornton had recognized the volatility of the computer industry and launched a program of expansion and diversification. Now TarrenTech produced all kinds of electronics— from television sets to abstruse gadgets involved in the space program—and had gone into consumer goods and services as well.

When Thornton had decided the company needed its own fleet of airplanes, he had simply bought an airline, then another and another. That had led to hotels, car rentals, and a string of other travel-related companies.

Next, as Thornton had recognized the aging population of

America, came the hospitals, nursing homes, and pharmaceutical companies. By now the Digital Division had become only a minor cog in the whole great machine, but Ted Thornton, partly out of a sense of nostalgia, and partly as a way of appearing a lot more humble than he was, still kept his offices in what had once been the entire space occupied by the beginnings of his vast conglomerate.

"Go right in, Blake," Anne Leverette told him from her guard post outside Thornton's door. "He's expecting you." Her smile alone made Blake relax, for it was well known that if Thornton was chopping off someone's head, Anne never smiled personally at the victim. Her loyalty to Thornton was legendary, and she was known to resent anyone she assumed had caused trouble for her boss.

Blake stepped through the double doors into the immense corner office and found Ted Thornton sitting behind a bare, black marble desk, a telephone cradled against his ear. Thornton signaled him to take a chair, then quickly wrapped up his phone call. As soon as he'd hung up, he stood, offering Blake his hand and asking if he wanted a drink.

Blake relaxed even more—the offer of a drink invariably signaled good news, and was not meant to be turned down.

"Chivas and water," Blake replied, and Thornton smiled.

"Never settle for less than the best," he said, pouring each of them a generous shot over a single ice cube. He grinned as he handed Blake one of the glasses. "It's a cliché, but then, your best moment has become one, too, hasn't it?" He held his glass up toward a large, framed mosaic on the wall. On a cobalt-blue background, the stylized white letters spelled out the slogan that Blake had dreamed up seven years before.

IF IT'S HI-TECH, IT'S TARRENTECH

"I guess you could say so," Blake agreed, raising his own glass slightly, then taking a sip of the whiskey. Surely, at this late date, there was a more important reason for this meeting than for Thornton merely to acknowledge the slogan that had, indeed, become a cliché over the years? He wondered what Thornton was leading up to as he watched the CEO seat himself behind his desk again and regard him appraisingly.

"Ever heard of Silverdale, Colorado?" he asked, and Blake's heart skipped a beat. This was something neither he nor Rosalie had thought about.

"Is there anyone at TarrenTech who hasn't?" he countered.

"Oh, I'm sure there are a few." Thornton chuckled. "I'm not sure most of the people in the Travel Division even know about Research and Development, much less care."

Blake permitted himself a small smile. "I'm afraid I'd have to disagree with you," he suggested. "After all, Tom Stevens runs Travel, and his last post was Silverdale." He didn't feel it necessary to add that it wasn't merely the Travel Division's chief officer who had once been posted in Silverdale, but virtually every senior man in the TarrenTech hierarchy. A posting in Silverdale, as nearly everyone in the company knew, meant that you were in line for the top jobs. As far as Blake knew, however, no one from Marketing had ever been sent there before.

"True enough," Thornton mused, then fell silent for a few moments as his gray eyes seemed slowly to assess Blake. "Jerry Harris has an opening out there, and he's asked for you."

Blake tried not to let his astonishment show. Until two years ago Jerry had run the Digital Division, and though he'd been several rungs above Blake on the corporate ladder, the two men had become good friends, largely due to the influence of their wives, neither of whom seemed to give a rap for Ted Thornton's general disapproval of his managers becoming too friendly with men they might someday have to fire.

As if reading his thoughts, Thornton spoke again. "If you'd been working for him here, of course, I wouldn't entertain the idea for a moment—I've never believed in letting people build empires within my own company. But you didn't work for Harris here, at least not directly, and he's a good man. If I trust him to run R and D, I have to trust him to choose his staff. Therefore, you'll be moving."

It wasn't a question, it was a command. Blake understood instantly that he wasn't being offered a new job; he was being informed that he had one. Not that he would have considered turning it down, he reflected, even for a moment. Aside from the fact that to refuse would have meant the end of his career at TarrenTech, he was as aware as anyone that being sent to Silverdale meant that, at the age of thirty-eight, he was already marked for a top position in the company. And top positions didn't come much larger than they did at TarrenTech.

He instinctively knew it would have been a mistake to ask just what the job in Silverdale would be. There was only one question that was relevant, so he asked it.

"When do I leave?"

Thornton stood up. "You report to Harris two weeks from today, so you'll want to get there by the end of next week. The arrangements have all been made. A house is waiting for you, and the movers will be at your place in San Marcos next week to do the packing."

Blake swallowed, his head suddenly spinning. What would Sharon think? Shouldn't he at least discuss it with her? But of course she knew how TarrenTech worked as well as he did, and he wouldn't be the first executive to be transferred on short notice. He stood up.

"Thank you, Mr. Thornton," he said. "I appreciate your confidence in me, and I won't disappoint you."

Thornton's brows arched slightly, and when he spoke, his voice held an acerbic note. "It's Jerry Harris I have confidence in," he said. "And it is Jerry you won't disappoint." Then he flashed a smile and extended his hand. "And call me Ted," he added.

The interview was over. Everything in Blake Tanner's life, and the lives of his family, had just changed.

2

It wasn't until they'd started south on Highway 50 out of Grand Junction that Sharon Tanner began to feel better. For two days, as they'd driven from San Jose to Reno, then across the seemingly endless wastelands of Nevada and Utah to Salt Lake City, she'd sat numbly next to Blake in the front seat of the station wagon, the desolation of the landscape perfectly reflecting the bleakness of her spirit.

Less than two weeks, and everything had turned upside down. Of course, there had not been any question of their going. After all, hadn't they talked about the possibility for years? But neither of them had ever seriously thought there was any chance of Blake being transferred to Silverdale—it was a research facility, and Blake's expertise in marketing had always seemed to both of them to preclude making the quantum leap within the company that an assignment at Silverdale represented.

And yet it had happened, and for the next ten days, until the movers arrived, Sharon had been far too busy dealing with the myriad details of winding up their affairs in San Marcos to deal with her emotions.

Only now, as they began making their way through the

foothills of the Rockies, did the reality of it all truly begin to set in. And as the scenery began to take on a majestic beauty, Sharon felt her spirits begin to rise.

Of the four of them, only Blake had seemed unaffected by the prospect of the sudden move.

Mark had immediately been excited about the change. For him the advantages had instantly overbalanced the disadvantages, since the prospect of living in the Rockies, with the mountains' towering peaks, broad valleys, and abundance of wildlife, had been irresistible.

For Kelly it had been something else entirely. The prospect of leaving her friends had at first infuriated her. Then, when she found that her anger wasn't going to change anything, she had sunk into a darkly sullen silence which was, Sharon reflected, at least better than the screaming tantrums of the first few days after Blake had come home with news of the transfer.

Her own reaction, she realized now, had been mixed. The advantages of the move had been obvious—the salary was a third more than Blake had been earning, and his future prospects were suddenly unlimited. Nor did the prospect of living in Silverdale upset her; indeed, she'd always been curious about the little town nestled in the mountains, which was so important to her husband's employer, and she would be reunited with her friend Elaine Harris. Nor was Sharon sorry to be leaving San Marcos, which long ago had been swallowed up in the urban sprawl around San Jose, losing whatever character it may once have had, disappearing into the faceless morass of subdivisions and shopping malls.

But simply to pack up and be gone in little more than the space of a week seemed somehow unnatural to her. Almost, in an odd way, like dying. She'd barely had time to let all her friends know she was leaving, much less see them all to say good-bye. There had, of course, been a farewell party, but by then the house was in too advanced a state of chaos for her to host it herself. In the end the Tanners' farewell had been thrown by John Ripley, Blake's boss, and most of the guests had been TarrenTech people, not the wide range of friends from the academic and arts community whom Sharon had always felt most comfortable with.

Still, the decision had been made, the movers had come, and now all their worldly possessions were in the van that had left San Marcos a few hours before they themselves had piled into the station wagon.

The car was crowded with the four of them, plus Chivas and the cage full of rabbits, which the movers had refused to be responsible for and which Mark, with her support, had refused to give up, despite his father's loudly voiced disgust. The rabbits proved to be a distraction for Chivas, who had spent most of the trip lying placidly in the back of the car, staring at the small animals as they huddled together in their cage, their eyes wide with fear, their noses twitching uncomprehendingly. Kelly's sullen silence had finally begun to evaporate—the energy of maintaining anger over a two-week period finally having proved too much for her—and Mark had spent his time with a collection of field guides that had appeared from God-knew-where, identifying every bush, tree, flower, and geological feature they passed. Now, thirty miles ahead, lay Silverdale.

Half an hour later Blake turned left off the highway and they started up the road toward the hidden valley in whose heart Silverdale lay. It had been a mining town once, but the ore had long since given out, and the town—like so many others in the area—had begun to die. Ted Thornton had discovered it a decade earlier, and then, after having lost three major projects to the sort of industrial espionage endemic to Silicon Valley, had decided to move his Research and Development arm out of the San Jose area.

He'd quietly bought up large tracts of land around Silverdale, and before the town knew quite what was happening, a strange sort of light-industrial complex had appeared on the west side of the crumbling village. The buildings, long and low, had been perfectly landscaped, but not so perfectly that the few remaining residents had been unaware of the cameras that photographed everything in the area. But along with the buildings had come jobs, and then people.

And suddenly Silverdale, after fifty years of slow and steady decline, had come to life again.

As they came over the pass that seemed to separate Silverdale from the rest of the world, Sharon got her first view of the town. She gasped, for it was not at all what she'd been expecting. It appeared before her like something out of a picture book: neatly laid out, its streets narrow and shaded by a profusion of aspens and pines. The houses, all of them centered on large lots, were of various forms of nineteenth- and early-twentieth-century architecture, each of them different, but with enough similarity to give the town a feeling of unity. All of them had large porches in front, and each yard was surrounded by a neat white picket fence. Before they dropped into the valley itself, Sharon could see that each of the main roads through the town seemed to lead somewhere—to the north was the high school and what looked like an old-fashioned Carnegie library; to the south a shopping area; everything within easy walking distance for everyone in town.

"It's incredible," she breathed as Blake brought their speed down to the posted limit of twenty miles an hour. "It looks like something out of the past."

Blake grinned across at her. "That, as I understand it, is the whole idea. Ted found a group of architects who seem to think we're lousing things up with shopping malls and subdivisions, and he turned them loose here. Told them he wanted a company town that wouldn't look like one or feel like one, and since he'd bought up nearly every parcel of land here, he was able to do it. Something, isn't it?"

Sharon gazed sharply at her husband. There was a look about him that told her all this wasn't a surprise to him. "You knew what it was like?" she asked.

"I saw a movie of it last week." He chuckled softly. "I think John Ripley was afraid I was going to change my mind, so he showed me some tapes. But I have to say, the place is even prettier than I thought it would be."

"It looks like pictures of where everyone's grandma is supposed to live," Kelly piped from the backseat. "Except no one's does. Anyway, no one I know. Everyone's grandparents live in condos."

"Where's our house?" Mark asked. He'd finally put his books aside and was gazing out the window with the same wonder as the rest of the family.

"Telluride Drive," Blake replied. "Two forty South." The road had narrowed sharply, and two blocks farther along he turned left, drove two more blocks, then made a right. The moving van was pulled up in front of a medium-sized Victorian house halfway along the block. Already, some of the Tanners' furniture was spread along the sidewalk. Blake pulled the station wagon into the driveway and the family, followed by Chivas, climbed out of the car to stare at their new house.

It was painted a pale green, with its trim done in a tone several shades darker, set off here and there by touches of an orange-rust color. A wide porch spread across the front of the house, curving gracefully around the turret that rose up from the southeast corner. There were small bay windows jutting out from the sides of the house, and on the second floor all the windows were framed by shutters. The roof rose in a steep pitch, the angles of which were softened with delicate latticework, and the roof itself appeared to be made of slate. The house was surrounded by tall aspens, whose narrow height complemented its design, and though the style of architecture had seen its most glorious days at least a hundred years before, Sharon could tell at a glance that the house itself was no more than five years old. She gazed at it in silence for several long minutes, taking in every detail. When at last she turned to Blake, a smile was playing around her lips.

"When I saw something like this in San Marcos last year, I thought it was so cute it would make me nauseated," she said. Then she shrugged helplessly and her smile spread. "But here . . . well, don't ask me what it is, but it seems just perfect."

With Kelly running ahead, they went up the front steps and across the porch. Inside there was a small foyer, opening onto a den on one side and a living room on the other. Through the living room, enclosed by the round turret, was a sunny breakfast room, with a large kitchen that opened into a dining and family room behind it.

Upstairs, the turret contained a small sitting room for the master suite, plus three other bedrooms and two bathrooms. There were two fireplaces downstairs and another in the master bedroom. And although the house had seemed somewhat fussy and cluttered from the outside, inside, the rooms were bright and airy, and larger than Sharon would have thought possible. By the time they had finished inspecting the house and returned to the front porch, all her misgivings about the move had faded. She put her arms around Blake and squeezed him hard. "I love it," she said. "The town's beautiful, and the house is perfect. How long will we be here?"

Blake shrugged. "At least a couple of years," he said. "Maybe five or six." Then his eyes flicked away from Sharon and a slight frown creased his brow. She turned to see Mark pulling the cage of rabbits out of the back of the station wagon.

As if feeling his parents' eyes on him, he turned and grinned happily. "Would you believe there's already a hutch next to the garage?" he yelled. "Thanks, Dad!"

Sharon gazed up at her husband, her eyes reflecting her puzzlement. "I thought you didn't want him to bring the rabbits."

"I didn't," he said. "Let's go take a look."

They followed Mark down the driveway and found him carefully transferring the rabbits from the cage into a perfectly constructed rabbit hutch that, quite obviously, had been finished only a day or two before their arrival. Chivas, his right forepaw quivering two inches above the ground, his tail held straight out, was gazing at the rabbits steadily, almost as if he were hoping one of them would escape so he could have the fun of capturing it and returning it to the hutch.

"I'll be damned," Blake breathed. "I never even mentioned the rabbits to anyone. How'd they know?" His expression cleared as the answer came to him. "Jerry," he said. "Of course! Jerry remembered. He never forgets anything." He reached out a hand and tousled his son's curly mop of dark brown hair. "Or did you write to Robb and remind him?" he asked.

Mark glanced up from the hutch, the last of the rabbits still held gently in his hands. "Not me," he said. "I wasn't even sure you'd let me bring them till the last minute." Then his own brows creased in a frown that was almost a perfect replication of his father's. "Where *are* the Harrises?" he asked. "Weren't they going to be here to meet us?"

"For that matter," Sharon added, "where is *everybody*?"

Blake looked curiously at his wife and for a moment wondered what she was talking about. Then he knew.

As they'd come into Silverdale and driven through the streets to their house, they hadn't seen another car, or another person.

It was, he realized, as if they'd come into a ghost town.

Elaine Harris sat in the grandstand of the Silverdale High School stadium, her husband on one side, her fifteen-year-old daughter Linda on the other. Below the stands, sitting on the bench while the offensive team took the field, was her son Robb. With only two more minutes left to play, and the Silverdale Wolverines winning the game by a score of 42–0, it didn't appear that Robb would be playing anymore that afternoon. "Don't you think we can go?" she asked Jerry, her eyes flicking nervously to her watch. "I promised Sharon we'd be there."

Jerry shook his head, his eyes never leaving the field. "They might not even get here till after dinner," he said. "Besides, how would it look? It's the first game of the season, Robb's playing, and I'm the head of the division."

"Well, even in Silverdale that doesn't quite make you the mayor," Elaine observed dryly, though she kept her voice low enough so no one but Jerry would hear. She was aware that his job might just as well have made him the mayor, since practically everyone in town was dependent on TarrenTech in one way or another. If they didn't work directly for the company, most of them provided services for those who did. And besides, even if he weren't head of the R&D Division, he still might as well be thought of as Silverdale's mayor since there wasn't a soul in town who didn't like her husband.

With a sigh she admitted to herself that he was right—the least they could do was stay till the end of the game. Resisting her impulse to glance at her watch once again, she shifted her slightly overweight body into a more comfortable position on the hard bench and turned her attention to the field, where the Wolverines, in possession of the ball, were poised on their own thirty-yard line. And knowing the team as well as she did, she decided it might just be worth watching. Phil Collins always liked his boys to keep up their drive till the final seconds ran out. It wouldn't surprise her at all if the team scored yet again before it was all over.

And no one else in the stands—which held practically everyone in town—was showing any sign of leaving early. Jerry was right, as he usually was: There was no point in leaving now.

On the field Jeff LaConner quickly outlined the play he had in mind, then clapped his hands to signal the end of the huddle. He trotted into his quarterback position as the rest of the team fell into their places along and behind the scrimmage line. He glanced at the Fairfield team and smiled to himself as they prepared themselves for what they were certain was going to be a passing play.

They were in for a surprise.

A moment later the center snapped the ball and Jeff faded

back, glancing around as if searching for a receiver. Then, tucking the ball under his arm, he ducked his head and charged the line.

Ahead of him the center and both guards had opened up a slot, and Jeff hurled himself toward it. To his left he sensed a flash of movement, but instead of dodging away from it, he threw himself toward it. He saw one of the Fairfield tackles tumble aside. Directly ahead two more Fairfield players were lunging at him, and he knew he was going down. But as one of the guards hurled himself at Jeff's legs, Jeff twisted sharply then let himself collapse, dropping his full 220 pounds onto the much smaller frame of his opponent. Another of the Fairfield players dropped on top of him, and at the same time three of his own teammates joined in the melee. The whistle blew, and Jeff lay still, certain that he had gained at least seven yards on the play. A moment later the players began sorting themselves out and Jeff scrambled to his feet, leaving the ball where it lay.

The player from Fairfield, on whom Jeff had dropped at the moment he was tackled, lay still, and a gasp rose from the crowd. Jeff looked down for a moment, his brow creased into a frown, then dropped to his knees.

"Hey, you okay?"

There was no answer from the other boy, but Jeff could clearly see his open eyes through the bars of his helmet.

He stood up and waved to the Silverdale coach, but Phil Collins was already shouting for a stretcher team. From the other side of the field Bob Jenkins, the Fairfield coach, was racing toward him from the sidelines.

"I saw that!" Jenkins yelled as he dropped to his knees next to his injured player. "For Christ's sake—he had you! You didn't have to drop on him like that!"

Jeff stared at the Fairfield coach. "I didn't do anything," he protested. "All I did was try to get away from him."

Jenkins only glared at him, then turned his attention to the boy, who still lay unmoving on the ground. "You okay, Ramirez?"

The boy said nothing, and then the stretcher team was there. Two boys from Silverdale started to reach out for the fallen guard, but Jenkins stopped them. "Don't touch him," he said. "I want a doctor. I want to know what's wrong with him before he's moved."

"We've got a doctor right here, and there's an ambulance on its way," Phil Collins said, dropping down onto the grass next to Jenkins. "Can you tell if anything's broken?"

"How the hell do I know?" Jenkins demanded, his angry eyes fixing on the Silverdale coach. "I'm gonna file a complaint this time, Collins. And I want that player on the bench for the rest of the season."

"Now, cool off, Bob," Collins replied. His fingers began running gently over the injured boy's legs, searching for a break, but he found none. "Your boy's going to be okay. Things like this happen all the time. . . ."

Jenkins seemed about to say something else, but before he could speak, a soft moan drifted from the lips of the boy on the ground, and for the moment the argument was forgotten.

"Is he all right?" Charlotte LaConner asked. She was standing up in the grandstands, shading her eyes against the late afternoon sun as she struggled to see what was happening on the field. In the row in front of her Elaine Harris turned and smiled encouragingly.

"He'll be fine," Elaine replied. "He just wound up on the bottom of the heap, and Jeff knocked the breath out of him."

Charlotte opened her mouth to say something else, then changed her mind. The truth of the matter, she knew, was that she just didn't like football. But in Silverdale that was the next thing to treason, and she'd long since learned to go to the games and cheer the home team on. Not that they needed much cheering, since the Silverdale team was one of the best in the state. Last year, in fact, the team had wound up in the state finals and lost by only a single point to a team from Denver.

But why did the game have to be so rough? That's what she didn't understand. It all seemed so pointless to her. All she'd ever been able to make of it was two tides of humanity moving up and down the field in a series of plays that she failed to comprehend, much less enjoy. Still, Jeff loved the game, and since he'd become the quarterback last year, her husband had become almost a fanatic. Even she had to admit there wasn't much else to do in Silverdale, so it was easy to understand why the whole town always turned out for the games, particularly since the team was very nearly certain to win. Indeed, she sometimes wondered if the town was so fanatic because the Wolverines were so good or if the team was so good because the town was so crazy about the game. But, it was a violent, dangerous game, and the clash of bodies on the field sometimes made her shudder. Now, as an ambulance came onto the field, her attention shifted back to the boy who still lay inert on the grass.

It wasn't just that he got the wind knocked out of him—they wouldn't have called an ambulance for that. When Jeff fell on him, he must have gotten seriously hurt. Without thinking, she squeezed hard on her husband's hand, and Chuck LaConner, knowing what was in her mind, returned the gesture.

"It wasn't anybody's fault," he assured her. "It's just the breaks of the game, and you've got to get used to it."

But Charlotte shook her head. "I'll never get used to it," she replied. "Can't we leave now?"

Chuck stared at her as if she'd spoken in a foreign language. "Leave? Honey, it's the first game of the year, and your son's the star. How can you want to leave?"

"But it's over, isn't it?"

"Still a minute and a half to go," he told her with an affectionate grin. "They stopped the clock at the end of the play. Look."

Charlotte gazed out at the field, and sure enough, the

injured boy had been put into the ambulance. As the ambulance left, the crowd shouted out a cheer for the fallen player. Then, almost as if nothing had happened, the two teams took up their positions for the final plays of the game.

On the last play Jeff LaConner hurled a forty-yard pass for a final touchdown, and was carried off the field on his teammates' shoulders as Silverdale's supporters, their cheers a roar, rushed down from the bleachers to congratulate their heroes.

In the stands Jeff's mother remained frozen in place. What, she wondered, counted for more? The fact that Silverdale had won? Or the fact that one of the Fairfield boys was now in the hospital?

It was Elaine Harris who finally provided her with the answer. "What are you doing still up here?" she asked, smiling broadly at Charlotte. "It's Jeff's big moment. Go down and congratulate him!"

With Chuck shouting happily and half pulling her through the crowd, Charlotte went down to tell her son how proud she was of him.

Except that she wasn't really sure she was all that proud.

"How do you do it?" Elaine Harris asked Sharon Tanner an hour later. The two women were alone in the Tanners' kitchen, searching through a box of towels clearly marked EVERYDAY CHINA, in the vain hope of finding coffee cups. Their husbands were in the living room, already discussing business, and Mark had taken Linda Harris outside to show her the rabbit hutch, with Kelly tagging along. Robb had not yet shown up, having gone out with the rest of the team for a celebratory hamburger in violation of their training diets. "You don't look a day older than you did three years ago," she went on, eyeing Sharon's svelte figure with undisguised envy. "And I suppose your hair's still its natural color, too, isn't it?"

Sharon chuckled. "As natural as it ever was. Nobody has natural auburn hair, and you know it. And you haven't changed either."

Elaine shrugged amiably and patted her hips. "If you call twenty extra pounds 'not changing,' I thank you. But I decided that if Jerry doesn't care, I don't either, so I eat what I want, and the hell with it." Then her expression turned serious. "Mark hasn't changed either, has he," she said, almost tentatively.

Sharon hesitated only a second, then shook her head, but her gaze shifted toward the window. By the garage, Mark was standing next to Linda Harris. Even Linda, who was not a big girl, was an inch taller. "But we're still hoping he'll do some growing," she said with forced cheerfulness, "and you can believe he's hoping so, too. What about Robb?"

Elaine grinned. "You won't recognize him. Six-foot-one, with shoulders a yard wide."

Sharon sighed ruefully. "Well, that's going to be something else for Mark to adjust to. I have a feeling he thinks Robb's going to be just the same as he was three years ago."

"Nothing stays the same," Elaine observed, then made an expansive gesture. "So what do you think of it all? Not like San Marcos, is it?"

"Not at all," Sharon agreed. "But I think I like it."

"You'll do more than like it," Elaine assured her. "Within a month you'll love it and won't know how you ever lived anywhere else. Clean air, a small town, nice people, skiing, hiking, the film festival at Telluride—it's like I died and went to heaven."

"And what if you get transferred?" Sharon asked, not trying to conceal the edge in her voice.

But Elaine only shrugged. "I'll deal with it when it happens, and from here there's nowhere to go but up. And speaking of things that have gone nowhere but up, look who's coming!"

Sharon glanced out the window, and barely recognized the boy who had left San Marcos three years before. The thin

and wiry Robb Harris who had been only a little taller than
Mark, and slightly asthmatic as well, was now a solidly built
young man whose features had matured into a husky hand-
someness. His wide-set blue eyes seemed to have become
brighter with adolescence, and his blond hair, cropped short,
appeared even lighter in contrast to his deeply tanned skin.
Catching sight of her through the open window, he grinned,
exposing a perfect set of even teeth.

"Hi, Mrs. Tanner," he called. "Welcome to Silverdale.
Where's Mark?"

"Out back," Sharon replied vacantly. The change in
Robb was so startling, she hardly knew what to make of it.
As he headed on down the driveway toward the garage, she
turned back to Elaine. "My God," she said. "He's gor-
geous! But what about his asthma? Ever since he was a
baby—"

"It was the smog," Elaine said. "As soon as we got him
out here, it cleared right up! I always half suspected it, but
that quack in San Jose always insisted it was psychosomatic.
But either way, it's gone."

Sharon shook her head, and when she spoke again, her
voice was almost wistful. "I wish it could be that easy for
Mark," she said. But unfortunately, there was nothing either
smog-related or psychosomatic about the aftereffects of rheumatic fever.

Elaine, understanding perfectly her friend's feelings, said
nothing.

There were times when silence was better than any kind
of sympathy.

3

Andrew MacCallum, who had been known as Mac almost since the day of his birth thirty-two years earlier, gazed glumly at the stack of X rays on his desk. When Rick Ramirez had first been brought into the hospital nearly three hours before, Mac hadn't thought the boy looked too bad. Indeed, his first instincts were that Rick had simply been knocked out.

Now he knew better.

Two vertebrae in the boy's neck were broken, one of his kidneys was ruptured, and three of his ribs had been cracked. Two of the ribs had punctured his left lung, which had collapsed, and in the few hours since he'd been in the hospital, his condition had deteriorated to the point where he was now on life-support systems.

The job of explaining to the boy's mother what had happened had, of course, fallen to Mac MacCallum. He left his office and turned down the hall toward the waiting room, then decided to have one more look at Rick. Perhaps, with luck, he might find some scrap of improvement that would soften the news he had to give to—he glanced quickly at the Next of Kin entry on the boy's chart—Maria Ramirez.

Susan Aldrich, whose shift had just been ending when the ambulance arrived with Rick Ramirez strapped to a stretcher, sat by the boy's bed. When Mac glanced at her questioningly, she only shook her head, her lips tightening.

Mac picked up the boy's limp left arm and quickly checked his pulse, then glanced at the array of displays on the monitors above Rick's bed. Nothing had changed: his pulse still erratic, his blood pressure low. Only his breathing, assisted by the respirator next to the bed, appeared normal. But Mac knew that without the machine, Rick's breathing would soon stop.

"No changes at all?" he asked, though he already knew the answer.

Susan shook her head again. "It's so strange," she said, her voice quavering. Her eyes wandered to Rick's face and she gazed silently at his calm expression, which seemed to indicate a peaceful sleep rather than a struggle for life itself. "I keep thinking he's going to wake up and say something, and everything's going to be fine. But he's not, is he?"

Mac shook his head. "I'd better go talk to his mother."

He gently closed the door behind him, then continued down the hall to the small waiting room where Maria Ramirez, her face pale, rose shakily to her feet as he entered. She looked so young to Mac—so vulnerable.

"Ricardo," she breathed. "Please—is he going to be all right?"

Mac gestured her back into her chair as his eyes shifted to the man who sat next to her. "You are . . . ?" he began, deliberately leaving the question hanging.

"Bob Jenkins," the man replied. "I'm the coach of the Fairfield team."

"I see," Mac replied. "I wonder if I might have a moment alone with Mrs. Ramirez?"

But now it was Maria who shook her head. "It's all right," she said, her voice so low Mac could barely hear it. "He's been a good friend to Ricardo—to both of us. . . ." Though her voice trailed off, Mac could read perfectly the situation as she gazed at the coach, who reached out and took her hand protectively in his own.

"I wish I could give you good news," Mac began, and winced inside as Maria Ramirez's eyes filled with tears.

"Ricardo," she whispered almost inaudibly. "He's . . . ?"

"He's alive," Mac quickly reassured her. "But he's in a coma, and he has a lot of internal injuries." As gently as he could, he outlined the extent of the damage Rick Ramirez had sustained, but before he was done, Maria had buried her face in her hands and begun quietly sobbing.

It was Bob Jenkins who questioned him when he was finished. "What are his chances for recovery?" he asked, and the steadiness of his gaze as he met the doctor's eyes told Mac he wanted no temporizing.

"Right now, I'd have to say somewhat less than fifty percent," he replied. A small cry of anguish escaped Maria Ramirez's lips, and Mac swallowed the lump that immediately rose in his own throat. "But that's not to say things couldn't change radically by tomorrow," he added. "I'm afraid, though, that even if he survives, his chances of walking again are going to be very slim. The breaks in his vertebrae have damaged some of the main nerves."

Jenkins's eyes clouded. "But what about surgery?" he demanded. "I thought—"

Mac shook his head. "Right now surgery is out of the question. There's no way Rick's body could withstand the shock. Perhaps later—"

"No!" Maria cried. Her hands fell away from her face, and her eyes, wide and beseeching, fixed on MacCallum. "He can't be crippled," she pleaded. "Not my Ricardo. He's all I have. . . . He—" But her voice failed her, and she collapsed against Jenkins, whose arm went around her to hold her close.

MacCallum watched them in silence for a moment, then signaled Jenkins that he'd like to talk to him alone. When he was sure the other man understood, he went back to his office.

Five minutes later Bob Jenkins let himself into MacCallum's office and closed the door behind him. "She'll be all right," he said, reading the unspoken question in MacCallum's eyes. He smiled tightly. "She's a remarkable woman. She's raised Rick by herself, and he was born when she was only fourteen years old." His voice hardened. "She never told anyone who his father was, and her own parents kicked her out when they found out she was pregnant. But she's never complained. She works as a waitress, and the last couple of years, since Rick's been old enough, she's been going to night school. She's absolutely determined that Rick should go to college, so she has to get another job."

"Jesus," MacCallum whispered. He gestured Jenkins into the chair on the other side of his desk. "The boy's going to need a lot of care. If he survives, and something can be done about his spinal injuries, he's going to need a lot of physical therapy. But before all that begins, he's going to be in the hospital for a long time. Perhaps," he added, his voice dropping, "permanently. There's a good chance he won't come out of the coma at all. And if he does . . ." He spread his hands in an eloquent expression of unanswerable questions.

"All of which costs money," Jenkins observed, and Mac immediately nodded. "Well, Maria doesn't have any," the coach went on.

"Insurance?" Mac asked.

Jenkins shrugged. "Maybe a little, but I'm sure it won't be enough. And the school has some insurance, too, I suppose." His lips twisted in an ironic smile. "I'm going to be in an interesting position," he said. "I've been trying to convince Maria to marry me for two years, but she's always said she won't until Rick's through college. She said it wouldn't be fair to me. If only she'd married me, she and Rick would both be covered by my own insurance. So now I'm going to have to advise her to sue the school district I work for."

MacCallum pursed his lips thoughtfully. "Or sue Silverdale," he suggested. "After all, what happened, happened right here, didn't it?"

Jenkins hesitated, then nodded. "I'd already thought of that," he said. "Frankly, I didn't mention it because of you. I mean . . ."

He hesitated, clearly uneasy, and MacCallum suddenly understood the man's discomfort: Obviously Jenkins had assumed that he would automatically adopt the same defensive posture as Phil Collins had on the field.

Except that Mac MacCallum had long since come to the conclusion that the Silverdale of the past, the Silverdale he had come to immediately after his residency, no longer existed. TarrenTech had changed it all—changed it beyond recognition—and MacCallum no longer felt any great loyalty toward the town. Indeed, if anything, he felt a deep resentment for the changes that had taken place in the village, and an even deeper anger toward the company that had brought them about.

"I don't work for the town of Silverdale," he finally replied. "I work for the county, and besides that, my only interest right now is Rick Ramirez. He's going to need a lot of help, and I intend for him to get it." He stood and held out his hand to the coach. "I've arranged to have another bed brought into Rick's room. I expect Maria will want to stay with him, at least for the moment."

Jenkins stood up and grasped MacCallum's hand. "Thank you," he said. "Maria and I both appreciate everything you've done—"

But MacCallum cut him off. "So far, I haven't done much, and I'm not at all sure of what I'm going to be able to do. But I'll do what I can, and I'll call in anybody else I think we might need. It's going to be a long haul."

When Jenkins had left, MacCallum returned once more to the room where Rick Ramirez lay unconscious in the bed.

In the half hour he'd been gone, nothing had changed.

MacCallum wasn't sure whether that was a good sign or a bad one.

*   *   *

Phil Collins was stretched out in the recliner that was the dominant feature of his living room, his fingers idly pressing the buttons of the television remote, when suddenly a low growl rose from the throat of the big German shepherd sprawled on the floor next to the chair. A split second later the dog rose to its feet, its hackles rising, and Collins kicked irritably at the animal. "Shut up!" he commanded as the door bell rang. "We're not living in Chicago anymore." He tossed the remote control onto the table next to the chair, then stood up. With the dog still growling softly, and preceding him by half a step, he went to the door and opened it. On the porch, his face only half lit by the dim glow of the porch light, he recognized Bob Jenkins. Collins's brow rose a quarter of an inch, but he opened the door wider. "Down, Sparks," he ordered curtly, and the police dog obediently dropped to its haunches. "Come on in," he said. "I was sort of wondering if you might stop by. How's your boy?"

Jenkins's eyes glittered angrily as he stepped into the house, but he froze when the dog growled a warning.

"Don't worry about Sparks," Collins told him. "He's all talk and no action. Anyway," he added, a crooked grin half forming on his face, "I think he is. So far, nobody's had the guts to challenge him." The grin faded. "Your boy okay?" he repeated.

"My 'boy' is named Ricardo Ramirez," Jenkins said, his voice tight. "And no, he's not okay. His neck is broken, he has a lot of internal injuries, and he's in a coma. Which you would very well know," he went on bitterly, "if you or anyone else from your school had bothered to show up at the hospital."

"Hey!" Collins protested, his eyes widening. "How was I supposed to know? For all I knew, the ambulance took him back to Fairfield!"

"Don't try to act stupid," Jenkins snapped, his voice rising. The dog, instantly sensing a threat to its master, snarled dangerously. "And get that dog outside, Collins," he went on in a more reasonable tone. "You're not going to like what I have to say to you, and neither is your mutt. And believe me, it would give me great pleasure to sue you for every cent you're ever going to be worth."

Collins's jaw tightened, but he said nothing. Instead, he led the dog to the kitchen, returning with two cans of Coors, closing the kitchen door behind him. He offered one of the beers to Jenkins but wasn't surprised when the other man refused it. Popping the top of his own beer, he settled his heavy frame back into his recliner and indicated another chair for the Fairfield coach. But Jenkins remained on his feet.

"I came over here to tell you I'm going to be filing a complaint against your team, and Jeff LaConner in particular," he said. "It seems like every year your team gets rougher, and now I've got a boy who's seriously injured."

Collins held up a conciliatory hand. "Now, hold on," he said. "I know you're upset, and I agree we better talk about this. But I don't think you want to start talking about complaints, or lawsuits, or whatever else you've got in mind. Football's a rough game—"

"We know that," Jenkins said, his voice icy. "And no one expects that there won't be some injuries now and then. But this one was absolutely inexcusable."

Collins frowned. "It was an accident, Bob. You know it."

"It wasn't an accident," Jenkins objected. "I saw it perfectly. Your boy was going down, and he deliberately threw himself onto Rick."

Collins took a deep breath, then rose and walked to the television set, on top of which sat a video-cassette recorder. "Why don't we just take a look?" he suggested.

Jenkins gazed at the other man in surprise. "You're kidding. You mean you tape your games?"

"Every one of them," Collins replied. "How can you correct errors if you can't even show the guys what they did wrong?'' He pressed the play button on the tape deck and a moment later an image of that afternoon's game flashed onto the screen. As both men watched, the penultimate play of the game unfolded before them.

''Right there!'' Jenkins suddenly said. ''Play it again. You got slow motion?''

Collins rewound the tape a few feet, then started the play over again, this time in slow motion. As they watched, they could both clearly see Rick Ramirez tackling Jeff LaConner. Jeff twisted slightly, then collapsed heavily onto Rick. And for just a split-second, before the rest of the two teams piled onto the heap, both men could see Rick's head twist at an unnatural angle. They watched the tape again, and then once more.

''Well?'' Collins finally asked.

Jenkins was chewing his lip thoughtfully, but Collins could see that much of his anger had drained away. ''I don't know,'' he said at last, his voice betraying his pain at having to make the admission of uncertainty. ''But it looks to me like he deliberately threw himself on Rick,'' he insisted.

''And it looks to me like he lost his balance,'' Collins replied, rewinding the tape yet one more time. ''Let's watch it again.'' Once more the image came on the screen, and once more the two men watched in silence. When it was over, Collins spoke again, choosing his words carefully. ''Look, Bob, I know what you're thinking, and I know how you feel. But all that happened there is that Rick—what's his name?''

''Ramirez,'' Jenkins replied almost tonelessly, his eyes still fixed on the screen, where Rick's head was frozen in a painfully grotesque angle.

''Ramirez,'' Collins repeated. ''Well, it looks to me like he just did his job, maybe a little too well, and wound up under LaConner when he went down. But it wasn't anyone's fault.''

Jenkins nodded slowly and finally turned away from the television set. ''Maybe,'' he said softly, ''I'll change my mind about that beer.'' He picked it up from the coffee table and jerked at the tab on its top, then took a long swig. ''It's been a bad day. Rick . . . well, if I had my way about things, Rick would be my stepson.''

''Oh, Jesus,'' Phil Collins groaned. ''I'm sorry. I can't tell you how sorry I am. If there's anything I can do—''

Jenkins abruptly met Collins's eyes. ''There is,'' he said. ''You can tell me what kind of insurance your school carries and if you'll fight a claim on this case. Rick's mother has no money at all and—''

But Phil Collins was already holding up a hand. ''Enough said,'' he assured Jenkins. ''I don't think any of us wants a lawsuit—mind you, I don't think the boy could win one, but I wouldn't want to have to fight it. All any of us wants is what's best for the boy. I'll start things rolling tonight and keep you posted. And if there's anything I can do personally, you just let me know. Okay?''

Jenkins hesitated a moment, then nodded, and standing, extended his hand. ''I guess I owe you an apology,'' he began.

But Collins brushed it aside. ''Don't even think about it,'' he said. He flopped back into his chair, then shrugged. ''In a way,'' he went on, ''I can't say I disagree with you. Sometimes I think the game *is* getting too rough. And every year it seems like the boys are getting bigger and bigger. But what can we do about it? For a lot of the guys in this part of the country, football's the only way they're going to get to college, and they can only get there if they play for a winning team. So they keep trying harder. But you can bet,'' he added, ''that my team will see that film and get a talking-to about dropping when they know they're hit. We shouldn't have accidents like today's.''

A few minutes later, when Jenkins had gone, Collins picked up the phone and dialed the number of the principal of Silverdale High. As briefly as possible, he recounted the conversation he'd had with Jenkins. When he was done,

Malcolm Fraser, whose concerns about the dangers of football were well known to everyone in Silverdale, clucked fretfully.

"I don't know," he sighed. "Perhaps we've been putting too much emphasis on winning—"

Collins cut him off. "Winning is the whole point of the game, Malcolm. If we're not out to win, there's no point in playing at all. So we'll just do what we can for Ramos, or whatever his name is, and forget the whole thing."

"Unless they decide to sue," Fraser replied.

"If they sue, they sue," Collins said flatly. "And that won't be our problem. That will be the lawyers' problem."

"I see," Fraser replied after a long silence. Then: "And what about Jeff LaConner? What are you going to do about him? He's playing awfully rough, isn't he?"

Collins chuckled hollowly. "That he is," he agreed. "And if he keeps it up, I can tell you what I'm going to do. Name him Most Valuable Player at the end of the season."

He was still chuckling when he hung up.

Charlotte LaConner watched her husband open another beer and pass it over to Jeff, then pop the top on yet another can for himself. It was the third beer for Jeff, the fourth for Chuck, and finally she could contain herself no longer.

"What do you think Phil Collins would say about that?" she asked, nodding toward the Bud her son was emptying into his glass.

But Chuck only grinned at her. "Come on, honey," he protested. "It's a big night for Jeff! First game of the season, and a perfect pass on the last play! And it was Phil who told the boys to go out and have a good time."

Charlotte took a deep breath, then let it out again. There was no point in arguing with Chuck, not after he'd had a couple of beers. And the fact that he knew as well as she did that the coach hadn't intended to include drinking in his lifting of the training strictures that afternoon wouldn't make any difference. But still, the whole thing bothered her.

The image of the injured boy lying motionless on the ground was still strong in her mind, and though Chuck had insisted she was wrong, she still felt that as Jeff's mother, she should have gone to the hospital to see if the boy from Fairfield was all right. But Chuck had wanted to go out with the parents of some of the other boys on the team, and in the end, as always, she had gone along.

As always, Charlotte had sat in the group of celebrating parents, feeling terribly alone amidst the talk, which never varied from an unending replay of that afternoon's game. Finally she let her mind drift away entirely, and Chuck had to shake her out of her reverie when the group at last began to break up.

Then, when Jeff had come home an hour ago, it began again. Play by play, father and son had relived the game.

At last they had come to the moment when Jeff plunged through the line, dropped on the other boy, and disappeared under a heap of other players.

"Did you see it, Dad?" Jeff asked now, his eyes glinting with the memory, a wide grin spreading across his face. "Thought he had me, but I fixed him! Just twisted around and dropped on him. Put a knee right into his kidney!"

Charlotte felt her stomach tighten, and suddenly knew she could put it off no longer. Wordlessly, she turned and left the room, went to the bedroom and closed the door. Taking the phone book out of the top drawer of the nightstand, she riffled through it, then dialed the number of the county hospital.

"This is Charlotte LaConner," she said. "I'm calling about the boy who was brought in this afternoon. After the football game?"

There was a momentary silence before the voice at the other end spoke coolly and impersonally. "And what is your relationship to the patient?"

Charlotte hesitated, then replied tightly, "It was my son who tackled the boy."

"I see," the voice said tentatively. Then: "Perhaps I'd better connect you with the duty nurse."

A few moments later, after explaining once more who she was, Charlotte listened numbly as the nurse summarized Ricardo Ramirez's injuries.

"But—But he'll be all right, won't he?" Charlotte finally asked, the question coming out as a plea.

"We don't know, Mrs. LaConner," the nurse replied.

Slowly, Charlotte replaced the receiver, too unnerved to do more than sit still on the bed. Minutes passed as she tried to collect her thoughts. Then, when a raucous laugh echoed from the den, she made up her mind. She stood, straightened her back, and left the bedroom. She paused at the door to the den and waited until her husband noticed her. For a moment he seemed puzzled, but when he saw the expression on her face, his smile began to fade.

"What's wrong?" he finally asked. "You look like you just saw a ghost."

"I just called the hospital," she said. She turned to her son. "The boy you tackled. His name is Rick Ramirez."

Jeff frowned. "S-So?"

Charlotte licked her lips nervously. "He might die, Jeff. His neck is broken and one of his lungs collapsed." Despite herself, her voice hardened. "And when you put your knee into his kidney, apparently you ruptured it."

Jeff's eyes widened, and Charlotte could see his fingers tighten on his beer glass. "Jesus," he whispered. But then, as she watched, a curtain seemed to fall behind his eyes. "It wasn't my fault," he said, his voice taking on a note of belligerence.

From his chair a few feet from Jeff, Chuck shot her a warning glance, but Charlotte chose to ignore it. "Not your fault?" she asked, no longer trying to contain the anger she was feeling. She moved closer to Jeff. "I heard you say you deliberately kneed him."

"Well, what if I did?" Jeff demanded, rising to his feet. He was big, nearly six-foot-three, and he towered over Charlotte's five-foot-four-inch frame. "Shit, Mom, he'd just tackled me, hadn't he? What did you expect me to do? Just stand there and take it?"

Charlotte reached out to grasp her son's arm. "But that's part of the game, isn't it? You try to get through, and he tries to tackle you. But you don't try to hurt him on purpose. . . ."

Jeff's jaw tightened and his eyes blazed with sudden fury. "And you don't know a goddamn thing about football!" he shouted. Abruptly, he shook his mother's arm off his own and hurled his still half-filled glass into the fireplace. The stein shattered against the bricks, then Jeff stormed out of the room, slamming the door behind him.

"Jeff!" Charlotte called too late. Already the back door had slammed as well. A moment later they heard his car start up and roar down the driveway. Furious, she spun around to face Chuck.

"That's it!" she snapped. "No more football! On Monday morning he's quitting the team. I've had it."

But her husband was staring at her as if she had lost her mind. "Hey, slow down, honey," he said, standing up and moving toward her. "Maybe he shouldn't have yelled at you and thrown the glass like that, but how do you think he feels?"

"*Him?*" Charlotte blazed. "What about Rick Ramirez?"

"Jeff didn't mean to hurt him," Chuck replied. "In the heat of a game, these things happen. And whose side are you on, anyway? You just as good as accused him of trying to kill that kid. Your own son! How the hell do you expect him to react?"

Charlotte was silent for a second, and when she spoke, her voice was tight. "I expect him to behave the way we brought him up. I expect him to be a good sport and to keep in mind the fact that he's a lot bigger than most kids and could hurt someone. And if he can't do that, I expect him to stop playing football."

Chuck LaConner gazed silently at his wife, then shook his head. "You mean you want to keep him tied to your apron strings and you don't want him to grow up," he said. "But you can't do that, Charlotte. He's not your little baby anymore." Picking up his own empty beer glass, he left the room.

Charlotte, not quite certain of what had gone wrong, but knowing that she had mishandled the situation very badly, began to clean up the shards of glass scattered across the floor of the den.

4

There was a sharp snap to the air on Monday morning, and as Mark Tanner stepped out the back door into the brilliant sunlight, the first thing he noticed was the sky. Cobalt blue, it had a depth to it that he'd never seen in San Marcos, where no matter how clear the day was, a vague haze always seemed to hang over the world. Here, the mountains to the east were etched sharply against the sky, and there was a different odor, too—not the pungent aroma of the bay, sometimes briskly salty, but more often carrying the faintly nauseating stench of the mud flats—but the clean scent of pine. Chivas, too, seemed to feel the difference, and uttered a joyful bark as he shoved his way past Mark and raced out to the rabbit hutch next to the garage.

But as he fed the rabbits, Mark's sense of exhilaration began to fade, for already he suspected he would have trouble fitting himself in with the rest of the kids in Silverdale.

He had begun thinking as much Saturday evening, when he'd seen Robb Harris. He'd tried to pick up their friendship where it had been left three years before, but quickly realized that it wasn't going to work.

Robb had changed.

He towered over Mark now, and it seemed he'd lost interest in a lot of the things they'd shared when they were growing up.

The rabbits, for instance. Robb had glanced at them for a moment, then asked Mark—and Mark was certain he hadn't mistaken the contempt in Robb's voice—why he was still "messing around" with them. Mark had frowned.

"You used to raise guinea pigs," he'd pointed out.

Robb had rolled his eyes. "Everybody did, when we were kids. Or hamsters, or gerbils." Then he grinned, but it hadn't been the kind of friendly grin Mark remembered from years ago. "Why don't we let 'em go?" he suggested. "Then we could hunt them."

Though Mark had felt a flash of anger, he said nothing. From then on, though, the evening had gone downhill for him. He tried to pretend he was interested in the football game Robb had played in that afternoon, but it hadn't really worked, and Robb finally asked what team he himself was going to try out for.

Then it was Mark who had grinned. "I don't know," he replied. "Debating, maybe?"

Robb looked at him as though he were some kind of alien. "We don't have a debating team," he replied. "And even if we did, nobody would care."

Mark had fallen silent then; and yesterday, when his mother had suggested he go over to the Harrises' and visit Robb, he'd shaken his head and made up an excuse. His mother had looked at him sharply, and it seemed she was about to say something but then changed her mind. So he had spent the day with Chivas, following a trail up into the foothills, enjoying the solitude and the majestic scenery, but already starting to worry about what would happen today.

Suddenly Kelly burst out the back door. "Mom says if you don't come in right now, you're going to be late!" She planted her feet wide apart and put her hands on her hips. "And she has to take me to school, so hurry up!"

Mark grinned at his little sister. "What if I don't?" he teased.

Kelly giggled, as she always did when he teased her. "I don't know," she admitted. "But I bet you'll get in trouble!"

"Then I'll hurry," Mark replied.

He finished hosing out the tray and slid it back beneath the hutch, then added some water to the rabbits' reservoir. In less than a minute he was back in the house, sliding into his place at the breakfast table. His father, already nearly done with his breakfast, glanced up at him.

"I talked to Jerry Harris yesterday," Blake said.

Mark frowned, but made no reply.

"He was thinking you might show up over there. Wanted to know if anything was wrong between you and Robb."

Mark shrugged, but still made no reply.

Blake leaned back in his chair and crossed his arms, and Mark felt himself tense. "I know this move is a big change for all of us," Blake began. "We're all going to have a lot of adjusting to do. But it's a big opportunity." He hesitated a moment, and finally Mark looked up. His father was staring straight at him. "Especially for you," Blake told him.

Mark shifted uneasily in his chair. What was going on? Had he done something wrong?

"I want you to fit in here," his father went on. "I know you've had some problems in the past—missing a year of school—and I know you've had some problems fitting yourself in. But this is a chance for you to start over again."

Suddenly Mark understood. "You mean you want me to go out for sports," he said.

Blake said nothing, but the long, questioning look he gave his son spoke for him.

"I thought we already talked about that—" Mark began

His father silenced him with a gesture. "That was before— and you were right. In San Marcos, you probably wouldn't have made the team. But this is a much smaller school, and Jerry tells me there's room for everyone."

Mark's eyes clouded. "But—"

Once again, Blake didn't let him finish. "All I want you to do is try. Okay?"

Mark hesitated, then reluctantly nodded, knowing there was no point in arguing with his father right now. Still, when he left for school a few minutes later, he was already starting to think of a way around the decision his father had so abruptly made for him.

"Hey! Wait up!"

Mark was still two blocks from the school when he heard the girl's voice. He ignored it until he heard the shout again, this time with his name attached to it, then stopped and looked back. Half a block away, running to catch up, was Linda Harris. She was breathing hard when she came abreast of him, and a sheen of perspiration glistened on her forehead. "Didn't you hear me?" she gasped. "I've been yelling at you for two blocks."

"I didn't hear you," Mark protested.

"You mean you weren't listening," Linda contradicted him, her blue eyes dancing mischievously. "I've been watching you, wandering along with your head in the clouds. You could have gotten run over by a bus, and you wouldn't even have noticed."

Mark felt himself flush, but it was more with pleasure than embarrassment. For Linda, too, had changed since the last time he'd seen her. In three years she'd grown from a gangly girl with braces on her teeth and her hair in braids into a gently curved fifteen-year-old whose blond hair—a little darker than her brother's—flowed softly over her shoulders. "There aren't any buses in Silverdale, are there?" he countered, simply to make conversation. He fell in beside her as she started walking once more.

"A couple," she told him. "There're a few kids who live out on ranches, and they have to go to school, too, you know." She glanced at him curiously. "So what were you thinking about?"

Mark hesitated. His first instinct was to tell her the truth—

that he'd been trying to figure out a way around his father's determination that he go out for football—but he wasn't sure how she might react to that. And, with a jolt, he realized that he didn't want Linda Harris to react badly to him. So he shrugged his shoulders amiably and smiled at her. "I don't know. I guess I was just looking around. You know, getting the feel of things. I . . . well, I do that a lot," he finished lamely.

To his surprise, Linda nodded. "I know. I do that, too. Sometimes people think I'm weird, 'cause I just all of a sudden tune everything out. But just because people are talking doesn't mean you have to listen, does it?" She looked at him so earnestly that he almost burst out laughing.

"I guess not," he admitted. "Not that I ever really thought about it, but I guess you're right. And most people don't seem to have much to say anyway. I guess that's why I like animals better than people."

They turned the last corner and Mark stopped short. "Jesus," he breathed. "Is that the high school?"

Linda stared at him blankly. "What's wrong with it?" she asked, her voice taking on a defensive note.

"N-Nothing," Mark stammered. "It's just—well, it's just not what I was expecting."

Without even thinking about it, Mark had supposed that the school in Silverdale would look like all the others in the innumerable small towns they had passed through since leaving San Marcos—a simple wood-frame structure, its paint peeling, sitting in the midst of a dying lawn on a dusty block on the outskirts of town, with a dirt playing field behind it.

But Silverdale High School resembled nothing he'd seen before. It was a red-brick building, rising three stories high in its central core, with two-story wings jutting out from it to form an imposing V shape. All the windows were framed by white shutters, and the high, peaked roof of the core structure was supported by six soaring columns.

The columns were made of white marble.

The building faced a velvety lawn that was crisscrossed

with winding brick paths, and in front of the building were gardens that, even in September, were ablaze with brightly colored flowers.

A flagpole stood in the center of the lawn. As Mark watched two boys slowly ran an American flag up the pole, as the strains of "The Star-Spangled Banner" began to sound. Next to him, Linda stood still, facing the flag, and a moment later Mark realized that on the lawn in front of the school, and on all the pathways, too, the other students had stopped as well, as though frozen in place, their eyes fastened on the flag. It rose slowly in the morning sun, then, as it reached the top, it began flapping in the breeze just as the last notes of the anthem sounded from the public address system. Only when the music had died away did the school come to life once more.

Mark blinked, then looked at Linda in puzzlement. "Everyone does that every day here?"

Linda frowned for a split-second, then nodded. "I guess it seems kind of dumb to you. Robb said it really bugged him when we first came. But it's a tradition now."

"And everybody does it?" Mark pressed. "They just all stop and face the flag?" He was trying to picture the kids at San Marcos High—the ones with their hair dyed green and orange, and rings through their nostrils—stopping their talk for the raising of the flag. But of course they wouldn't have: They would have turned their ghetto blasters up louder and kept right on with whatever they were doing.

But then, as he and Linda started across the wide lawn toward the school building itself, he realized that none of the kids here wore punk hairstyles, or leather jackets covered with studs. Everywhere he looked he saw only boys in chinos and sports shirts, and girls in sweaters and skirts or carefully pressed slacks and crisp blouses.

They mounted the flight of steps that led to a wide, terracelike porch between the marble columns and the main doors of the school. "Well, do you like it?" Linda asked eagerly.

Mark grinned. "What's not to like?"

Linda waved to a group of her friends who were standing next to one of the columns but made no move to join them. Instead, she took Mark's arm and edged him toward the door. "Come on, I'll show you where the office is."

Inside the front doors was an enormous hall whose ceiling rose the full three floors to the roof. A broad staircase at the end of the hall rose to the second floor, and above that, split into two narrower flights, one on each side of the hall that led to the third floor. The ceiling itself was made of white plaster, but was decorated with an ornate molding around its edges.

The floor beneath Mark bore a complicated geometric design of black and white marble. He paused for a moment, trying to take it all in, but Linda urged him on. "The principal's office is down this way," she said, leading him off to the right. A moment later they'd stepped through a white paneled door with a fanlight above it and were facing a smiling secretary.

"This is Mark Tanner, Miss Adams," Linda said. "He's starting today."

The secretary nodded. "Your father called me last week," she said, then turned to Mark. "Did you happen to bring your records with you?"

Mark shook his head blankly, but the secretary seemed unconcerned. "Just start filling these out, and I'll have them before you're done," she said. She pushed a small stack of forms and cards toward Mark, then turned to a computer terminal on her desk. Her fingers flashed over the keyboard, and a few minutes later a printer on a table next to the wall clattered to life.

"See you at lunchtime," Linda promised. Then she was gone and Mark was filling out the numerous questionnaires and forms that would get him enrolled as a student at Silverdale High.

Half an hour later Shirley Adams quickly went over the forms he'd completed and handed him yet another stack.

"Take these to the nurse—two doors down, on the left—then come back here after you're done. By then we should have a schedule for you."

"Wh-What about photography?" Mark asked hesitantly. "Back in San Marcos I was taking my second year of it."

Shirley Adams's smile widened. "Then you'll be in it here, too."

"You mean you really have a darkroom?"

Miss Adams looked astonished. "This is Silverdale," she said. "We have everything here."

Mark, dressed only in a pair of gym shorts that were two sizes too large, was standing on the scales when Robb Harris walked into the nurse's office. Robb glanced at the scales, then smirked at Mark.

"A hundred and five?" he asked. "You're even scrawnier than I was when I came here." Before Mark could say anything, Robb turned to the nurse. "The coach wants me to go over to the clinic this morning. Can you write me a pass?"

"In a minute," the nurse replied, not glancing up from the clipboard on which she had been noting Mark's height, blood pressure, lung capacity, reflex responses, and myriad other details pertaining to his health.

"Maybe you'd better write one for Mark, too," Robb went on, dropping onto a chair and stretching his long legs out in front of him. "I bet Dr. Ames could fix him up in no time."

Mark frowned. "Dr. Ames?" he asked. "Who's he?"

"The sports clinic. Didn't your dad tell you about it?"

Mark shook his head, but already a tight knot of anxiety was forming in the pit of his stomach.

"It's a couple of miles out of town. It's a sports camp all summer, and kids come from all over the country. But the rest of the year we get to use it."

Mark stared at Robb. "Use it for what?"

"For training," Robb replied. The look of scorn that had

needled at Mark on Saturday evening came into his eyes once more. "Dr. Ames knows practically everything there is to know about sports medicine, and he's got all kinds of special equipment out there. It's neat."

"And," the nurse added with a knowing glance at Mark, "the fact that the boys get a morning off from classes when the coach sends them out there doesn't make it any tougher for them."

"Time off from classes?" Mark echoed. "Just so you can go out and train for football?"

"And basketball and baseball," Robb replied.

Mark frowned. "So what's wrong with you that you're going today?"

Robb shrugged. "Nothing. It's just a checkup. All of us on the football team get one every week."

"Every *week*! What for?"

Robb rolled his eyes impatiently. "Because you can get hurt playing football, dummy. Christ, look what happened to that guy from Fairfield on Saturday. He's all torn up inside, but he looked just fine."

The nurse put her clipboard aside for a moment, scribbled something on the top sheet of a small pad of paper, and handed it to Robb, who stood up and stretched lazily, then grinned at Mark.

"Sure you don't want to come along?" he asked. "It sure beats sitting in a math class."

Mark shook his head. "Guess I'll have to do without weekly checkups, since I'm not going out for football."

Robb looked at him sharply. "Oh, yeah? That's not the way I hear it."

And then he was gone. Mark stared at the closed door where Robb had stood a moment before. The other boy's last words echoed in Mark's mind.

The knot of anxiety in his stomach tightened.

Robb Harris pedaled his bicycle slowly out of town, enjoying the warmth of the sun on his back, feeling no rush to reach his destination. That, he decided, was one of the best things about being on the football team. You never had to rush to get anywhere except practice, and at least one day a week you could count on half a day off from classes. Not, of course, that you could let your grades slip—Phil Collins was an absolute fanatic about that. Drop below a B average, and you were off the team. But if you were on the football team, the teachers were always ready to give you a little extra help, so it was really no sweat. And in the end the best football players from Silverdale always got their pick of where they wanted to go to college.

They might not get scholarships, but they all at least got their choice.

He breathed deeply of the mountain air, enjoying the rush of oxygen filling his lungs.

Not like before, when he'd been growing up in San Marcos. From the time Robb had been seven years old, almost every breath had been an agony. He could still remember the terrible panic he felt whenever an attack began, the helpless, horrible fear as he gasped for air. It had been that way here, too, for the first few months. But then he'd started going to Dr. Ames, and been put on a regimen of exercise.

For the first six weeks he'd absolutely hated it. But then the coughing had begun to ease and he'd started feeling better. A few months later, as he'd put on weight and grown out of his clothes, he decided that all the exercise was worth it.

Then, summer before last, his dad had gotten him into the football camp, even though he'd never really played the game before. At first he felt clumsy and stupid, but as the summer progressed, he began to catch on. For the first time in his life he felt like everyone else.

Maybe, he thought, that would happen to Mark, too. Except that Mark didn't seem to care if he fit in or not. Robb snickered softly to himself, remembering Mark showing off his rabbits the other day.

Christ, that was kid stuff. And if the other guys found out about it, Mark had better watch out.

He turned off the narrow road that led up the valley toward the foothills, and steered the bike up the lane to the gates of the sports clinic, barely glancing at the sign he knew so well:

ROCKY MOUNTAIN HIGH
Mens Sana in Corpore Sano

Robb still thought it was a dumb name but he hadn't been able to convince Marty Ames that none of the kids cared about that old John Denver song anymore.

The gates under the arching sign stood open, and Robb rode through with a wave to a gardener who was working on the turf of the playing field to the right. He parked the bike in the stand next to the entrance and pushed open the glass door into the lobby. It was large and airy, and furnished with an assortment of comfortable furniture. During the summer the lobby served as a lounge for a motley collection of husky youths. But now, during the school year, it was deserted, and Robb hurried through it, then turned left, passed the dining hall, and entered the waiting room next to Dr. Martin Ames's office. Marjorie Jackson smiled up at Robb from behind the clutter on top of her desk. She was a middle-aged woman whose title was Assistant to the Director, and it was she, as all the boys knew, who actually took care of the day-to-day running of the camp, with little direction from her employer.

"He's in the rowing room," she said without waiting for Robb to ask. "And," she added, glancing at the clock on the wall, "you're ten minutes late."

Even before Robb could begin to make up an excuse, she had gone back to her work, pointedly ignoring him. Only slightly abashed, Robb turned and left the office, then broke into a trot as he cut through the dining room and kitchen, toward the large training section at the back of the building. Marjorie might forgive him for the ten minutes, and Dr. Ames might not even mention it, but still, Robb would see the hurt look in the doctor's eyes and know that he'd let him down.

Robb, and most of the other boys on the team, far preferred Phil Collins's shouting at them to Marty Ames's grave look of abject disappointment.

Today, though, Ames seemed not to have noticed Robb's tardiness. When Robb came into the rowing room, the tall, dark-haired doctor merely looked up from the computer terminal he had been staring at and smiled a welcome.

"Good game Saturday," he commented.

Robb shrugged modestly. "I didn't really do much. A dozen plays, and that was about it."

Ames chuckled. "If you don't let the other team keep the ball, the defense is going to sit on the bench." His face turned more serious then. He was a good-looking man, though not quite handsome, and he appeared to be no more than thirty-five, though he was actually nearing fifty. He always joked to the boys that he had to work hard to keep as fit as his patients. "How are you feeling?" he asked.

"Fine," Robb replied. Without being told, he stripped down to his underwear, then stretched out on a treatment table next to the wall. An osteopath as well as an M.D., Ames ran his fingers expertly over Robb's spine, then instructed the boy to roll over on his right side and draw up his left knee. Wrapping his arms around Robb's torso, Ames applied a quick but gentle twist to the boy's back, and Robb felt just a hint of something like vibration as one of his lower vertebrae adjusted itself back into perfect alignment.

"Looking good," Ames commented, then began wrapping the sleeve of a sphygmomanometer around his upper left arm. Satisfied, he nodded toward one of the rowing machines, and Robb, after pulling on a pair of gym shorts, took his position at the mechanical oars. He waited patiently as the doctor inserted an I.V. needle into his thigh, not even flinching as Ames expertly found the vein. "We'll be monitoring your blood today," he said, and Robb nodded, used to the procedures after more than a year.

Facing him was a wide, curving screen whose sides were just beyond the reach of his peripheral vision. At a signal from Ames, Robb began rowing. With the first stroke, the screen in front of him came to life.

It was a river scene, and though it looked to Robb like it might have been the Charles River in Boston, he knew that it was actually a computer-generated graphic, thrown onto the screen by three separate projectors. From where he sat, the illusion was almost perfect. He felt as if he were actually on the water. A few yards away he could see three other sculls, keeping pace with him.

He applied himself harder to the oars, and immediately the other sculls seemed to drop behind, until the other rowers, too, picked up their pace, and one of them began gaining on him.

Robb could feel himself sweating now, and he began working harder. Once again he pulled ahead, but then, while two of the other boats continued to drop back, the third once more began catching up with him. Cursing silently to himself, Robb renewed his efforts.

At the computer terminal, Marty Ames studied the graphic readouts of the changes in Robb's blood chemistry as the boy punished himself even harder. The blood-sugar level began dropping, and then he watched as Robb's adrenal gland kicked in and a short burst of adrenaline shot into the boy's system.

Then, as the adrenaline faded from Robb's circulatory system, Ames's fingers flew over the keyboard.

Once more the graphics on the screen changed.

Robb's eyes narrowed angrily as he saw his computer-generated competitor gaining on him. He leaned into the oars harder, but he was getting tired now and didn't seem to be gaining any speed. He looked up from his labors to see the other boat catch up with him and move off to the right to pass him.

"No!" Robb shouted out loud, then bit his lips in angry determination as he realized how much energy he'd wasted on the useless outburst. The tendons of his neck standing out, he forced himself to row harder. Once more he caught up with the other scull.

Abruptly, the screen went blank. It was over.

He was back in the rowing room at the sports clinic and Marty Ames was smiling at him, his expression reflecting his pride in Robb.

"Not bad," he said, which, coming from Marty Ames, was considered high praise. "How'd it feel?"

Robb rested against the oars for a moment, panting, then shook his head. "I don't know," he said. "This setup really gets to me sometimes. I *know* nothing's real, but when I'm doing it, I get so into it I could swear I was in a real race. And that guy in the number-three boat almost beat me."

"How come he didn't?" Ames asked with deceptive mildness as he began removing the needle from Robb's thigh.

Now it was Robb who grinned. " 'Cause I got pissed at him," he confessed. "I just got pissed off at losing."

"And that," Ames said, "is exactly the point. Your anger released a shot of adrenaline, and the adrenaline was just enough to put you across the line. In case you're interested," he added, glancing once more at the computer screen, "you beat him by exactly thirteen hundredths of a second."

"Not much," Robb commented, standing up and stretching his tired muscles.

"It was enough to win," Ames told him. "And it'll get better. If you just keep at it, it'll keep getting better."

As Robb headed for the shower a few minutes later, he knew he'd keep at it, because he knew how much he liked winning.

He liked it a lot.

A whole lot.

5

Charlotte LaConner knew that Chuck wouldn't approve of what she was about to do, and she was equally certain that he would find out about it. In Silverdale, after all, everyone always knew what everyone else was doing. Not that she particularly objected to the close scrutiny of a small town, she reflected as she put the final touches to the quarterly expense report she was compiling for the R&D Division. It was just that every now and then—times like today—she would have preferred a little more privacy.

She pressed the enter key on her computer, waited until the machine announced that the expense report had been successfully transmitted back into the main tank of the TarrenTech computer, then logged off for the day.

Charlotte had been working for only a few months, part of an experiment the company was conducting that, if successful, would allow women in Silverdale to work part-time at home. For now, the experiment was limited to the wives of men working for the company; only one man was participating—Bill Tangen, whose wife, Irene, was a pharmaceutical expert, working full-time while Bill took care of their baby daughter. For Charlotte, the program was working out perfectly. She discovered she liked working alone and got far more done in the space of a few hours than she'd ever accomplished while working full-time in the division offices. This morning, however, she'd found it hard to concentrate, and after finishing the expense report, she decided to call it a day.

It was Rick Ramirez who had been preying on her mind all morning. Indeed, the injured boy had never really been out of her mind. Not that his name had even been mentioned yesterday. Silence had fallen over the LaConner household since the angry scene when Jeff had stormed from the house.

Neither Chuck nor Jeff would discuss it with her.

And that, Charlotte now realized, was what bothered her the most. Her husband and her son had clearly put the terrible incident out of their minds as though nothing at all had happened. But she herself had been unable to escape the image of the Fairfield player lying hurt on the field, and had awakened this morning determined to go to the hospital to see how he was doing.

But why did she feel so guilty about it? What on earth could possibly be wrong with visiting an injured boy?

She could almost see Chuck gazing at her with that look of his, the look that told her he couldn't fathom her thought processes, and that, therefore, there must be something wrong with them. And she could hear him, too, his voice taking on what she thought of as his "logical tone." "But don't you see? If you go to the hospital, it's as much as admitting that Jeff was somehow responsible for what happened. And even if he were responsible—which he's not—it would still be a mistake. The lawyers could make hay with something like that."

Or was it Chuck's voice she was hearing? Was that really what he'd say, or was it how she herself felt, deep inside?

It didn't matter. Right or wrong, she was going.

Thirty minutes later, forcing herself not to glance around to see who might be watching, she pushed through the doors into the lobby of the small county hospital and stepped up to the counter. From behind the glass Anne Carson smiled at her, then rolled her eyes and pointed meaningfully at the phone she was cradling against her ear. Several times, as Charlotte watched, Anne opened her mouth to say something then closed it again as the person at the other end apparently went right on talking. Finally, though, Anne wearily put the phone back on the hook and slid open the glass panel that separated the waiting room from the office.

"Charlotte! What brings you down here?" Concern spread over her face. "You're not sick, are you?"

Charlotte shook her head. "I . . . well, I wanted to find out how the Ramirez boy is. From Fairfield?"

"Not good, I'm afraid," she said, then forced a small smile. "He's in room three, down the hall." She hesitated, then understanding Charlotte's distress, said, "It's against the rules, but you can look in on him if you want to."

Charlotte's step slowed as she moved down the corridor, and she came to a complete stop in front of the half-open door to the boy's room. At last, steeling herself, she pushed the door open and stepped inside. There were two beds in the room, but only one of them was occupied. Covered only with a light blanket, his head held rigid in a metal brace, his eyes closed, Rick Ramirez had a strange stillness about him that told Charlotte instantly that he was not merely asleep. She stepped forward and stood beside the boy, gazing down into his face. A lock of curly black hair lay over one eye, and Charlotte instinctively reached out to brush it back.

"Don't touch him," a soft but urgent voice said behind her. Gasping with surprise, Charlotte turned to see a pretty young woman, no more than thirty, coming out of the bathroom that connected this room and the next. "Please," the woman went on. "I can do it." She moved to the bed, and Charlotte stepped aside. Gently, her hand barely caressing the boy's cheek, the woman carefully moved the lock of hair. Then she looked up, her dark eyes meeting Charlotte's. "Who are you?" she asked.

"Charlotte LaConner," Charlotte replied. "I—my son is Jeff LaConner. He was in the game—"

Instantly the other woman's eyes flashed with anger. "I know who he is," she said. "He's the boy who hurt my son. I am Maria Ramirez," she added, the words sounding to Charlotte almost like a challenge.

Charlotte swallowed, struggling to control her emotions. "I—I just came to see how your son is." She spoke softly, her voice little more than a whisper. "Is he going to be all right?"

Maria Ramirez's eyes glistened with tears, but when she spoke, her voice was perfectly controlled. "No," she said. "He's not going to be all right. He may never walk again." Though she saw Charlotte recoil from her words, Maria went relentlessly on. "He might not even live, Mrs. LaConner. Your son might very well have killed my boy."

Charlotte closed her eyes, as if the gesture might shut away the reality of Maria Ramirez's words. But when she opened them, the slim Chicano woman was still staring at her. "Is—Is there anything I can do?" Charlotte whispered. "Anything at all?"

Maria Ramirez shook her head. Charlotte moved forward then and reached out as if to touch the woman, but Maria shrank away from her. Silently, Charlotte turned to go. But when she was at the door, Maria spoke once more.

"Make him stop, Mrs. LaConner. Make your son stop playing that game. If he doesn't, he'll hurt someone else."

Charlotte turned back and nodded. "I will, Mrs. Ramirez. You can be very certain of that. Jeff has played his last game."

But as she walked out of the hospital and into the bright glare of the high, noonday sun, Charlotte wondered whether or not she would be able to back up her words. In the twenty years she'd been married to Chuck, she had yet to win a major argument. Inevitably his logic won out over her own emotionalism.

*   *   *

Blake Tanner had spent the morning touring the TarrenTech facility with Jerry Harris. At almost every turn his amazement had increased.

When he'd arrived that morning, he'd been surprised at the apparent lack of security in the building, but Jerry had quickly disabused him of that notion.

"The television cameras have been tracking you since you came within a quarter of a mile of the shop," he explained. "A description of your car and its plate number is already in the memories, and it also did a match to a photograph of you. In addition, we have a whole series of perimeter alarms buried in the ground around the building, and backup systems in case anyone is smart enough to get around the main system. Not that we've ever had a problem," he added, a note of smugness coming into his voice. "In all the years we've been here, there hasn't been so much as a single attempt to breach our defenses."

Jerry Harris spoke as though TarrenTech were a fortress and he its commanding officer. And as they began their tour of the building, Blake saw that the comparison was apt. Deceptively small when viewed from the outside, the building extended four floors below ground level. "No point alerting anyone as to how much we're doing here," Jerry had pointed out, chuckling softly.

They'd gone first to the software section, where a group of top programmers, all of them casually dressed, were working at computer terminals or whispering quickly to each other in the strange programming language that Blake had never been able to comprehend. "We have an Artificial Intelligence unit working here," Jerry said in reply to Blake's inquisitive glance. "We're far ahead of the guys in Palo Alto and Berkeley, but of course they don't know it. In fact, as far as they know, we're only working on a new operating system to compete with Microsoft."

Blake nodded. He'd heard the rumors himself and had already begun working on marketing strategies.

"Except," Jerry went on, smiling broadly, "it's a bunch of bullshit."

Blake gaped at him, and his boss laughed out loud.

"Do you think Ted Thornton's dumb enough to go up against Microsoft on their own turf? We started the rumor ourselves, and managed to get it going really well by sending a few guys to Berkeley and Palo Alto." His eyes fairly glittered with pride and amusement as he told the story. "The reason they wanted out of TarrenTech, supposedly, was that they were bored with operating systems and wanted to get into A.I. So we now have our men in both places, and no one has caught on yet."

Blake shook his head in wonder. They moved on then, wandering through a maze of laboratories. One of them was experimenting in superconductors, concentrating on ceramics, and others were experimenting with new forms of bubble technology. Finally, they entered the pharmaceutical labs and at last encountered a security guard. Though he didn't ask them for any identification, he watched carefully as they donned lab coats and covered their faces with masks.

"Of course, this isn't much protection if anything's loose in here," Jerry said, "but it's better than nothing. And our containment has been about as good as it can get. In five years we've never had a bug get loose. Not even within the lab itself."

"Bug?" Blake asked, hesitating at the door. "What's going on in there?"

Jerry's smile was hidden by his mask. "Research. The big push right now, of course, is AIDS, but we're involved in a lot of other things, too. And you don't have to worry about AIDS—in the conditions here, it would be next to impossible for you to be exposed to it. Come on."

He opened the first of a double set of locked doors; as soon as they had stepped inside, the doors automatically closed behind them, sealing them in the antechamber. A moment later the second set of doors was released. Then they were in the lab itself. Jerry did his best to explain what was going on, but when the talk began to involve DNA and genetic engineering, Blake was lost.

"And now," Jerry Harris announced nearly an hour later, after they'd left the labs and returned to the first floor, "we come to my personal favorite part of the whole installation." He pushed open a door and they stepped into a long, sky-lit room, with cages along one wall. "The animal room," Jerry said, his voice taking on a note of excitement that went beyond anything Blake had heard before that morning. He grinned like a kid. "I must come in here at least three times a day," he said. They walked slowly along the row of cages. At almost every one of them Jerry stopped to murmur to the mice, rats, or guinea pigs. When they came to a cage full of white rabbits, Jerry opened the door and carefully lifted one of the animals out. He cradled it gently in his hands, and Blake was instantly reminded of his own son. Jerry seemed to read his mind.

"It was Mark who got me started. I always liked Robb's guinea pigs, but there's something about rabbits that always gets to me. I guess they always seem so friendly or something."

Blake's brows pulled together in a puzzled frown. "But they're lab animals, aren't they?"

Jerry's eyes clouded for a moment, then cleared. "I guess I just try not to think about that," he said quietly. "I try not to get too attached to any of them, but sometimes, well—" He broke off suddenly and put the rabbit back in the cage. "Come on," he said. "Let's go take a look at the monkeys."

They moved to the end of the room where, in a large cage well equipped with rings, bars, and branches of trees, a small troop of spider monkeys chattered amongst themselves. As they approached, the monkeys fell silent, their wary eyes gazing suspiciously at the two men for a long moment, until, as if satisfied about something, their attention shifted back to one another and they returned to their grooming and murmuring.

"They recognize people, you know," Jerry said quietly. "They were looking to see if one of us was the lab tech. They always know that that means one of them is going to be taken away and not brought back. I've been thinking of having someone different do it each time, but I'm afraid if I did, the troop might become frightened of everyone.''

They watched the monkeys silently for a few minutes, then Jerry Harris turned away. ''Well, back to the grind, I suppose,'' he sighed.

They were no more than five steps from the big cage when they heard a loud screech of pure animal fury and both men spun around to see a large male—almost a third larger than any of the others—reach out and grab one of the smaller males around the neck. Its eyes glittering with rage, the larger one sank its teeth into the smaller one's shoulder, and then, as the smaller one began to scream in agony, the larger animal began shaking it.

Blake stared at the two monkeys in shock, but Jerry Harris instantly reached out and hit a button on the wall. A loud bell began to ring, the doors at the far end of the room flew open, and three attendants came running toward them.

''The hose!'' Harris called. ''Bring the hose!''

While two of the attendants advanced toward the cage, the third wheeled back and disappeared for a moment. When he returned, he was clutching the nozzle of a fire hose that snaked out behind him.

The smaller of the two monkeys was already dying, blood spurting from the torn artery in its neck. But the bigger one, apparently oblivious to the crimson fluid with which it was being drenched, kept shaking the body of the smaller one.

Finally, the attacker dropped the limp body of its victim to the floor of the cage. Grasping the now-dead creature by its feet, he began swinging it around, maniacally smashing its head against the bars of the cage.

Fighting down a wave of nausea, Blake turned away from the gruesome spectacle, but Jerry Harris, his face ashen and his jaw tight, kept watching, directing the activities of the three attendants.

''Turn on the water,'' he shouted. ''He'll drop it as soon as you hit him.''

The blast of water nearly knocked the attendant who was holding the nozzle off his feet. But as Harris had predicted, the large monkey, still screaming with rage, dropped the corpse of its victim. Immediately he was pinned against the bars at the far end of the cage.

While the attendant with the hose kept the animal immobile with the pounding stream of water, another quickly fired a tranquilizing dart into the raging creature. Not more than three seconds later the large monkey slumped to the floor.

"Jesus," Blake breathed when it was all over. "What the hell happened in there?"

Harris hesitated a moment while he seemed to regain control of himself. As the attendants began the work of herding the rest of the troop into the sleeping quarters behind the main portion of the cage so they could remove the bodies of the two fallen monkeys, he took Blake's arm and drew him toward the door.

"It happens sometimes," he said, his voice quavering. "Something happens to an animal when it's kept in a cage. It might seem perfectly normal for years, but then, all of a sudden, it can just go berserk." He glanced at Blake. "Haven't you ever seen the big cats pacing back and forth in a zoo? Especially in the small cages? Well, I don't think they're just exercising. If you ask me, they've just gone completely psychotic. They'd be better off dead."

They were back in Jerry Harris's office before Blake spoke again. "If you feel that way," he said, "then how can you stand to know that every one of those animals back there is going to die in our labs?"

Harris managed a thin smile. "It's my job," he said, a trace of bitterness apparent in his voice. "And I keep telling myself that the research we do, and the lives we might save, are worth what we're doing to the animals."

Blake thought about it for a moment, then slowly nodded. "And what am I doing out here?" he finally asked. "From what I've seen, you don't need a marketing man at all."

Apparently relieved to have the subject changed, Jerry

Harris tossed a file across his desk to Blake. "You're going to be doing a lot," he said. "You're going to know every facet of what's going on out here, and even if you don't understand the technology—which I don't, myself—you're at least going to know what we're trying to do. You've always been good with people, Blake, and whether you agree or not, that's what marketing is all about. Showing people why they need what you have. Out here, of course, you'll be doing a lot of what you might call public relations as well. And you can start with that." Harris nodded toward the file, and Blake picked it up. He opened it curiously, and was surprised to find that it was a medical file.

It was the file on Ricardo Ramirez.

Puzzled, Blake Tanner gazed questioningly at Jerry Harris.

"TarrenTech will be picking up every one of the medical costs for that boy," Harris told him. "Whatever he needs—surgeons, specialists, physical therapists—the works."

Blake smiled cynically, certain he understood. "On the theory that it can't cost more than a lawsuit," he commented. But to his surprise, Harris shook his head.

"There won't be any lawsuit," he said. "No grounds. It was clearly an accident." He leaned back and put his hands behind his head. "We're in a unique situation here, Blake," he said. "Silverdale was a tiny town when we arrived. TarrenTech came in and changed everything. Essentially, we rebuilt the town from scratch, right down to the schools and library. There was some opposition at first, but we asked the people who were here to trust us, and they did. And we've never failed in that trust." He pointed to the file in Blake's hands. "Legally, no one in Silverdale is responsible for what happened to that boy. But that isn't going to help him, is it?"

Blake shifted in his seat, feeling suddenly embarrassed about his own cynicism of a moment ago. "No," he agreed, "I don't suppose it is."

Harris's voice took on a heavy note of authority. "So as far as I personally, and this company as an entity, are concerned, since the accident happened here, we have a moral responsibility. Ricardo Ramirez will be taken care of, and there will be no cutting of corners. Whatever he needs, he'll get, and for as long as he needs it. If it comes to the worst, the company is prepared to set up a permanent annuity for him.'' Once again his eyes met Blake's. ''His mother says Rick intends to be a doctor when he grows up. He has the grades for it, and he seems to have the drive as well.'' He paused for a moment, then went on. ''Keep that in mind when you start thinking about how to set up a trust. I should imagine a boy like Rick would have treated his mother pretty well, all things considered. In the event that he can't, we will.''

Blake Tanner blinked. The implications of what Jerry Harris was saying could be enormous. ''Have you talked to Ted Thornton about this?'' he asked.

Harris smiled thinly. ''I didn't have to,'' he said. ''It's Ted's policy. And it's a policy,'' he added, ''that I happen to be in one-hundred-percent agreement with. TarrenTech made this town. We are, one way or another, responsible for everything that happens here. And we don't shirk that responsibility.''

When he left Harris's office that morning, Blake Tanner had a new respect for the company—and the people—he worked for. Silverdale, he was beginning to suspect, was not simply going to be a new step in his career.

It might very well change his life.

Mark Tanner found himself walking home alone after school. He had waited in front of the building for Linda Harris for twenty minutes, and when she hadn't shown up, he'd finally wandered around to the back. Just as he'd rounded the corner of the building, the door from the boys' locker room had flown open and the football squad, dressed in practice gear, had trotted out onto the playing field. He'd called out to Robb Harris, but either Robb hadn't heard him or had chosen to ignore him. He was about to call out again when the coach appeared and Mark realized that perhaps neither had been true. For as the coach had approached the squad, all of whom were standing in a neat formation, he had suddenly stopped and glared at one of the boys in the rear rank.

"Fifty push-ups!" he'd shouted. "Now!"

As Mark watched, the boy had immediately dropped to the ground and begun pumping his body up and down. It wasn't until he'd already completed ten of the push-ups that Mark realized what the boy's infraction had been.

He'd waved to one of the girls on the drill team, which was already in the midst of its practice session on the next field. "Holy shit," Mark whispered to himself. He started to turn away, then heard Linda calling his name. Looking up, he saw her waving to him.

"Hi," he said as he walked over to where she was standing with three other girls and two boys. "I was sort of looking for you."

"Cheerleading practice," Linda told him. "And then I have to go over to the library. Want to wait for me?"

Mark shook his head. "Can't," he said. "Mom needs me to help her with the unpacking." He hesitated. "Do you practice every day?"

Linda smiled and shook her head. "Just three days a week, and once during the evening before a game." Their eyes met for a moment, and then, feeling himself reddening, Mark turned away.

"Well, see you tomorrow, I guess," he mumbled.

He didn't see Linda smiling after him, nor did he see Jeff LaConner, who had paused on the football field for a moment, staring speculatively in his direction.

Instead of going directly home, Mark decided to walk down Colorado Street to the shopping district, look around for a few minutes, then cut back over to Telluride Drive. He walked slowly, gazing at each of the houses as he passed, his mind already framing the ornate Victorian-style buildings in the lens of his camera. Almost every one of them, he decided, was worth a picture.

Calendar shots, that's what they looked like.

He filed the idea away, wondering what you did to sell pictures for calendars.

A quarter of an hour later he came to the small collection of buildings, all facing on a little square, that served as Silverdale's downtown section. Like the rest of the town, the commercial area looked like something out of another century. It was a series of free-standing buildings, most of them of wood-frame construction in a style that reminded Mark of a western movie. Wooden sidewalks, raised above the narrow, bricked street by a couple of steps, connected the buildings, and there was a large parking lot laid out behind the Safeway store. The street itself seemed only to be used by pedestrians and a couple of dogs that lay sunning themselves in the middle of the road. Mark stopped to scratch one of the dogs. When he looked up, he saw a camera shop, the name SPALDING'S emblazoned in bright blue letters over the door. The shop was small, tucked into the narrow space between the drugstore and the hardware store.

It was then the idea came to him.

If he had a job after school, there was no way his father could insist that he go out for sports.

Straightening up, he tucked his shirt neatly into his jeans, then walked into the camera store. From behind the counter a friendly-looking man with gray hair and wire-framed glasses smiled genially at him.

"What can I do for you?" the man asked.

"Are you Mr. Spalding?" Mark asked.

The man nodded. "None other. And who might you be?"

"Mark Tanner," Mark replied. "I just moved here, and I was wondering if maybe you needed some help. Just part-time, after school and maybe on weekends."

Henry Spalding's brows arched skeptically. For a moment Mark was certain he was going to be turned down flat. Then, to his surprise, Spalding cocked his head thoughtfully. "Well, actually, I've been thinking about some help. Ski season is coming, and that always brings some people around. Then there's Christmas, and whatnot.'' His gaze sharpened slightly. ''But it's evenings I'd need.''

Mark thought quickly. What difference did it make? If he was working in the evenings, he'd have to do his studying in the afternoons. ''That's okay,'' he said. ''That would be perfect.''

Spalding disappeared into the tiny office at the back of the store and returned with a crumpled and stained job-application form. ''Well, why don't you fill this out, and then we can talk,'' he said, handing the application to Mark. As Mark fished a pen out of the bottom of his book bag, Spalding regarded him speculatively. ''What team are you on?'' he asked. ''You look kind of small for football. Tennis, maybe? Or baseball?''

Mark shook his head, not looking up from the form. ''I'm not on any of the teams,'' he said. ''I'm . . . well, I guess I'm a lot better at photography than I am at sports.''

Suddenly Mr. Spalding's hand appeared in Mark's line of sight, pulling the application back.

''Not on any team?'' he heard the man asking, and looked up to see Spalding gazing quizzically at him.

''N-No,'' Mark stammered. ''Why?''

''Why, because it makes all the difference in the world,'' Spalding told him. ''This is Silverdale, son. Here, we support our teams. And that includes making sure they get first pick of the part-time jobs.'' Then, seeing the look of disappointment in Mark's eyes, he tried to soften the blow. ''Tell you what,'' he said. ''I'll give the school a call tomorrow and sort of see what's what. Maybe nobody on the teams will want the job here. And if they don't, then you can surely have it yourself.''

Mark bit his lip and managed to thank Henry Spalding before he picked up his book bag and backed out of the little shop. But as he started home, he knew that there would be no job for him at Spalding's camera shop.

After all, he'd overheard one of the boys in his photography class talking that morning about looking for a job until baseball season started.

As he turned onto Telluride Drive, Mark began to wonder if maybe he wasn't wrong about Silverdale after all. A week ago it had all seemed so exciting.

Now it didn't seem exciting at all.

6
___

Sharon Tanner stood at the kitchen sink, her lips pursed, her brows pulled together in a worried frown. Though there were four steaks sizzling on the grill behind her, she had forgotten them for the moment, for she was watching Mark, who was seated cross-legged on the lawn near the garage, staring blankly at the rabbit hutch. Though she'd been watching him closely for only a few minutes, she'd been vaguely aware of his presence in the backyard for at least half an hour. That in itself wasn't unusual; Mark usually spent at least an hour a day taking care of the rabbits, petting them, checking them, or just playing with them, letting them run free in the yard for Chivas to chase, confident that the dog would bring them back unharmed.

But today something was different. Instead of frolicking around Mark and sniffing eagerly at the hutch, Chivas was sprawled out on the ground beside his master. The dog's forelegs were stretched out in front of him and his massive head rested quietly on his paws. Behind him, his tail lay limply on the ground, and though he looked as if he might be asleep, Sharon could see even from the kitchen that his eyes were open and staring up at Mark's face.

Chivas, too, apparently sensed that something was wrong. And now that she thought about it, Sharon realized that it wasn't only today. All week, it seemed in retrospect, Mark had grown quieter and quieter, spending more and more time by himself, wandering around in the hills with Chivas after school, or just sitting by himself in the backyard, staring at the rabbits in their cage. But she was almost certain he wasn't seeing the rabbits at all. No, something else was on his mind, something he hadn't been willing to talk about. When Kelly came into the kitchen, demanding to know when dinner was going to be ready, Sharon made up her mind.

"In a few minutes, honey," she told the little girl. "How'd you like to take care of the steaks for me?"

Kelly's eyes glittered with pleasure, and she instantly picked up the large fork from the counter by the grill and stabbed experimentally at one of the thick T-bones that were just barely beginning to brown. "Is it time to turn them?"

"Every four minutes," Sharon replied, glancing at the meat and deciding she had at least fifteen minutes in which to talk with her son. Leaving Kelly alone in the kitchen, she went out into the yard and dropped down on the lawn next to Mark. As if sensing that help for his master had arrived, Chivas sat up, his tail wagging, his big trusting eyes fixed on her expectantly.

"Want to talk about it?" Sharon asked.

Mark glanced at her curiously. "Talk about what? Did I do something wrong?"

"No," Sharon replied. "But I'm your mother. I can tell when something's bothering you. You get quiet. But quiet won't fix anything."

Mark took a deep breath, then sighed. "I—I guess I'm just not sure I like Silverdale," he said, looking away.

"This is only Thursday. In less than a week you've already decided you don't like it? You were the one who was so excited about coming, remember?"

Mark nodded glumly. "I know. And I know how much Dad likes it. Even Kelly's stopped sulking about her friends at home."

"And you don't want to rain on anybody's parade. Right?"

Mark hesitated, then nodded. "I guess so," he admitted. But then, as he met his mother's gaze, everything that had been building up inside him since Monday came pouring out. "All anyone here thinks about is sports," he said. "Mom, I can't even get a job, 'cause I'm not on any of the teams."

Sharon stared at him in confusion. What on earth was he talking about? "A job?" she asked. "Why are you looking for a job?"

Mark flushed self-consciously. "I—Well, I thought if I had a job, Dad might get off my back about going out for sports. I mean, if I was working, I wouldn't have time to play, would I?"

Sharon could hardly keep from laughing out loud, but the look of appeal in her son's eyes stopped her. "Well, aren't you the devious one," she said, allowing herself a small chuckle. "I have to admit, it would probably work. So what's the problem?"

Mark shrugged, and told her what had happened at the camera store on Monday afternoon. The scene had been repeated on Tuesday and Wednesday afternoons, as he'd presented himself at other shops. Today, Henry Spalding's words had been repeated to him again, this time at the drugstore. "What am I going to do? I'm not going to make any of the teams, and I'm not going to be able to get a job, and Dad's going to start riding me."

The two of them sat without speaking for a few minutes, as if the silence itself might provide a solution. Finally, Sharon shrugged. "I wish I knew what to tell you," she said. "I'll try to keep your father from pushing you too hard. But you know your father." She gave Mark an affectionate pat on the back, then scrambled to her feet. "Come on. Supper's almost ready."

But Mark shook his head. "I'm not very hungry," he said, looking up at her. "Is it all right if I just skip dinner? Maybe I'll take Chivas up into the hills."

Sharon considered it for a moment, then made up her

mind. He's almost sixteen, she told herself. He has to start working things through for himself. "Okay," she agreed. "But just make sure you get back before dark. I don't want you getting lost up there."

Mark grinned at her, and the change in his expression alone was enough to make Sharon certain she'd made the right decision. "I won't. But even if I did, Chivas would get us back."

As Sharon started back to the kitchen where Kelly was already yelling that the steaks were going to burn, Mark and Chivas disappeared down the driveway.

Mark wasn't certain how long he'd been gone. In fact, he hadn't really been paying too much attention to how they'd gotten here. With Chivas romping ahead of him, he'd walked north until he'd come to the edge of town, then followed the winding course of the river for a quarter of a mile to a small footbridge. Crossing the bridge, he'd found three paths leading in as many directions, and chosen the one that would take him uphill. Within twenty minutes they'd come to the edge of the valley and started up into the mountains.

The tree-dotted meadowlands of the valley quickly gave way to thick stands of pines interspersed with groves of aspen. Chivas, his whole body quivering with pleasure at the strange aromas that filled his nostrils, kept bounding off into the woods, giving chase to the squirrels and birds, or anything else that moved. Mark himself kept to the trail, working ever higher. Then, as he came around a tight bend, he found himself standing at the top of a steep bluff that commanded a view of the entire valley. For some reason the crest of the bluff was clear of trees, but in several places the tall grass had been matted down where deer had apparently bedded for the night. Mark glanced around for Chivas, but the big dog was nowhere to be seen. The sun, still a little above the horizon, felt warm after the deep shade of the woods, so he dropped down onto one of the deer beds and gazed out over the valley.

A few minutes later he stretched out on his back and let his eyes close. Just for a few seconds . . .

It was with a start that he realized the sun had dropped below the horizon. Chivas, a low growl rumbling in his throat, was standing next to Mark, his body trembling as he gazed off into the distance, one forepaw raised slightly off the ground, his tail dropping in a slight curve behind him, every muscle in his body tense.

Mark shook the sleep out of his head, then got to his knees. Squinting in the fading daylight, he followed Chivas's steady gaze but could see nothing.

Still, something had alerted the dog, and jarred Mark himself out of his light sleep.

But what?

And then he heard it.

It was a low, vaguely wailing sound, and when it first drifted up to him out of the valley, he wasn't sure he'd heard it at all. But then, as he strained his ears and Chivas's growl grew louder, the sound changed, becoming a scream of something that sounded like pain.

Pain, or fury.

It was an animal sound, vicious and feral, and Mark felt a chill in his body as the howl slashed through the peace of the evening.

A split-second later the howling abruptly ended, leaving not even an echo to reverberate through the hills.

Chivas, at his side, barked once then fell silent.

The two of them stayed where they were for several long minutes, listening for the sound again, but a silence seemed to gather, and as the sun continued to set and the sky in the west took on a brilliant, pinkish tinge, long, deep shadows could be seen in the valley below.

"Come on, boy," Mark said, instinctively dropping his voice to little more than a whisper. "Let's get home." He rose to his feet and started back along the path through the woods. This time Chivas, instead of bounding off on a path of his own, stayed close to his master. Every few yards the dog paused to look back, a soft whimper rising in his throat.

Mark hurried his step, but it wasn't until they'd crossed the bridge once again and were back in the more familiar surroundings of the town that he finally felt himself begin to relax.

Linda Harris watched anxiously as Tiffany Welch took a deep breath, ran three quick steps, jumped, then hit the end of the springboard perfectly. The board launched her upward, and she executed a near-perfect flip in the air before landing unsteadily on the shoulders of Josh Hinsdale and Pete Nakamura. The two boys, feeling Tiffany's legs tremble, grasped her ankles to steady her, and she threw her arms wide as she remained on their shoulders for a moment before losing her balance. Yelling for them to let go, she jumped back to the mats that covered the floor of the gym.

"All right," she said, reading the look in Linda's eyes. "So it wasn't perfect. But at least I got up, and by the time we have the homecoming game, I'll be able to stay up."

Linda shook her head. "Or you'll wind up with a broken back. I'm telling you, Tiff, if Mrs. Haynes finds out what you're doing, she'll kill us all."

"So we won't let her find out," Tiffany said. "I'll just keep practicing until I get it right, and then we'll show her."

"Well, I'm not practicing anymore tonight," Linda told her. She glanced up at the clock. "It's almost nine, and I still have to do my algebra. Come on."

The two girls said good-bye to Josh and Pete, then hurried into the locker room, showered quickly, and dressed. "Want to grab a Coke?" Tiffany asked as they left fifteen minutes later, their hair still wet, but drying quickly in the dry mountain air.

Linda shook her head. "Can't. Besides the algebra, I've got an English paper due."

" 'My Summer Vacation, by Linda Jane Harris'?" Tiffany asked, her voice edged with sarcasm. "Don't you just hate those things?"

Linda giggled. "Except that this one's even worse," she said. "I have to come up with a thousand words on 'The Most Important Person In My Life.' Maybe," she went on, as a sudden image of the English teacher's humorless face came into her mind, "I'll do my paper on Mr. Grey himself."

Tiffany shook her head. "My brother tried that two years ago. Mr. Grey gave him an F and made him do it over again."

As they turned the corner around the school building, a figure suddenly stepped out of the shadows ahead. Both the girls froze for a second, but then they heard, "Hey! It's just me."

The figure moved fully out of the shadows, and Jeff LaConner appeared in the light of the streetlamp above. "I was waiting for you," he said to Linda.

Tiffany glanced at Linda out of the corner of her eye. "How about Jeff?" she said. "You could write the paper about him, couldn't you?" Then, before Linda could think of a good retort, Tiffany said a quick good-bye and hurried away, leaving Jeff and Linda alone.

Jeff fell in beside her and slipped his arm around her shoulders. It wasn't the first time he'd put his arm around her as they'd walked, but tonight, for some reason, it made her feel uncomfortable. Almost instantly she realized why.

Mark Tanner.

Linda had been dating Jeff LaConner since last spring. But even during the summer, when they'd spent time together almost every day, she hadn't been certain how she felt. Of course, at the beginning she'd been thrilled that Jeff was interested in her at all, since she was only a freshman and he was a junior. And a football star, at that. And she'd loved the envious looks Tiffany Welch and the other girls had given her when Jeff came over to sit with her at lunchtime. But as the summer wore on and Jeff began spending more and more time practicing football, she'd had misgivings. It wasn't that she didn't like him—she did. It was just that he didn't seem to be interested in anything but football, and half the time, when he'd come over to see her, he and Robb ended up out in the backyard, passing a ball back and forth while she sat on the porch wondering why he'd come at all.

And then last weekend Mark had come to town, and on Saturday, before Robb had arrived and Mark had gotten so quiet, she'd enjoyed talking to him. Not that they'd really talked about much. But it had been easy for her to talk to Mark, because unlike her brother, or Jeff most of the time, he really listened when she talked to him. It had been the same every morning this week, when they'd walked to school together. Even at lunch hour, though most of the time she was with Jeff, she'd found herself looking around for Mark.

"We still on for the pep rally tomorrow night?" she heard Jeff asking now. As he spoke, she felt his hand tighten on her shoulder, and there was a roughness in his voice she couldn't remember having heard before.

"T-Tomorrow night?" she asked, stammering slightly. "But you didn't ask me, did you?"

Jeff stopped walking and turned to face her. They were a few yards away from a streetlight, and though Jeff's face was partly in shadow, his expression appeared angry. "I didn't think I had to," he said. "You're going to be there, and I'm going to be there, and we always go out afterward, don't we?"

"Do we?" Linda asked, then felt stupid at the sound of her own question. Of course they did—everyone knew they did. Why had she said something so dumb?

Mark Tanner: that was why.

"What do you mean, do we?" Jeff asked. There was a definite tinge of anger when he said, "You're my girlfriend, aren't you?"

Linda swallowed. "I—I don't know," she replied. All of a sudden it seemed as if her mind had gone off on its own and she no longer had any control over her own thoughts. "I think—well, maybe we've been spending too much time together. . . ." Now, why had she said that? Sure, she'd been thinking about Jeff, wondering how she really felt about him, but she hadn't really been thinking about breaking up with him, had she?

Maybe she had.

Jeff's eyes were glittering angrily now, and he reached out, putting his hands on her shoulders. "It's that Tanner creep, isn't it?" he demanded. "If that little shit's been trying to hit on you—"

"Stop it!" Linda hissed, glancing around, hoping no one was watching. "It doesn't have anything to do with Mark."

But it did, and Jeff seemed to know it. His hands tightened on her shoulders, and she felt a stab of pain where his fingers dug into her flesh. The streetlight was full on his face now, and suddenly he looked different to her. His anger had done something to his features, and his face—the face that she had always before considered so handsome—seemed coarse.

"I don't want you talking to him anymore," Jeff was saying now, and suddenly Linda's own anger rose inside her. Who was Jeff LaConner to tell her what she could do and whom she could talk to?

"Let go of me," she demanded. "I'll talk to whoever I want—"

But she couldn't finish her sentence, for Jeff's face had darkened with rage and he was shaking her.

His hands dug deep into her arms now, and she felt flashes of pain shooting down into her hands. Her head was flopping back and forth and her eyes filled with tears.

"Stop it!" she screamed. "You're hurting me! Jeff, stop that right now!"

It was her cry of pain that penetrated Jeff's anger. As suddenly as he had begun shaking her, he stopped and released her. Her face was streaked with tears, he saw, and she was rubbing her left shoulder, her fingers kneading at her own flesh as she tried to massage the pain away. Jeff stared at her mutely for a moment, then abruptly turned, smashed his fist into a tree, and with a cry that was half pain and half frustrated anger, broke into a run and plunged away into the night.

Linda, breathing hard, her heart pounding, watched him go. After a while the pain in her shoulders began to ease, and finally she resumed walking home. What on earth had happened just now? Jeff had never acted like that before—never!

Tonight she'd actually been terrified of him. And she hadn't done anything, not really. But if he was going to act like that . . .

My God, what if he came back?

She quickened her step, finally breaking into a run. By the time she got home, hurrying to her room without even speaking to her parents, she had made up her mind.

She picked up the telephone and dialed the Tanners' number, only realizing when their phone started to ring that, without even thinking about it, she'd already committed their number to memory.

"Mrs. Tanner?" she asked a moment later. "This is Linda. Can I talk to Mark?"

It was nearly midnight, but Mark still hadn't been able to fall asleep. He'd been in bed for more than an hour already and still couldn't stop trying to figure out what had happened that night. When he'd first heard Linda's voice on the phone, he hadn't thought much about it. But when she'd asked him if he was going to the pep rally tomorrow night, then asked him if he'd go out for a hamburger with her afterward, he'd started to wonder what was going on. He'd accepted the invitation before he'd even thought about it, but as soon as he hung up the phone, the questions had started coming into his mind.

Why had she called him?

She was Jeff LaConner's girlfriend, wasn't she?

And her voice had sounded kind of funny, too, as if there were something wrong.

Eventually he concluded that his mother, worried about him after this afternoon, had called Mrs. Harris and asked her to have Linda call him.

But his mother had denied it, and Mark was pretty sure she wouldn't lie to him. She might try to explain why she'd done it, and try to keep him from breaking the date, but she wouldn't lie about it.

Still, it had to be a mercy date. Linda probably just felt sorry for him and had asked Jeff if it would be all right if she invited him along.

That was it! She intended to have him tag along with her and Jeff! He'd look like some kind of an idiot!

He'd almost called her back right then, but as he reached for the phone, he'd changed his mind. Linda wouldn't do a thing like that, would she? He thought about it for a long time and finally decided she wouldn't.

He'd spent some time on his homework, then gone to bed. But he still couldn't figure it out—Linda was a cheerleader, and going out with the star of the football team. And even though she wasn't very tall, she was still an inch taller than he was. So why would she want to go out with him?

Giving up on sleep, he switched the light on, got out of bed, and went to stare at himself in the mirror.

Skinny. Not wiry, like his mother always told him. Just skinny. His chest looked narrow, and his arms were much too thin.

Unbidden, an image of Jeff LaConner came into his mind. Was there really a chance he'd ever look like that?

Then he remembered Robb Harris. Three years ago, when the Harrises had lived in San Marcos, Robb had been just as skinny as Mark was now. But Robb had put on weight, and looked great.

Maybe he could do it too, Mark thought as he stared unhappily at his own image.

And it wasn't just Linda, he told himself. It was everything. He knew he'd been thinking about it all afternoon while he and Chivas were walking in the hills. He just hadn't admitted he was thinking about it. But there wasn't any point in putting it off any longer.

He was in Silverdale, and he wasn't going anywhere else. And if he was going to live here, he was going to have to fit in with everyone else, even if it meant learning to like sports.

Even if he didn't learn to like sports, he could fake it. He could go to the games and cheer as loudly as anybody else.

And he could start doing exercises. He'd been doing them in gym since seventh grade, and he could do them again.

That was the whole thing, he decided. He didn't like the way he was, so he would change himself.

Lying down on the floor, he braced his feet under the lowest drawer of his desk, then folded his arms behind his head. Taking a deep breath, he began to do sit-ups.

To his own surprise, he managed twenty-five of them before his stomach began hurting so much he couldn't go on. But tomorrow, he told himself as he climbed back into bed, he'd do thirty. And the day after that . . .

His thoughts were interrupted by a sound that cut sharply through the night, instantly silencing the insects that had been buzzing softly outside.

It was the same piercing, agonizing scream he had heard earlier, when he'd been up in the mountains.

Except that now, in the darkness of the night, the scream sounded different.

It sounded almost human. . . .

7

Charlotte LaConner glanced at the clock that glowed dimly next to the bed. Nearly one-thirty. Beside her, Chuck was snoring softly. How could he sleep, knowing that Jeff had still not come home? Charlotte got up, slipped her arms through the sleeves of a light robe, then went to the window and peered out at the street. The night was quiet. A gentle stillness lay over the valley that seemed totally at odds with the turmoil in her mind.

It had been a bad week for her, and every day things seemed to be getting worse. It had begun on Monday evening, when she'd tried to talk things over rationally with Chuck. He'd listened patiently while she'd told him about seeing Ricardo Ramirez. But when she'd gone on to say that she'd decided Jeff was going to have to quit the football team, his expression froze and a hard look came into his eyes.

"That's the stupidest thing I've ever heard," he'd said.

His words had lashed her like a whip, but she'd bitten her lip, then tried to argue with him.

It had done no good. "It was an accident," he'd insisted.

"You don't ask a kid to give up his favorite sport just because of an accident."

As far as Chuck had been concerned, that was the end of it. If he'd even noticed the tension in the house since then, he'd given no sign, acting as if nothing had changed. But Charlotte, unable to get Rick Ramirez out of her mind, had grown quieter through the week, and become acutely aware of changes in Jeff.

If they were really changes.

For by now, she wasn't sure. Perhaps Jeff hadn't really changed at all, and she was simply reading things into his behavior. Still, she believed his personality actually was changing. Jeff's temper—always so even when he'd been younger— appeared to flare up now at the least provocation, and twice this week, when she'd asked him to do something, he had yelled that he already had too much to do, then slammed out the door. On both occasions he'd come back a few minutes later and apologized, and she'd been quick to forgive him. A repeat of the scene on Saturday night was the last thing she needed.

But her son's sudden rage had led Charlotte to watch him closely, searching for clues to his mood before she spoke to him. And as she observed him, often when he wasn't aware that she was watching, she'd begun to feel that it wasn't just his personality that had undergone a transformation—he seemed to be changing physically as well.

His eyes seemed to her to have sunk slightly, and his brow, always strong, now seemed to have thickened and grown heavier. His jaw, carrying the same square line as his father's, had a slight jut to it, giving him an aggressive look that became even more pronounced when he lost his temper.

When Jeff had come home after football practice today, his hands looked swollen, and when she'd asked him about it, his eyes flashed with quick anger. "Anything else?" he demanded. "Got any more problems with me, Ma?"

Charlotte had recoiled from his words, then tried to tell him she was only worried about him, but it had been too late.

He'd already disappeared into his room to spend the hours until dinner working out on the Nautilus equipment Chuck had bought him the previous summer. Immediately after dinner he left the house, and she'd neither seen nor heard from him since.

She heard the faint sound of the big clock at the foot of the stairs striking two, and finally turned away from the window. With mixed emotions—part trepidation, part anger that she'd come to fear her own husband—she went to the bed and shook Chuck. He stopped snoring, then wriggled away from her and rolled over. She shook him again, and he opened his eyes and looked up at her.

"What is it?" he mumbled. "What time is it? Christ, Char, it isn't even light out!"

"It's two in the morning, Chuck. And Jeff isn't home yet."

Chuck groaned. "And for that you woke me up? Jeez, Char, when I was his age, I was out all night half the time."

"Maybe you were," Charlotte replied tightly. "And maybe your parents didn't care. But I do, and I'm about to call the police."

At that, Chuck came completely awake. "What the hell do you want to do a thing like that for?" he demanded, switching on the light and staring at Charlotte as if he thought she'd lost her mind.

"Because I'm worried about him," Charlotte flared, concern for her son overcoming her fear of her husband's tongue. "Because I don't like what's been happening with him and I don't like the way he's been acting. And I certainly don't like not knowing where he is at night!"

Clutching the robe protectively to her throat, she turned and hurried out of the bedroom. She was already downstairs when Chuck, shoving his own arms into the sleeves of an ancient woolen robe he'd insisted on keeping despite its frayed edges and honeycomb of moth holes, caught up with her.

"Now just hold on," he said, taking the phone from her

hands and putting it back on the small desk in the den. "I'm not going to have you getting Jeff into trouble with the police just because you want to mother-hen him."

"Mother-hen him!" Charlotte repeated. "For God's sake, Chuck! He's only seventeen years old! And it's the middle of the night, and there's nowhere in Silverdale he could be! Everything's closed. So unless he's already in trouble, where is he?"

"Maybe he stayed overnight with a friend," Chuck began, but Charlotte shook her head.

"He hasn't done that since he was a little boy. And if he had, he would have called." Even as she uttered the words, she knew she didn't believe them. A year ago—a few months ago; even a few weeks ago—she would have trusted Jeff to keep her informed of where he was and what he was doing. But now? She didn't know.

Nor could she explain her worries to Chuck, since he insisted on believing there was nothing wrong; that Jeff was simply growing up and testing his wings.

As she was searching for the right words, the words to express her fears without further rousing her husband's anger, the front door opened and Jeff came in.

He'd already closed the door behind him and started up the stairs when he caught sight of his parents standing in the den in their bathrobes, their eyes fixed on him. He gazed at them stupidly for a second, almost as if he didn't recognize them, and for a split-second Charlotte thought he looked stoned.

"Jeff?" she said. Then, when he seemed to pay no attention to her, she called out again, louder this time. "Jeff!"

His eyes hooded, her son turned to gaze at her. "What?" he asked, his voice taking on the same sullen tone that had become so familiar to her lately.

"I want an explanation," Charlotte went on. "It's after two A.M., and I want to know where you've been."

"Out," Jeff said, and started to turn away.

"Stop right there, young man!" Charlotte commanded.

She marched into the foyer and stood at the bottom of the stairs, then reached out and switched on the chandelier that hung in the stairwell. A bright flood of light bathed Jeff's face, and Charlotte gasped. His face was streaked with dirt, and on his cheeks there were smears of blood. There were black circles under Jeff's eyes—as if he hadn't slept in days—and he was breathing hard, his chest heaving as he panted.

Then he lifted his right hand to his mouth, and before he began sucking on his wounds, Charlotte could see that the skin was torn away from his knuckles.

"My God," she breathed, her anger suddenly draining away. "Jeff, what's happened to you?"

His eyes narrowed. "Nothing," he mumbled, and once more started to mount the stairs.

"Nothing?" Charlotte repeated. She turned to Chuck, now standing in the door to the den, his eyes, too, fixed on their son. "Chuck, look at him. Just look at him!"

"You'd better tell us what happened, son," Chuck said. "If you're in some kind of trouble—"

Jeff whirled to face them, his eyes now blazing with the same anger that had frightened Linda Harris earlier that evening. "I don't know what's wrong!" he shouted. "Linda broke up with me tonight, okay? And it pissed me off! Okay? So I tried to smash up a tree and I went for a walk. *Okay?* Is that okay with you, Mom?"

"Jeff—" Charlotte began, shrinking away from her son's sudden fury. "I didn't mean . . . we only wanted to—"

But it was too late.

"Can't you just leave me alone?" Jeff shouted.

He came off the bottom of the stairs, towering over the much smaller form of his mother. Then, with an abrupt movement, he reached out and roughly shoved Charlotte aside, as if swatting a fly. She felt a sharp pain in her shoulder as her body struck the wall, and then she collapsed to the floor. For a split-second Jeff stared blankly at his mother, as if he was puzzled about what had happened to her, and then, an anguished wail boiling up from somewhere deep within him, he turned and slammed out the front door.

Chuck, stunned by what had happened, stared at the closed door for a moment, then knelt down to help his wife to her feet. As Charlotte began sobbing quietly, he led her upstairs.

First he'd get her calmed down and back in bed. Then he'd start hunting for Jeff.

Jeff shambled away from the house, stumbling down the sidewalk to the street. But as the glow of the streetlight struck his eyes, he blinked dazedly then quickly ducked away, darting across the street and disappearing into the deep shadows between two houses.

His head was pounding with a dull throbbing pain that seemed to penetrate the very bones of his body, and tears were streaming from his eyes. How could he have done that? It was bad enough shaking Linda Harris like she was some kind of rag doll, but to have hit his own mother that way . . .

He tried to force the thought from his mind. He couldn't have done that—he couldn't have! It must have been someone else.

That was it. There was someone else inside him—someone evil—who was making him do things he never would have done himself.

But if there were someone else inside him, it meant he was going crazy. He was losing his mind, and they'd lock him up. That's what they did with crazy people, he knew—at least if they got violent.

He crouched in the shadows for a moment, his eyes darting like those of a wild animal that knows it's being hunted. How long did he have before they would start looking for him, how long before they'd come for him? He had to get away, had to find someplace to hide.

He kept low to the ground, balanced on the balls of his

feet, then darted across a backyard, vaulting over the low
fence that separated one yard from the other. He crossed two
more yards that way, then slipped once more between the
houses, pausing to search the street for signs of life before
dashing across its open expanse to the welcome darkness on
the other side. He wasn't certain where he was going yet, but
his instincts seemed to be leading him to the other side of
town, out near the school.

And then he knew.

There was someone he could go to, someone he trusted,
someone who would help him. His breathing eased slightly as
his panic began to subside and his mind to clear. Even the
terrible pain in his head was lessening, and he broke into a
loping stride, slipping from one shadowed area to the next,
carefully avoiding the bright pools of yellow light that illuminated the sidewalks. No more than ten minutes later he
reached his destination.

He paused across the street from Phil Collins's house,
huddling close to the trunk of a large cedar tree, watching not
only the coach's house, but the houses on either side as well.

The buzzing of insects seemed amplified in his ears, and
in his paranoia he couldn't imagine how anyone could sleep
through the din. Yet all the houses on the block were dark,
nor could he see signs of movement on the streets.

Perhaps, after all, they weren't looking for him yet.

He crouched for a moment, then darted across the street
and around to the back of the coach's house. He tapped softly
at the back door, then harder.

Instantly, the house came alive with the sound of a dog
barking, and a second later lights came on. Then the door
opened a crack and Jeff recognized the coach's familiar face
peering out at him.

"It's me, Coach," he said, his voice trembling. "I—I'm
in trouble. Can I come in?"

The door closed for a second, and Jeff heard Collins
mumble something to the dog, then the door opened wide and
Jeff stepped into the kitchen of Collins's little house. The big

German shepherd crouched at its master's feet, its teeth bared, a low growl rattling in its throat.

"Easy, Sparks," Phil Collins said. "Take it easy." The dog visibly relaxed, then slunk forward to sniff at Jeff's hand.

Jeff sank into the single battered chair that stood next to the kitchen table and held his head in his hands.

"I—I hit my mother," he said, his eyes avoiding the coach's. "I don't know what happened. But—Well, sometimes it's like I just go crazy." Finally he looked up, his expression beseeching. "What's wrong with me?" he asked. "I get so mad sometimes I just can't control myself. All I want to do is start hitting things. I just want to start hitting, and I don't care what happens."

Collins placed his hand on the boy's shoulder. "Now, just take it easy," he said, unconsciously repeating the same words he'd used to the dog only a moment before. "There's nothing wrong with you, Jeff. You're just going through a tough time in your life, that's all. Now just try to tell me what happened."

Half sobbing, Jeff did his best to tell Collins what had happened that evening, from the time he'd started talking to Linda Harris until the moment hours later when he'd suddenly, without thinking about it, struck his mother. But in the end he knew the story didn't make much sense—there were a lot of blank spots, times when he couldn't remember where he'd been or what he'd been doing. To his relief, the coach didn't seem too upset by what he'd done.

"Sounds to me like you just had an overreaction to breaking up with your girlfriend," he said. "Happens all the time with kids your age—hormones are flying all over your body and you never know what they're going to do to you. Tell you what," he went on. "I'll call Marty Ames and we'll take you out there and have him look you over. Believe me," he added with a wink, "if you're cracking up, Marty will be able to spot it in a minute. But you're not," he added quickly, as Jeff paled. "I'll bet he says the same thing I just said."

"But what about my folks?" Jeff asked, his voice anxious. "After what I did to my mom, my dad's going to kill me!"

"No, he's not," Collins assured him. "If we need to, I'll talk to him, or Marty Ames will. But I'll bet we won't even have to do that. Your old man's pretty proud of you, Jeff. And he's sure not going to turn against you now. He's not, and your mom's not."

As Jeff seemed to calm down, the coach went to the phone and made a quick call. A quarter of an hour later, with Jeff sitting next to him, Collins pulled his car to a stop in front of the clinic gates and rolled the window down to speak to the guard who was waiting for them. The guard pressed a remote control and the front gates swung slowly inward to let Collins drive through.

Martin Ames was waiting for them in the lobby of the sprawling main building and immediately led Jeff back to the examination room. "Strip down to your shorts," he told the frightened boy, "and let's have a look at you." He turned to Collins. "Tell me what happened." While Jeff peeled off his clothes, Collins briefly repeated what Jeff had told him earlier. "Okay," Ames said when Collins was done. "Let's get started."

It was as Ames began checking the reflexes in his legs, tapping his knees with the small rubber mallet, that the rage suddenly began to build in Jeff again. He could feel it coming on but could do nothing about it. And yet there was no reason for it—he'd been through this procedure hundreds of times before and it had never bothered him. But not this time.

This time it infuriated him.

"Stop that, goddamn it!" he shouted. "What the fuck do you think you're doing?" Kicking the tiny mallet in Ames's hand aside, Jeff jumped off the examination table, his eyes blazing with fury, his hands clenching into fists.

Ames took a quick step backward and glanced at Collins, who instantly threw his arms around Jeff in a powerful bear hug. In the brief moment before Jeff could recover from the sudden action, Ames jabbed his arm with a hypodermic needle and pressed the plunger. Jeff froze in Collins's grasp, and as the drug began to take effect, felt his rage ease and his body relax. As Collins released him, Jeff sank back onto the treatment table.

The last thing he heard as he drifted into unconsciousness was the sound of Ames's voice telling Collins to call his parents and explain to them where he was. He was going to be all right, Ames said, but he would have to spend the rest of the night at the clinic.

But was he going to be all right?

Martin Ames didn't know.

He knew it was a nightmare, knew it had to be. Surely what was happening to him couldn't be real.

His entire body was racked with pain, blinding, searing pain that tore at the depths of his soul.

He seemed to be surrounded by darkness, and yet, even in the pitch-black of the torture chamber, he could see perfectly.

He was not alone.

He could see the others, some of them chained to the walls, others strapped to the rack in the center of the floor. And he could hear their cries—agonized shrieks that bellowed from the depth of their souls, reverberating through the stone room but never fading away, only being built upon by more screams, more pitiful wails.

The chamber masters were there, too, oblivious to the keening pleas of their victims, each of them carrying a different tool of torture. One of them was approaching Jeff now, a red-hot branding iron balanced delicately in his hands. He seemed to smile at Jeff for a moment, and through the cacophony, Jeff almost imagined he could hear the man laugh before he pressed the glowing metal against his thigh.

The sweet smell of burning flesh filled his nostrils then, his gorge rising as a wave of nausea swept over him. "Nooo!"

he wailed, and his whole body jerked and thrashed against the chains that bound him to the metal table on which he lay. *"Nooo!"*

It was his own scream that finally released him from the grip of the terrible dream, and he sat bolt upright.

A blinding stream of white light shone in his eyes. He blinked several times and his vision began to clear.

He was breathing hard; his lungs felt as if they might explode as he gasped for air.

There were people around him, and for a moment the dream closed around him again and he opened his mouth to scream out once more. But then he caught hold of himself.

They weren't the torturers. These men were real, and they wore white coats—as white as the room in which he sat.

Hospital.

He was in a hospital.

Then, slowly, it came back to him, and as his memory returned in bits and pieces, he began to calm down.

He was at the sports clinic. The coach had brought him here, and Dr. Ames was taking care of him. So he was going to be all right.

He looked around now.

There were three attendants, three men he recognized immediately.

They were part of the staff; his friends.

But they were looking at him strangely, almost as if afraid of him.

He raised his hand to shield his eyes against the brilliance of the light, and it was then that he saw the leather strap.

It was buckled tightly around his wrist, but the free end was torn and ragged, almost as if . . .

As if he'd been strapped down and managed somehow to rip himself free.

He swallowed hard and felt a soreness in his throat, the kind of rawness he always felt after he'd spent an afternoon shouting at a football game.

Puzzled, he tried to swing his legs off the table and sit up straight, but found that he couldn't. And when he looked down at his feet, he saw that his ankles, too, were wrapped in leather straps.

Just as in the nightmare, he was bound to a metal table.

A wave of anger built up inside him, and he gathered himself together to jerk his legs free.

Once more a needle was plunged into his arm and he quickly felt himself sink back into the strange, soft darkness of unconsciousness.

Mercifully, the nightmare did not come back to haunt him.

8

Mark Tanner woke up early the next morning, but instead of rolling over to catch an extra ten minutes of sleep, he threw the covers off, sat up and stretched. As Chivas gazed curiously at him from his place next to the bed, he dropped to the floor and began doing push-ups, his resolve of the night before still strong within him. He kept at it, grunting with the exertion, until his arms ached. Then, though he knew it was impossible for his body to have changed yet, he glanced in the mirror. But this morning, instead of being depressed by what he saw, he only grinned at himself encouragingly. "It'll work," he muttered. "If it worked for Robb, it'll work for me, too."

"What'll work?" he heard Kelly's voice ask.

Flushing beet red, he spun around to see his sister staring at him from the door. "What are you doing?" he demanded. "If my door's closed, you're not supposed to come in."

"I had to go to the bathroom," Kelly replied, as if that explained everything. "You were making funny noises. Are you sick?"

"Don't be dumb," Mark told her. "If I were sick, wouldn't I be in bed? Now get out of here, or I'll tell Mom you came into my room without knocking.'' Of course he knew he wouldn't, but he also knew the threat would be enough to send Kelly scuttling back to her own room.

As soon as she was gone, he stripped his underwear off, tossed it into the corner with the rest of his dirty laundry, then pulled on his robe and headed for the bathroom. He was already in the shower, the bathroom was clouded with steam, when he heard the door open. ''That you, Dad?'' he yelled over the noise of the spray.

''Got to shave,'' Blake replied, then frowned uncertainly. ''What are you doing in there? Didn't you shower last night?''

''Uh-huh,'' Mark replied. A minute later he shut off the needle spray and stepped out of the shower, grabbing a towel off the rack. ''Dad?''

Blake, his face covered with lather and his head tipped back as he drew the safety razor carefully over his neck, grunted a response and glanced at his son in the mirror.

''Do you suppose maybe we could start practicing football again? I mean on weekends or something.''

The razor stopped in midstroke as Blake's gaze fixed on Mark. ''I thought you didn't want to do that,'' he remarked. But as Mark flushed scarlet, his father thought he understood. ''Linda Harris, right? She's on the cheerleading squad, isn't she?''

Mark's flush deepened, and he nodded.

''How about tomorrow?'' Blake asked. ''Or maybe Sunday?''

Mark hesitated. For a moment Blake thought he was going to change his mind, but then the boy nodded briefly, pulled on his robe and left the bathroom. As he went back to his morning shave, Blake felt a sense of satisfaction. Silverdale, he decided, was going to be the best thing that had ever happened to his son.

Forty minutes later Linda Harris fell in beside Mark. They were three blocks from the school and still had plenty of time before the first bell would ring. ''C-Can I talk to you about something?'' Linda asked, stopping in the middle of the block and turning to face Mark.

Mark's heart sank. She'd already made up with Jeff LaConner and was going to break their date.

"It—Well, it's about last night," Linda went on, and Mark knew he was right.

"It's okay," he mumbled, his words barely audible. "If you want to go out with Jeff tonight, I don't care."

"But I don't," Linda protested, and Mark, who had been staring uncomfortably at the ground, finally looked at her. Though her eyes looked sort of worried, she was smiling at him. "I just wanted to tell you what happened, that's all." As they resumed walking slowly toward the school, she told him everything that had happened after she'd left the gym with Tiffany Welch the night before. "I was really scared of him," she said. "It just seemed like he went nuts."

"Did you tell your folks?" Mark asked.

Linda shook her head. "They think Jeff's the next thing to God," she said, her voice trembling. "Just because he's a big football player, they think I should be thrilled to death that he wanted to take me out."

"Well, you went with him, didn't you?" Mark asked, doing his best not to let his voice betray him. "I mean, if you didn't like him, how come you went out with him?"

"But he was different," Linda insisted. "He always used to be real mellow. But now . . ." She shrugged helplessly. "I don't know, he's just changed, that's all. He gets mad for no reason at all."

Mark couldn't resist a slight dig. " 'Course, telling him you're breaking up with him isn't any reason for him to get upset, is it?" he asked.

Linda started to say something, then saw his grin. "All right, so last night maybe he had a reason," she admitted. "But that isn't what I'm worried about," she went on, her eyes growing serious.

"Then what is it?" Mark asked.

"I just—" Linda began, then faltered, wondering how to say it.

"You just what?" Mark pressed. "Come on, spit it out."

"It's you," Linda finally said, her eyes avoiding him. "When he finds out about tonight, I don't know what he might do."

Mark felt his face reddening, and tried to control it. "You mean he might try to pound me?" he asked.

Linda nodded, but said nothing.

"Well," Mark went on, feigning a bravado he wasn't feeling, "if he tries, I guess there isn't much I can do about it, is there? Maybe I could just roll over and play dead," he suggested. "Think he'd buy it?"

In spite of herself, Linda giggled. "He's not dumb, Mark." Then her giggle faded away. "Anyhow, if you want to change your mind about tonight, it's okay."

Mark shook his head. "What are we supposed to do, pretend we don't like each other just because of Jeff LaConner?"

As they approached the school, Mark stopped walking. Parked in front was a sky-blue station wagon with the words ROCKY MOUNTAIN HIGH emblazoned on its sides. Someone Mark didn't recognize was behind the wheel, but Jeff LaConner was getting out of the passenger side. Mark frowned. "What's that?" he asked.

Linda frowned. "Rocky Mountain High—it's the sports clinic," she said, "and that's one of their cars. Jeff must have been out there this morning." Glancing nervously at Mark, she added, "M-Maybe we ought to go around to the side door."

But it was already too late. Jeff LaConner had seen them and, after saying something to the driver, was starting toward them. To their surprise, he was smiling. Despite Jeff's smile, however, Mark could sense Linda's tension as the big football player approached.

"Hi, Linda," Jeff said, and when she made no reply, his smile faded and was replaced by an embarrassed look. "I—Well, I wanted to apologize for last night."

Linda's lips tightened, but she still said nothing.

"I wasn't feeling very good," Jeff went on. "Anyway, I shouldn't have done what I did."

"No," Linda said stiffly. "You shouldn't have."

Jeff took a deep breath, but didn't argue with her. "Anyway," he went on, "after I got home I got worse, and finally I had to go see Dr. Ames."

Linda frowned uncertainly. "How come? What was wrong?"

Jeff shrugged. "I don't know. He gave me a shot and I spent the night at the clinic, but I'm fine now."

Mark had only been half listening, for he'd been preoccupied by the mark he'd noticed on Jeff's wrist. The skin was abraded and bright red. Now he asked: "What did they do? Tie you down?"

Jeff gazed at him curiously, and Mark nodded at the other boy's wrist. Still not sure what Mark meant, Jeff looked down. Seeing the red mark on his right wrist, he raised his other hand, and as his arm bent, the cuff of his sleeve moved up a couple of inches. His left wrist, too, was ringed with an angry red welt.

He stared at the marks blankly.

He hadn't the slightest idea where they might have come from.

Sharon Tanner collapsed the last of the packing boxes, added it to the immense pile next to the back door, then wiped her brow with the back of her hand. "You were right," she said, glancing at the clock over the sink. "Only eleven-thirty, and it's all done. And dear God," she added, dropping into the chair opposite Elaine Harris, "don't let me have to do this again for at least five years!" She took a sip of cold coffee from the mug in front of her, grimaced, spat the coffee back into the mug, then got up and emptied the mug into the sink.

"All it takes is organization," Elaine replied.

"And extra hands," Sharon told her. "Why don't you show me around the stores, then I'll treat you to lunch." She looked down at her jeans and sweatshirt and smiled ruefully. "But nowhere fancy. I just don't feel like changing."

Fifteen minutes later Sharon pulled her car into the nearly empty lot behind the Safeway store and shook her head in amazement. "Not like San Marcos. There, I'd be lucky to find a spot after cruising the lot for ten minutes."

"Here, everybody walks," Elaine reminded her.

"Great," Sharon groaned. "And how do you get everything home?"

"Ever heard of a shopping cart?" Elaine retorted. "You know, the little wire gizmos old ladies drag around? Well, prepare yourself to enter the world of old-ladydom!" She laughed out loud at the horrified expression on Sharon's face. "Don't worry. I felt like an idiot the first time I did it, but now I've gotten so I like it. Of course," she added, patting her ample thigh, "I ought to walk even more than I do, but I figure I should get full credit for making the effort. Come on."

They crossed the parking lot, rounded the corner of the market, then came out into the tiny village itself. Although she'd been in the village almost every day this week, Sharon still gazed at it in wonder, for unlike the strip malls of San Marcos—where everyone seemed to be in a hurry to get somewhere else, moving quickly, oblivious to everything around them—here she saw small clusters of people, sitting on the wrought-iron-and-wood benches that had been placed on the boardwalk in front of almost every store, or chatting idly in the middle of the brick street itself. Practically everyone either waved or spoke to Elaine as the two women wandered among the shops, gazing into the windows. Sharon made a few purchases at the drugstore and stepped into what was labeled a hardware store, but actually seemed to have a little of everything, including books, clothes, and furniture—and where, at Elaine's insistence, Sharon bought a collapsible shopping cart—then they went back to the Safeway.

At first it appeared to Sharon to be very much like any other supermarket she'd been in. But as she moved through the aisles, checking items off the long list she'd been building up all week, she noticed something strange.

In the bakery department, she searched in vain for a loaf of white sandwich bread. Finally deciding the store was out, she was about to settle for a loaf of whole wheat instead, when she realized that all the shelves were full, as if the department had just been stocked. Frowning, she asked Elaine if she'd seen any white bread.

Elaine shook her head. "There isn't any around here. The store gets all their bread from a bakery in Grand Junction. Super sourdough and great seven-grain. But no white bread."

"Swell," Sharon commented. "I don't suppose Mark will mind, but what am I going to tell Kelly? She loves peanut-butter-and-honey sandwiches on white bread, with no butter on the honey side, so by the time she eats it, the bread's like eating honeycomb."

"It does the same thing with whole wheat," Elaine replied.

Sharon shook her head dolefully. "Obviously you've forgotten what nine-year-olds are like. Substitutions of what they like are 'gross,' and mothers who make substitutions obviously have no regard for their children's health, because there's no way the kid will eat it, even if he—or in this case, she—starves to death." She took a deep breath, dropped a loaf of honey berry into her cart, then chuckled. "Well, at least she can't give me the 'everybody else has white bread' line."

They moved on through the store, and Sharon paused in front of a small display of soft drinks.

There was nothing there except mineral water, in an array of different natural flavors. She looked at it with disgust. "I hate this stuff," she said. "Where's the real pop?"

Elaine shook her head. "This is it. Anybody who wants anything else brings it in from outside. But nobody does. Mineral water's good for you, and once you get used to it, you get so you like it."

Sharon stared at her friend. Was she serious? She couldn't be! This was a Safeway, wasn't it?

As they kept moving through the aisles, Sharon noticed more and more discrepancies between this market and the ones she was used to.

The fresh-produce department was twice as large as any she'd seen before, and she had to admit that the fruits and vegetables were better than any she'd seen in California. The same for the meat department.

But in the frozen-food section, she found the supply limited to a few vegetables and a little premium-brand ice cream—the kind with no preservatives in it. She turned to face Elaine squarely, her expression quizzical. "What is this?" she asked. "A supermarket or a health-food store?"

"It's a supermarket," Elaine protested. "But they just don't carry any junk food, that's all."

"Junk food!" Sharon protested. "They barely carry anything at all that my family likes! Don't get me wrong, I'm all for fresh vegetables. But Kelly likes popsicles, and Mark is absolutely crazy about frozen fried chicken. And what are the kids supposed to do if Blake and I want to go out by ourselves? Where are the TV dinners?"

Elaine shook her head. "There aren't any. Nobody in Silverdale buys any of that kind of thing, so why should the store stock it? Besides, look at our kids. Have you ever seen a healthier bunch? They're big, and they're strong, and they practically never get sick. If you ask me—"

Sharon felt a surge of exasperation. "If you ask me," she interrupted, "you're starting to sound just like all those health-food nuts we used to laugh at back home. And maybe if the store stocked what you call junk food, people might buy it! What kind of manager do they have here, anyway? Don't all Safeways have to stock the same things?"

"Hey, it's not my fault—" Elaine started to protest.

"I didn't say it was," Sharon snapped. "I know Jerry runs TarrenTech around here, but I wasn't assuming he ran the Safeway, too!"

A strange look came into Elaine's eyes, and for a moment Sharon had the bizarre notion that somehow she'd struck a nerve. Then she realized that Elaine wasn't looking at her at all, but was staring past her at someone who had just turned into their aisle.

"Charlotte," she heard Elaine gasp. "What happened? You look awful!" Elaine clapped a hand over her mouth as she heard the tactlessness of her own remark. "Oh, dear," she said quickly. "I didn't mean—"

Sharon turned to see a small, blond woman, her hair drawn back in a ponytail to expose a face that would have been pretty if it didn't look so tired. Her eyes were rimmed with red, the black circles under them only partly hidden by a thick layer of makeup, and her left arm was held immobile by a sling.

"Sharon, this is Charlotte LaConner," she heard Elaine saying. "Sharon is Blake Tanner's wife. You know, Jerry's new number two?"

Charlotte managed a wan smile and extended her right hand. "It's a pleasure to meet you," she said, the words coming automatically. Her eyes shifted back to Elaine. "And you don't have to apologize," she said. "I know how I look."

"But what happened?" Elaine asked again.

Charlotte shook her head. "I—I'm not sure, really." She looked sharply at Elaine. "Didn't Linda tell you what happened last night?"

Elaine shook her head uncertainly. "Linda? What does she—"

"Apparently she broke up with Jeff after practice last night," Charlotte went on. "Anyway, when he came home, he . . . well, he was pretty upset, and he gave me a shove."

Elaine's face turned slightly pale. "My God . . ." She glanced at Sharon. "Jeff's big," she said. "He's the captain of the football team—"

"Not anymore!" Charlotte said with vehemence. "All week I've been telling Chuck I want Jeff off that team!" She was trembling now, and her eyes glistened with moisture. She glanced nervously around, and her voice dropped to an urgent whisper. "He was never like this before," she said. "Never! He was always such a sweet-tempered boy. Of course, Chuck still insists that it's just hormones—that he's just going through adolescence. But it's not. It's more than that, Elaine. It's that damned game, and Phil Collins, too! He drives them so hard—always yelling at them that the only thing that counts is winning! He's turned Jeff into a stranger, Elaine! A stranger, and a bully, and I don't blame Linda for not wanting to go out with him anymore."

"Charlotte—" Elaine began, but the other woman shook her head bitterly, pressing her hand against her mouth as if to hold back her own angry words.

The tension was almost palpable, and Sharon Tanner quickly searched her mind for a way to break it. Then she remembered the words she'd exchanged with Elaine just before Charlotte had arrived. "Maybe it's the food around here," she suggested, struggling to keep her tone light. "Elaine was just telling me how big and healthy all the kids are. Maybe they've finally gotten too big."

Charlotte shook her head. "It's football," she said bitterly. "That's all anyone around here cares about, and the biggest mistake I ever made was letting Jeff get involved with it."

"Now, come on, Charlotte," Elaine soothed. "It's not as bad as all that."

"Isn't it?" Charlotte asked, her voice bleak. She turned to Sharon Tanner. "I was wrong just now," she said softly. "Letting Jeff get involved in football wasn't my biggest mistake. My biggest mistake was coming to Silverdale at all!"

Then she turned and hurried away.

All afternoon Sharon heard Charlotte LaConner's words echoing in her head.

"My biggest mistake was coming to Silverdale. . . ."

She would have dismissed the words, since the woman had been terribly upset, perhaps even in pain.

Still, even before she and Elaine had run into Charlotte in the market, Sharon had begun to have misgivings.

Although she couldn't argue that the town wasn't beautiful, perfectly planned, and perfectly built, there was still something wrong.

And that, she suddenly realized, was it.

It was too perfect, all of it.

The homes, the shops, the schools, even the food in the market.

Too perfect.

Jeff LaConner knew he'd fouled up at football practice that afternoon. His concentration had been way off, and even though Phil Collins had yelled at him, sent him on extra laps around the track, and finally benched him, it hadn't helped. Now, in the locker room, he was staring curiously at the marks on his ankles. He hadn't noticed them until the last period of the day, when he'd stripped down for his regular gym class. But once he'd seen them, he couldn't get them out of his mind.

They were faded, barely visible now, as were the marks on his wrists. Four strange bands of reddened skin, almost as though they'd been bound up with adhesive tape the night before.

Adhesive tape, or something else.

At times throughout the day, his whole body would shudder. Strange flickers of images would come into his mind, then disappear before he could get a good look at them. But they were frightening images, and as the afternoon wore on, he'd finally begun to remember the nightmare he'd had the previous night.

The nightmare in which he'd been bound to a table, and someone—a man whose face he couldn't remember at all— had been torturing him.

He stripped off his practice uniform, then went to the

shower. There were a dozen other guys still there, but instead of joking with them as he usually did, Jeff only soaped his body down and stood for a long time under the hot needle spray, letting the water relax his sore muscles. Finally, when everyone else had left, he shut off the water, toweled himself dry, then dressed. Instead of leaving the locker room, however, he went to the coach's office and knocked on the door.

"It's unlocked," Collins barked. Jeff let himself into the room, and Collins looked up at him from behind his desk, his expression souring. "I don't want to hear any excuses," he growled. "All I want is for you to keep your mind on the game."

"I—I'm sorry," Jeff stammered. "I just wanted to talk to you for a minute."

Collins hesitated, then his shoulders hunched in a gesture of impatient resignation and he waved to the chair opposite him. "Okay, shoot. What's on your mind?"

"These," Jeff said, holding out his wrists so Collins could clearly see the marks on them. "They're on my ankles, too."

Collins shrugged. "So am I supposed to know where they came from?" he asked.

Jeff shook his head uncertainly. "I just—well, all day I've been having these funny feelings . . . like all of a sudden I get scared. And I had a nightmare last night," he went on. He told Collins as much as he could remember of the dream. Then: "The thing is, could the dream have caused the marks? I mean, in the dream they had me strapped down to the table. And I was just thinking—"

"You mean maybe they're psychosomatic?" Collins asked. Again he shrugged, his hands spreading wide on the desk. "You got me, Jeff. I don't know anything about that sort of stuff. If you want, we can call Ames and ask him." He reached for the phone, but Jeff shook his head.

"No," he said. "That's okay. I'll be going out there tomorrow or the next day, and I can ask him then."

Collins gazed at him speculatively for a moment, then

nodded. "Okay," he said. "But I want you to take it easy tonight, okay? No fights, and early to bed. I want you in prime shape for tomorrow's game."

Jeff stood up to go, then turned back. "What about my mom?" he asked. "What if she still wants me to quit the team?"

Collins's eyes met Jeff's steadily. "That's not her decision, is it?" he asked. "Isn't that pretty much up to you and your dad?"

Jeff hesitated, a slow smile spreading across his face. "Yeah," he said. "I guess it is, isn't it?"

When Jeff was gone, Collins sat quietly for a few minutes, thinking, then picked up the phone and dialed Dr. Martin Ames's private number at the sports clinic.

"Marty?" he said when the doctor came on the line. "It's Phil." He hesitated a moment, wondering if there was really any reason for him to be calling the doctor. But those marks on Jeff's ankles had certainly been real. "I was just wondering if there's a reason why Jeff would have marks on his wrists and ankles today."

There was a momentary silence, then Ames spoke, his voice tinged with condescension. "Are you asking exactly what we did to Jeff last night?"

Collins's jaw tightened. "I'm just asking if there's an explanation for the marks."

Again there was a momentary silence, and when Ames spoke again, his tone was gentler. "Look, Phil, you know how Jeff was last night. You had to restrain him, and after you left, he had another attack. Nothing to worry about, but we had to restrain him, too, until we could get him calmed down. Sometimes the straps leave marks. What's the big deal? Isn't he all right today?"

"Seems okay," Collins admitted. "But he had a nightmare —a really bad one. I guess I was wondering if the marks could have come from that."

Now Ames chuckled. "You mean you were wondering if Jeff's cracking up?"

Collins flinched, for that was exactly what he had been thinking. And yet when Ames actually spoke the words out loud, they sounded ridiculous. "I guess maybe I overreacted," he replied.

Now Ames's voice became reassuring. "No, you did the right thing. You know I always want to know what's going on with the boys, no matter how insignificant it might seem. Not that bruises on Jeff's arms and legs are insignificant," he quickly added. "You did the right thing to call me. But it's nothing to worry about. Okay?" When the coach made no reply for a moment, Ames spoke again, his voice carrying a harsh note of challenge. "I know what I'm doing, Collins," he said.

Phil Collins's lips compressed into a tight line. If the arrogant bastard was so sure of himself . . . He put the thought out of his mind. Ames, after all, had done more for the team than any other single individual, himself included. "Okay," he said at last. "I just wanted you to know what's happening, that's all."

"And I appreciate that," Ames replied, friendly again. The conversation ended a moment later, but even after he'd hung up, Phil Collins still felt uneasy.

What if something really was wrong with Jeff?

What if Jeff LaConner was getting sick the way Randy Stevens had last year?

Just the thought of it made Collins shudder.

9

The last days of Indian summer had faded away, and as September gave way to October, the aspens began to change color. Now Silverdale was ablaze with the brilliant reds and golds of autumn, and the mountain air had taken on a brisk snap, harbinger of the winter to come. Already some of the mountain peaks to the east of the little valley were brushed with snow, and the long evenings of summer were a thing of the past.

For the Tanners, Silverdale was finally beginning to feel like home, and they had fitted themselves comfortably into the pace of the little town. Kelly, her friends in San Marcos all but forgotten, was insisting that if her parents didn't buy her skis immediately, it would be too late, her life ruined forever.

Blake, though still in the throes of sorting out the masses of detail his new job entailed, managed to come home by five-thirty or six every day, and he was never required to work on weekends. Indeed, the first time he tried to go to his office on a Saturday afternoon, he quickly discovered that working on weekends in Silverdale was impossible, for a security guard had stopped him just inside the front door, informing him that all the offices were locked up for the weekend. When he'd protested that he had work to do, the guard had shrugged impotently and suggested he call Jerry Harris. Jerry had laughed at him and told him to go home. "As far as I'm concerned," he said, "there isn't anything we're doing out here that can't wait until Monday. So enjoy your family while you can. The kids grow up too fast anyway."

That afternoon they'd gone to the high school football game, and the following weekend they'd driven down to Durango to watch the Wolverines play there. To Blake's surprise, Mark had actually shown some interest in the games, although at first he suspected that Mark's major interest was in Linda Harris rather than the game itself. Yet, every Sunday afternoon, it had been Mark who insisted on spending a couple of hours on the high school practice field, working once more on his place kicking.

For Sharon, the misgivings she'd felt in the Safeway the day they'd run into Charlotte LaConner had retreated to the back of her mind, and when she'd seen Charlotte at the football games—noting that despite Charlotte's words that day, Jeff was still quarterbacking the team—she decided that perhaps Elaine Harris had been right when she'd said that Charlotte had a tendency to overreact to things.

Now, on the second Thursday in October, Mark glanced at his watch, scraped the last mouthful of potatoes off his plate, and slid his chair back. "Got to go," he announced.

Kelly's face creased into a scowl. "How come I can't go to the pep rallies?" she demanded. "I go to the games, don't I?"

Mark grinned at his little sister. "You wouldn't like them," he told her. "It's a bunch of people jumping up and down and yelling all the time."

"Then how come you like them?" Kelly countered.

" 'Cause they're kind of fun," Mark admitted. "And besides," he added, "I'm taking pictures for the annual tonight."

Kelly cocked her head. "I bet Linda Harris is going to be in every one of them, isn't she?"

"Maybe," Mark said, a faint blush spreading over his face.

"Mark's got a girlfriend, Mark's got a girlfriend," Kelly chanted.

Mark rolled his eyes and turned his back on his sister. "We're gonna go out and get a hamburger after the rally," he told his mother. "What time do I have to be home?"

"Eleven," Sharon replied. Then, as Mark started toward the front door, she called after him, "And if you're going to be late, call!"

"I will," he called back. A moment later the door slammed behind him.

The pep rally was just beginning when Mark got to the school. As he came into the stadium, he saw Linda waving to him from the field. He smiled, waved back, then broke into an easy run. Until tonight he'd watched the pep rallies from the stands with the rest of the kids, but now he, too, would be on the field. Finding a spot on the bench, he opened his camera bag and quickly selected a zoom lens for his Nikon. He screwed on the flashgun, checked his film supply, then moved out to the field itself. By now he knew the routines by heart, and last week he'd decided which would be the best shots. By the time the band started to play the Silverdale alma mater and the drill team was marching onto the field, he was ready. He grinned to himself as he realized that he'd just proved Kelly wrong. Linda Harris wasn't on the drill team, so he'd have at least one picture that didn't include her.

The rally went on. Half an hour later Mark had shot three rolls of film and there was only one roll left in his gadget bag. He sat down on the bench next to Linda, and while the song leaders began dancing their routine to the major fight song, fumbled to get the last roll of film into the camera. By the time the song was over and Peter Nakamura had picked up a megaphone to introduce the team, Mark was ready. He took up a position next to the main gate, and as Peter called out the names of the boys on the team, their numbers, and the positions they played—and the players, in full uniform, trotted out onto the field—Mark resumed shooting pictures.

Some of the players paused for Mark, others waved to him as they trotted past. One or two ignored him completely, and Robb Harris, timing the action perfectly, flipped him the finger at the exact moment the flash went off.

Finally, after a long pause accompanied by a drum roll, Peter Nakamura called Jeff LaConner's name. As the crowd of teenagers in the stands got to their feet and their cheering rose to a crescendo, Mark focused the zoom lens on Jeff, who was running in place a few yards away. As his name was called, Jeff turned, dropped low to the ground for a moment, then broke into a dead run. As he came abreast of Mark he turned his head, and as the flashgun went off, he was facing the camera squarely.

The look of pure hatred in his eyes almost made Mark drop his camera.

But then Jeff was gone, and as the Wolverines' star quarterback ran onto the field, his arms spread, his hands held high over his head, Mark decided he must have been wrong. After all, it had been a couple of weeks since Linda had broken up with Jeff, and despite Linda's fears, Jeff had been perfectly friendly toward both of them.

No, he was wrong, Mark decided. He had to be. Jeff had just been putting on a ferocious expression for the sake of the camera.

Jeff LaConner stood at the end of the long row of football players, his hands clenched at his sides. Though the strains of the Silverdale fight song were filling the air, and the other members of the team were singing along with the crowd, Jeff was oblivious to all of it.

His eyes were fixed on Mark Tanner, who was now standing next to Linda Harris, whispering in her ear. The familiar anger, the anger that was getting harder and harder for him to keep under control, was building inside him again.

It had happened once during the week after he'd spent the

night at Rocky Mountain High. He'd been on the practice field, and was playing well. He'd been working on his passes that day, taking the ball on the snap from Roy Kramer, fading back a few yards with a quick look to see if the wide receiver was keeping to his pattern, then hurling the ball with almost perfect accuracy toward the spot where Kent Taylor would be a few seconds later.

In eleven tries, they'd completed the pass eleven times.

On the twelfth try, as he'd scanned the field, he caught a glimpse of Linda Harris and Mark Tanner, both of them laughing, walking away from the school. The play had fallen apart, his pass falling short by a good ten yards. Instantly, Phil Collins had blown his whistle and stormed onto the field, demanding to know what had happened. Jeff said nothing, barely even hearing the coach's tirade, for a wave of pure fury was sweeping over him. His vision almost seemed to desert him, his focus telescoping to the point where all he could see was Mark and Linda.

They were laughing at him—he was as certain of it as he had ever been of anything in his life.

And then, as abruptly as it had come on, the anger had drained out of him. He'd stood still for a moment, his body suddenly tired, as if he'd just run a ten-mile race.

He could still see Linda and Mark. They had paused by the corner of the building and were looking toward him. When Mark raised his hand to wave, Jeff found himself waving back. For the rest of the session Jeff's concentration was shot, his mind totally occupied with trying to figure out what had happened. He wasn't mad at either Linda or Mark. Or, anyway, he didn't think he was.

From then until the past week, he hadn't had any problems with anger. But on Monday morning, then again at lunchtime on Tuesday, he'd lost control for a moment. And yesterday it had happened twice, and today he'd carefully avoided both Linda and Mark, afraid the sudden rage might come over him again and that this time he wouldn't be able to control it at all.

Now, as he stood with the rest of the team facing the
stands, it was happening again.

His eyes were fixed on the two of them, his fury tingeing
their images with red. He could almost hear them talking
together, and he was sure they were talking about him.

"Little prick," he muttered out loud.

Next to him, Robb Harris turned to glance at Jeff out of
the corner of his eye. He thought Jeff had spoken to him, but
now Jeff was looking away. From the expression on his face,
it seemed Jeff was angry about something. But what? He'd
been fine a few minutes ago, when they'd all been in the
locker room, putting on their uniforms. Puzzled, Robb glanced
around to see what Jeff was staring at.

All he could see was his sister, sitting on the bench next
to Mark Tanner. But that was no big deal—Jeff had told him
only a couple of days ago that he didn't blame Linda for
breaking up with him. Now, though, he was glaring furiously
at Mark, and when Robb glanced down, he saw that Jeff's
hands were curled like claws, the knuckles white, the tendons
standing out like steel wires drawn too taut.

The last notes of the fight song faded away, and the rest
of the players turned, ready for Jeff LaConner to lead them
off the field and back to the locker room.

But Jeff didn't move. He stood where he was, as if rooted
to the ground, his eyes still fixed glassily on Linda and
Mark.

"Come on, Jeff," Robb whispered. "Let's go!"

Jeff didn't seem to hear him. Finally, Robb nudged him.
"Will you move your ass, man? What the hell's wrong with
you?"

It took a moment before Robb's words seemed to penetrate Jeff's hearing, and the bigger boy swung around to face
him.

"I'm gonna get that little bastard," he said. "I'm gonna
smash him up so bad, nobody's ever going to want to look at
him again!"

*   *   *

"So what's up?" Blake Tanner asked Jerry Harris. They were sitting in the Harrises' oak-paneled den, and though Blake had been there for almost an hour, Jerry still hadn't gotten to the point. And there *was* a point to this visit, Blake was almost certain, for when Jerry had called him after dinner that evening and asked him to drop by, there had been something in his voice that told Blake it was to be more than just a visit between friends.

Nor did he think it had anything to do with the office, for even in the few short weeks he'd been in Silverdale, Blake had learned that if something came up in the office, Jerry Harris left it there. Of course, they talked business all the time, no matter where they were, but if the situation was primarily social, important issues were never brought up. Nevertheless, as he walked the six blocks from his own house to the Harrises', he wondered what might be on Jerry's mind.

It was Ricardo Ramirez, he decided first, and Blake shook his head sadly as he thought about the boy. Rick was still in the hospital in Silverdale, his head held perfectly still in the metal embrace of a Stryker frame. Given his condition, Blake had come to think that the fact the boy was still in a coma was a kind of left-handed blessing, for at least Rick was totally unaware of how serious his injuries were. As far as the specialists Mac MacCallum had called in could tell, Rick was nearly totally paralyzed from the neck down, and without the respirator, he would die very quickly. But his heart was still strong, and so far Maria Ramirez had refused even to consider the possibility that her son might never wake up. Indeed, she was at his bedside every day, holding her son's hand, murmuring softly to him in Spanish, certain that somehow, even through his coma, he could hear and understand what she was saying.

The trust fund was all set up, a massive insurance annuity that would continue paying every possible expense both Maria and Ricardo could possibly incur for the rest of their lives. Though Blake was certain that Maria didn't yet understand the full extent of her affluence, he was also certain that she would never abuse it. Indeed, after his initial shock at the instructions Jerry Harris had issued on his first day at work, Blake had come to believe that Ted Thornton was correct in his policy, for without the aid of TarrenTech, Maria Ramirez would have had no resources at all. And now Maria had a trust fund and nothing to worry about in the future except the welfare of her son.

If her son lived.

But when he'd gotten to the Harrises', Jerry made no mention of the Ramirez family, or anything else pertaining to business. Instead, he seemed more interested in how the Tanners were adjusting to Silverdale. And now, finally, in answer to Blake's question, Jerry mixed them each a third drink and got to the point.

"I've been thinking about Mark," he said.

Blake's brows arched questioningly.

"I've been wondering if you've had a chance to look over what we're doing at Rocky Mountain High," Jerry went on, "the sports center."

Blake shrugged noncommittally. "Other than the fact that we fund a lot of it, I don't know that much about it yet."

"It's sort of an experimental camp," Jerry told him. "Martin Ames has some interesting ideas about athletic training, and we've been letting him put them into practice." He grinned, his eyes sparkling. "And since you've been going to the football games, you can see how well it's working out. In fact," he went on, "it's exceeding all our expectations."

Blake sat forward in his chair. "What's the deal?" he asked. "What's he doing?"

"Synthetic vitamins," Jerry replied. "He's been finding a lot of links between physical development and certain vitamin complexes, and for the last few years he's been developing a series of new compounds that are helping us compensate for a lot of genetic deficiencies." He paused a moment. "Such as Robb's asthma, for instance."

The words seemed to hang in the air for a moment before their import sank into Blake. "You mean it wasn't just the change of climate and good, clean mountain air that cleared it up,'' he said.

Jerry shook his head. ''I wish it had been that simple. But it wasn't. Ames found all kinds of things wrong with Robb. It wasn't just the asthma—he was having some problems with his bones that might have been precancerous conditions, and ever since he was a baby, he'd been a little slow to develop. Ames's theory was that it was all linked to the way Robb's body handled certain vitamins.'' He smiled. ''And, as I'm sure you've noticed, all that's been taken care of.''

The implication was clear, and Blake didn't need Jerry to spell it out for him. ''But it's a sports center,'' he said, ''and you know how Mark feels about sports.''

Now it was Jerry Harris who looked surprised. ''Isn't that you and Mark I see out on the field every Sunday afternoon? Looks to me like he might be changing.''

Blake shrugged with careful indifference, unwilling to expose even to Jerry Harris his hopes that perhaps Mark would, after all, follow in his own footsteps. ''He's a bit small for the team here, don't you think? I mean, all our guys are so big, they'd run right over Mark.''

''Exactly,'' Jerry replied, setting his glass down. ''And I know it's really none of my business, but I've been talking to Marty Ames about Mark—the rheumatic fever and all that. I even went so far as to get Mark's medical records sent to him.''

Blake frowned. ''Aside from the fact that I thought medical records were supposed to be confidential, why would you want to do that?''

''Because I wanted to get Marty's opinion before I talked to you. I didn't want to get your hopes up, then not have it amount to anything.''

Blake put his own drink aside. ''All right,'' he said. ''So, just for the sake of discussion, what did he say?''

Jerry Harris's eyes met his. ''He thinks he can help Mark. He doesn't think Mark's problems from the rheumatic fever have to be permanent, and he thinks he can bring Mark's growth rate back up to normal.''

Blake's face took on a quizzical expression. "Are you serious?"

"Absolutely," Jerry replied. "He's come up with a variant of the same vitamin complex Robb was treated with, and he's ninety percent certain it will be effective with Mark."

Blake gazed at his friend. None of what he was saying made sense. If there really was such a complex, he and Sharon would have heard of it by now. Unless . . .

"Are you telling me you want me to let somebody use an experimental drug on Mark?" he asked.

Harris shook his head as if he'd been expecting the question. "It's hardly experimental," he said. "And it has nothing to do with drugs, either. It's just a new way of combining certain vitamins, allowing the body to achieve its full potential. All the vitamins do is act as a sort of trigger, releasing hormones that are already present, but not fully functional." Reading the doubt in Blake's eyes, he went on: "Do you really think I'd let Ames give my own son a compound I didn't have full faith in? He's my son, Blake, not a guinea pig."

"Well, I don't know," Blake replied. "But it's certainly something to think about. And I'd like to see all the material on it." He grinned a little self-consciously. "I'm no doctor, but after all Mark's problems, I can tell you I know more about growth problems than the average layman."

"Just like Elaine and I knew everything there was to know about asthma," Harris agreed. "You'll have all the material on your desk Monday morning. Plus, you might want to go out and talk to Ames about Mark. Just listen to him, then make up your own mind."

A few minutes later the talk turned to other things, but Blake barely listened, for his mind kept going back over what Harris had told him.

And he remembered the sounds he'd heard emanating from Mark's room every morning for the last few weeks.

The sound of Mark's labored breathing as he struggled with his push-ups and sit-ups, and the soft grunts that broke from the boy's throat as he worked with Blake's own set of weights.

If there were really a way to help him . . .

Maybe he wouldn't wait until Monday. Maybe he'd go to the office tomorrow and take a look at Ames's material.

It was a little after ten-thirty when Linda and Mark left the little café next to the drugstore and started home. They still had plenty of time for Mark to walk Linda to the Harrises' without missing his eleven o'clock curfew, but they walked quickly. A breeze had come up, and Mark turned his collar up as the chill of the night made his cheeks tingle.

"I still don't think Jeff's mad at you," he heard Linda say as she tucked her hand into his jacket pocket and meshed her fingers with his own. "He didn't say anything, did he?"

"He didn't have time," Mark told her, not for the first time. "He was running. But I'm telling you, the look on his face almost scared the hell out of me. Wait till Monday, when I develop the film. You'll see."

They turned the corner off Colorado Street. There, the night seemed darker, with only a few pools of yellow light dotting the sidewalk ahead. Instinctively, Jeff glanced around, then felt foolish. This was Silverdale, he told himself as they walked on, not San Francisco, or even San Marcos. But after they'd walked nearly two blocks, a figure stepped out from behind a bush up ahead.

Linda and Mark stopped, startled but not yet frightened.

The figure took a step toward them.

"H-Hello?" Mark asked.

The looming figure said nothing, but as it came closer, both Linda and Mark suddenly knew who it was.

"Jeff?" Linda asked. "Is that you?"

Still there was no reply, then the figure stepped into one of the pools of light beneath a streetlamp and Linda and Mark could see Jeff's face clearly.

His eyes were glassy and his heavy features were contorted with fury. At his sides his big hands were already working themselves into fists.

"Oh, Jesus," Mark whispered. "Let's get out of here."

With Linda at his side, Mark spun around and ran toward Colorado Street and the bright lights that lined its sidewalks. There would be people there—the rest of the high school crowd leaving the café, and the audience from the movie theater across the square.

His breath was coming hard as he ran, and his heart was racing. Although Linda was keeping up with him, he could hear Jeff's feet pounding on the sidewalk behind them, closer every second.

There was only another block to go, and then half a block.

It was too far. Suddenly Jeff crashed against him from behind. Letting go of Linda's hand, he yelled at her to keep going, then crumbled to the ground as Jeff LaConner's furious blows struck him in the stomach.

10

"Stop it!" Linda Harris screamed. "Jeff, what are you doing?"

Mark was on the ground now, facedown, and Jeff LaConner sat astride him, his fists pummeling the smaller boy. Linda yelled at Jeff again, and when he seemed not even to hear her, she tried to pull him away from Mark. One of Jeff's arms came up, swinging wildly, and caught Linda's rib cage. Stunned, she fell to the pavement, too, then staggered to her feet, gasping for air. Her eyes burning with tears, one hand clamped against her bruised ribs, she staggered the rest of the block, then turned onto Colorado Street.

"Help!" she called out, but even to herself her voice sounded like no more than a hoarse whisper. She paused for a moment, bracing herself against the post of a streetlamp, fighting to fill her lungs with air. Then, once more, she shouted, "Help! Someone, please help me!"

A block away she saw three boys come out of the café, and waved frantically to them. For a single, awful moment she thought they were going to turn the other way, but then they saw her, and in seconds her brother and two of his friends were running toward her.

"Down there," she gasped, pointing into the darkness of

the side street. "It's Jeff! He's gone nuts! He's beating Mark up!"

Robb Harris stared at his sister uncomprehendingly until a sudden image of Jeff exploded into his mind—an image from earlier that night, when he'd seen Jeff gazing at Mark and Linda, his whole body trembling, his face blazing with anger. "Holy shit," he muttered. "Call Dad," he told Linda, then shouted to his friends, "Come on!" With Pete Nakamura and Roy Kramer chasing after him, Robb dashed down the sidewalk toward the spot where he could now see Jeff and Mark struggling on the ground.

Linda, her ribs starting to ache now, ran down Colorado Street toward the brightly lit café, stumbled through the door and reached for the pay phone. It was only when she fumbled for a quarter that she realized she no longer had her purse. She uttered a sob of frustration and turned toward the counter at the back, where Mabel Harkins was slowly counting the money in the cash register. Except for Mabel, the café was empty.

"Sorry, honey, I'm all closed up," Mabel said, glancing up from her counting as Linda approached the counter. Then she stopped counting and stared. "Jeez, hon, what happened to you?"

Linda ignored the question. "Can I use your phone, Mabel? I have to call my dad."

Immediately, Mabel pushed the phone by the cash register across to Linda, but when the girl, her fingers trembling violently, tried unsuccessfully to punch the buttons, Mabel pulled it back. "I'll do it," she said. "What's the number?"

On the third ring Jerry Harris answered. "It's Mabel Harkins," the waitress said. "Down at the café?" Without waiting for Jerry to respond, she continued, "Linda's down here, Jerry, and she's awful upset. Just a sec." She handed the phone to Linda, then listened as the girl tried to tell her father what had happened.

"I don't *know* why he did it," she said at last. "We were just walking along the street and he was up ahead of us.

It was like he was waiting for us or something. Anyway, Robb and some other guys are trying to break it up. Can you come over, Daddy?''

She listened for a moment, then told her father where Jeff and Mark were. Finally, her hands still shaking, she hung up.

Mabel handed her a glass of water. ''Here, hon,'' she said. ''You just sit down and drink this, and try to calm down.''

But Linda shook her head. ''I can't. I—I have to get back there. I can't just leave Mark alone—''

''He's not alone,'' Mabel said firmly. ''And there's nothing you can do right now. You just sit down and get yourself calmed down for a minute, then we'll both go see what's going on.''

Jerry Harris appeared upset as he hung up the phone. ''What is it?'' Blake Tanner asked. ''What's going on?''

''I don't know, exactly,'' Jerry replied. Already on his feet, with Blake right behind him, he went into the living room, where he told Blake and his wife what Linda had said.

''Oh, Lord,'' Elaine breathed. Her eyes shifted to Blake. ''You go with Jerry and I'll call Sharon.'' She was already picking up the telephone as the two men hurried out into the night.

Mark had managed to wriggle free of Jeff twice, but it hadn't done him any good. Neither time had he managed to get more than a few feet away before Jeff tackled him again. Now, with Jeff's fists pummeling him, he gave up trying to get away from the larger boy and was instead merely doing his best to defend himself from the rain of blows that seemed to come from every direction.

His nose was bleeding and he could taste the salty flavor

of blood in his mouth. He thought there was a cut over his right eye, too, and his ears were still ringing from a blow to his head.

Now Jeff was on top of Mark again, his eyes fixed blankly on the object of his rage. His mind had almost ceased to function, but as he felt his fists hammer into Mark again and again, a sensation of satisfaction coursed through him. He'd show the little jerk—he'd show everyone!

A few seconds later, when Robb Harris, Pete Nakamura, and Roy Kramer arrived on the scene, Jeff wasn't even aware of their presence, so engrossed was he with the damage he was inflicting on Mark Tanner.

Nor did Jeff hear Robb's voice as Robb shouted at him. "What the hell are you doing, Jeff? You're going to kill him!"

Robb stared at the struggling figures, only half recognizable in the darkness. It wasn't even a fight, he saw instantly, for Mark, pinned to the ground, was doing little more than trying to shield his face. And Jeff, his own face a nearly unrecognizable mask of mindless fury, seemed oblivious of what he was doing. It was like watching a dog worry a half-dead rat, Robb realized with a sickening sensation. At any moment he expected Jeff to pick Mark up and start shaking him.

"Help me!" he shouted to Pete Nakamura. "We've got to get him off Mark."

As a porch light snapped on across the street, and then another one farther down the block, Robb moved in on one side of Jeff, grasping his arm.

With one quick movement, Jeff twisted himself loose from Robb's grip, then swung at him, his fist clipping Robb's jaw. Robb howled with the sharp pain and reeled back, his right hand automatically coming up to touch his injured jaw.

Jeff's first swing at Pete Nakamura caught the other boy in the left eye. Roy Kramer hurled himself onto Jeff's back, his arms snaking around Jeff's neck.

As Roy's grip tightened around Jeff's neck, Jeff seemed

to hesitate for a moment, his arms dropping to his sides. Then a gurgle of fury erupted from Jeff's strangled throat. Heaving with exertion, he thrust himself upright, carrying Roy Kramer on his back. He spun around, as if expecting to find this new enemy behind him, then dropped to the ground and rolled over. As his weight pressed down on Roy, the other boy's arms loosened for a moment, and suddenly Jeff was free. He rolled again, then crouched low to the ground. His eyes, glistening in the light of the streetlamp, darted from Robb to Pete, then back to Roy, who was lying on his back now, trying to catch his breath.

Mark Tanner, whimpering with pain, had drawn himself into a tight ball, his knees drawn up against his chest.

People were emerging from the houses on the block now, and shouts were beginning to fill the night as one person called out to another, asking what was happening.

Jeff's head swung around and his eyes took in the gathering crowd. Then a strange, animallike sound emerged from his throat, and he was gone, dashing down a driveway, disappearing around the corner of a house.

Jerry Harris turned the corner into Pueblo Drive and instantly braked the car to a stop. A few yards away a crowd was gathering and he could see Robb, massaging his jaw with a hand, standing in the middle of someone's lawn.

Blake Tanner was already out of the car, running toward Robb. It was only when Blake dropped to his knees that Jerry realized the dark form at Robb's feet must be Mark. Leaving the engine idling, he ran over to his son.

"What happened?" he asked. "Are you all right?"

Robb nodded, but said nothing for a moment. When at last he spoke, his voice was shaking. "It was . . . nuts," he breathed. "Jeff was just pounding him into the ground, and he wouldn't stop—"

"Where is he?" Blake demanded.

"Gone," Robb told him. "It was really weird, Dad. Roy finally jumped him from the back and got him off Mark, but then he rolled over and Roy had to let go. And then he started looking at us like he didn't even know who we were. Then he started running." Robb pointed to the two houses between which Jeff had dashed, and Jerry nodded.

"Okay," he said. He glanced quickly at the gathering crowd, then recognized one of the staff from TarrenTech. "Call an ambulance," he told the man. "Then let's get some people together and see if we can find Jeff LaConner. And somebody call his folks," he said to no one in particular, but almost immediately a woman split away from the crowd around Mark and hurried across the street.

Finally Jerry joined Blake Tanner at Mark's side. "Is he okay?"

Blake glanced up, his expression tight with anger. "How okay can he be with his nose bleeding, his face cut up, and one of his eyes swollen shut? And where the hell is that LaConner kid, anyway?"

"Now, take it easy," Jerry replied. "Let's just take one thing at a time and try to get this straightened out. And the first thing is Mark. I've got an ambulance coming, just in case we need one."

On the ground, Mark moved and his right eye opened slightly. "D-Dad?" he asked. "Is that you?"

"It's okay, Mark," Blake assured him. "I'm here, and it's all over. You're going to be okay."

A sob, half pain, half simple relief, erupted from Mark's throat. Slowly, almost as if he were afraid he might break into pieces, he straightened his legs. Then, with almost no warning at all, he rolled over, dragged himself onto his hands and knees, and threw up.

He gagged for a moment, coughed, then sank back down to the lawn.

A few people, sensing Mark's embarrassment, turned away.

There was the wail of a siren in the distance, and a couple

of minutes later the street was filled with flashing lights as the ambulance rounded the corner and screeched to a stop at the curb.

Sharon Tanner's face was pale as she opened the front door for Elaine Harris. "Where is he?" Sharon asked. "Where's Mark?"

"Just put on your coat and let's go," Elaine told her. "Jerry and Blake are already there. Everything's going to be all right, I'm sure."

Sharon reached for her coat, then remembered Kelly, who was upstairs in her room, sound asleep. "Just a second," she said. "I have to get Kelly."

While Elaine waited in the foyer, Sharon hurried up the stairs, then reappeared a moment later. Kelly, still in her pajamas, and tying the belt of a bathrobe around her waist, trailed after her.

"But where are we going, Mommy?" she asked.

"Never mind, honey," Sharon told her. She rushed down the stairs and put on her coat. "It's going to be all right. We're just going for a little ride, that's all."

Kelly, still fogged with sleep, followed her mother out to the Harris's station wagon and climbed into the backseat. By the time Sharon had settled herself into the passenger seat, Elaine had started the engine and put the transmission in gear. The car lurched as Elaine's foot hit the accelerator, then they were out of the driveway.

"What happened?" Sharon asked as they drove down the street. "Why would Jeff want to pick on Mark?"

Elaine shook her head. "I just don't know," she said. "Unless he's been brooding about Linda all this time. But that's not like Jeff. He's always been an easygoing—"

Then, as both she and Sharon simultaneously remembered their encounter with Charlotte LaConner in the Safeway a couple of weeks ago, she fell silent.

Within a couple of minutes they came to Pueblo Drive and Elaine pulled the station wagon behind Jerry's car. Telling Kelly to stay in the backseat, Sharon opened the door and scrambled out. She scanned the crowd quickly, then spotted Blake standing with Jerry Harris. Next to them two white-clad attendants were gently moving Mark onto a stretcher.

"My God," Sharon breathed. Breaking into a run, she pushed her way through the crowd of onlookers, then had to grasp Blake's arm to steady herself as she looked down at Mark's battered face. She stifled the scream building in her throat, then dropped to her knees and gently touched her son's cheek.

"Mark?" she asked. "Honey? Can you hear me?"

Mark's left eye fluttered open and he forced the barest trace of a grin. "I—I guess I didn't make curfew, did I?" he managed to say.

A wave of relief swept over Sharon, and she gently patted Mark's hand, which was resting on his chest. "Don't you worry about that," she said. "Are you all right? Does it hurt terribly?"

Mark swallowed, and his shoulders moved slightly as he attempted a shrug. "Ever been hit by a bus?" he asked.

Sharon's eyes watered and she shook her head.

"Well, if you ever get curious, pick a fight with Jeff LaConner." Then his eye closed again and he winced as the two attendants lifted the stretcher off the ground and started toward the ambulance. Sharon walked next to the stretcher and Blake fell in on the other side, but neither of them spoke until the stretcher had been placed inside the vehicle and the doors closed. "Where are you taking him?" Sharon asked.

One of the attendants smiled at her. "County Hospital, ma'am. Don't worry—it's not as bad as it looks. Maybe a couple of stitches over his right eye and some tape on his ribs. But he's gonna be fine."

Sharon sighed with relief. Then, as she glanced around, she realized something was wrong. She frowned and turned to face Blake. "Where are the police?" she asked.

It was Jerry Harris, standing a couple of steps behind Blake, who answered her. "It was just a fight between a couple of high school kids, Sharon. I didn't think we needed the police."

Sharon glared at him. "You mean nobody even called them?" she asked, her voice reflecting disbelief.

Jerry Harris frowned uncertainly. "Come on, Sharon, things like this happen all the time—"

"And when someone gets beaten up as badly as Mark did tonight, the police get called!" Sharon snapped. "And where's Jeff LaConner? What did he do, just walk away from all this?"

"He's gone, honey," Blake said, trying to soothe her. "Robb and some other kids showed up, and Jeff took off."

"But we'll find him," Jerry told her. "He's probably at home right now, trying to explain to his parents what happened."

Sharon's expression tightened further. "He'll do a lot more than explain to his parents," she said. "He'll explain to the police, too. As soon as I get to the hospital, I'm going to call them. And then we're going to find out exactly what happened here tonight."

"We know what happened," Jerry began, but once more Sharon cut him off.

"We know that Jeff LaConner beat up on a boy who's only about half his size," she said. "And I don't care what provocation Jeff may or may not have thought he had. He's not going to just get off scot-free."

"Honey, no one's even suggested that he should," Blake said now. "But let's just take one thing at a time, okay? Go to the hospital with Mark, and I'll get a ride with Jerry. When we know exactly what happened, we'll take it from there."

Sharon seemed about to say something more, then appeared to change her mind. One of the attendants opened the back of the ambulance again and she climbed inside, crouching by her son. A moment later, moving quickly but with its siren silent, the ambulance pulled away.

11

It seemed to Sergeant Dick Kennally as if half of Silverdale had tried to jam themselves into the tiny waiting room of County Hospital. When he'd first heard the wailing of the ambulance's siren a little more than an hour before, he'd half expected the phone to ring, summoning him to the site of an automobile accident. But when the phone hadn't rung, he'd decided that whatever had required an ambulance wasn't a police matter, and gone back to the crossword puzzle he'd been half-heartedly working on ever since he'd come on shift at four o'clock that afternoon. Indeed, he'd all but forgotten the siren when the call finally came shortly after eleven.

Why did situations like this always have to come up just before the end of a shift? he wondered as he drove to the hospital. Why couldn't people wait until after midnight to call the cops? Wes Jenkins, who usually took the graveyard shift, was always complaining he didn't have anything to do, anyway. But of course after ten years on the tiny Silverdale force, Kennally knew the answer—by midnight most of the town was already in bed, and those who were up and about weren't the sort who would call the police. Rather, they were the sort other people would call the police about.

He'd been surprised to find Jerry Harris, together with his wife and kids, sitting with the Tanners when he'd arrived. Harris tried to explain what had happened, but even as he listened to Jerry's words, he found himself watching Sharon Tanner. Her eyes were flashing with barely suppressed anger, and several times she seemed about to interrupt Harris. Each time, her husband stopped her. Finally, after Jerry had sketched the situation for him, Kennally turned to Linda Harris.

"Can you tell me exactly what happened?" he asked, his voice gentle.

Linda shrugged helplessly. Her face was pale and her cheeks stained with tears. "I don't *know* what happened," she said unhappily. "We were just walking down the street on the way to my house, and Jeff came out from behind a bush. It—Well, it was almost like he was waiting for us. At first we didn't think anything about it. But then we saw his face—" She stopped talking and her whole body shuddered violently.

"His face?" Kennally repeated. "What about it?"

Linda struggled to find the right words. "He—I don't know. He just looked crazy. His eyes were all glassy, like he didn't really know who we were. It was Mark who figured out he was coming after us. We got scared and started running, but Jeff caught up with us right away."

"Why?" Kennally asked bluntly. "Why was he mad at Mark Tanner? What did he say?"

Linda shook her head. "Nothing. He didn't say anything at all. It was—well, it was really spooky. He just jumped Mark and started beating up on him."

Kennally chewed thoughtfully at his lower lip. "You were dating Jeff, weren't you?" he asked.

Linda hesitated, then nodded. "But that was over weeks ago. Jeff was mad at me when I told him, but he got over it. He's been fine ever since."

"No, he hasn't," Robb Harris interjected. Until now he'd been silent, sitting quietly by his father. When Kennally looked at him questioningly, Robb tried to tell him what had happened at the pep rally earlier. "It was weird," Robb concluded a couple of minutes later. "It's like Linda said—his eyes were kind of glassy and he was just staring at them like he wanted to kill them or something. Then all of a sudden he was fine. In the locker room afterward he was acting like nothing had happened."

Kennally's brows knit into a deep frown. At first, listening to Jerry Harris, he'd thought maybe the fight had been nothing more than a squabble between a couple of schoolboys. But now . . . He sighed heavily, and finally turned to face Sharon Tanner, who had called him as soon as she'd gotten to the hospital—exactly as she had promised Jerry Harris. "You're sure you want to press charges?" he asked, though the expression on her face answered his question clearly enough.

To his surprise, Sharon's eyes reflected a degree of uncertainty. "I—I didn't say that," she said. "But I certainly think you ought to talk to him. I'm willing to listen to his side of the story, and then we can decide what to do. But if what Linda and Robb say is true, certainly something has to be done about him."

Kennally reluctantly nodded. He liked Jeff LaConner—always had. It was a shame to have to pick him up tonight. Saturday, after all, was a game day, and without Jeff playing . . .

Still, Kennally had no choice. Letting himself into the small office adjoining the waiting room, he first called Chuck LaConner, who told him that Jeff wasn't home yet. Briefly, Kennally told Chuck what had happened and heard LaConner curse softly.

"How's the Tanner boy?" Chuck asked a moment later.

"Don't know yet," Kennally replied. "MacCallum's still working on him." His voice dropped and he turned away from the window to the waiting room. "If I were you, Chuck, I'd get down here pretty fast. Mrs. Tanner's mighty upset, if you know what I mean."

There was only the slightest pause before Chuck LaConner replied that he'd be at the hospital within minutes.

Next Kennally called the police department, and when Wes Jenkins answered, filled him in on what had happened. "Call some of the boys," he said. "We're going to have to go out looking for him."

"Any idea where he might have gone?" Jenkins asked.

"Not really. But it shouldn't be too hard to track him. We know which way he headed after the fight." Kennally finished issuing his instructions to the night sergeant, then left the hospital. But he drove only a few blocks before pulling into a deserted parking lot illuminated by the soft glow of a phone booth in one of its corners. Stepping into the booth, he dialed the department number once again.

"Wes? Me again. One more thing—tell the boys that if they get hold of Jeff LaConner, I want him taken out to Ames at the sports center."

"Ames?" Jenkins replied. "How come? The LaConner kid sick?"

Kennally hesitated. "Dunno," he said finally. "But I just have a feeling, okay? I'm gonna call Ames right now, and if there's any change, I'll let you know."

He hung up, then fumbled in the inside pocket of his jacket for the small book of unlisted phone numbers he always carried with him, on duty or off. Flipping through it, he squinted at a number, then dropped another quarter in the phone. A sleepy voice answered on the sixth ring.

"Yeah?"

"Dr. Ames? It's Dick Kennally. From the police department. Sorry to have to call you so late."

Instantly, all vestiges of sleep drained out of the doctor's voice. "What is it?" he asked. "Has something happened?"

Kennally talked steadily for five minutes, even consulting his notebook to be sure he'd forgotten none of the details. "I've already told Jenkins to bring the LaConner boy out there if we find him. I can change that, if you think it's best."

"No," Ames said immediately. "You did the right thing. I'll get a team ready to admit him, and keep me posted. And Dick?" he added.

"Yeah?"

"Be careful," Ames told him. "From what you said, it sounds like Randy Stevens all over again. And if it is, Jeff LaConner should be considered very dangerous."

Kennally was silent for a moment, then grunted and hung up.

Did Ames really think he was telling him anything he didn't already know?

Even now, nearly a year after it had happened, he could still remember the night Randy Stevens cracked up. It had been a quiet night in Silverdale, at least until around eleven o'clock, when Kennally had gotten a call from the Stevenses' neighbors, reporting a disturbance. It had struck Kennally as odd, since in the two years the Stevenses had been in Silverdale they had never been anything less than model citizens. Randy, indeed, had been the boy other Silverdale parents always pointed to as a role model for their own children. Handsome, polite, an A student—Randy had been the star of the football team as well.

And never caused so much as a hint of a problem for either his parents or anyone else.

But that night something had snapped in Randy, and when Kennally arrived at the Stevenses, a small crowd of frightened onlookers had already gathered around the house.

Inside the house it was apparent that a major fight was taking place.

When Kennally forced his way in, he found Phyllis Stevens, her face bleeding, sobbing on the sofa in the living room. In the den, Tom Stevens and Randy were struggling on the floor.

Except that it wasn't really a struggle, for Tom was sprawled on his back, doing his best to fend off a rain of furious blows as his son straddled him, pounding at him mercilessly.

Kennally had known instantly that this was no simple fight, no argument between father and son that had gotten out of hand. For there was a look in Randy's eyes—a cold emptiness—that told Kennally that Randy wasn't even aware of what he was doing.

His mind was gone and he was simply lashing out at whomever was at hand.

It had taken three men to subdue the boy, and he was finally taken away from the house strapped to a stretcher. At Tom Stevens's request, Randy had been taken to the sports center and put under the care of Marty Ames.

The next morning Randy was transferred to the mental hospital at Canon City.

Though such a thing had never happened before in Silverdale, Marty Ames had explained that it wasn't all that uncommon. Randy, after all, had always been too perfect, meeting his parents' every expectation. But along with those expectations there had been pressure, and Randy never allowed himself to vent that pressure. And so, finally, he turned on his parents, his emotional structure collapsing in a shambles.

He had tried to kill them.

He had almost succeeded.

And now, tonight, Kennally could see the parallels between Randy Stevens and Jeff LaConner quite clearly.

Overachievers, both of them.

Neither of them ever in any trouble, neither of them ever showing signs of problems.

When Randy had finally blown, he'd come close to killing his own father.

Would Jeff have actually killed Mark Tanner tonight? Kennally didn't know, but he suspected he might well have done exactly that, given the chance.

So he would, indeed, take Ames's advice, and consider Jeff LaConner extremely dangerous.

It promised to be a long night.

Mac MacCallum smiled encouragingly at Mark Tanner, who was lying on his back on the examining table. The boy's chest was heavily taped, but Mac had assured him that none of his ribs was actually broken. Four of them, however, were cracked, and MacCallum had warned him that they would hurt for a while, especially if he laughed, coughed, or sneezed. Now he was working on Mark's face, carefully stitching up the cut over his right eye. "Only a couple more stitches and we'll have it," he said. "How're you holding up?"

Mark winced as the needle penetrated his skin once again. "Okay," he said between his clenched teeth. "Next to Jeff, this is a piece of cake."

Mac said nothing more until he'd taken the last stitch, tied off the thread with a neat surgeon's knot, then covered the stitches with a bandage. Mark started to try to raise himself to a sitting position, but MacCallum stopped him.

"Just lie there. I want to take some more X rays."

"How come?" Mark asked. "Nothing's broken, is it?"

"Not that I can see from the outside," MacCallum agreed. "But judging by what happened to your face and your ribs, it seems a good idea to take a look." In fact, MacCallum was almost certain the boy's jaw had sustained a hairline fracture, and there was still a strong possibility of internal injuries, particularly to the boy's kidneys and spleen. He washed his hands, then picked up Mark's chart and began writing instructions on it. When he was done, he handed the chart to the night-duty nurse, Karen Akers. "Can you handle all that?"

Karen glanced quickly down the chart, then nodded. Disappearing into the corridor, she returned a moment later, wheeling a gurney in front of her. Holding it steady next to the examining table, she helped Mark transfer himself. Mark winced at almost every motion, but when he'd finally made it, he forced himself to grin at the nurse. "See? Nothing to it. I could run a ten-K if I had to."

"Right," Karen replied dryly. "But the question is, can you hold still while I take your picture?"

MacCallum followed them into the corridor, but as they turned right toward the X-ray room, he took the other direction. A few seconds later he entered the waiting room where the Tanners and the Harrises were waiting. In the far corner he also recognized Chuck LaConner.

"Is he all right?" Sharon asked anxiously.

MacCallum glanced once more at Chuck LaConner, then turned his attention to Sharon. "All things considered, I'd say he doesn't look too bad." He detailed the stitching and bandaging he'd already done, summarizing Mark's injuries in the most reassuring way he could. "Of course," he went on, "I'll want him to stay the night, just so I can keep an eye on him. He's in X-ray right now, and we'll know a lot more after we see the results of those." Raising his voice, to be absolutely certain that Chuck LaConner would hear what he said next, he added, "Frankly, considering what happened to him, he's in pretty good shape."

Sharon's eyes clouded. "Considering what happened?" she repeated. "What does that mean?"

"Considering it was Jeff LaConner he ran up against," MacCallum said heavily. "The last boy who came in here wasn't so lucky."

"Now wait a minute," Chuck LaConner interrupted, rising to his feet and taking a step toward the doctor. "Everybody knows what happened to the Ramirez kid wasn't Jeff's fault."

The color drained from Sharon's face, and her eyes shifted quickly between LaConner and her husband. "Rick Ramirez?" she asked, her voice hollow. "The boy who's in a coma?"

MacCallum nodded briefly.

Sharon's legs suddenly felt weak, but she refused to allow herself to drop back onto the sofa. Even angrier now, she turned to Blake. "I thought you told me the Ramirez boy was an accident victim," she said, a note of uncertainty in her voice, as if she were trying to put something together in her mind.

"He was—" Blake began, but MacCallum interrupted.

"He may have been," he corrected.

Chuck LaConner's eyes were blazing now. Before he

could say anything, however, Sharon Tanner whirled on him, furious. "Is that what you want us to say happened to Mark, too?" she demanded. "That Jeff accidentally beat him up? And what about your wife?" she added, her voice bitter. "Was that an accident too?"

Blake stared at his own wife in bewilderment. "His wife?" he echoed. "Honey, what are you talking about?"

"I'm talking about Jeff LaConner," Sharon said, her voice harsh with anger. "Mark's not the only person he beat up, you know." She turned again, her eyes fixing on Chuck LaConner once more. "Or are you going to claim that was an accident, too?" she demanded.

LaConner seemed to pull back. "He didn't mean it," he said, but his voice was defensive. "He was upset that night. It was the night he and Linda broke up—"

"He hurt me that night, too."

Though she'd uttered the words softly, almost apologetically, Linda Harris, who had been sitting quietly between her father and her brother, suddenly had the attention of everyone in the room.

"He hurt *you*?" Jerry Harris asked. "Honey, you never said anything."

"I—I guess I just didn't think it was very important," Linda replied, her voice trembling. "I mean, he didn't really hurt me. He was just real mad, and he started shaking me. But . . . well, when I yelled at him, he stopped."

"And you never told us?" Elaine asked. "Darling, it must have been awful for you!"

"I guess I just didn't want to get him in trouble. He got sick that night, and afterward he seemed . . . well, he seemed okay, I guess."

"Well, he's in trouble now," Sharon Tanner stated. "I don't suppose I'm going to make myself very popular in Silverdale, what with Jeff's being a big football hero and all that," she said, making no attempt to mask the sarcasm in her voice. "But even if none of the rest of you will do anything about it, I intend to make as much trouble for Jeff

LaConner as I can.'' She turned to Blake. ''We're going to
press charges against him,'' she said. ''It sounds to me like
Jeff thinks he can do anything he wants as long as he's the
star of the team. Charlotte as much as told me so herself, the
day after he slammed her against a wall.'' She turned back to
Chuck now, her eyes challenging. ''That *is* what happened,
isn't it, Mr. LaConner?''

LaConner hesitated, then nodded.

''Then that's it,'' Sharon said quietly. ''It sounds to me
like Jeff needs to be locked up for a while, and allowed to
think things over.''

''And that's what's going to happen to him, honey,''
Blake reminded her. ''As soon as the cops find him.''

''Will it?'' Sharon asked. ''Or will he just be given a
little slap on the wrist and sent out on the football field to try
to kill someone else?''

Her words silenced everyone in the waiting room. When
Karen Akers appeared a few moments later to tell MacCallum
that the X rays were finished and Mark was back in his room,
no one had yet spoken another word. But as Blake rose to
follow Sharon down the hall to their son's room, Jerry Harris
put a hand on his arm and Blake paused for a moment. His
eyes met Jerry's, and he could almost read his boss's mind.

''I know,'' he said, his voice tired. ''If Mark were in any
kind of shape, this wouldn't have happened. He might not
have been able to beat Jeff, but he at least could have
defended himself.'' He'd been thinking about his conversation with Jerry almost from the moment he'd seen Mark lying
helpless on the lawn an hour ago. Now his mind was all but
made up.

Jeff LaConner crouched behind a large boulder. He had
run blindly at first, racing from the darkness of one backyard
to the next, pausing only briefly to cast a wary glance into the
streets before dashing across to take shelter once again in the
comforting shadows of the darkened houses.

He'd come to the edge of the town, then moved along the riverbank until he reached the footbridge. It was the wailing of the ambulance siren that finally made up his mind, and he'd hurried across the bridge and started up the path into the hills.

He was having no trouble seeing, even though the moon was no more than a quarter full, and he moved easily, fatigue from the fight he only dimly remembered dissipating as he loped along the trail. At last he'd come to the boulder, and with an almost animal instinct, crouched low against it, his back pressed close to the stone. There he'd waited, and watched.

For a long time nothing happened, and then he'd seen a police car moving through the streets, disappearing toward the county hospital a half mile out of town. After a while the patrol car had come back, stopping briefly in a darkened parking lot. Then it began moving again, and a moment later another car joined it.

He was certain he knew where they were going, and was not surprised when they came to a stop on the now nearly deserted block where the fight had occurred.

They were hunting for him.

He shrank closer to the boulder.

Wes Jenkins arrived at the scene of the fight only a few minutes after Dick Kennally. With him in the car were Joe Rankin, and in the screened-off back section of the black and white station wagon, Mitzi, the large police dog whose primary function had turned out to be keeping the night sergeant company during his normally boring shift. Tonight, though, Mitzi seemed to sense that something was happening, and as she leaped from the back of the station wagon, she barked eagerly.

Frank Kramer, Roy's father, was already there, having walked the three blocks from his house after Wes Jenkins had called him.

"Roy says he took off that way," Kramer said as the men gathered around him. He pointed across the street, and Wes Jenkins squatted down to snap a heavy leather lead to the collar around Mitzi's neck.

"Come on," he said. "Let's see what she can find."

As Kramer and Jenkins led the dog across the street, the other two men got into the black and white station wagon. Joe Rankin took the wheel and Dick Kennally switched on the radio, tuning it to the frequency of the portable unit Kramer was carrying with him.

"She's already got a scent," Kramer's voice crackled from a speaker a moment later. "She's heading east."

Joe Rankin put the car into gear, turned it around, and started slowly down the street, keeping abreast of the unseen men who were following the dog through the backyards.

"Turning north," Kramer said a few seconds later. "We're cutting across Pecos Drive."

The pursuit went on, Kramer keeping the men in the car posted as to his position, Rankin doing his best to anticipate their moves. At last the cruiser was parked on the street a few yards from the footbridge, where Frank Kramer and Wes Jenkins were waiting for them. Mitzi, straining at the end of her leash, was struggling to reach the bridge itself.

Kennally and Rankin left the car and joined the two men already at the bridge.

"I don't know," Kramer said doubtfully, gazing up into the darkness on the other side of the bridge. "Why would he go up there? All that could happen to him is that he'd get lost."

"Maybe Mitzi's following a 'coon or something," Jenkins suggested.

But Kennally shook his head. "I don't think so. I think he's up there, and I don't think he's thinking straight. Come on."

Taking the leash from Jenkins, Kennally started across the bridge. The dog, her nose close to the ground, whined eagerly.

Mitzi didn't so much as hesitate at the fork in the path on

the other end of the bridge. Instead, she started up the center trail, and Kennally heard a groan from Frank Kramer.

"Told you you were letting yourself go," he said over his shoulder. "Maybe you'll get lucky tonight and we can do five miles."

As the streetlamps of the village faded away behind them, the men switched on flashlights and started up the trail, soon disappearing into the deep darkness of the woods.

Jeff's eyes flickered as he watched the flashlights approach. He could barely make out the shapes of the men hunting him, but he had seen the dog clearly when one of the lights briefly flashed across its lithe form.

He stayed by the rock for a moment, trying to decide what to do. But his mind was fuzzy and he couldn't think clearly. Finally, following his instincts, he started uphill once again. Almost immediately the path grew sharply steeper, and within a few minutes his breath began to come in gasping pants. Still, he forced himself onward.

A few minutes later he missed his step and felt a sharp pain as he twisted his ankle. Stifling the yelp that rose in his throat, he lowered himself to the ground and rubbed at the injured joint. He rested there a moment, then heaved himself back up, resting all his weight on his good leg.

Gingerly, he tried to take a step forward.

He couldn't walk.

"He'd better be up here," Frank Kramer groused fifteen minutes later. They had come out into a clearing on a bluff above town, and Mitzi was sniffing eagerly at the base of a large boulder. Kramer wiped the sheen of sweat from his brow and tried to catch his breath, silently promising himself that after tonight he'd get serious about the diet and exercise he'd been putting off for longer than he cared to admit.

The other three men, he noticed, didn't even seem to be breathing heavily.

"He's up here," Kennally replied, maliciously shining the light on Kramer's face. "Look how Mitzi's acting. Wouldn't surprise me if Jeff sat here for a while, watching us hunt for him."

"How can I look with that damned light in my eyes?" Kramer muttered. Then: "How long do we keep looking? He could be anywhere up here."

Kennally tilted his head in a gesture of indifference. "Anywhere he could be, Mitzi can find him."

The dog had abandoned the boulder now and was once again pulling at the lead as she tried to scramble up the steep trail. The four men followed her for another ten minutes, until she stopped abruptly, her whole body rigid as she stared into the darkness ahead.

Kennally played his light over the trail, and then all four men saw what they were looking for.

He was crouched down by another large boulder, and in the glare of the flashlight his eyes seemed to glint unnaturally. As he gazed silently at the boy, a strange thought flitted into Dick Kennally's mind.

A cornered animal. He looks just like a cornered animal.

"It's okay, Jeff," he said out loud. "We're not going to hurt you. We're just going to take you back to town."

Jeff LaConner said nothing, but in the glow of the flashlight, they could see him press closer to the shelter of the boulder.

Kennally hesitated a moment, then spoke again, his voice low. "Okay, you guys. Let's spread out and move in slowly. I don't want anyone getting hurt."

Joe Rankin glanced at him curiously. "Hurt? Christ, Dick, he's not Charlie Manson. He's just a kid."

But Kennally shook his head, Martin Ames's words fresh in his mind. "Just do what I tell you, all right?"

Kramer and Rankin moved off to the left and Wes Jenkins

slipped into the woods to the right as Kennally moved slowly up the trail, keeping his flashlight trained on Jeff LaConner. The boy's eyes never blinked, but his head began to move in a strange weaving pattern that reminded Kennally of a snake preparing to strike. Out of the corner of his eye he kept track of the men's progress, and when they had fanned out, cutting off any possible avenue of escape for the boy, he signaled them to move forward.

He began talking to Jeff, speaking in the soothing tones he'd use on a frightened animal.

As Frank Kramer drew close, Jeff suddenly struck out with his right fist, clipping Kramer on the shoulder, sending him reeling back. "Shit!" he heard Kramer exclaim. "What the hell's wrong with you?"

But Jeff didn't hear, his eyes now fixed warily on Wes Jenkins.

Then, as Joe Rankin approached from the opposite side, Kennally saw their opportunity. "Now!" he snapped. Dropping the light in his hand, he leaped forward.

Jeff, ignoring the injury to his ankle, scrambled to his feet and pressed closer to the boulder. His fists began to lash out as the three men closed on him.

It finally took all four of them to subdue the furiously fighting teenager, and in the end they had to carry him back down the hillside, his hands cuffed together behind his back, his ankles manacled with a second set of handcuffs. Even as they carried him across the footbridge and worked him into the back of the station wagon, he was still thrashing in their arms, twisting wildly as he tried to escape their grasp.

From his throat emerged a series of feral howls, like the anguished cries of a coyote whose foot has been clamped in a trap.

12

"What the hell's wrong with him?" Frank Kramer asked. He glanced nervously over his shoulder. In the rear compartment of the station wagon Jeff LaConner was still struggling against the handcuffs that manacled his hands and feet. His right ankle was swelling rapidly, and though the metal band dug deeply into his flesh, he was apparently oblivious to the pain of his injury. He was curled up tightly in the confining space behind the heavy wire mesh, but as Kramer watched, the boy suddenly wrenched himself around and his feet lashed out at the barrier itself. The mesh bulged slightly, but held firm. In Jeff's throat a strange, keening wail was building.

"Some kind of mental breakdown," Dick Kennally replied tersely. They were through the town itself now, and the road narrowed as they headed east toward Rocky Mountain High, where a few lights glowed dimly in the darkness. He grimaced as he heard Jeff's feet crash once more into the mesh of the barrier. Then Mitzi, sitting up on the seat between Kramer and Joe Rankin, began barking. "Can't you shut that dog up?" Kennally asked.

"It's better than listening to the racket the boy's making,'' Rankin replied sourly. Then, catching Kennally's glare in the rearview mirror, he laid a hand on the dog's bristling hackles. "Easy, Mitzi," he murmured. "Nothing to worry about.''

Mitzi's barking subsided to a low growl, but as the station wagon gained speed and they left the town behind, Rankin could still feel the tension in the dog's muscles.

Kennally slowed the car and made the turn into the narrow driveway that led to the sports center. He sounded the horn, but even as its blare momentarily drowned out Jeff's anguished wails, the gates were beginning to swing open. Kennally waited impatiently, then gunned the station wagon through the gap even before the gates had opened fully. As he sped through, an attendant signaled him to go around to the back of the building.

He braked to a stop in front of an open door. The harsh brilliance of halogen floodlights cut through the darkness, and Kennally had to shield his eyes as he stepped out of the car. The others were on the driveway now, too, but Mitzi had remained where she was, her watchful eyes on Jeff LaConner.

The white glare of the lights shone brightly through the car's windows, and the sudden illumination seemed somehow to have affected the boy, for suddenly he was lying still, his eyes clamped shut, his neck twisted at an unnatural angle—as if he were trying to escape the light.

Martin Ames, wearing a white lab coat unbuttoned down the front, only partially covering his flannel shirt, stepped out of the door and peered into the station wagon. His lips tightened into a grim line, then he glanced at Kennally. "How bad was it, Dick?''

Kennally shrugged, as if to belittle the struggle that had taken place on the hillside half an hour earlier. "Well, let's just say he wasn't too interested in coming with us," he finally answered. He gestured to the other three men. "Let's get him inside.''

Joe Rankin carefully raised the station wagon's rear door.

Almost instantly Jeff twisted himself around and his legs lashed out. Rankin dodged away from the boy's flailing kicks, and with Wes Jenkins's help, pinioned his legs to the floor of the car. A moment later Kennally and Kramer had grasped Jeff's arms. With the boy still struggling to free himself, they carried him inside the building.

"In there," Marty Ames instructed, nodding to an open door a few yards down the hall. The four policemen carried Jeff into a small room, its white walls shadowlessly illuminated by overhead fluorescent tubes. In the center of the room stood a large table with heavy mesh straps laid neatly across each of its ends. As two attendants moved the straps aside, the officers placed Jeff LaConner on the table. The attendants, working quickly, bound Jeff's legs tightly to the table, immobilizing them. Only then did Kennally remove the leg manacles.

The bruise on Jeff's sprained right ankle, swollen large now, had turned an ugly purple, and there was a deep mark where the metal of the cuff had cut into his damaged flesh.

"Okay," Ames said. "Let's get the cuffs off his wrists."

As soon as his arms were free, Jeff sat bolt upright and began flailing out at the men around him, his eyes glowering angrily in the bright light. Kennally and Jenkins moved in behind him, each of them grasping one of his shoulders, and managed to force him down, holding him still while his arms, like his legs, were secured to the table with the heavy straps.

Only when they were certain Jeff was immobile did the two men step back. Their foreheads were beaded with sweat, and Jenkins's arms were trembling with the strain of fighting against Jeff's strength.

"All right," Ames said. "I think we can take it from here." He moved to a small cabinet against the wall opposite the door and picked up one of several hypodermic needles laid out on its white enamel surface. One of the orderlies cut the sleeve of Jeff's shirt away from his arm, and Ames slid the needle expertly into a vein.

The drug seemed to have no effect whatever on the boy, whose eyes, wild and glazed, darted about the room as if still seeking a means of escape.

It wasn't until Ames had administered the third shot that Jeff's struggles finally began to abate. As the group around him watched, the strength seemed to drain out of him. Finally, his head dropped back onto the hard metal of the table and his eyes closed.

"Jesus," Frank Kramer finally said in the sudden silence that hung in the room. "I never saw anything like that before. And I hope I never do again."

Marty Ames met Kramer's gaze. "I hope you don't either," he quietly agreed.

Fifteen minutes later, after Dick Kennally and his men had left the sports clinic, Marty Ames went back to the examining room. The two orderlies were still in the small cubicle, one of them cutting away the last of Jeff's clothing as the other finished setting up a complicated array of electronic monitoring devices. As Ames watched silently, they began attaching sensors to Jeff's body. Only when they were done and Ames was satisfied that the equipment was functioning properly and that Jeff was in no immediate danger, did Ames finally start toward his office, preparing himself for the call he now had to make to Chuck LaConner.

He considered these calls the worst part of his job. But they were also part of the deal he'd made with himself five years before, when Ted Thornton had approached him about heading up the sports center Thornton had envisioned for Silverdale.

Thornton had seduced him, of course, as Thornton managed to seduce so many men, but in the moments when Ames was being completely honest with himself—moments that were becoming more rare as he approached the success that was now almost within his grasp—he had to admit that he'd been willing to be seduced. Thornton had promised him the world, almost literally. First, a lab beyond his wildest dreams, far beyond anything the Institute for the Human Brain in Palo Alto would ever be able to provide. Anything he needed, anything he wanted, would be provided.

Unlimited funds for research, and nearly total autonomy.

If he were successful, a Nobel prize was not out of the question, and certainly he would be able to write his own ticket, both professionally and financially.

Best of all, the project was a direct extension of his work at the Institute, where he had been working with human growth hormones in an effort to correct the imperfections of the human body.

It was Ames's theory that there was no reason why every human being should not possess an ideal body, no reason why some people should be undersized, or overweight, or prone to any of the myriad physical defects and weaknesses that plagued mankind.

Ted Thornton had recognized the commercial value of Martin Ames's studies and hired him away from the Institute, sending him to Silverdale. Immediately, the town itself had become his own private laboratory.

He'd limited his most advanced experiments to the children of TarrenTech's own personnel. Thornton had decreed that early on, explaining that it was merely a matter of damage control: they both understood that things would go wrong; some of the experiments would fail. But when such things happened, Thornton wanted to be in a position to deal with the fallout immediately and effectively.

So far it had worked just as Thornton had planned. Most of the experiments had gone well. But when things had gone awry, when some of his subjects had developed serious side effects from his treatments—extreme aggression being the most common—Thornton had kept his promise. The boys were quickly and quietly taken care of in whatever manner Ames deemed appropriate, and their families were immediately transferred out of the area, with large enough promotions and raises so generous that so far no one had so much as whispered that the financial remuneration was nothing more than a payoff for the loss of a son.

His failures had been so few—only three in nearly five years—that Ames considered his program at Rocky Mountain High a complete success. Most of the boys had responded well to his treatments, and for some of them—Robb Harris, for instance—growth hormones had not been indicated at all. Which was perfect, for it meant that Jerry Harris was able to explain exactly what had been done to his son with complete honesty.

For Jeff LaConner the treatment had been the norm— massive infusions of growth hormones—and until just two weeks ago it appeared Jeff was going to be a success. But now things had gone sour, for the first time since Randy Stevens—and Marty Ames had to make the onerous phone call. Quietly, he'd explain to Chuck LaConner that Jeff would have to spend a certain amount of time in an "institutional environment."

That was the phrase Ames had come to prefer. It allowed the boys' parents a vague hope that perhaps someday their children would be well again.

And perhaps, if Ames were lucky, it could be true for some of the boys. Perhaps he would find a way to reverse the uncontrolled growth and unbridled fury to which they fell victim.

Indeed, during the past few months he'd even begun to hope that there might be no more Randy Stevenses, no more necessity for calls such as he was about to make. He was so close—so very close.

Perhaps tonight's call would, after all, be the last.

But of course, with experimental science, you never really knew.

Sharon sat quietly on a straight-backed chair next to the bed in which Mark lay sleeping. He looked younger than his sixteen years, and the bruises on his cheek, the bandage over his right eye, and the swelling on his jaw only made him look more vulnerable. Sharon was no longer certain how long she'd been sitting with him, how much time had passed since he'd finally drifted into a sedated sleep. His breathing, the loudest noise she could hear, sounded labored, and although she knew he felt nothing, she imagined she could feel the pain that each of his shallow gasps must be inflicting on his bruised chest.

Behind her there was a soft click, and she sensed rather than saw the door opening. A moment later she felt Blake's hands resting gently on her shoulders; automatically her own hands went up to cover his. For a moment neither of them spoke, then Blake's hands slipped away. "Don't you think we ought to go home?" he asked, moving around to the other side of the bed so she could see him.

Sharon shook her head. "I can't. If he wakes up, I want to be here."

"He's not going to wake up tonight," Blake replied. "I talked to the nurse just now, and she says he'll sleep through till morning."

Sharon sighed heavily. Her eyes left her son and she looked up at her husband. "It doesn't make any difference. I just want to be here for him, that's all."

Blake hesitated, then nodded. "I know," he said. "Tell you what. You stay here, and I'll go on over to the Harrises and pick up Kelly." He was silent for a moment, then added: "Walk me to the door?"

For a moment he thought Sharon was going to refuse, but then she stood up, reached down and touched Mark's cheek gently, and nodded. Neither of them spoke again until they had reached the nurses' station. The waiting room beyond was now deserted.

"How's he doing?" Karen Akers asked, looking up from the computer terminal that glowed on the desk in front of her.

Sharon managed a wan smile. "Still asleep."

"You really should go home, Mrs. Tanner," Karen urged.
"There isn't much you can do for him right now." Even as
she spoke the words, Karen knew they would have no effect.
After all, if it were her own son sleeping in the room down
the hall, would she leave? Not a chance. "Tell you what,"
she said, not waiting for Sharon's reply. "I'll put on a fresh
pot of coffee and bring you a cup when it's ready." Then she
disappeared down the corridor to the small kitchen at the back
of the building.

Sharon and Blake stood in silence at the door, then Blake
drew her close, kissing her softly. "It's going to be all
right," he assured her. "In a few days you'll hardly know
anything happened to him."

Sharon nodded automatically, though she didn't agree.
She knew that the sight of Mark lying on the stretcher, his
face bruised and bloodied, would never leave her. As Blake
was about to leave, a thought that had been lurking in the
back of her mind almost since the moment she'd left the
waiting room to take up her vigil at Mark's bedside suddenly
emerged.

"Blake . . ." she said. "Do . . . do you know exactly
what happened to the Ramirez boy?"

Blake hesitated, then nodded. "I saw the tape," he said,
and braced himself for the question he knew was coming
next, the question he'd been trying to answer for himself
since he had first heard of the fight between Jeff and
Mark.

"Well?" Sharon asked. "*Was* it an accident? Or did Jeff
deliberately hurt the Ramirez boy?"

Blake didn't answer for a moment, letting his mind rerun
the cassette Jerry Harris had played for him the day after he'd
begun working on the Ramirez case. "I don't know," he said
at last. "It could have been. But there's the possibility it
wasn't."

Sharon said nothing, but even before she kissed him once

again and sent him on his way, Blake could see the shadow come into her eyes. Invariably that look meant that she had zeroed in on something and would now begin to examine it, worrying at it until she'd solved whatever her problem might be to her own particular satisfaction.

When he was gone, Sharon leaned against the heavy glass of the front door for a while. Then, her mind made up, she started back down the hall. But instead of returning to Mark's room, she let herself into the room across the way.

The room where Ricardo Ramirez lay, his body still held rigid in the grotesque mechanism of the Stryker frame, was nearly identical to her son's, and the similarities sent a chill through Sharon's body.

That's what could have happened to Mark tonight, she thought. She scanned the monitors over the bed, their green displays glowing eerily in the darkened room, the endlessly repeating patterns of Ricardo Ramirez's artificially sustained life forces crossing the screens with an almost hypnotic rhythm. Once again Sharon lost track of time as she stood silently watching.

What was happening inside the boy's mind? she wondered. Was he aware of anything? Was he dreaming, suffering from nightmares from which he could never escape? Or was he simply lost somewhere in a gray void, suspended from all reality, unaware of anything? She didn't know—couldn't know.

Perhaps no one could ever know.

"Mrs. Tanner?" Karen Akers's soft voice penetrated Sharon's reverie, startling her. "Are you all right?"

Sharon nodded. Turning away from Ricardo Ramirez, she stepped into the corridor, blinking against its brightness. "I—I just wanted to see him," she said, her voice quavering. "It's so horrible."

"And it could have been your son," Karen said, voicing the thought that had been so powerful in Sharon's mind a few moments before. "But Rick's not your son, Mrs. Tanner. And Mark's going to be just fine."

Sharon nodded, then forced a tiny smile as she gratefully took the mug of steaming coffee from the nurse's hands. "Of course he is," she said. She went back to Mark's room and once more took up her vigil next to his bed. But as the minutes slowly crept by, she found herself still thinking about Ricardo Ramirez.

She knew what TarrenTech was doing for the boy, and until tonight had never thought to question the company's generosity and sincerity. Now she found herself wondering.

Her mind went back over the football games she'd watched over the past weekends, and she had an image of the Silverdale team trotting out onto the field like a troop of gladiators.

They were big boys—all of them—and now she recalled noticing, as each game began, how unevenly matched the opposing sides appeared to be. The Silverdale boys, towering over their opponents, easily overwhelmed them by the sheer force of their size alone.

And they played rough, too. No matter how far ahead the Wolverines might be on the scoreboard, they never eased up, never stopped pressing their opposition, never waited out the clock at the end of the game.

She shivered in the darkness of the hospital room as she thought about it.

Big, strong, healthy boys.

And, apparently, dangerous boys as well.

For if TarrenTech truly believed that what had happened to Ricardo Ramirez was an accident, why were they so willing to pay any price in order to avoid a lawsuit against the school, or possibly even against the LaConners themselves?

Was it because a lawsuit, in the end, would turn on TarrenTech itself?

Suddenly Sharon Tanner was more frightened than she had ever been in her life.

*   *   *

Chuck LaConner tried not to let his expression reveal his emotions as he listened to Marty Ames talking to him on the telephone. In the chair facing him from the opposite side of the fireplace, Charlotte was sitting straight up, her face ashen even in the orange glow of the fire burning on the hearth. When he at last hung up, she immediately spoke.

"What is it?" she demanded. "That was about Jeff, wasn't it? Is he in jail?"

At Ames's suggestion, Chuck had been careful not to reveal to whom he was speaking, and now he shook his head, at the same time rising to his feet. "He's not in jail," he told her. "He's had some kind of breakdown. Apparently he lost his temper completely this time, and they've taken him to the doctor." He moved out to the hall closet, with Charlotte following right behind.

"I'm going with you," she said. But to her unbelieving dismay, Chuck shook his head.

"Not now," he said. "They specifically asked me to come out alone. I guess—" he began, then stopped, unwilling to repeat to Charlotte what Ames had told him. "I guess it's pretty bad," he said at last. "They . . . well, they said Jeff might have to be in the hospital for a while."

Charlotte sagged against the wall. "And I can't even see him?" she whispered hoarsely. "But he's my son!"

"It's just for tonight," Chuck promised her. "They just want to get him calmed down a little, that's all." He reached out and touched Charlotte's chin, not ungently, tipping her head up so she couldn't avoid looking into his face.

"It's going to be all right, sweetheart," he promised her. "We're going to get this thing straightened out. But you've just got to trust me. Okay?"

Her mind too numb to think clearly, Charlotte automatically nodded. It wasn't until she heard Chuck's car starting up a minute later that she slowly began to come back to life.

She and Chuck had been sitting by the fireplace for hours, ever since Dick Kennally had called, asking if Jeff were at

home. Chuck had left for a while, then come back to assure
her that Mark Tanner was all right, that his injuries weren't
serious. She'd wanted to leave then, to go to the hospital
herself, if only to apologize to Sharon Tanner for what had
happened, but Chuck had refused to allow it. He'd gone to
the hospital alone, while she waited anxiously, worrying
about her son and the boy he had injured.

But she couldn't wait any longer. Now it wasn't just
Mark Tanner who was in the hospital; it was Jeff, too.
Only five minutes after Chuck left, she hurried out into the
night.

She pulled into the parking lot of County Hospital ten
minutes later, not even pausing to glance around for her
husband's car before hurrying through the doors into the
waiting room. From behind the glass partition Karen Akers
looked up curiously, then, recognizing Charlotte, stood up
and came out of the little office.

"Why can't I see him?" Charlotte asked without pream-
ble, her voice trembling. "What's wrong with him that they
won't let me see him?"

Karen stared at Charlotte in bewilderment. What on earth
could the woman be talking about? "Wh-Who?"

"Jeff," Charlotte said. "Chuck said they took him to the
doctor . . ." Her voice trailed off as she realized that the
waiting room was empty and the building itself was totally
silent. "Isn't my husband here?" she asked, but knew the
answer even before Karen Akers spoke.

"There's no one here, Charlotte, except Mrs. Tanner.
She's sitting with Mark."

Tiredly, her mind reeling helplessly, Charlotte sank down
into one of the Naugahyde-covered chairs that lined a wall of
the waiting room. She was silent for a moment, gathering her
wits about her. "But he said—" she began, her voice taking
on a note of desperation. And then she knew. They hadn't
brought Jeff here at all—they'd taken him out to the sports
center, to Dr. Ames, just like the last time, when Jeff

had slammed her against the wall then stormed out into the night.

Somehow, the knowledge made her feel better. After all, Jeff had come home the very next day—not even come home, actually, but gone straight to school. And he'd been fine. Maybe Chuck was right.

She looked up at Karen Akers, feeling foolish. "I don't know what's wrong with me," she said, then saw the look of concern in the nurse's eyes, as if Karen thought she were losing her grip. Charlotte forced a lame smile. "I mean, I'm sure Chuck must have told me where they were taking Jeff. It—Well, I guess it hasn't been an easy night for any of us."

Karen Akers's expression cleared a little.

"How is he?" Charlotte asked then. "Mark Tanner, I mean?"

Karen hesitated, uncertain what to say. But as she saw the genuine worry in Charlotte's eyes, she nodded toward the corridor. "He's sleeping now. But if you want to peek in, I don't suppose Mrs. Tanner would mind."

Charlotte got to her feet and started down the hall, pausing next to the door to Ricardo Ramirez's room. Taking a deep breath, she crossed the hall and gently opened the door to Mark's room. It was almost dark inside; only a single, small night-light cast a soft glow from the corner next to the bathroom door. Mark lay motionless on the bed, and on the chair next to the bed, Sharon Tanner was nodding fitfully. Charlotte hesitated, and was about to back out of the room when Sharon's head came up and her eyes opened.

"H-Hello?" she asked tentatively.

"It's me," Charlotte whispered. "Charlotte LaConner."

Charlotte could see Sharon stiffen, and suddenly she wished she hadn't come into the room. But then Sharon stood up and came toward her. "I just wanted to see how he was," Charlotte said. "And to tell you how sorry I am. . . ."

Charlotte's words trailed off, and to Sharon's surprise, she found herself feeling a pang of sympathy for the woman. She eased Charlotte out into the hallway, then pulled the door closed. "He's going to be all right," she said. Keeping her voice as neutral as possible, she asked, "Have they found Jeff yet?"

Charlotte swallowed the lump in her throat and nodded. "They took him out to Dr. Ames," she said. "He . . . I don't know what happened to him, Mrs. Tanner."

"Sharon," the other woman replied.

"Sharon," Charlotte repeated, pronouncing the name carefully, almost experimentally. "He—Well, I guess it was like the night he hit me," she said. "It's his temper. He just can't seem to control it anymore. Something sets him off, and he just blows up." She frowned, as if a distant memory were coming back to her. "Like Randy Stevens," she went on, speaking slowly now. "That's what he's like. Like Randy, before they took him away . . ."

Sharon stared at Charlotte. Randy Stevens? Who was he? She'd never heard the name before in her life.

Chuck LaConner stared dully at Dr. Martin Ames. They'd been sitting in Ames's office at the sports center for thirty minutes, while Ames had gone through the speech he'd rehearsed so many times, a speech carefully designed to accomplish both his own aims and those of Ted Thornton.

"Of course, I won't be able to release him," Ames had concluded, spreading his hands helplessly on the desktop. "We'll do the best we can to correct the chemical imbalance in his brain, but I'm not at all certain that anything will be effective."

It had taken a while for it to sink in, but now Chuck straightened in his chair. "But you said nothing could go wrong," he protested. "When I agreed to put Jeff into the program, you promised me—"

"I didn't promise you," Ames interjected. "I told you we were ninety-nine percent certain we had the compound perfected, but that there was always the chance there might be some side effects. And you understood that there were still some"—he hesitated, casting around for the right words— "some, shall we say, experimental aspects to the treatment."

Chuck rested his head in his hands. It was true, of course. He could remember the day three years ago when he'd first talked to Ames, and Ames had told him there was a good chance that Jeff could overcome the congenital deficiency that had plagued him almost from birth. It wasn't that Jeff was small—his size was perfectly normal, and always had been. But there was a brittleness to his bones that came close to turning him into an invalid, and almost from the day he'd learned to walk—and broke a leg in his very first tumble—he had been wearing a cast on one or another part of his body practically every day of his life. None of the doctors the LaConners had taken him to held out any hope at all. So when Jerry Harris had told him about Ames's program—a new process of combining vitamins with a hormone that could stimulate calcium production, Chuck had instantly agreed to try it. The worst that could happen would be that it would fail.

But it hadn't failed. Within a month Jeff's bones had almost miraculously begun strengthening. He'd shot up that summer when he was fourteen, and even during the awkward period while he was adjusting to his full stature, he'd broken no bones. Indeed, his skeleton—always looking so frail in the X rays Chuck had been shown from the very beginning—had taken on a solid look, the long bones thickening visibly, giving Jeff added weight and a degree of toughness he'd never before possessed. His shoulders, always so narrow when he was a little boy, had broadened, and along with the vitamin/hormone program, Ames had put him on an exercise regimen.

Until a few weeks ago there had been no reason to suspect that the treatment was anything but totally successful. But now . . .

Chuck rose to his feet, struggling to control his emotions. "Can I see him?" he asked.

Ames hesitated for a moment, then he, too, stood up. "Of course," he said. "But I want you to prepare yourself. He's under sedation right now and probably won't be conscious. Even if he is, he might not recognize you."

As they moved through the maze of corridors that made up the sports center, Chuck tried to prepare himself. But when at last they entered the clinic and Marty Ames opened the door to the room in which Jeff was still lying strapped to the metal table, Chuck felt a wave of nausea rise up in him.

His son was naked, his arms and legs still strapped tightly to the table. Every part of his body seemed to have sprouted wires, and there were I.V. tubes in both his forearms. But it wasn't the mass of equipment, nor even the straps securing him to the table, that staggered Chuck LaConner.

It was Jeff himself.

He'd changed in the past hours, changed so much that Chuck hardly recognized him.

His hands appeared to have grown.

His fingers were longer, and his knuckles stood out like twisted knots of wood. Even in sleep Jeff's hands were working spasmodically, as if trying to free themselves from the bonds that held them.

His face, too, had changed. His eyes had sunk deeper into their sockets and his brow jutted out sharply, giving him a faintly simian look. His jaw, always strong, seemed to be too big for his face, and now it hung slack, exposing his teeth and tongue.

His breathing was coming in strange rasps.

"My God," Chuck breathed. "What's happening to him?"

"His bones are growing again," Ames said. "Only this time it seems to be out of control. It's starting with his extremities—his fingers and toes, and his jaw. If we can't get it under control, it will spread to the rest of his body."

Chuck LaConner stared at the doctor, fear naked in his eyes. "And then what will happen to him?" he asked.

Ames fell silent for a moment, then decided there was no point in keeping the truth from Jeff's father. When he spoke, his voice was clinically cool.

"And then he'll die."

A silence fell in the room, disturbed only by the dank rasping of Jeff's labored breath. As Chuck stared hopelessly down at his son's distorted face, Jeff's eyes suddenly opened.

They were wild eyes, the eyes of an animal.

And they glinted with a rage Chuck LaConner had never seen before. His face ashen, his whole body suddenly seized by an icy chill, Chuck LaConner shrank away from his own son.

13

Mark Tanner's eyes flickered, then came open. For a moment he wasn't certain where he was. Sunlight was pouring in a window, and he instinctively raised his right hand to shield his eyes from the glare.

A spasm of pain wracked his body, and he dropped his hand back to the bed, closing his eyes once more. Slowly, his mind began to clear, and in bits and pieces the events of the previous night came back to him.

He was in the hospital. He remembered it now—remembered the fight with Jeff that really hadn't been a fight at all. Remembered the ride in the ambulance with his mother crouched on the floor next to him, acting like he was going to die or something.

Remembered the doctor—what was his name? Mac . . . MacSomething, working on his face. He winced at the memory of the sharp pain when the needle pierced his skin. Then they'd X-rayed him, and finally, mercifully, he'd been put to bed and allowed to go to sleep.

His eyes still closed against the brilliance of the sun, he began experimentally moving his limbs. It wasn't too bad, really. His chest hurt whenever he moved his arms, but not too badly, and if he was careful not to take really deep breaths, he could hardly feel his cracked ribs at all.

His jaw was sore, and he touched it gingerly, then moved it. That, too, wasn't so bad. Just sort of like a toothache. Finally, steeling himself against the pain in his ribcage, he raised his hand once more and brushed his fingers over the bandage on his forehead. Then, at last, he opened his eyes again.

Or, anyway, he opened his left eye. His right eye would hardly open at all, and when he saw nothing but a red haze through it, he let it close again. Finally he turned his head and looked around.

His mother, her head nodding on her chest, was slumped in a chair next to his bed, but even in her sleep she seemed to feel his eyes on her. Abruptly, she came awake and quickly straightened up.

"You're awake," she declared in a surprised voice that made Mark wonder if she hadn't expected him ever to wake up at all.

"I guess I am," he admitted. "You been here all night?"

She nodded. "I didn't want you to wake up and be frightened."

Mark groaned inwardly. Did she think he was still a baby? He tried to raise himself up, but fell back as a sharp pain shot through his chest.

"Try this," Sharon said, handing him the controls for the bed.

Mark experimented for a moment, then the head of the bed rose slowly until he was half sitting up. The pain in his chest eased and he managed a weak grin. "I guess I didn't come off very well last night, did I?"

"Don't you worry about that," she told him. "And if Jeff LaConner thinks he's going to get away with this—" She broke off her sentence as the door opened. Mac MacCallum strode in, picked up the chart suspended from the end of Mark's bed, scanned it quickly, then shifted his attention to the boy himself.

"How are you doing this morning?" he asked as he picked up Mark's wrist and took his pulse. "Sleep okay?"

"Never woke up at all," Mark replied. "How long do I have to stay here?"

MacCallum's brows arched. "Already got a taste of the food here, did you?" he inquired dryly. When Mark only looked faintly confused, his tone turned more serious. "I'd say until tomorrow, just offhand. It doesn't look like anything's seriously the matter with you, but it won't hurt to keep you around for a day, just so I can keep an eye on you." He nodded toward the television suspended from the wall opposite Mark's bed. "How's a day off from school with TV thrown in for nothing extra sound?"

Mark shrugged. "Okay, I guess. What happened to me? I mean, what's wrong with me?"

Briefly, MacCallum summarized the list of injuries. "From what I understand," he finished, "you got off lucky. Jeff LaConner's a big fellow, but he seems to have messed up your looks more than your innards." He turned to face Sharon. "I've already gone over his X rays and other tests, and unless something shows up today, there's no reason why he shouldn't go home tomorrow. Maybe even this evening."

"What sort of something could show up today?" Sharon immediately asked.

"Nothing terribly serious," MacCallum assured her. "But if there happens to be kidney damage—which I don't think there is—blood could show up in his urine. Frankly, I'm not expecting anything. And if I were you," he added, "I'd be thinking about going home and getting some sleep myself. Mark's going to be dozing on and off until noon, and there's no use your sitting here any longer."

"I want to be here," Sharon insisted.

"Go *home*, Mom," Mark said. "All I'm gonna do is lie here."

Sharon was about to protest, then realized that MacCallum was right. She could feel her exhaustion in almost every fiber of her body, and her back was stiff from sitting up in the hard chair all night. She stood up. "Okay," she agreed. "But if you need anything, or want anything, call me. All right?"

"Sure," Mark replied, then flushed as she bent over to kiss his cheek.

As she followed MacCallum out of the room, she heard the television go on. Smiling ruefully to herself, she walked with Dr. MacCallum into the waiting room, thanked him once more for all he'd done for Mark, and called Elaine Harris to come and pick her up. Then, while waiting for Elaine, she recalled her conversation with Charlotte LaConner. Her brow creasing into a deep frown, she hurried after MacCallum, catching up with him just as he was going into his office.

"Dr. MacCallum," she said, "did you ever have a patient named Randy Stevens?"

MacCallum glanced at her sharply. "Randy Stevens? What did you hear about him?"

Quickly, she told him about Charlotte LaConner's visit to the hospital the night before. "The way she was talking," Sharon said, "it sounded like something was wrong with Randy."

MacCallum nodded. "I remember him, of course. He was the biggest star the football team had a year or so ago. Almost another Jeff LaConner. And I guess he could be just as mean, too. But then the Stevenses moved away. I think his father got transferred to New York or something."

Sharon hesitated, puzzled. "But you never treated him?"

MacCallum's lips tightened. "No one ever asked me to." He seemed about to say something more, but the intercom buzzed loudly and a disembodied voice demanded MacCallum's response to a phone call. Feeling vaguely dissatisfied by what the doctor had told her, and somewhat distracted by the interruption, she thanked him for his time, then hurried out of the hospital. She didn't notice the twin station wagons with ROCKY MOUNTAIN HIGH emblazoned on their sides pull into the hospital driveway as she got into Elaine's car.

Dr. Martin Ames, his eyes rimmed with red, emerged

from the first of the two wagons. Waving to the occupants of the other car to stay where they were, he strode into the waiting room of County Hospital. He paused near the receptionist's window, inclining his head toward the hall that led to MacCallum's office. "He in?" The nurse glanced up from her work, recognized him, and nodded.

A moment later Ames tapped at MacCallum's door, then let himself in as the other doctor called a cheerful, "Come on in."

MacCallum's expression registered a degree of surprise as he recognized Ames, but with a smile he gestured him into the chair opposite his desk. "What brings you out so early?"

Ames reached into his pocket and pulled out an envelope, which he lay on MacCallum's desk. "Mark Tanner," he said. "I understand he's fit to be moved?"

MacCallum frowned as he picked up the envelope. "Sure he is," he replied. "But I'm afraid I don't understand . . ." He pulled a single sheet of paper from the envelope, and his frown deepened as he read an order, signed by Blake Tanner, transferring Mark from County Hospital to the small clinic housed within the sports center. "What's this all about?" MacCallum asked, his gaze shifting from the paper to Ames. "Jeez, Marty, I was going to release the boy tomorrow."

Ames shrugged, his features twisting into a sympathetic grimace. "Search me, Mac. All I know is, I got a call from Jerry Harris out at TarrenTech late last night, asking me if I'd mind taking the case. And you know me—when Jerry Harris calls, I answer. So this morning, one of their guys showed up with that. And here I am."

"But there's no point to it," MacCallum protested. "There isn't anything seriously wrong with the boy. A few bruises and a couple of cracked ribs."

"Try telling that to a worried father," Ames replied. "Anyway, there's the order. Unless he's not fit for a ten-minute ride, it isn't up to either one of us."

"Unless you refused the case," MacCallum pointed out dryly, but knew even as he said it that he was wasting his breath. Even if Ames wanted to—which MacCallum suspected he didn't—Martin Ames would be a fool to jeopardize the generous underwriting of Rocky Mountain High that TarrenTech provided each year by refusing to do a favor for Jerry Harris.

And Martin Ames was no fool.

"We'll get things started," MacCallum said. Sighing, he picked up the phone.

Robb Harris approached Phil Collins's office with trepidation. He'd been worried ever since his English teacher had handed him the note halfway through the hour, instructing him to report to the coach during the break before second period. He was almost certain he knew what it was about—Collins was going to want an explanation of his part in the fight last night. But when he entered the office, Collins only told him to take a seat, something he never did if he was going to chew you out. His nervousness giving way to curiosity, Robb dropped his book bag onto the floor and sat down.

"How do you feel about taking over as quarterback?" Collins asked.

Robb stared at him. What was he talking about? Nobody could replace Jeff LaConner. And himself? He wasn't even on the offensive team. All he'd ever played was defense.

"LaConner's out," Collins told him. "At least for now, and maybe for the rest of the season." He chewed at his lower lip for a moment, as if trying to decide how much to tell Robb. But in fact he'd made up his mind an hour ago— the best way to spread the word was by telling one of the kids. "I guess you know what happened last night. Anyway, Jeff's in pretty bad shape. I hear he may wind up in a hospital for quite a while." He didn't have to specify what kind of hospital he was talking about; his tone of voice made it clear.

"Wh-What happened to him?" Robb asked. "Did he just crack up?"

Collins shrugged. "How would I know? I'm a coach, not a shrink. Anyway, I've been going over the line-up, and your name came to the top of the list. Not that I think you're ready," he added deliberately as Robb flushed with pleasure, "but I can't move anybody else from the positions they're already playing. And your passing's not bad, all things considered." He leaned back in his chair and clasped his hands behind his head, sizing Robb up. "How about last night?" he asked finally. "I heard you were involved, too."

Robb's shoulders moved dismissively. "Jeff took a swing at me, but it wasn't too bad."

"Well, why don't we let the computers be the judge of that," he said.

Five minutes later, stripped down to his gym shorts, Robb met Collins in the tiny exercise room off the boys' gymnasium. Despite its small size, it was packed with a large variety of workout equipment, all of it attached by a series of cables to a small computer on a desk in one corner. Robb began a familiar routine of exercises, ones he'd performed hundreds of times before, quickly moving from one machine to the next. Here, his progress was monitored by the movement of the machines themselves, rather than of his own body. Though he knew the measurements taken were nowhere near as exact as the ones the machinery at Rocky Mountain High were capable of, it was still always interesting to see the results which came out on a series of graphs and charts the printer spewed forth at the end of each session.

Fifteen minutes later he was done, and a moment after that the printer came to life, chattering madly for nearly another full minute. At last Collins tore off the printout, studied it for a moment, then handed it to Robb. "Not bad," the coach commented. "But not really great, either."

Robb looked at the graphs and found that while he'd done as well as ever on most of the routines, his bench presses were off from his norm, as were his leg lifts. The vague ache in his jaw, where Jeff's fist had connected with him the night before, told him what the problem was. He looked up at the coach, who was already scribbling a note on a pad of paper.

"This'll get you out of classes for the rest of the day," Collins told him. "I want you to go out to the center and let Ames look you over. If you're going to play tomorrow, you've got to be in top condition."

Grinning happily, Robb Harris returned to his locker, dressed, and headed to the bike rack behind the gym.

"What's this all about?" Mark asked from the backseat of one of the station wagons. There were orderlies on both sides of him, and though his chest ached a little, the pain wasn't really too bad. But he felt crowded, and wondered why both the orderlies had gotten into the car with him. The other station wagon, ahead of them, was occupied only by its driver.

"Your dad just wants me to have a look at you, that's all," Dr. Ames told him from the front seat.

"But why?" Mark pressed. He'd been trying to get a straight answer out of Ames since the doctor had first come into his room half an hour after his mother had left. He'd introduced himself and told him he was being transferred to Rocky Mountain High. It still didn't make any sense to Mark—Dr. MacCallum had said he'd be able to go home tomorrow morning.

"I think your dad wants me to recommend some exercises for you," Ames told him now. "And I have a vitamin complex that might help you get over your growth problem."

Mark frowned. His father hadn't said anything to him about it at all. "When did he come up with that?" he asked. And then, of course, he knew. Last night, after the fight, when he hadn't even been able to run away from Jeff LaConner. Still, if his folks had decided to send him out to the sports center, why hadn't his mother told him about it? His eyes fixed on the back of Ames's head. "Does my mom know about this?"

As if feeling Mark's eyes on him, Ames turned around to

give the boy a friendly smile. "Your dad, as I understand it, would like you to be able to defend yourself, and I assume your mother feels the same way. And since I understand you've started exercising on your own," he added dryly, "I'm also assuming you're getting a little tired of being the smallest kid on the block, too."

Almost in spite of himself, Mark found himself laughing. He had to admit it was true—well, he didn't have to admit it to Dr. Ames, but he'd already admitted it to himself. And his dad must have figured it out, too, even though he'd tried not to make a big deal out of what he was doing.

He leaned back in the seat then, and tried to relax, but still felt crowded by the two orderlies on either side of him. It was almost like they were taking him to prison, he suddenly thought, and were afraid he might try to escape.

When they came to the high gates protecting Rocky Mountain High from the rest of the valley, the image of a prison grew stronger in his mind. "What is this?" he asked. "A sports center or some kind of concentration camp?"

He heard Ames chuckle in the front seat. "Actually, it does look sort of like a prison, doesn't it?" he heard the doctor say. "But it's to keep people out, not in. We have a lot of valuable equipment out here and a lot of programs we'd just as soon not let anybody else in on." He turned and winked at Mark then, and Mark thought he understood. It was like TarrenTech, and all the other companies in Silicon Valley that spent half their time trying to keep their new ideas from being stolen and the other half trying to steal everybody else's stuff. To him the whole thing had always seemed kind of dumb. After all, everybody eventually found out what everyone else was doing anyway, didn't they?

The gates swung open and Mark gazed curiously at the big building that housed the center. It looked nice—like a lodge, not a hospital. Then he remembered what Robb Harris had told him about it.

"How many kids come here in the summer?" he asked.

"Almost fifty this year," Ames replied, grinning at him.

"Of course, we don't give them the full benefit of everything we know. If we did, the home team might get some competition." He paused, gazing speculatively at Mark. "You interested in football?"

Mark shook his head. "Not really," he admitted. "In fact, I've always thought it was kind of stupid." The car he was in passed the front of the building and drove toward the rear while the other car pulled up near the main entrance. "Where are we going?"

"Around in back," Ames replied. "We'll go in through the garage." A few seconds later the car pulled up to a pair of imposing metal doors, then the doors swung slowly upward. As soon as they were open, they drove inside. The doors closed behind them with a heavy metallic clang.

"Here we are," Ames told him. One of the orderlies slid out of the backseat and held the door open for Mark. He followed the orderly through a door and then down a hall, turning finally into a treatment room very much like the one Dr. MacCallum had examined him in the night before.

Except that in this room there were heavy straps made of thick webbing attached to the examining table.

Mark frowned at the straps, and suddenly recalled the strange marks he'd seen on Jeff LaConner's wrists the morning after he'd spent the night here.

"Wh-What are those?" Mark asked, his voice betraying the fear that had begun to play once more around the edges of his mind.

"Nothing to worry about," Ames told him. "Just take off your clothes and put on this," he went on, handing Mark a pale green hospital gown.

"Why?" Mark demanded. "You already know what's wrong with me, don't you? I just got beat up. I'm not sick."

Ames's voice hardened. "Just do what you're told, Mark. We're not going to hurt you. All we're going to do is help you."

Mark's eyes flicked toward the door, but one of the orderlies was blocking it, his eyes fixed on Mark as if he knew what he was thinking. Mark hesitated for a moment, his heart pounding.

Then he reminded himself that it was his father who had sent him here. So whatever this was all about, it had to be okay, didn't it? Still, his nervousness only increased as he slowly took off his clothes and put on the hospital gown.

It wasn't until he was already stretched out on the table that the orderlies suddenly jumped him, one of them holding him down while the other strapped his legs and arms securely to the metal surface.

"What the hell—" Mark shouted. Then a gag was placed over his mouth and he felt a needle slipping into a vein in his forearm.

"You're going to be fine," Ames assured him once more. "Believe me, Mark, you're going to feel better than you've ever felt before in your life."

Mark struggled against the heavy straps for a moment, but as he tried to pull himself free, a stab of pain lashed through his chest.

Even before the searing pain had faded away, Mark Tanner sank into the dark abyss of unconsciousness.

14

Linda Harris already had her book bag packed by the time the lunch bell rang. She'd been thinking about it all morning, but had finally made up her mind only fifteen minutes ago. She was going to skip lunch and go out to the hospital to visit Mark Tanner. She didn't have time, really, but her class after lunch was only a study hall, and she could always say she'd spent the time in the library. In fact, if she had to, she could get Tiffany Welch—who always spent that hour helping the librarian—to back her up. As the clanging of the bell faded away, Linda hurried out of the classroom and toward the wide staircase that led to the main floor. She was halfway down the stairs when she heard Tiffany calling to her from the mezzanine above.

"Linda? Wait up!"

Linda hesitated, half tempted to pretend she hadn't heard, then thought better of it. "Hi," she said as the other girl caught up with her. "Look, I need a big favor. If I miss my study hall, will you tell Mr. Anders I was in the library?"

Tiffany's oval face reflected confusion for a moment, then her bright blue eyes took on a conspiratorial quality. "Where are you going? Are you cutting the whole afternoon?"

The eagerness in her friend's voice told Linda that Tiffany was considering coming with her; to Tiffany, practically anything was more interesting than school.

"I'm just going to the hospital," Linda said.

Tiffany's face brightened. "To see Jeff? I'll go with you."

"Why would I want to see Jeff?" Linda demanded, her eyes flashing angrily. "After last night, I hope I never see him again!"

The eager look faded from Tiffany's eyes. "Then who?" At last, the light dawned. "You mean you're going to see Mark?" she asked, her voice traced with scorn.

"Well, why shouldn't I?" Linda snapped.

"He's just such a . . . well, he's kind of a wimp, isn't he?" Tiffany said.

Linda's features congealed coldly. "Just because he isn't a sports nut like everyone else around here doesn't mean he's a wimp. He happens to be a real nice guy. And he doesn't go around jumping guys who are a lot smaller than he is, either."

Tiffany couldn't resist the opening. "There *aren't* any smaller guys," she said, "unless you go over to the junior high." Seeing Linda's eyes glitter with tears, she relented. "I'm sorry," she apologized. "And I'll cover for you, too. Say hi to him for me, okay?"

Linda nodded, then turned away and hurried out of the school building.

Twenty minutes later she came to the small county hospital and pushed her way into the waiting room. Except for a Chicano woman—her face pale and her eyes sunken and tired—the room was deserted. Linda looked around uncertainly for a moment, then went to ring the bell on the counter separating the reception area from the office.

"She's in Ricardo's room," the fragile woman suddenly said. "She's giving my son a bath."

Linda turned to face the woman, realizing who she was but not knowing what to say to her. Before she could say anything at all, Susan Aldrich appeared. "All done, Mrs. Ramirez," she said, then recognized Linda. "Well, hello. What brings you out here?" She glanced instinctively at the clock.

"It's lunch hour," Linda explained. "I thought I'd come out and say hello to Mark."

"Mark?" the nurse replied blankly, then understood. "Oh, you mean Mark Tanner. He's not here."

Linda looked at the nurse in confusion. "But they brought him in last night."

Susan Aldrich nodded. "And he left this morning, so I guess he must not have been hurt very badly."

Linda could barely believe it. She remembered the glimpse she'd caught of Mark last night as they'd moved him out of the emergency room, his face bruised and swollen, his chest swathed with heavy tape. "But where'd he go?" she breathed.

"Home, I suppose," Susan replied. "I could check if you want. He was already discharged when I got here this morning."

Linda shook her head. If she hurried, she still had time to get to the Tanners', say hi, and be back at school in time for her fifth-period class.

Sharon Tanner was just coming out of the house when Linda arrived. "Hi!" she greeted her. "You just caught me in time. I was going over to the hospital." She held up some magazines and a book. "Mark must be getting bored with TV by now, don't you think?"

Linda gaped at Sharon. What was she talking about? "B-But isn't he here?" she asked. "I was just at the hospital and they told me he was discharged this morning!"

Now it was Sharon who stared dumbly, her mind reeling with confusion. There must be some mistake—when she'd left the hospital, Dr. MacCallum had made it clear that Mark wouldn't be out until tomorrow, or this evening, at the earliest. "But that's crazy!" she protested. "Of course he's there. Whom did you talk to?"

Linda repeated what had happened at the hospital. As Sharon listened, her eyes darkened with worry, but she still clung to the idea that it was some kind of mistake. "Come on," she said to Linda, and turned back to the house. "I'm going to call the hospital and get this straightened out. My God," she added, forcing a brittle laugh. "They can't have lost him, can they?"

Five minutes later, when she finally got Dr. MacCallum on the line, she was no longer laughing. "But why wasn't I told?" she demanded. "I've never even talked to Dr. Ames!" She listened impatiently as MacCallum explained what had happened. "But it's all ridiculous," she protested when he was finished. "You said yourself there's nothing seriously wrong with him. And why would he need a sports specialist? He was beaten up, not injured in a football game."

"I don't know," MacCallum replied honestly. "All I can tell you is that your husband's signature was on the release. I even matched it against the forms he filled out here last night, just to be sure. It never occurred to me that he didn't tell you this morning, or I would have called you myself."

When at last Sharon hung up, her worry of a few minutes earlier had been replaced with a hot anger. For her husband to have had Mark transferred to another hospital without even telling her—it was outrageous!

She dropped Linda Harris off at the school, feeling no better for Linda's assurances that Ames had been working with Robb almost since the day they'd moved to Silverdale, and that Robb was crazy about the program Ames had put him on.

"But that's not the point," she'd tried to explain. "I'm sure there's nothing wrong with it at all. It just burns me up that no one told me what they were doing with Mark, that's all!"

Linda scrambled out of the car and slammed the door.

"Tell Mark I'll come and see him after school," she called, but it was too late. Sharon's anger in firm control of the accelerator, she sped away from the school, the tires of her car shrieking in protest.

Mark lay in a haze, gazing glassily at a large television monitor that was suspended from the ceiling above his head. His ears were covered with a pair of headphones, and through the fog of drugs that clouded his brain, only the images on the screen and the sounds in his ears were real.

It was like a dream—a pleasant dream in which he walked along a shady riverbank, pausing now and then to watch the water tumble over rocks or a turtle bask in the sun on a log. Birds flew overhead, and their sounds, mixed with the soothing babble of running water, filled his ears.

A deer stepped out of a clump of aspens ahead, and Mark came to a halt, watching the animal as it grazed languidly on a clump of grass near the stream. Then other images began to flicker vaguely in his mind, images he couldn't quite see but which his subconscious nevertheless registered and remembered.

It was these images—the ones he couldn't quite see—that he would remember later. All the rest of it, the vision of the stream and the birds singing, would fade away.

As would the reality of what was happening around him, and to him.

He was still strapped to the metal table, but he was no longer in the examining room to which he'd been brought on his arrival at the sports center. Nor, in reality, were the straps necessary, for Mark had ceased struggling against them immediately after that first shot—the first of more than half a dozen he'd received in the few hours he'd been there. Mark's body, as relaxed now as his mind, was submitting nervelessly to the treatment it was undergoing. But they'd left the straps in place as they moved the metal table from room to room, more as precaution than anything else.

Mark's body, like Randy Stevens's and Jeff LaConner's on other, earlier days, was wired to an array of meters and monitors. An I.V. dripped into a needle taped securely to his upper right thigh, and another I.V. took a slow but continual sampling of his blood, a sampling that was being analyzed almost as quickly as it moved through the tiny capillary tube attached to the needle.

A scanner hovered above his body, moving slowly up and down the length of the table, feeding a constantly changing series of data to a softly humming computer which, as fast as the digitalized images were absorbed into its memory banks, expanded and exaggerated them, then fed them onto an over-sized monitor.

Changes—drastic changes, even though they were imperceptible to the naked eye—had already taken place inside him.

The hairline fracture in his jaw had all but disappeared, and the cracks in his ribs were healing rapidly.

His bones, stimulated by the massive doses of synthetic hormones that had been dripping steadily into him since early that morning, had begun to respond, reproducing their own cells at an accelerated rate that had already added a sixteenth of an inch to Mark's total height, and nearly a pound to his total weight.

For nearly five hours Martin Ames had been overseeing Mark's treatment, watching for the slightest sign of an adverse reaction. So far everything was proceeding beyond even his own highest expectations. Though few people would even have known what to look for, Ames was able to watch the changes in Mark's body almost as they happened.

His lung capacity had increased slightly, as had the size of his heart. His blood pressure—somewhat high when he had been brought in that morning—was normal now, and Ames felt pleased as he noted that the compensations he'd allowed for Mark's emotional state just before his blood pressure was first measured had apparently been exactly precise.

Even Mark's brain showed minute chemical changes, changes that would soon embody themselves physically.

And yet, Ames knew, without the enhancement of the bank of computers, Mark would appear no different now from the boy he had been a few hours ago.

A soft electronic chime sounded, disturbing Ames's concentration, and he glanced up irritably. A blue light was flashing on the wall. Could it really have been five hours that he'd been in the treatment room, his aides surrounding the examining table and making continuous, minute adjustments to the chemicals dripping into Mark's body as he'd quietly issued a steady stream of orders? The strain in his muscles told him it was true.

"All right," he said, stretching his six-foot frame, massaging a knot in his right shoulder. "That's it for now."

Immediately, one of the aides stopped the flow into Mark's thigh from the I.V., and another slid the needle out of the vein, then swabbed the spot with a wad of cotton soaked in alcohol. It was a tiny needle, the mark barely visible in the center of a small bruise that would disappear within a few hours.

Other aides began removing the monitoring devices. One by one the screens went blank, all except the one displaying Mark's cardiovascular activity. That would be the last to be removed, when the final phase of Mark's treatment had been completed.

Ames watched the activity impassively. The session had gone perfectly. He was certain the prognosis for Mark Tanner was good.

Unless . . .

His mind shifted gears, and he thought of Jeff LaConner, who had been in this same room only hours before, wired to the same equipment. He still didn't know what had gone wrong with Jeff. He'd been so careful, adjusting Jeff's treatment after the first signs that the boy was developing a reaction to the therapy. It hadn't worked; Jeff's condition had only deteriorated.

Somewhere there was an answer, and he was determined to find out what that answer was, to discover the miscalculation in the mix of hormones that had triggered the explosive response in Jeff LaConner and all the others.

In the meantime, Mark Tanner, with his history of rheumatic fever and retarded growth, would provide more data, more knowledge, more progress.

As Jerry Harris had promised, Mark was a perfect experimental subject. And in the end, Ames thought, Mark might benefit from the experimental treatment as much as he himself.

Unless . . .

He put the thought out of his mind as the team of aides finished their work. The monitor above Mark's head had gone dark now, and the earphones had been removed from his head. The boy was stirring as the consciousness-suppressing drugs were filtered out of his bloodstream. In a few minutes he would awaken.

"Unstrap him before he starts struggling," Ames said as he stepped forward and took a hypodermic needle from the hand of his chief assistant. "We don't want any marks on him at all." Checking the needle carefully, he slid it into one of the veins of Mark's right arm, then pressed the plunger.

Almost as soon as the insulin hit Mark's bloodstream, the boy broke out in a cold sweat and his body shook with tremors.

The tremors increased. Abruptly, the dreamy look on Mark's face was replaced with a grimace of fear and pain.

The convulsions began then, Mark's body jerking spasmodically as he went into the third phase of insulin shock. Only when he had finally fallen unconscious and his body relaxed did Ames nod.

"All right," he said. "Take him in and get him dressed. By the time he wakes up, he won't remember a thing." A sardonic smile twisted his lips. "In fact," he added, "he'll probably feel better than he's ever felt before in his life."

*   *   *

At first Sharon Tanner wasn't certain she'd come to the right place. She'd driven the two miles out of town almost unconsciously, simply following the road as her anger—most of it directed toward Blake—grew within her. Why would he have done such a thing without asking her? It wasn't like him; wasn't like him at all. But even as her anger built, the rational part of her mind answered her own question. Had he sought her agreement, she'd have simply assumed it was one more step in his ongoing campaign to get Mark involved in sports, and automatically objected.

And she would have been right.

She braked the car suddenly and stared at the building off to the right. The sports center appeared more like a campus than a clinic, completely surrounded by well-kept lawns. But then, as she drew nearer, she realized that these weren't just lawns: they were playing fields, acres and acres of them. At least two football fields, a baseball diamond, and a hockey field. There was a track, too, with an infield that boasted an array of both high and low hurdles, a broad-jump track, and a high jump, as well as various exercise bars.

In the center of all this was what looked like a lodge, but between her and the building were a pair of closed gates. She pulled the car up to the gates, rolled down the window and pressed a button on a large metal box mounted on an iron post. A moment later a male voice scratched from a speaker within the box: "Can I help you?"

"I'm here to see Dr. Ames," Sharon said, her voice a little louder than she'd intended. "My name is Sharon Tanner. I'm Mark Tanner's mother."

"One moment, please," the voice replied. The speaker went dead. The seconds ticked by, and after nearly a minute, Sharon wondered if she was, indeed, at the right place. She was considering what to do when the speaker came to life again; at the same time, the gates began to swing open.

"Just park in front of the building and come in the front door, Mrs. Tanner," the disembodied voice instructed her.

She took her foot off the brake and drove slowly down the drive, impressed with what she saw, even in spite of her anger. It was a graceful building, fitting well into the surroundings of the rising mountains, and whatever it was all about, it was obviously successful. She parked the car, hurried up the front steps and across the wide veranda, pushing through the heavy glass door into the lobby. A smiling woman who wore a lab coat open over a tailored dress was waiting for her.

"Mrs. Tanner?" the woman asked, then went on without waiting for a reply. "I'm Marjorie Jackson, Dr. Ames's assistant. Everyone calls me Marge. Won't you come with me?"

Sharon's lips tightened, but despite her urge to vent the anger that had been building inside her, she found herself obediently following Marge Jackson through the lobby and what was apparently a dining room, then down a hall into one of the building's large wings. "It seems awfully empty, doesn't it?" Marge asked, glancing back at Sharon. "But you should see it during the season. Last summer we had to feed the boys in two shifts!"

A minute later Sharon found herself being led into a suite of offices. Marge Jackson seated herself behind a desk. "I assume you're here to see"—she paused to glance down at a file on the desk in front of her—"Mark, isn't it?"

"I'm here for a lot more than that," Sharon replied, her voice cool. She was pleased to see Marjorie Jackson's smile fade uncertainly away.

"I beg your pardon?" she said. "I'm afraid I don't understand—is something wrong?"

"Wrong?" Sharon repeated, making no attempt to veil her anger. "Why should anything be wrong? I left my son in County Hospital this morning, and by lunchtime I find he's been moved. Nobody asked me—nobody even told me! And you want to know if something's wrong?"

Marge Jackson's uncertain expression gave way to one of

genuine concern, and suddenly Sharon felt foolish. Whatever had happened, it obviously wasn't this woman's fault. Letting out her breath in an explosive sigh, she sank into a chair and apologized. As briefly as she could, she explained exactly what had happened. By the time she was done, Marge Jackson was nodding sympathetically.

"But how terrible for you," she said. "If my husband had done something like that, I think I'd kill him. But I'm sure it was just a mix-up, and I can tell you that everything's just fine."

"But why was Mark brought here?" Sharon asked. "It all seems so, well, so unnecessary."

"I'm afraid you'll have to talk to Dr. Ames about that," Marge replied. Her expression brightened and she nodded toward someone who had just come through the door. "Here he is now. Dr. Ames, this is Sharon Tanner, Mark's mother."

Sharon rose to her feet, surprised to find a genial-looking man in his mid-forties—with gray eyes that fairly twinkled as he smiled at her—extending his hand. She automatically accepted the greeting, only then realizing that subconsciously she had expected some sort of Machiavellian monster who had coldly abducted her son and would now make smooth excuses for what he'd done.

Ames ushered her into his office, offered her a cup of coffee, and after listening to her story, assured her it was his own fault. "I should have had Marge call you myself, just to make sure you knew what was going on. And call me Marty," he added. "Everybody else does, even a lot of the kids." He smiled, then leaned back in his chair. "Anyway," he went on, "you'll be glad to know that there's nothing wrong with Mark."

"I already knew that," Sharon told him. "Dr. MacCallum worked on him most of the night, you know."

Ames looked abashed. "I know, and I certainly didn't mean to imply that there's anything wrong with Mac. There isn't. In fact, he's a damned good doctor."

"Then why did my husband want you to see Mark, Dr. Ames?" Sharon asked, not yet won over.

Ames shrugged. "I suppose he just wanted a second opinion," he said. "And I assume Jerry Harris told him that my specialty is working with kids who have had physical and developmental problems."

Sharon was startled. So she'd been right, at least partially. Blake was, indeed, still looking for a way to overcome the residual effects of Mark's rheumatic fever. "And do you have an opinion?" she asked, doing her best to keep her voice neutral.

Marty Ames spread his hands noncommittally. "It's hard to say, really. But I've given him a complete examination, and I'm pleased to be able to tell you that there's nothing seriously the matter with him. In fact, given his early medical history, he's remarkably healthy."

Sharon felt herself relax. "Then when can I take him home?" she asked.

"No reason you can't take him home now," Ames said pleasantly. "I've given him some codeine to keep the pain in his ribs from bothering him. In a couple of days he should be as good as new."

Sharon stared at Ames. This was it? She'd built herself into such a fury, been so certain that somehow Blake and this doctor had cooked up some sort of scheme. And now . . .

"Tell you what," Ames said, standing. "Why don't I give you a tour of the place, show you what we're doing out here. By the time we're done, Mark should be all set to go."

"I don't really think I need a tour," Sharon began, but Ames held up a protesting hand.

"We kidnapped your son, remember?" he asked. "The least we can do is set your mind at ease."

To her own surprise, Sharon found herself obediently following Ames out of his office and listening intently as he gave her a tour of the facility and spoke about the summer program.

"What I try to do," he said as they entered a gym filled

with equipment the like of which Sharon had never seen before, "is treat each of the kids as an individual. It's always seemed to me that to claim there's a single diet, or exercise regimen, or even medication that will work for every kid, is just plain nuts. And since almost every kid who comes here has a special problem of one sort or another, I try never to view them as simply kids. They're individuals, and have to be treated as such."

Sharon paused, staring at a stationary exercise bicycle that had a large screen curved around its front. "What on earth is that for?" she asked, pointing to the screen.

Ames grinned. "Ever used one of those things?" he asked.

Sharon nodded. "I tried one a few years ago. Bought the bike, used it about three times, and sold it. It was the most boring thing I've ever done in my life."

"Try this one," Ames suggested. Sharon hesitated, but then, curious, mounted the bike. To her surprise, she found that the handlebars were not stationary, but moved easily both left and right. Ames crossed to a small computer console and switched it on. "Like San Francisco?" he asked.

Sharon's brows arched. "Who doesn't?"

A moment later the lights dimmed in the gymnasium and the screen in front of Sharon lit up with a bright image of Market Street. She felt as if she were on the right side of the street, facing Twin Peaks, and cars were streaming in both directions. "Start pedaling," she heard Ames tell her.

Her feet began slowly turning the pedals, and to her surprise, the picture on the screen changed.

It was as if she were moving along the street itself.

"Speed up a little and move out into traffic," Ames instructed her. Frowning, Sharon increased the speed of her pedaling, then twisted the handlebars to the left.

The picture shifted, and she felt as if she were in the center of the right lane. She kept pedaling, then heard Ames telling her to turn right up Van Ness Avenue. As the handlebars turned in her hands, the image swung around and she could see the vista of the broad avenue stretching northward. She kept pedaling, watching the familiar scenery of the city unfold before her. She made several more turns, then finally brought the bike to a stop, feeling silly as she realized she had actually pulled it over to the curb again. When the screen went blank and the lights came up, she looked at Ames with awe.

"What is it?" she asked. "How does it work?"

"It's all done with computers," Ames explained. "Practically the whole city north of Market Street and east of Divisidero is on a laser disk, and the handlebars control it. You can ride all over San Francisco, looking at anything you want. And it simulates the hills, too, so you never have to change the tension on the wheel yourself." He grinned at her. "Now I ask you, was that boring?"

Sharon shook her head. "It's great. I could have kept at that for a couple of hours."

"You and everybody else," Ames observed wryly. "Out here, the problem isn't getting the kids to exercise. It's getting them to stop." He glanced at his watch. "Well, that's about it. Let's go see how Mark's doing."

They started back toward the offices, but as they came into the main lobby, Mark jumped up from a sofa he'd been sprawling on.

"Hi, Mom," he said, grinning at her.

Sharon stared at him.

The bruises on his face looked much better, and where this morning his face had been pale, almost pasty, his cheeks were now tinged a healthy pink. His right eye was still a bit swollen, but he was able to open it, and the shiner glowing darkly beneath it seemed to be healing.

"Mark?" she breathed. "Honey, are you all right? Your chest—"

But Mark only grinned at her. When he'd bounded off the sofa, he hadn't felt a thing in his chest. "I'm fine," he said. "Marty gave me something for my ribs, and they don't hurt at all."

Sharon stared at him for almost a full minute. He looked better than she'd imagined possible.

It wasn't until half an hour later, when they were driving back through the village, that a sudden thought came into her mind.

After his morning at Rocky Mountain High, Mark was almost like the town itself.

Perfect.

Too perfect.

15

"It doesn't matter what you thought, or what Jerry Harris told you," Sharon insisted. "I'm your wife, and I'm Mark's mother. You had no right simply to make a decision about Mark without even telling me!"

They were in the small sitting room area of the master suite. On the hearth, a fire was slowly dying. Blake had lit it when they'd come upstairs an hour before, for that afternoon a cold front had moved in from the north and a light snow was falling outside. But Sharon was oblivious to both the snowfall and the fire, her eyes fixed angrily on her husband. "Don't you even understand what I'm saying?"

Blake shrugged tiredly. It seemed to him that the argument had long ago become circular, but once more he reiterated what he'd already told her three times: "You've already admitted that nothing terrible happened to him out at the center. In fact, all things considered, he looks pretty damned good. And you were exhausted this morning—you'd been up all night and you wouldn't have been thinking straight."

"But you still—" Sharon began.

"Enough!" Blake said. He'd been pacing the room, finally pausing at the window to watch the snow float to the ground outside. Now he turned to face her, his jaw set firmly in an expression that told her his patience had run out. "For Christ's sake, Sharon, what do you think I intended? It's not like I was trying to do something terrible! Jerry just suggested I have Ames look him over, and it sounded like a good idea! If I was wrong, I was wrong, and I apologize. But I wasn't wrong!"

"Can't you keep your voice down?" Sharon asked, her own dropping to a harsh whisper. "We don't have to tell the whole neighborhood we're having a fight, do we?"

It was a mistake. Sharon knew it was as soon as she'd uttered the words. Blake's jaw tightened and his eyes glinted with anger. "No," he said, "we certainly don't. In fact, we don't have to have a fight at all. I'll see you later."

Before Sharon could say anything else, he was gone. She listened as he stamped down the stairs and the front door slammed. From the curved window of the turret she watched him walk away from the house, his shoulders hunched, his head down. He was walking quickly, and she was certain she knew where he was going.

To the Harrises, where Jerry would assure him that he had indeed done the right thing, whatever his wife might think.

She turned away from the window and added a log to the fire as if the gesture itself would put a period to the fight. She wasn't being fair, she chided herself. If Jerry thought Blake was wrong, he wouldn't hesitate to say so.

She curled herself up in a small chintz-covered chair in front of the fire and tried to sort her thoughts out rationally, firmly putting aside the anger she felt over Blake's failure to consult her before sending Mark out to Marty Ames.

Overall, she had to admit that Blake was right—certainly the doctor had done Mark no harm; indeed, from all appearances, he had done him a lot of good.

And from what Mark had said on the way home, Ames hadn't really done all that much. In fact, in retrospect she found herself chuckling at Mark's exasperation when she'd pressed him for details as to precisely what had happened at the sports center.

It wasn't any different from asking Kelly what had happened at school on a given day.

"Nothing" was her daughter's invariable answer, as it had been Mark's when he was the same age.

Finally, as she'd driven him home that afternoon, he'd turned to her with a teenager's scorn for his mother's silliness clear in his eyes.

"I keep telling you, Mom, nothing happened at all," he insisted. "Dr. Ames checked me over and gave me a shot of codeine for my ribs, and then I did some exercises. That was all."

"Exercises?" Sharon had echoed, glancing at him doubtfully out of the corner of her eye. "My God, Mark, you've got three cracked ribs. It must have hurt like—"

"It didn't hurt at all," Mark interjected, not about to admit to his mother that he'd actually passed out for a minute while working on a rowing machine. She'd go nuts and put him to bed for the rest of the day. Besides, it hadn't been any big deal. He'd just opened his eyes, and one of Marty Ames's assistants had been grinning at him. For a moment he'd wondered what had happened, then his memory had come back to him in bits and pieces.

He had no idea that those memories were only the ones carefully and subliminally planted in his subconscious during his long hours on the metal table in the treatment room. Of that ordeal he had no memory at all.

Sharon had finally dropped the subject as she turned into their driveway and pulled the car into the garage. Chivas, lying sleepily by the back door, had gotten lazily to his feet. As Mark got out of the passenger seat of the car, the retriever barked joyfully at the unexpected appearance of his master. He'd bounded forward, his tail wagging, then suddenly stopped.

His tail dropped and the fur on the nape of his neck had risen slightly as an uncertain growl bubbled in his throat.

"Hey, fella, don't you recognize me?" Mark asked. He

squatted down, and Chivas, dropping low to the ground, had slunk forward, sniffing warily at Mark's outstretched hand.

"What's wrong with him?" Sharon asked.

Mark reached out and scratched the dog's neck, then grinned up at his mother.

"I'm supposed to be at school, and I bet I smell really weird after a night in the hospital. I probably smell just like the vet's office, and you know how he hates that."

Sharon had all but forgotten the incident until dinnertime, when Mark, who had been closeted in his room most of the afternoon, had come down to the dining room table. Throughout dinner Sharon noticed that Kelly seemed unusually subdued. Several times she caught her daughter eyeing Mark surreptitiously, her expression puzzled. It wasn't until the two of them were alone in the kitchen, washing the dishes, that Sharon finally asked Kelly about it.

"I don't know," Kelly had said, gazing up at her mother through serious-looking eyes. "He just looks sort of different, I guess."

"Well, of course he does," Sharon replied. "He's got a black eye and a bad cut."

"I don't mean that," Kelly protested. "It's just the way he looks. He's just not the same."

That was the real reason behind her argument with Blake, Sharon decided now, as she sat staring into the fire. She'd tried to tell him about it, tried to explain what had happened with Chivas and what Kelly had said after dinner, but he'd brushed it all aside.

"Of course Mark's different," he'd said. "He got beat up and bandaged up, and even if the injuries didn't change him, you can bet the fight did. You don't get pounded the way he did without it changing you inside."

"But it's not inside," Sharon had insisted. "Chivas saw it, and Kelly saw it, and I think I can see it, too. He's just not the same as he was."

In the end she hadn't been able to put her finger on just what it was about Mark that had changed, and finally she'd given up trying to make Blake see what she herself couldn't describe. If the truth be known, she finally admitted to herself, perhaps there really was nothing at all. Perhaps she wanted to see something, simply to justify her anger toward Blake for having sent Mark to Ames without talking to her about it first.

She took a deep breath and stood up, making an almost physical effort to shake off the last vestiges of her anger and her vague, indescribable misgivings. Certainly Mark had seemed perfectly happy all day, and not the least concerned about his hours at the sports center. If anything, he had actually enjoyed them. So why should she keep on fretting?

She poked at the fire, settling the burning log well back against the fire wall, then arranging a screen on the hearth. Going downstairs, she saw Kelly standing at the living room window, gazing wistfully out at the snow. Reading her mind, Sharon smiled at her daughter. "Want to go for a walk in it?" she asked.

Kelly's eyes glowed eagerly. "Can we?"

"Come on," Sharon replied. Several minutes later, bundled up in the parkas Sharon had purchased only a few days earlier, mother and daughter stepped out into the snowy evening. The flakes were large and fluffy, and as they started down the sidewalk, the cold air stung their cheeks and they were quickly enveloped in the gentle silence that always comes with the first snow of the year.

Kelly reached out and took her mother's hand. "I love it here," she said, gazing around in happy wonder. "Aren't you glad we moved?"

Sharon said nothing for a moment, then the peacefulness of the snowfall overcame her as well.

"Yes," she said. "I guess I am."

Yet even as she said the words, she wondered.

Charlotte LaConner shivered as she gazed out at the snow slowly building on the front lawn. Under normal circum-

stances she would have been thrilled to see it, for it meant the
skiing season was almost upon them, and that Christmas—
always her favorite season—was just around the corner. Tonight, though, the whiteness outside only reflected the chill
she was feeling in her own soul, and at last she turned away
from the window to face her husband. Her eyes, she knew,
had turned an angry bloodshot red, and her cheeks were still
stained with tears.

"But it's not right," she pleaded once more. "I'm his
mother, Chuck. Don't I have a right to see him?"

Chuck LaConner, the memory of his son's distorted features still etched deeply in his mind, forced himself to look
directly at Charlotte as he once more repeated the story he
and Ames had agreed upon late the night before. He rational-
ized to himself that at least she would be spared having to see
what Jeff was turning into. Better she should live in ignorance than have that terrible image engraved on her heart
forever. "It wouldn't do you, or him, any good," he said
once more. "Char, he wouldn't even recognize you."

"But it's not possible," Charlotte whimpered, cowering
away from his words as if she'd been struck. "I'm his
mother, Chuck—he needs me!"

"He needs rest," Chuck insisted. "Honey, I know it
seems crazy, but sometimes these things happen. Jeff's been
under a lot of pressure lately—"

"And is that my fault?" Charlotte suddenly flared. "I
wanted him to quit the team, remember?"

Chuck swore silently to himself. Remember? How could
he forget? The argument had gone on almost every day since
she'd gone to visit that boy in the hospital, and he still hadn't
been able to convince her that whatever had happened wasn't
Jeff's fault. Then he realized that perhaps there was a way to
turn her own words against her and once and for all put an
end to this discussion. "Did it ever occur to you that your
nagging might have contributed to what's happened?" he
asked, deliberately putting an icy edge on his words. As she
recoiled, he repeated to himself yet again that all this was for
her own good.

Charlotte dropped limply onto the sofa and stared at him bleakly. "Is that what he said?" she asked in a hollow voice. "That all this is my fault?"

Chuck licked nervously at his lips. "Perhaps not in so many words," he temporized. "But what it comes down to is, for the moment the best thing we can do—both of us—is let the doctors take care of Jeff. And it's not forever, honey," he went on. "After a while, when he gets better . . ."

He let the words trail off. Part of his mind told him that he had just told his wife an outright lie; Jeff was never going to get better. But there was another part of him that wanted to believe that somehow Marty Ames would come up with a solution to the terrible thing that was happening to their son.

The important thing right now, though, was to keep Charlotte from finding out exactly how bad Jeff's situation was. Of course, he would never forgive himself for what had happened, never forgive himself for enrolling Jeff in a medical program that carried any risks whatsoever, no matter how slight they might have been.

He'd lost his son. He'd understood that in the dark hours before dawn this morning, when Marty Ames had finally let him see Jeff. His first instinct had been to turn on Ames, to strike out at the man who had done this. But in the end, as always happened with him, reason had prevailed. He'd come to understand that in the final analysis it was he himself who was culpable, he who had made the final decision to allow Jeff to be treated with Ames's experimental compounds.

He'd wanted it to work so badly, wanted so much for Jeff to be like all the other boys—especially like all the other boys in Silverdale—that he'd deliberately shut his mind to the possible side effects of Ames's treatment.

And so he'd lost his only child.

And if Charlotte found out what he'd done, found out what had really happened to Jeff, he'd lose her, too.

But it didn't have to be that way, he thought. If he could only convince her that Jeff's problems weren't physical at all, convince her that their son had simply suffered a mental breakdown and needed a period of rest, perhaps she would never have to know the truth.

Perhaps Ames would find a cure and Jeff would be fine.

Or perhaps . . .

He deliberately shut his mind to the other possibility, telling himself that it wouldn't happen. It would be just as Jerry Harris had told him that afternoon.

"I don't want you to worry about a thing," Harris said after calling Chuck into his office. "I've talked to Marty Ames, and he thinks there's a good chance of turning this around. And you can count on TarrenTech. Whatever Jeff needs, he's going to get." They'd talked for a while, and Harris assured him that no matter what happened, both Jeff and the LaConner family would be taken care of. "And after this is over," Harris had said, "you can take Charlotte anywhere you want to go. I can't imagine you'll want to stay in Silverdale, not after this. But it's a big world, and we're a big company. And we take care of our own."

Even through his grief and guilt, Chuck had understood the message perfectly. What had happened to Jeff was going to be swept under the carpet, and neither the situation—nor his part in it—were ever going to be made public.

For a moment he'd hated Jerry Harris, hated him as much as he'd ever hated anyone in his life. But then, once more, that pragmatic core deep within him—the cold, analytical aspect of his personality that had not only made him valuable to TarrenTech over the years, but had led him to weigh the odds for Jeff three years ago and then take what he had thought was an almost risk-free gamble with his own son's life—came to the fore.

There was no point in hating Jerry. After all, hadn't Jerry himself taken the same gamble with Robb's life? And Tom Stevens, with Randy? And how many others?

They were the same, all of them. All of them had the same hopes and aspirations for their sons; the same ambitions for themselves. All of them had gambled.

Most of them had won.

Tom Stevens had lost.

Now he had lost.

But he didn't have to lose everything. He still had his career, and he still had his wife. And he intended to lose neither of those, no matter what it took.

He went to Charlotte and slipped his arms around her. "He'll get better," he promised. "And as soon as he does, then I know he'll want to see you. But for now we just have to let him be." He hugged her close and felt her draw in a deep breath.

"I'll try," she promised. She gazed up at him, her eyes flooding with tears. "But I miss him, Chuck," she went on, her voice bleak. "I miss him so much, and he's only been gone one day."

Chuck said nothing, suddenly unable to speak to her again or even look at her.

Mark closed the book he'd been reading and sprawled out on the bed, his eyes closed. He hadn't been able to concentrate on his homework, and knew he'd have to read the same section over again tomorrow night.

But he didn't care, for while his eyes had been scanning the pages, seeing the words but not really taking them in, his mind had been going back again and again over the events of last night and today.

He remembered the fight—remembered every humiliating moment of it. He'd never had a chance, not from the very beginning, when Jeff had first tackled him. And when it was finally over and he was in the ambulance on the way to the hospital, he'd felt like he was going to die. Nor had he felt much better when he woke up this morning.

But now, after the hours at the sports clinic, he felt fine. Sure, he had a few marks on his face, but the pain was gone, and the wounds seemed to be healing rapidly.

He'd come to a decision sometime during the morning:

never again would he allow himself to be beaten up the way Jeff LaConner had beaten him up. Even now the memory of it made him angry, and he clenched his right hand into a fist and punched his left palm with a sharp smack.

Startled by the sound, Chivas growled softly. Mark sat up and swung his feet off the bed.

"Things are going to change, boy," he muttered to the big dog, and reached down to scratch the animal's head. Chivas's ears dropped back against his skull. He whined softly, then slithered away from Mark's touch. Mark frowned, annoyed with the dog. But then, noticing the snow for the first time, he forgot his annoyance and went to the window to gaze out at the backyard.

The snow was nearly an inch deep on the roof of the rabbit hutch. Even from here Mark could see the little creatures huddling together in one corner of the cage. "Damn!" he muttered. "They're going to freeze to death. Come on, Chivas."

He left his bedroom and hurried down the stairs, Chivas trailing half-heartedly after him. It was only when he was at the hall closet, fishing his jacket out of the row of coats that hung there, that he noticed the hollow silence in the house. He called out, then shrugged indifferently when there was no answer. Putting on his jacket, he moved through the dining room and kitchen and opened the back door. Chivas barked happily, his mood suddenly changing as the blast of cold air from outside struck his nostrils. He bounded outside, coming to a sudden stop as his feet plunged into the icy chill of snow for the first time in his life.

The dog sniffed at the strange white stuff cautiously, then his tongue came out and licked tentatively at the wet, soft blanket that covered the yard. He took a step forward, hesitated, and with a leap, bounded out into the center of the yard, made three wide loops and rolled in the snow, working his shoulders deep into it. Regaining his feet, Chivas rushed toward Mark and dropped low to the ground, his tail wagging furiously. Mark grinned at him.

"You like this, huh?" he asked. "Well, let me take care of the rabbits, and then we'll find your ball."

Chivas, instantly understanding the reference to his favorite toy, hurtled out toward the back fence, snuffling wildly as he hunted for one of the well-chewed tennis balls he'd hidden in the yard.

Mark zipped his jacket up to his chin and walked quickly out to the rabbit hutch. The rabbits, still huddled together and shivering in the cold, seemed to be looking up at him expectantly.

"You guys getting a little cold?" he asked. "Well, we can fix that, can't we. 'Course," he added, glaring at the little creatures with mock severity, "you might have been warmer if you'd thought of going into your house."

He opened the door of the large cage, reached inside and turned the switch that controlled the single bulb suspended from the roof of the little shelter in the far corner.

The light came on but the rabbits didn't move.

"Come on," Mark urged them. "Don't be so dumb you stay out here and freeze to death!"

He reached toward them to herd them into the shelter. For a moment nothing happened. Then, before Mark could jerk his hand away, the big white male with black spots darted his head toward Mark's hand and nipped his finger. Reflexively, Mark jerked his hand back and stuck his bleeding finger in his mouth. He sucked for a moment, then pulled the finger out and stared at it.

The cut was small but deep, and as he watched, it began to bleed profusely.

"Goddamn it!" he swore out loud, his eyes fixing on the rabbit as a surge of unreasonable fury overwhelmed him. "I'll teach you!"

Reaching into the hutch, he seized the offending rabbit by the ears and dragged it away from its shivering companions. It squirmed in his hands, its hind legs kicking out as it tried to escape. But Mark was oblivious to the little animal's struggles.

He stared at it for a moment, his eyes cold and dead, then he grasped it by the neck.

A high-pitched squeal erupted from the rabbit's throat as Mark began to squeeze, the squeal cut off as Mark's other hand released the rabbit's ears and gave its head a sudden twist.

There was a soft cracking of bones. The rabbit went limp in Mark's hands.

He gazed at the little animal blankly for a moment, as if he weren't quite certain what he'd done.

Then, tossing it back into the hutch, he turned and started slowly back toward the house.

Chivas, a ball in his mouth, caught up with him at the back door and whined eagerly.

Mark ignored him.

16

Charlotte LaConner eyed the image in the mirror with lethargic disinterest. Could what she saw really be herself? But she knew the answer. The Charlotte LaConner she had grown up with—the gently smiling woman whose soft brown eyes had invariably gazed out at the world with calm acceptance—had disappeared almost completely over the past week. In her place was a pale ghost of her former self. The smile was gone, and around her lips a harsh picket fence of tiny lines had appeared. Her eyes, sunk deep from lack of sleep, flickered with suspicion, seeming even when at rest to be constantly moving, searching for some unseen enemy that must be lurking just out of sight, ready to spring out at her, to attack her if her vigilance flagged for even a moment.

The image in the mirror wore no makeup, its sallow complexion exposed for all the world to see, its stark features framed by a limp tangle of unwashed hair that bore a faintly oily sheen. But it didn't matter what that image looked like, Charlotte realized, for no one had seen it. After all, she hadn't been out of her house for more than a week.

It was Saturday afternoon, though Charlotte was only vaguely aware of it. Time, for her, seemed to have slowed down. Now, as she turned away from the mirror and its strange reflection of a person she was quite certain she didn't know, she felt herself moving with the slow rhythms of someone mired in a swamp. There were things she should be doing; she'd been keeping a mental list, adding items to it each day, as each day none of the previous items were checked off. The cleaning, for instance.

Newspapers were piled neatly by Chuck's favorite chair, the stack growing as each day she reminded herself to take them out but didn't. A thin layer of dust lay over the furniture, and wisps of lint had gathered in the corners. With a desperate effort, Charlotte tried to pull herself together to begin her chores, then sank down in front of the television, her hand automatically reaching for the remote control to flick it on. She sat still, her eyes fixed on the flickering image on the picture tube, but she didn't quite comprehend what she was seeing; the thick cobwebs that had settled over her mind effectively blocked out the inane stimulus of the cartoon on the screen.

Chuck had been patient with her, silently accepting her excuses at the beginning of the week that the snow was keeping her from going out. But the snow had melted by Tuesday morning and still Charlotte remained closeted within the house, retreating deeper and deeper within herself, desolated by her sudden and complete isolation from her son.

She was dimly aware of the back door opening and closing. When Chuck came into the little den where she sat—perched rigidly on the edge of the chair, as if afraid she might collapse completely if she let herself relax at all—her eyes slowly left the television set and focused on her husband.

Chuck gazed at her worriedly. She looked worse today, worse even than when he'd left this morning for a quick meeting with Jerry Harris. She was barely even speaking to him now, and as he'd watched her sitting at the kitchen table earlier, slowly stirring a cup of coffee long after it had turned cold, he'd wondered if she was lost to him, too, as Jeff was lost. But now, after meeting with Jerry, he had a fragile ray of hope. "Honey?" he said softly. "How are you feeling?"

Charlotte forced a wan smile. "There's so much to do," she replied, her eyes uncertainly scanning the room. "But I just can't make myself do it."

Chuck drew in his breath, then crossed to her, lowered himself to the arm of the chair and slipped an arm protectively around her. "You don't have to," he murmured. Her neck twisted and she gazed up into his eyes. "We're going away, honey. I've been transferred."

A look of confusion came into Charlotte's eyes, as if she weren't sure what the words meant. "T-Transferred? But we can't go anywhere now—it's the middle of the year. Jeff . . ." Her voice trailed off, as if the mere mention of their son's name had reminded her that he was no longer going to school.

"It's going to be all right," Chuck assured her. "All the arrangements have been made. We're going to Boston."

It was where Charlotte had grown up, and he'd hoped that the prospect of moving back home would snap her out of the depression that had closed around her during the past week, but she only stared at him for a moment, then shook her head.

"But of course we can't go." She spoke the words hollowly, as if repeating something Chuck must already know.

"No, darling," Chuck told her. "That's what the meeting this morning with Jerry was about. It's all set—we can leave any time. Even today, if you want to."

At last his words seemed to penetrate her fog. She looked at him again, almost suspiciously, like a mouse sniffing around the cheese in a trap before trying to snatch it. Then her eyes cleared.

"But we can't do that!" she exclaimed. She shook Chuck's arm away and rose to her feet. "We can't just pack up and go—what about Jeff? We have to make arrangements for him—find a hospital for him. . . ." Then, seeing the bleak emptiness in her husband's eyes, the full truth of what he was saying sank into her. "Dear God!" she breathed. "You don't mean for us to take him at all, do you? You think we're just going to go away and leave him here—"

"No," Chuck protested, though he knew her words were the truth. It wasn't meant to be the way Charlotte made it sound. "We can't take him with us now," he admitted. "But when he's better, Jerry says—"

"Jerry!" Charlotte spat the name at him. "I might have known Jerry Harris was part of this." Her eyes glowed with fury. "It's all part of another one of TarrenTech's grand schemes, isn't it?" Her voice rose dangerously and her eyes darted about the room as if she half expected to see Jerry Harris himself watching her from a corner. "Is that what it is?" she demanded. "They did something to Jeff, didn't they? And now they want to buy you off. What are they going to do, Chuck? Are they going to make us disappear, just like Tom and Phyllis Stevens did?"

It had been a wild stab, but she saw that it struck home. Her hand flew to her mouth at the look that came into Chuck's eyes, a look that was part pain, part fear.

"Don't be ridiculous," Chuck snapped, but his controlled reaction had come too late. She stood frozen where she was for a moment, listening to the lies that issued from his mouth. "Nothing happened to Tom and Phyllis. They're in New York. Tom is running the Travel Division and I saw Phyllis at a meeting in San Marcos not five months ago. She looks great."

Charlotte's eyes narrowed. "And what about Randy? Did they tell you how he is?" she fairly hissed at him. "Did you even ask?" He didn't answer for a moment, and her voice rose perilously. "Did you?" she screamed.

Chuck was on his feet now, and he took a step toward her. "No, I didn't," he began, "but—"

Charlotte backed away from him, then spun around and fled from the room. It was a trap! She knew it now. All of it was a trap. She had to get out, had to get out of the house, away from Chuck and everything that was happening. She ran to the front door, not even pausing to grab a jacket. It didn't matter, for she didn't even feel the chill of the air as she burst outside.

She paused in the middle of the street, her eyes darting toward the other houses on the block. Who was watching her? How many of them? Did they know what had happened? Were they all a part of it?

She started running, half staggering as her feet struck the uneven bricks of the pavement. She had to find help, find refuge.

But where?

Whom could she turn to? Whom could she trust?

Elaine Harris. Elaine had been her friend since . . .

She abandoned the thought. Elaine couldn't be trusted—she must be part of it. If Jerry was, Elaine must be, too.

And then she remembered.

There was one person she knew who might help her, might at least listen to her. Her breath coming in choking sobs, she turned and ran down the street.

Mark had left the house immediately after breakfast that morning, and Sharon had had to remind him to feed his rabbits, as she had every morning that week. His eyes had rolled with irritation and he'd suggested that Kelly do it, but Sharon had shaken her head. "They're your rabbits. You can't just dump them on your sister." He'd sighed heavily, but headed out to the backyard and quickly refilled the food and water containers inside the hutch. There were only five rabbits now, and as Sharon watched Mark hurriedly clean out the hutch, her eyes wandered to the small cross that marked the spot behind the garage where Kelly had insisted they bury the rabbit she'd found dead in the hutch last weekend.

It had been Mark who'd gone out to take a look when Kelly came running in that Saturday morning—the morning after the snowfall—crying that one of the rabbits had frozen to death. When he'd come back in, both Sharon and Blake looked inquiringly at him, but he only shrugged, seeming unconcerned. "I guess he didn't go in with the others," he said. "I turned the light on last night, and the rest of them are fine. I dumped him in the trash barrel."

Kelly, outraged at the indignity of the treatment accorded the dead animal, had insisted on a funeral for the rabbit, so after breakfast they all trooped out behind the garage and buried the little corpse in a shoe box. Only when Kelly had gone off to play with one of her friends had Sharon dug up the box, replacing it with a stone, and redeposited the rabbit in the trash barrel so Chivas wouldn't be tempted to dig it up and bring it into the house, proudly presenting it to her like a child who has just won a trophy.

But as the week had gone by, and it became increasingly clear that Mark's interest in the creatures was waning, she'd wondered what to do with the small colony that still survived. Blake had suggested eating them, and though Sharon could still remember eating rabbit when she was a little girl, the thought of devouring what had been family pets turned her stomach. Now, as Blake sat in his chair in the family room going over a stack of files, and Kelly sprawled on the floor staring at a cartoon on television, she gazed out the window at the furry creatures—all too unaware that their future had suddenly become uncertain—who were peacefully munching on their food. Perhaps they could simply release them and let them join the large colonies of jackrabbits that proliferated all over the valley. Her reverie was suddenly interrupted by a pounding at the front door. Before she had risen to her feet, Kelly was dashing out of the room. A minute later the little girl was back, her eyes wide and her voice trembling.

"There's a lady here," she said. "And she looks like she's crazy or something." She hesitated a second, then went on proudly, "I didn't let her in."

Frowning, Sharon went to the front door, Kelly trailing after her, and opened it a couple of inches. For a moment she didn't recognize Charlotte LaConner standing on the front porch, her face ashen, her dark-circled eyes reddened with tears. But at last Charlotte spoke. Gasping, Sharon pulled the door wide.

"Please," Charlotte rasped, her voice strained and her eyes darting back over her shoulder, as if she thought she were being followed. "I don't have anywhere else to go. You've got to let me in . . . please?"

As Kelly pressed close to her, Sharon held the door with one hand and drew Charlotte in with the other. "Charlotte! What is it? What's wrong?"

"They're making me go away," Charlotte sobbed. "They want me to just go away and forget about Jeff. But he's my son, Sharon!" she wailed. "I can't just forget him. I can't!"

Sharon stared at Charlotte LaConner, her mind whirling. What was the woman talking about? Jeff was in a hospital somewhere, wasn't he? She began guiding Charlotte gently toward the kitchen and the family room beyond, then realized that Kelly was still beside her, gazing curiously at the distraught woman. "Go up to your room, sweetheart," she said. "Just for a little while. All right?"

For a second she thought Kelly was going to protest, but then, as if she knew that something was happening that she didn't need to know about, she trotted up the stairs. When she got to the top, she turned and looked back. "Is she Jeff LaConner's mother?" she asked.

Sharon hesitated, then nodded. Kelly seemed on the verge of saying something else, but abruptly changed her mind and disappeared down the hall toward her room.

Blake was on his feet when Sharon and Charlotte came into the family room. When he saw the state Charlotte was in, he quickly began stuffing files back into the briefcase. "I'll be out of here in a second," he mumbled. He fell silent as Charlotte LaConner's bleary eyes fixed on him.

"Are you in on it, too?" she demanded, her voice reduced now to a hoarse rattle. Gasping for air, nearly spent from her wild run through the streets, she allowed herself to collapse onto the sofa. But her eyes never left Blake.

"I . . . in on it?" Blake asked. What was the woman talking about? Of course, he knew about Jeff LaConner's breakdown. He'd even helped set up the boy's admission to a private mental institution near Denver.

Charlotte LaConner's eyes were wild now. "They're all part of it, you know," she rasped, her eyes flicking toward Sharon. "They did something to Jeff, and they don't want me to find out what it is. They won't let me see him. They even say it's my fault!" She buried her head in her hands and began sobbing. Sharon reached out, wanting to comfort her, but Charlotte shrank away from her touch.

The door bell rang, and Charlotte flinched visibly at the sound. Wordlessly, Blake hurried out of the room, and a moment later Sharon heard the faint sounds of whispered conversation. Then Blake was back.

Behind him, his eyes veiled with worry, was Chuck LaConner. As soon as he saw Charlotte, his sigh of relief filled the room.

"I'm sorry," he said to Sharon, going to sit next to his wife. But as he tried to slip his arm protectively around Charlotte, she shrank from him as a moment ago she had from Sharon. "I wasn't sure where she went. I've been driving around, looking for her." He paused, then reached out to Charlotte once again. "Honey, it's going to be all right. I'm here, and I'm going to take care of you."

"No!" Charlotte lurched to her feet and scuttled away until she had backed herself into a corner of the room and could go no farther. She froze there for a moment. Dimly, as if from a great distance away, she could hear her husband's voice.

"You have to understand," he was saying. "Ever since the trouble with Jeff started she's been getting worse and worse."

She had to get hold of herself—she had to! He was going to convince them that she was crazy, and if that happened . . .

She drew a deep breath, then another. She stood quite still for a moment more, then slowly, her hands held carefully at her sides, turned to face the three people who were watching her. Though every one of her frayed nerves demanded she turn away once again, cried out for her to give in to the panic that was building inside her, she knew she couldn't. She swallowed, trying to clear her throat of the lump that threatened to cut off her breathing, then took another breath.

"I'm all right," she said, praying that her voice didn't betray her now. "I just . . . well, it's been a terrible week for me, and I guess I just came apart for a minute."

Her eyes held Chuck's as she silently pleaded with him to say no more. If he understood the look, he chose to ignore it.

"It's the strain of the last week," he said, his eyes meeting Blake's. "You know the situation—Jeff's in isolation and—" He stopped, his gaze shifting away from the Tanners. "Well," he finally went on, "I'm afraid Charlotte's begun imagining things." He moved across the room and took his wife's hand. "Come on, darling," he said quietly. "Let's go home and let you get some rest."

When they were gone, the house seemed oddly silent. It was Blake who finally spoke, after shaking his head sadly. "I've been working on it all week," he said. "Something just snapped in Jeff's head." He ran his tongue thoughtfully over his lower lip. "And I guess it's pretty obvious where the instability came from, isn't it?"

Sharon said nothing, for while Chuck LaConner had tried to explain what was happening to his wife, her eyes had remained on Charlotte.

And in Charlotte's eyes, she had read a clear message.

Don't believe him. Please . . . don't believe him.

Mark Tanner and Linda Harris were coming down out of the hills above Silverdale. They'd been hiking for an hour, and though Mark had taken his camera with him, so far he hadn't taken a single picture. Even when a large buck with antlers spread proudly above his head had emerged from a grove of aspens and instantly frozen in place, staring at them, Mark had made no move to capture the image.

"What's wrong with you?" Linda finally demanded, her voice sharp with exasperation. The buck, after nearly two minutes, had bounded away and disappeared, Chivas half-heartedly chasing it for a few yards before giving up and rejoining them as they started back toward town. "I thought you liked to take pictures of everything."

Mark shrugged laconically. "I did," he agreed. "But I don't know—lately it seems like taking pictures is just like everything else I used to do." He fell silent, trying to find the words to explain to Linda what was happening to him. "Taking pictures is sort of like standing on the outside, looking in," he went on. "And I'm just tired of feeling like I'm left out of everything."

Linda glanced at him out of the corner of her eye. Ever since the night he'd gotten beaten up, he seemed different, but so far he hadn't been willing to talk about it. In fact, she'd hardly seen him all week; three times she'd had to go to cheerleading practice after school, and the other two days Mark had gone out to the sports center to keep his appointments with Dr. Ames. "You mean like sports?" she asked now, keeping her voice as casual as possible. To her surprise, Mark only nodded.

"I guess so," he admitted. "I mean, always before, I didn't really care about being so small, 'cause I didn't want to go out for anything anyway." He grinned at her then, and exaggeratedly flexed one of his arms. "But all of a sudden I'm starting to work out, and I'm putting on some weight. Watch!" He dropped to the ground and did fifty push-ups while Linda watched, astonished. He was barely even breathing hard when he was done. "What do you think of that?" he asked. "Three weeks ago I couldn't even have done ten."

"Big deal," Linda commented sourly. "So you can do push-ups. Who cares? Jeff LaConner used to be able to do a hundred. And look what happened to him!"

"Aw, come on," Mark replied, suddenly deflated. He'd been so sure she'd be at least a little bit impressed. "Just because I'm trying to get in shape doesn't mean I'm going to turn into an asshole like Jeff!"

Linda glared at him. "He wasn't always an asshole, you

know. When I first started going out with him, he was really nice. In fact," she added pointedly, "he was real nice till he turned into a sports nut!"

Mark felt his cheeks burn. "Well, I'm not going to do that," he protested. They were walking along the river now, the Harrises' house only a block away. "And what's wrong with trying to be like everyone else?" he demanded. "Maybe I'm sick of not fitting in!"

Linda said nothing until they were a few yards from her house, then she turned to face him. "Look," she said. "I'm not mad at you or anything like that. I'm just worried about you, okay? And if you want to 'fit in'—whatever that means—I'm sure it's all right with me. But if you're going to turn into another Jeff LaConner, you might as well tell me right now."

Mark stared at her, baffled. Turn into Jeff LaConner? He wasn't anything like Jeff, and never would be. "But I'm not," he protested. "I'm still me, and I always will be."

They turned up the driveway of the Harrises' house. From the apron in front of the garage, Robb waved to them. "Hey, Mark!" he called out. "Want to shoot some baskets?" He took aim and tossed the basketball in his hands expertly through the hoop. When his eyes met Mark's, Mark was certain he saw a challenge in Robb's look. For a split-second he hesitated. Then a grin spread across his face. "Sure," he called back. "Why not?" He sprinted down the driveway, Chivas trotting after him, and didn't notice the look of disappointment that came into Linda's eyes before she turned away and hurried into the house.

Ten minutes later Mark was beginning to breathe hard, but he was pleased that despite Robb's size and ability, he'd still managed to score three baskets. Now, dribbling the ball carefully and edging toward the basket, he searched for an opportunity to duck around Robb. He made his move, feinting left, then dodging around to the right, but just as he leaped toward the basket, he felt Robb's elbow dig sharply into his ribs. He grunted as a stab of pain shot through him and the ball went wild, bouncing off the backboard and dropping into Robb's hands. Robb immediately rose into a smooth lay-up, and the ball sailed through the hoop.

"Doesn't count," Mark yelled. "You fouled me!"

"Tough shit," Robb grinned. "You see a referee anywhere around?"

A flash of anger swept over Mark. "What the hell are you talking about?" he demanded. "A foul's a foul."

Robb shrugged. "I play to win," he said, idly flipping the ball through the hoop once more.

Mark stared at him. "There are rules to this game, you know."

The grin faded from Robb's lips, and his eyes hardened. "The only rule I know is the one about winning," he said. He dropped the ball and gave Mark a shove. Surprised by the sudden move, Mark staggered backward.

Robb shoved him again, and now Mark's back hit the garage door. "Come on," he said, "what's going on?"

"Chicken?" Robb asked. "Is the little boy mad 'cause he lost a point?"

Mark's jaw tightened, and before he truly realized what he was doing, his fist flashed out, catching Robb on the jaw. Robb's eyes widened slightly, then his lips twisted into a malicious smile.

"So you want to fight, huh?" he mocked. "Is the little boy finally growing up?"

He began throwing punches then, his jabs barely touching Mark as he taunted the smaller boy. Finally he moved in close, and Mark seized his opportunity. Clenching his right fist tight, he threw himself toward Robb, plunging his fist into the other boy's stomach. A burst of air erupted from Robb's lungs and he lurched back, clutching his stomach and struggling to recapture his breath. Just as he was about to strike out at Mark once more, the back door of the house opened and Elaine Harris rushed out.

"Stop it!" she demanded. "Stop it this instant!" Both boys, startled by the sharpness of her words, turned to face her. She glared angrily at Robb. "I don't want to hear any excuses at all," she declared. "You're nearly a foot taller than Mark and you outweigh him by fifty pounds. Now you get into the house, and when your father gets home, you can explain this to him!" She waited, her hands planted on her hips, and finally Robb, his head ducked low, hurried past her and disappeared inside. When Elaine spoke again, her voice was gentle and apologetic.

"I'm sorry," she said. "Whatever happened, he shouldn't have taken a punch at you."

Mark felt his face burning with shame. What did she think he was, some kind of little kid who couldn't even defend himself? As he wordlessly turned away and hurried down the driveway, he remembered what had happened on the night when he *hadn't* been able to defend himself.

But today had been different. Today, even after Robb had taken a swing at him, he hadn't tried to run away.

This time he'd stood his ground and fought back.

And for a moment, after he'd landed the blow to Robb's belly, it looked like he might have won the fight. Of course, Robb had already been recovering from the blow when Mrs. Harris had come out, and he might yet have taken a pounding.

But still, at least he'd tried this time.

In fact, he'd sort of enjoyed the fight, he realized as he started home.

The feeling of pleasure in physical combat was something he'd never experienced before.

It had certainly never before occurred to him that he might like it.

17

It had been a quiet morning in the county hospital, and when Susan Aldrich glanced up at the clock suspended on the wall above her desk behind the admissions counter, she was surprised to see that it was only nine-thirty. That was the problem on the quiet days, she reflected—time seemed to crawl. She glanced out at the waiting room, then smiled almost ruefully when she saw that it had already been cleaned up. Nor could she fill a few minutes by setting up a fresh pot of coffee, either, for she had seen Maria Ramirez heading for the kitchen only a few moments ago.

Maria had become a fixture in the little hospital, and as the endless days of sitting next to the bed close by her son had turned into weeks, Maria had slowly begun developing a routine of her own. It had started with the simple housekeeping of Ricardo's room, but slowly she had expanded her domain, never asking if anything needed to be done, but simply watching the duty nurse and the orderlies as they went about their chores, then quietly relieving them of some of their tasks. At first Susan had tried to assure Maria that she needn't bother with the work she had cut out for herself, but she had only smiled at the nurse.

"You do so much for my son," she had replied. "And if I can't help him, at least I can help the people who can." So Susan, like Karen Akers and the other members of the staff, had left Maria alone to fill her time as she saw fit. By now, much of the routine work of the day shift—and the evening shift, too—was being expertly done by the slim and graceful woman whose dark eyes never seemed to miss anything.

Susan had come to realize that, in a way, Maria was helping her son as well, for all the staff had taken to dropping into Ricardo's room several times a day, sometimes simply standing next to his bed for a moment, at other times taking a few minutes to talk to him, even though all of them were privately certain that he was oblivious to their presence. Mickey Esposito—the day orderly, many of whose duties had quietly been usurped by Maria—had fallen into the habit of bringing a book to work and spending several hours quietly reading aloud to the inert form held motionless in the Stryker frame. The first time Mac MacCallum had stopped in while Mickey was reading to Rick, the orderly had looked up guiltily and closed the book, but Mac had told him to go on. "None of us knows what's going on in his mind," he'd assured Mickey. "We don't think he can hear us, but we don't know. And if he can, he must be eternally grateful for what you're doing."

Ricardo's room had become the focal point of the hospital. The small staff no longer gathered around the Formica table in the kitchen on their breaks, but gathered at Ricardo's bedside instead. Now, with a few extra minutes on her hands, Susan automatically wandered down the hall to look in on the boy. Her eyes, as always, quickly scanned the monitors over his bed, and she frowned. His heartbeat, always so perfectly regular, was fluctuating madly, and his eyes, which had remained closed and still since the moment he'd been brought into the hospital, were moving spasmodically behind his closed lids.

Even as she stared unbelievingly at the screen, an alarm bell sounded outside the room, alerting the tiny hospital to a

Code Blue. Within a few seconds MacCallum appeared, followed by two orderlies and Maria Ramirez.

"What is it?" Maria asked, her voice fearful, her eyes locked on the still form of her son. Then his eyes moved again, and Maria gasped. "He's waking up!"

She pushed close to the bed and leaned down just as MacCallum turned to Susan Aldrich and began snapping out orders for emergency equipment to be brought in. Maria looked up, the eagerness that had filled her eyes a moment ago now replaced with fear. "What is it?" she asked. "Is something wrong?"

MacCallum's lips tightened. "He's going into cardiac arrest," he said.

Maria's eyes widened and her face went ashen. Then she looked down at Rick again, and as she watched, his eyes suddenly blinked open and his mouth began to work. A sound—faint and rasping—rattled in his throat. Maria leaned closer, her hand closing on her son's. "I'm here, Ricardo. It's going to be all right."

Ricardo blinked then, and once more his lips moved. Maria pressed her ear close. Even as an orderly hurried into the room with a cart bearing the equipment to apply electroshock to Ricardo's heart, she thought she heard her son breathe a single word.

"Good-bye . . ."

For a split-second Maria wasn't certain she'd heard the word at all, but then, as MacCallum moved her aside so he could rip the gown from Ricardo's chest and press the electrodes against the boy's skin, she made up her mind.

"No!" she said sharply, her voice echoing oddly in the small room.

Everyone around the bed stopped what they were doing and stared at Maria.

"But he's going to—" MacCallum began. He stopped as Maria nodded.

"He's going to die," she said softly. "I know it. He knows it. We must let him go."

Susan Aldrich gasped, and MacCallum himself flinched at Maria's words. He glanced at the monitors once more. Ricardo's blood pressure was dropping rapidly and his heartbeat was coming only spasmodically now. "Are you sure?" he asked.

Maria hesitated only the barest fraction of a second. Her eyes were flooded with tears, but she nodded. "I'm sure. We must let him go. He has said good-bye to me, and so I must say good-bye to him." Then, as the others watched in silence, she leaned down and gently kissed Ricardo's lips.

Susan Aldrich took one of the boy's hands in her own, and Mickey Esposito took the other. Mac MacCallum reached down to lay his hand on the boy's forehead. Though all of them knew that Ricardo was totally incapable of any kind of speech, none of them was willing to take Maria's single consolation away from her. A moment later Ricardo Ramirez's eyes opened once more and appeared to come into brief focus.

What might have been only a spasmodic twitching—but could also have been the barest trace of a smile—worked at the corners of his mouth.

Then his eyes closed once more. The line on the heart monitor went flat. And a single steady note—almost like a dirge—began to sound.

Ricardo Ramirez was dead.

Half an hour later Mac MacCallum sat in his office, numbly staring at the completed death certificate. Like the rest of the staff at County Hospital, he had been taken completely by surprise by the boy's sudden death. Like the others, Mac had also taken to dropping by Rick's room several times each day—not because there was anything specific that needed to be done for the boy, but simply because even in his comatose condition, there was something about the boy that reached out to him. He, too, had come to regard

Rick as more than simply a patient. Quite simply, even though he and Rick had never exchanged so much as a single word, Mac MacCallum had come to regard him as a friend.

Now his friend was dead, and Maria Ramirez, whom MacCallum also had come to think of as a friend, was sitting in the waiting room, only her eyes betraying the depth of her grief, trying to come to terms with the loss of the single thing in her life she had truly loved and believed in. Finally, his features setting harshly, MacCallum reached for the phone and called Phil Collins at Silverdale High School, then waited impatiently, drumming his fingers on his desktop while the coach was summoned from the playing field.

"It's Dr. MacCallum," Mac said when Collins came on the line. "I know you don't really care, but Ricardo Ramirez died half an hour ago."

"Christ," Collins swore, but MacCallum was certain the only emotion in the coach's voice was worry, not regret. "What's going to happen now?"

"I don't know," MacCallum replied. "But I can tell you that I'm very well aware of what you and Ames and TarrenTech have lined up for Maria, and I don't think it's enough." His voice hardened. "I've had it with you and your football team, Collins. We had a broken leg in here last weekend, and a ruptured spleen day before yesterday." He hesitated, briefly wondering whether or not he would be able to back up his next words, then plunged on. "I'm going to suggest to Maria that she institute a wrongful death suit against you, the school, Jeff LaConner, his parents, Marty Ames, and Rocky Mountain High. I don't know what you're all up to, but it's got to stop right now."

"Now wait a minute," Collins began, but MacCallum cut him off.

"No, Collins," the doctor breathed, and gently replaced the phone in its cradle. He didn't know what, if anything, he'd accomplished, didn't even really believe a wrongful death suit would get anywhere. But at least he felt better.

In his own office, Phil Collins stared at the dead phone in

his hand for a moment, then rattled the button on the cradle until a dial tone buzzed. He punched the digits for Marty Ames's private number, then waited, drumming his fingers impatiently in unconscious duplication of Mac MacCallum a few minutes earlier. When Ames came onto the line, Collins repeated MacCallum's words almost verbatim.

Two minutes after that, Ames was repeating them to Jerry Harris.

"All right," Harris replied tiredly. He thought a moment, then spoke again. "We'll have to clean up the LaConner situation right now. Can you make whatever preparations we might need?"

"Of course," Ames replied.

Before he called Chuck LaConner into his office, Jerry Harris made arrangements for one of the TarrenTech corporate helicopters to prepare to make a flight to Grand Junction, where a Learjet would be waiting.

Charlotte LaConner felt an empty hollowness in her stomach. She couldn't have heard Chuck right—it had to be a mistake. Perhaps, after all, she *was* beginning to imagine things, as he'd been insisting since that terrible moment at the Tanners' the other day—she could no longer quite remember which day it was—when Chuck had as much as told Blake and Sharon that she was losing her mind. Maybe she was even imagining that he'd come home from work in the middle of the morning today. Maybe he wasn't really here at all.

She shook her head dazedly. "Pack a bag?" she asked. "Now?"

Chuck nodded. "That's right," he said. "I'm leaving."

"But, I don't understand."

"I'm being transferred, honey, remember?" Chuck said. "I'm going to Boston."

Charlotte's hands fluttered in a helpless gesture. "But I thought—I thought we were waiting for Jeff. . . ."

"I can't, Charlotte," Chuck replied. "I have to go now. Today. There's a chopper waiting for me."

Charlotte sighed with relief. Then it was all right. He was leaving, but she didn't have to. She could stay here and wait until Jeff got better. "M-Maybe I'll go to Boulder," she said. "I could be closer to Jeff then." The fingers of her right hand were working at her left now, the nails—ragged and unkempt from the totally unconscious habit she'd developed over the past few days of biting at them as she sat staring vacantly at nothing—digging into her skin, leaving angry red marks.

But Chuck shook his head. "I'm sorry, Charlotte," he said softly. He couldn't look at her now, couldn't bring himself to watch the pain in her face as he told her what was about to happen to her. "You're going to have to go into the hospital for a while. I've discussed it with Jerry and Marty Ames, and we all agree that you need a good rest. A period of time to adjust to what's happened and get over these paranoid ideas."

Charlotte recoiled from the words as if she'd been struck. "No," she whimpered. "You can't do that to me! I'm your wife, Chuck—"

"Honey, be reasonable," Chuck pleaded, but Charlotte was no longer listening to him. She ducked around him, rushing out of the room and stumbling up the stairs to the second floor, where she ran into the master bedroom, locking the door behind her.

She was in a state of panic now. They were going to take her away and lock her up, just like they'd taken Jeff away. But why? What had she done? All she'd wanted to do was see her son, talk to him, tell him she loved him.

But they wouldn't let her!

Why?

She knew now. It was suddenly clear to her; she should have realized it long ago! They were lying to her, had been lying to her right from the start. Jeff wasn't in a private hospital at all, not in Boulder or anywhere else. They had him locked up somewhere, where neither she nor anyone else could see him. He wasn't sick! He was being held prisoner somewhere!

Help! She had to get help before it was too late. She scrabbled around in the top drawer of her nightstand, where she was certain she'd hidden the scrap of paper on which she'd scribbled Sharon Tanner's phone number. She found it at last, then fumbled with the phone as her trembling fingers refused to obey her churning mind.

It was at that moment, while she frantically tried to dial the number, that she might have looked up and glanced out the window; might have seen the ambulance approaching the house and turning into the driveway. But she didn't look, didn't see, didn't have time to flee from the house.

Her fingers finally found the right buttons, and she waited in panic as the phone at the other end rang four times, then five, then six. What if Sharon wasn't home? What would she—

Then, to her relief, she heard a breathless voice at the other end.

"Sharon?" she said. "Sharon, you have to help me. They're going to send me away. They've done something terrible with Jeff, and they don't want me to find—"

"Charlotte?" Sharon Tanner's voice broke in. "Charlotte, what's wrong? You're not making any sense."

Charlotte forced herself to stop talking and willed her body to stop trembling. She focused her mind, drew a deep breath, and was about to begin again when she heard a banging at the bedroom door. "Charlotte?" It was Chuck's voice. "Charlotte, you have to let me in." Then she heard Chuck speaking to someone else, and her carefully constructed calm shattered like a house of cards.

"Oh, God," she whimpered. "Sharon, they're here! They've come for me, Sharon! What will I do?"

There was a crash, and the bedroom door burst open. Chuck, followed by two attendants, burst into the room, stared bleakly at her for a moment, and while she stood speechlessly watching him, came over, took the phone from her hand and replaced the receiver.

"It's going to be all right, darling," he told her, putting

his arms around her and holding her gently as he nodded to the two other men. As one of them disappeared from the room, the other came forward and slipped a needle into her shoulder.

Too stunned by what was happening even to protest, Charlotte began sobbing silently as the drug took quick effect. A moment later the second attendant reappeared with a collapsible gurney.

Charlotte was already unconscious when they lifted her onto the stretcher.

Sharon gazed dumbly at the phone that had gone dead in her hand, as if she didn't quite understand what had happened. But a moment later she made up her mind, riffled through the pages of the thin Silverdale phone book until she found the LaConners' address, then hunched into her jacket as she ran out of the house, cursing softly under her breath over the fact that she and Blake had decided against replacing the worn-out Subaru he'd used for commuting in San Marcos. Right now, the last thing she needed was a leisurely walk. By the time she reached the corner, she was already half trotting, the memory of the crash she'd heard over the phone still ringing in her ears. And Charlotte had sounded so frightened, so utterly terrified.

She broke into a jog, moving through the sharp mountain air completely oblivious to the biting cold. She paused at the corner of Colorado Street, and was about to cross it when an ambulance, its lights flashing but its siren silent, sped through the intersection. It turned left and disappeared around a bend. She swore again, suspecting that Charlotte was in the vehicle, knowing that if she'd had a car, she would have followed it. But there was nothing she could do now, and catching her breath, she trotted across the street then on toward Pueblo Avenue and the LaConners' house.

From the outside it looked no different from the other

houses on the block. Set well back from the sidewalk, it was almost an exact copy of the Tanners' own house. Yet there was something about the house—a sense of something wrong—that made Sharon uneasy. She glanced at the car in the driveway, then hurried up the front steps and pressed the door bell. There was no answer. After a moment Sharon pressed the bell again, then tried the door and found it unlocked. Her heart quickening, she pushed the door open and leaned inside.

"Charlotte?" she called out tentatively. "Charlotte, it's Sharon Tanner. Are you here?"

There was still no answer. Sharon stepped over the threshold, pushing the door closed behind her. She heard a movement upstairs, and a moment later Chuck LaConner appeared at the top of the steep flight of stairs, a suitcase in his hand. He paused, startled to see her.

"Sharon," he said. Then his eyes clouded. "That was you Charlotte was talking to on the phone, wasn't it?"

Sharon nodded. "What's happened to her?" she asked. "Is she all right?" Her eyes shifted to the suitcase.

Chuck held it up as if offering it as proof of something. "I'm afraid I'm in a hurry," he said, starting down the stairs.

"Where is she, Chuck?" Sharon asked. "What's going on?"

Chuck said nothing for a moment, then his shoulders slumped and he lowered himself wearily to sit on the stairs, still halfway up. "I guess there's no point in not telling you," he said at last, his voice hollow. "I—Well, I've had to have Charlotte institutionalized."

The sharp intake of Sharon's breath made a gasping sound, but Chuck shrugged helplessly. "There was nothing more I could do," he said. "You saw how she was on Saturday, and since then it only got worse. This morning she seemed a little better, so I went to work. And then an hour ago she called me. She was making all kinds of wild accusations, claiming the telephone was tapped and there were people watching the house." He shook his head sadly. "It didn't make any sense, of course, and finally I called a friend down in Canon City."

Sharon frowned. "Canon City?"

"It's over on the other side of the mountains, near Pueblo." His eyes met Sharon's. "There's a state mental hospital there," he said. "My friend is on the staff."

"I see," Sharon breathed, licking her lips.

"Anyway," Chuck went on, "he told me I'd better have Charlotte sent over there. So I called an ambulance, then came home." His lips tightened. He glanced at his watch, then stood up. "Come on up," he said. "You won't believe it."

Silently, Sharon followed Chuck to the master suite. The door, hanging crookedly from a single hinge, was pushed back against the wall, and the room itself was in chaos.

Chuck's clothes were strewn all over the floor, and even the drawers had been pulled from the dresser by the wall. "She had the door locked," he explained. "She told me she was throwing me out, that I was part of some plot she'd dreamed up. She wasn't anything like rational, and finally, well . . ." Again, he shrugged then glanced at his watch. "Look, I've got to go. I've got some of Charlotte's things here, and I have to take them over to Canon City."

"I see," Sharon whispered. She gazed around the ruined room once more, then followed Chuck back down the stairs and out of the house. "It—It must have been terrible for you," she said at last as Chuck tossed the suitcase into the backseat of the LaConners' Buick.

"It hasn't been easy," Chuck agreed as he slid in behind the wheel. His eyes met Sharon's gaze, and he hastily looked away. "But it's been a lot worse for her," he said. "I—I guess I just don't know what we're going to do now."

"If there's anything I can do," Sharon began, but Chuck waved her words away.

"I wish there were," he said sadly. "But I'm afraid there isn't. Not right now, anyway."

He started the car, then offered Sharon a lift, but she refused, and a moment later he drove away.

Sharon stood on the sidewalk, watching the Buick until it disappeared, then turned to look at the house once again.

In her memory she heard once more the disjointed telephone call in which Charlotte had pleaded for her help, and once more saw the look that had been in Charlotte's eyes on Saturday, just before Chuck had led her out of the Tanners' home.

Don't believe him, that look had said. *Please don't believe him!*

Then she pictured the chaos of the master bedroom. Though Chuck's clothes had been scattered everywhere, she hadn't seen so much as a trace of Charlotte's own clothing.

Charlotte's closet hadn't even been opened.

And yet Chuck had said he was packing Charlotte's things to take them to the hospital.

"Don't worry," Sharon said now, speaking out loud even though there was no one to hear her. "I don't believe him. I don't believe a single word he said!"

18

Sharon gazed uneasily at the TarrenTech building. She'd seen it before, of course, even admired it. It had been so perfectly designed for its environment that it almost looked like an outgrowth of the landscape itself. But now it seemed to have changed, taking on the appearance of an animal crouching in the undergrowth, awaiting its prey. But that was ridiculous, of course—it was nothing but a building, and nothing about it had changed. It was she herself who had changed, and even as she'd walked the half mile from the town out to the low building set amidst landscaped acreage, she'd felt the difference in herself. She'd tried to walk slowly, as if out for nothing more than a leisurely stroll, just in case someone happened to be watching her.

And that, too, was silly, she reminded herself now as she approached the front doors. She'd done nothing except respond to a call for help from an acquaintance. Why should people be watching her? Yet as she drew close to the entrance, she found herself glancing around uneasily, searching for the hidden cameras she knew were trained on her. But the cameras had no personal interest in her; they were nothing more than inanimate objects, continuously scanning the area around the building, alert for nothing in particular, but nevertheless recording everything that crossed their paths.

It was Charlotte LaConner's words that had put Sharon's nerves on edge, and they still echoed in her mind: "They're going to send me away. They've done something terrible with Jeff, and they don't want me to find out."

Had she meant TarrenTech, or had she meant the sports center?

Sharon had turned the words over in her mind, looking at them from every direction, and finally come to the conclusion that it didn't matter exactly what Charlotte had meant, for she was certain that one way or another the sports center, like nearly everything else in Silverdale, was totally dependent on TarrenTech for its survival. An operation like Marty Ames's couldn't possibly survive on the fees it could collect as a summer training camp for high school kids.

Unconsciously straightening her posture, Sharon pushed through the door and stepped up to the information desk, where she was met by a smiling receptionist.

"May I help you, Mrs. Tanner?"

Sharon frowned, then glanced instinctively at the girl's lapel, searching for the identification badge that all TarrenTech employees wore.

This girl wore none.

The girl's smile broadened as she realized Sharon's dilemma. "I'm Sandy Davis," she said. "And you don't know me. The security system did a photo comparison on you, so I knew who you were even before you came into the building."

Sharon's body stiffened. A photo check of *her*? But why? And how? She'd never given the company a picture of herself—they'd never even asked for one. But of course the answer was obvious: the cameras in San Marcos had recorded her comings and goings, and no doubt images of her had been transmitted to Silverdale along with the personnel files on Blake. Still, there was something eerie about it all, something creepy about knowing that she'd been spotted and identified even before she'd entered the building. She returned Sandy Davis's smile, hoping her nervousness wasn't showing.

"If you'll just tell me where my husband's office is?"

"Just down the hall to the left, turn right, and it's in the far corner, near Mr. Harris's."

Sharon started walking down the long corridor, but now that she was inside the building, the strange sensation of being watched was even stronger. She felt the hairs on the nape of her neck standing on end. Her step instinctively quickened, and she had to remind herself to appear as though nothing was wrong. By the time she reached Blake's suite, she was walking at a normal pace again. As soon as she stepped into the outer office, his secretary—another woman whom Sharon had never met—offered her a warm smile that was almost an exact copy of Sandy Davis's. "He's on the phone right now, but I slipped him a message that you're here," she said, after introducing herself with a firm handshake. "Would you like a cup of coffee?"

Sharon shook her head, and almost immediately the inner door opened and Blake stepped out. "This is a pleasant surprise," he said, smiling a welcome. "What are you doing all the way out here?"

Sharon quickly blurted out the first thing that came into her mind. "The car," she said. "I wanted to do some shopping, and the list was too long for my cart." Then she glanced at the secretary out of the corner of her eye. "Could we go inside?"

Blake looked puzzled, but he nodded and held the door open for her. It was Sharon herself who closed it when they were both in his office. He cocked his head. "What's going on that you don't want Ellen to hear?"

"It's Charlotte LaConner," she said, automatically lowering her voice. Carefully trying not to betray the emotions churning inside her, she explained to Blake what had happened. When she was finished, Blake looked at her, bewildered.

"You came all the way out here to tell me that?" he asked. "That Charlotte's had a breakdown? Honey, we both saw that coming a couple of days ago."

"It's not that," Sharon said nervously. "At least not

quite. It's what she *said*. That 'they' had done something to Jeff. I think she must have been referring to the sports center.''

"Or the great communist conspiracy," Blake observed archly. At the hurt he saw in Sharon's eyes, he tried to soften his words. "I didn't mean that," he said apologetically. "But we know Charlotte was getting paranoid, and with paranoia—"

"Was she?" Sharon interrupted. "I don't think we know that at all. We know she was upset, and she had every right to be. After what happened with Jeff, why wouldn't she be?"

Blake took a deep breath, then lowered himself into the chair behind his desk. "All right," he said. "What's on your mind? It's not just Charlotte, is it?"

Sharon hesitated, then shook her head. "I guess not," she said. "It's all kinds of things—things that wouldn't have bothered me at all if it were only one or two of them. But I keep getting the feeling that something's wrong out here, Blake." She made an expansive gesture, her trembling hands betraying her worry. "It's the whole thing—the town, the school, even the kids. Everything is too perfect."

Blake smiled wryly. "Apparently Jeff LaConner isn't perfect," he interjected. Then his expression turned serious. "The Ramirez boy died this morning," he went on. "I understand his mother is still trying to blame Jeff."

Sharon's eyes clouded with tears as she remembered the sad form of Rick Ramirez, but then her thoughts shifted back to Jeff LaConner. "But Jeff's gone, isn't he?" she asked. "And Charlotte started making a fuss about Jeff, and now she's gone, too."

"Now wait a minute," Blake began. "It's starting to sound like you're buying into—"

Sharon didn't let him finish. "I'm saying I'm not sure we did the right thing in coming here," she said. "At first, everything was fine. But now even Mark is starting to change. And it's happened since he started going to Dr. Ames."

"He's doing some exercises, and building himself up."

But again Sharon cut him off. "Yesterday he got into a

fight with Robb Harris. That's not like Mark—he's never fought with anyone in his life.''

Blake's jaw tightened and his arms folded over his chest. "What is it you want?" he asked. "You want me to pull Mark out of the sports center? Maybe we shouldn't stop there. Maybe I should quit TarrenTech and we should move back to California.''

"Maybe we should," Sharon heard herself blurt out. Was that what she'd really been thinking all along? She wasn't sure.

Suddenly she thought she saw Blake's eyes flick nervously around the room, almost as if he were afraid that even in the privacy of his own office they were being observed. He fumbled in his pocket a moment and tossed her his key ring. "Look," he said. "I know you're upset right now, and maybe you even have a right to be. But this is something we can discuss later, when we're at home. Okay? Take the car—I'll either walk or hitch a ride with Jerry this evening.''

It was a dismissal. For a moment Sharon was tempted to argue with him, to demand that they talk it out right now. But the expression on his face—and the strange flicker of nervousness in his eyes—made her keep silent. "All right," she said at last. She went over to kiss him, and for a fraction of a second thought he started to duck away from the gesture. "But I'm not kidding," she whispered into his ear. "Something's going on around here, Blake. I don't know what it is, but I'm going to find out.''

A moment later Blake walked her to the door and kissed her good-bye. Even as she left the office, she had the strange feeling that he hadn't really meant the kiss, that it had been given more for the benefit of some unseen audience than as a gesture of affection for her.

In his office next to Blake Tanner's, Jerry Harris switched off the tiny machine that had been recording every word spoken in the office next door. He leaned back in his chair, his hands clasped behind his head as he thought over what he'd just heard. Finally coming to a decision, he leaned forward and picked up the phone, dialing a series of digits from memory. A moment later Marty Ames came on the line.

"We may have another problem on our hands," he said, neither speaking Ames's name nor identifying himself. "I'll be out there within the hour. We can talk about it then."

"I've got a couple of things scheduled—" Ames began, but Harris cut him off abruptly.

"Change them." Harris hung up the phone, then removed the tiny microcassette from the recorder in the bottom drawer of his desk and slipped it into his pocket.

Charlotte LaConner had been dealt with.

And if it came to that, Sharon Tanner could be dealt with, too.

Sharon wasn't certain if she'd deliberately turned the wrong way when she left Blake's office, but she suspected she had. Nor did she know exactly why it was that she wanted to explore the offices of TarrenTech. Was she really looking for something specific, expecting to find some clue that would trigger the answers to all the vague and indefinable questions churning in her mind?

Of course not.

The building, like any other office complex, was just that: a maze of corridors with doors leading off them, some of them open, most of them closed. But still she moved on, wandering in the halls until even she was no longer certain where she was.

Then, in the distance, she heard a sound, as if some kind of an animal were in pain.

She hurried her step, moving toward it. A few seconds later it was repeated. She was in a wide corridor now, and ahead of her was a closed door with a wire-meshed window mounted in it at eye level; a few feet from the door was an elevator. Sharon paused for a moment, waiting for the sound to come again. While she was waiting, the elevator doors opened and a man dressed in what looked like a lab coat stepped out.

He was carrying a cardboard box—no more than a foot square—but even from where she stood, Sharon could clearly read a single word printed on its side in large red letters:

INCINERATE

As she watched, the eerie sound came again. The man frowned, then glanced toward the door with the reinforced window in it. When the sound came again, he set the box down on the floor, used a key to unlock the door, and pushed his way through.

Barely even considering her action before carrying it out, Sharon hurried to the box and picked it up. Lifting the lid, she peered inside, then nearly dropped the box as a gasp of surprise burst from her lungs.

She hesitated a split-second, her eyes flicking toward the ceiling as she searched for security cameras.

She saw none.

Making up her mind, she rummaged in her purse for the packet of Kleenex she always carried with her. Taking a deep breath, she reached into the box with trembling fingers, removed two of the objects it contained, and carefully wrapped them in a wad of tissue. Finally she gingerly placed the two wrapped objects in her purse. Putting the lid back on the box, she carefully replaced it on the exact spot from which she had picked it up a few seconds before, and hurried down the corridor.

She had just disappeared around the corner when the door near the elevator opened again and the lab technician emerged, picked up the box, and continued on his errand to the incinerator at the rear of the building.

Sharon had turned two more corners when she saw a man

in a guard's uniform coming toward her. Her first instinct was to duck through the nearest door, but she thought better of it.

"Excuse me," she said, only slightly too loudly, as the guard came near.

He eyed her suspiciously, then seemed to figure out what her problem was. "Lost?"

Sharon called forth an embarrassed smile. "I feel like a fool," she said. "I'm Mrs. Tanner. I stopped in to speak to my husband, and I must have turned the wrong way. . . ." She shrugged helplessly, and the guard's expression softened into an amused grin.

"Happens all the time," he told her. "One wrong turn around here and you can wander for twenty minutes before you find the lobby. Come on—I'll show you."

He walked along beside her, made a left turn then a right, and a moment later they were back in the main lobby. "Thank you," Sharon said as the guard held the door open for her. His fingers touched his hat politely and he turned away. Her heart pounding, Sharon stepped out into the chilly fall afternoon and scanned the parking lot for the station wagon.

It wasn't until she was well out of sight of TarrenTech that she pulled the car over to the side of the road, left the engine idling, and reached for the purse she'd dropped on the floor in front of the passenger seat.

Her fingers trembled as she opened the bag and pulled out the first of the two objects she'd removed from the box by the elevator.

It was a tiny white mouse, weighing no more than a couple of ounces.

It was dead, its body stiff with rigor mortis.

Sharon gazed at the tiny corpse for a moment, then carefully laid it on the car seat next to her.

The other object was larger, weighing nearly half a pound. It looked very much like the mouse, except that its feet and claws seemed abnormally large and its whole body had an oddly deformed look to it. Sharon's hands trembled even more violently as she held it, as if her hands themselves sensed something wrong.

The white rat—if that indeed was what it was—was also stiff with the rigor of death, but there was one other difference between it and the mouse.

The fur on the rat's neck had been shaved away and there was a dark bruise, in the center of which was a puncture mark, as if a needle had been used to pierce the rat's skin.

Both the animals had small metal tags attached to their right ears. Sharon had to fish in her purse once more to find her reading glasses before she could make out the tiny letters stamped on each of the tags.

The tags were nearly identical. Each bore the same series of numbers and letters: 05-08-89/M#61F#46.

But on the tag on the rat there was an additional number: GH13.

Sharon stared at the creatures for a moment, trying to figure out what the numbers might mean. The first six digits, she was absolutely certain, were a date. But the rest?

And then she thought she knew the answer, but it didn't quite make sense.

Quickly returning the two small corpses to her purse, she put the car in gear and sped away, her mind already trying to figure out a way to confirm her suspicions.

Was it really possible, she wondered, that the two animals could have come from the same litter? And if they had, what had been done to the second creature that could have made it grow so large?

She shuddered, knowing already that she didn't want to know the answer—and at the same time knowing that nothing would stop her from finding out exactly what that answer was.

Mark closed his notebook as the three-ten bell rang and fished under his desk for his book bag. He hadn't taken much in the way of notes today; indeed, he'd found it hard to concentrate on the history class at all. Instead he'd found himself fidgeting and glancing at the clock every few minutes, waiting eagerly for the bell to ring. Now, as the last echoes of its shrill clanging died away, he was on his feet and out the door. He took the stairs to the main floor two at a time, then paused as he heard Linda Harris calling his name. She hurried up to him, her expression apologetic.

"I'm sorry about this morning," she told him. For the first time in nearly three weeks, she hadn't met him at the corner three blocks from the school so they could walk the rest of the way together. He'd waited a few minutes, then decided she wasn't coming at all. When he'd gotten to school he found that she was already there, sitting on the steps with Tiffany Welch. When he'd spoken to her, she pretended she didn't hear him for a minute, then been cool when she finally acknowledged his presence. "I—I guess I acted like a kid this morning, didn't I?" she asked now.

Mark shrugged. "I just don't see why you're so mad," he said.

Linda fell in beside him as he started toward the main doors. "I guess I'm not mad, really," she said. "I just . . ." She looked at him a moment, her brows knit into a frown, and decided not to utter the words hovering on the tip of her tongue. "Never mind," she said. "Where you going? Want to go get something to eat?"

Mark shook his head. "Can't. I have an appointment with Dr. Ames."

Suddenly the frown was back on Linda's brow. "How come?"

"He's just checking me over," Mark replied distractedly as his eyes scanned the crowd of students that filled the hallway. "Did you see Robb anywhere?"

Now Linda's expression grew bewildered. "Robb?" she asked. "I thought you and Robb had a fight yesterday!"

"We did." Mark grinned. "And I could have taken him, too, if your mom hadn't stopped us. Anyway, he's going out to the center, too. He said he'd meet me here."

Just then Robb came around the corner from the eastern wing and tossed his book bag to his sister. "Take it home for me?" he asked. Linda gave him a sour look.

"What if I don't?" she challenged.

"But you will," Robb teased. "You don't want to look like a brat in front of your boyfriend, do you?" He snickered as both Linda and Mark reddened, then delivered a light rabbit punch to Mark's upper arm. "Come on—Ames hates it if we're late."

Mark hesitated only a second, turning away before he saw the dark look that came into Linda's eyes. Following Robb, he trotted down the steps toward the rack where the other boy's bike was parked. As Robb got the bike moving, Mark jumped onto the rack on the back, feeling the metal tubing give slightly as it accepted his weight.

"Jesus Christ," Robb complained. "How much do you weigh?"

"Five pounds more than last week," Mark replied. "And it's all muscle, so you'd better watch out!"

Linda, standing at the top of the steps as she watched the two boys ride away from school, felt a strange mix of emotions. She supposed it was nice that Robb and Mark were becoming friends again, and she'd already decided that she couldn't expect Mark never to change, but still, there was a little voice inside her that kept telling her something was wrong, that Mark wasn't really changing at all.

Instead she had the weird feeling that he was *being* changed, and that he didn't even know it. Disconsolately, she slung Robb's book bag over her arm and started home.

"There's my boy!" Marty Ames exclaimed as he strode into the examining room where Mark was stripped down to his underwear. A nurse had already checked his blood pressure and pulse, weighed him, measured him, and checked his lung capacity. "How're you feeling?"

"Great," Mark told him. "I'm up another couple of pounds, and I've grown almost half an inch."

Ames's brows arched appreciatively and he scanned the newest statistics the nurse had entered into Mark's computerized medical record. "Lungs up a few cc's, too," he commented. His eyes shifted to Mark. The bruises on his face had almost completely disappeared, and only a thin scar marked the spot where his forehead had been cut. "Any pain in your ribs?" Mark shook his head. "Well, in that case, I pronounce you healthy."

Mark's face registered his disappointment. "You mean that's it?" he asked uncertainly. "I'm done out here?"

"I didn't say that." Ames chuckled. "In fact, now's when the real work begins. The vitamins are all fine, but you still have to do most of the work. Pull on a pair of shorts and come with me."

Mark fished in his book bag for the gym shorts he'd started carrying with him the previous week, then put on his socks and tennis shoes. Leaving the rest of his clothes and the book bag where they were, he followed Ames out of the examining room and through the halls to the gym. He'd spent time here before, learning how each of the machines worked and how it acted on his muscles, but today Ames led him through a door into a smaller room where Robb Harris was already working out on a rowing machine, his eyes fixed on the screen that curved around in front of him.

Mark hesitated as he saw the needles in Robb's thighs and the I.V. tubes attached to them. "What's going on?" he asked.

As Mark settled himself onto a rowing machine that was an exact twin of the one Robb was using, and one of the aides began adjusting it to fit his body, Ames explained the monitoring system and its purpose.

"We need to know exactly what happens to your body when you work out. The easiest way to do that is to analyze the chemical changes in your blood. And for that," he added, grinning in a parody of sadistic pleasure, "we have to puncture your veins and stick needles in your flesh."

Mark chuckled at Ames's exaggerated villainy, but still winced as the needles were slipped into him then taped securely in place. A moment later, as he began rowing, the first of the images flashed on the screen, and soon he found himself involved in the illusion that he was actually competing in a race with other rowers.

He leaned into the machine, increasing his pace, and a sheen of sweat broke out on his brow.

Then, as one of his two-dimensional competitors slipped by him on the left, he felt a surge of anger. Swearing silently, he pulled yet harder on the oars and a moment later overtook the image on the screen.

He rowed steadily for a while, keeping pace with the other oarsmen, but then they began to creep up on him, and he felt his anger begin to grow once more.

Almost imperceptibly, the image on the screen flickered. It happened so quickly that Mark was barely aware that it had occurred at all. The other boats were gaining on him now, and the muscles in his arms and legs were beginning to ache. Sweat dripped from his forehead, stinging his eyes, and he could feel it running down his back and under his arms as well.

The image on the screen kept flickering, but he was oblivious to it, his anger growing steadily as the other boats inexorably overtook him. He was furious now, almost trembling with the rage he felt toward the other rowers.

Then, slowly, he began to think of his mother.

He didn't know why she came into his mind, for he was totally unaware of her image as it was flashed subliminally on the screen, far too quickly and too briefly for his conscious mind to register.

But deep inside himself he was becoming convinced that it was her fault he was losing the race against the other rowers.

Her fault—for babying him all his life, for making excuses for him, for insisting that he was different from the other kids.

But he wasn't different.

He was only smaller, and weaker.

He rowed harder, grunting with the strain, trying to catch up with the other rowers. He would catch up—he knew it.

He was growing now, and getting stronger, and maybe it wouldn't happen today, but in the end he would win.

And he wouldn't let his mother stop him.

An hour later, after Mark and Robb had left the sports center and were on their way home, Marty Ames called Jerry Harris. "I think it's going to be all right," he said. "I have a feeling our latest problem may just solve itself after all."

Ames smiled to himself as he hung up. The experiments with Mark had taken a new turn. He was already feeling the tingle of anticipation that always came to him when he was on the verge of discovering something absolutely new.

If it worked—if the aggression that he was able to induce in his subjects could truly be focused on a specific object . . .

He put the thought out of his mind, refusing to savor it fully until he knew whether or not the experiment had succeeded.

19

Kelly Tanner knew they were out there, knew the creatures were hunting for her. She didn't know how she'd gotten there—wasn't even quite certain where she was.

Mark had taken her for a hike up in the hills, and at first it had been fun. Chivas had been with them, and they'd followed the stream up into the hills and found a little waterfall. A grove of pines was clustered around the pool beneath the falls, and she and Mark had sat down in the scented bed of needles beneath the trees while Chivas sniffed around the boulders at the edge of the river, scratching at a hole some animal had dug there. Suddenly Mark had picked up a rock and hurled it at Chivas. The dog, yelping in pain, had whirled around, crouching low to the ground, stared at Mark for a moment then slunk off into the woods.

"Why did you do that?" Kelly had asked.

Mark hadn't answered her. Instead, he'd just gotten up and walked away, disappearing into the foliage after Chivas.

She hadn't liked that—she knew Mark wasn't supposed to leave her alone—but at first she wasn't worried. He'd come back in a few minutes, she thought, and Chivas would be with him. Then they'd start back home.

But Mark hadn't come back. She'd waited and waited.
And suddenly everything had changed.

The branches of the pines—so sheltering only a moment
before—now seemed like arms reaching out to grab her.

The sun, too, had disappeared, and at first she thought it
was nothing more than a cloud drifting by. But then the
darkness had closed in on her and she felt the first pangs of
fear.

She called out to Mark then, but there was no reply.

She scrambled to her feet. All she had to do was follow
the stream, and pretty soon she would be out of the hills and
back in the valley, and there would be the familiar houses and
stores of the town.

Except that as she walked, the trail seemed to change,
growing narrower and narrower, until she could barely make
out where it was at all.

That was when the sounds had started.

They were faint cries at first, coming as if from a great
distance away. Then she heard them again, nearer this time,
and Kelly froze in the path to listen.

The sounds came ever closer, and began changing.

First they were moans—strange, strangled sounds, like
someone crying. But then the moans shifted into a cacophony
of shrieks that echoed in the hills around her, and Kelly
shuddered.

She searched the cloying darkness around her, looking for
the source of the terrifying sounds.

A twig cracked somewhere behind her, and she spun
around, but could see nothing.

Another twig cracked, but this time the sound came from
a different direction.

She started running then, but every step seemed to take
forever. Her feet felt heavy; she could barely move them. She
tried to cry out herself, tried to scream for Mark to come and
help her, but her voice strangled in her throat and all that
emerged was a faint rasp.

They were all around her now—whatever they were—and

she thought she could hear them sniffing at the air, searching for her scent.

She knew what would happen when they found her. They would circle around her, closing her in, then come to get her, their yellow eyes glowing evilly in the darkness, their fangs dripping with saliva.

Suddenly she saw one of them.

It was big—bigger than anything she'd ever seen.

It had long arms, with curving claws extending from the fingers, reaching almost to the ground.

It was grunting, pushing its way through the brush, and she could smell a sour odor in the air as it breathed.

It was almost there, almost upon her, and she gathered what was left of her strength for a final scream.

That was when she woke up, her whole body jerking in a spasm of fear.

In the darkness the image of the monster still lurked, and in the distance she could still hear the cries of the others. She whimpered, gathering her blanket close around her, and then another, softer scream burst from her throat as her bedroom door opened.

"It's all right, darling," her mother told her, snapping on the ceiling light and filling the room with a brilliant glow that washed away the terrifying shadows. "You were just having a nightmare, that's all." Sharon came and sat on the edge of the bed. She put her arms around her daughter and held her close. "Do you want to tell me about it?"

Shakily, Kelly tried to repeat what had happened in the dream, and finally she looked up at her mother, her eyes large. "Why did Mark just leave me like that?" she asked.

"But he didn't, sweetheart," Sharon reassured her. "It was just a dream, and the things in dreams aren't real."

"B-But it *felt* real," Kelly protested. "And Mark was so different from the way he really is. At least," she added, her voice dropping and her eyes shifting away from her mother's, "he was different from the way he used to be, before we moved here."

Sharon felt a knot of tension twist in her stomach, but when she spoke, she did her best not to betray her own feelings. "What do you mean?" she asked.

Kelly shrugged elaborately, then snuggled down into the bed, pulling the covers up under her chin. "I don't know," she said, her small face screwing up into an expression of intense concentration. "He just seems different, that's all. I mean, he doesn't even care about his rabbits anymore, and I don't think Chivas likes him the way he used to."

Sharon laid her hand on the little girl's cheek. "What about you?" she asked. "You still like Mark, don't you?"

"Y-Yes," Kelly replied, but there was a hesitation in her voice, as if she weren't really sure. "But he *is* different. He—He even looks sort of different."

Sharon smiled tightly. "That's because he's getting a lot of exercise, and because he's starting to grow faster."

Kelly scowled and shook her head. "It's not that," she said. "It's something else. It's like—"

She suddenly stopped speaking as a sound drifted through the night. Though it seemed to come from far away, Kelly recognized it instantly.

It was the same high-pitched scream of fury she'd heard in her nightmare only a few minutes before. Her eyes widened into fearful circles and she clutched the covers tighter. "D-Did you hear that?" she asked.

Sharon hesitated, then went to the window and opened it. The chill night air poured in from outside, and she drew her robe tight around her. It was silent outside, and in the east the first faint hints of dawn were silhouetting the mountains against a brightening sky. She listened for a moment, but heard nothing.

She was just turning away from the window when the sound came again.

There was no mistaking it this time. It was some kind of animal out hunting in the night, but it sounded now as if it were in pain. An image came suddenly into Sharon's mind of an exhibit she'd seen in a museum years ago. It had been a diorama, and behind the glass, caught forever in a moment of agonizing pain, had been a stuffed mountain lion, its mouth agape in a silent roar, one of its immense feet caught in the jaws of a trap. Smears of realistic blood stained the fur of its foot, and the skin was torn away from its leg above the trap, where the creature had tried to gnaw itself loose.

The sound that rent the night as Sharon stood at Kelly's window was exactly the sound she had imagined coming from that trapped and wounded cougar's throat.

The cry died away, and Sharon closed the window tightly. "It's only an animal, darling," she told Kelly, who was sitting straight up in bed now, staring at her with frightened eyes. "It's up in the mountains somewhere, and it can't hurt you."

"B-but what if it comes down?" Kelly asked, her voice quavering.

Sharon glanced at the clock on Kelly's dresser. It was almost six, the sky outside was brightening by the minute. "Tell you what," she said. "Why don't you and I get dressed and go downstairs? We can fix a nice breakfast, and surprise your father and Mark."

Kelly brightened immediately, and she instantly slithered out of the bed, stripped off her pajamas, and began pulling on her clothes.

"A shower first," Sharon reminded the little girl. As Kelly headed for the bathroom, she went downstairs and started a pot of coffee. But even after Kelly joined her a few minutes later, Sharon found herself not saying much, her mind still occupied with what Kelly had said about Mark.

For Sharon, too, had been acutely aware of the changes taking place in her son. She'd tried to attribute them to the hormonal imbalances of adolescence, and yet even as she'd insisted to herself that nothing was wrong, she knew she was lying to herself.

The changes were coming too fast and were too marked to be anything normal.

Indeed, she'd even tried to talk to Blake about it the night before, but he'd put her off, as he seemed to lately about anything but the most banal of topics. "Be happy," he'd advised her. "He's finally growing up."

Growing up into what?

She opened the freezer and reached for a can of frozen orange juice, her eyes resting for a second on the small package, wrapped in butcher's paper, that was tucked away at the back of the freezer. Though it looked for all the world like nothing more than a small steak ready to be thrown away, she knew it wasn't.

Wrapped inside the butcher paper were the corpses of the two rodents she'd retrieved from the trash at TarrenTech.

She'd told nobody about them yet, hadn't even looked at them again herself. And yet she was certain they were very important, and that until she'd decided exactly what to do with them, she shouldn't even mention them to her husband.

An hour later, when Blake and Mark came down for breakfast, Sharon found herself surreptitiously watching her son, searching his face for signs of change.

This morning she thought she saw them.

There was a hardness about Mark's gentle features that she didn't remember seeing before.

Three hours later Mark trotted into the locker room to strip down for his P.E. class and realized that this week, for the first time in his life, he had actually begun to look forward to the hour on the practice field. He was still among the last to be chosen as the class was split up into teams, but yesterday there were still four guys standing unhappily, waiting to see which of them would be the "stuck-with" for the day (an honor that had, until this week, invariably been Mark's), when to Mark's surprise one of the team captains had actually called out his name.

Nor had he played football badly yesterday. He'd caught two passes, one of which had developed into a touchdown when he'd successfully evaded the two opponents who'd attempted to bring him down.

So today he put on his shorts and T-shirt eagerly, then trotted out onto the field with the others. Again to his surprise, immediately after he'd fallen in for the ten minutes of calisthenics that began each hour, the teacher called him out of the ranks and sent him to the gym.

His heart sank as he saw Phil Collins waiting for him, and he wondered what he might have done wrong that called for a dressing-down from the football coach. But to his surprise, Collins was smiling amiably at him.

"I've been hearing good things about you, Tanner," Collins called to him. The coach was at the far end of the gym, idly hefting a large leather-covered medicine ball. "Marty Ames tells me you're putting on a lot of muscle."

Mark grinned bashfully. "I guess so," he admitted.

"So let's see what you can do," Collins went on. Without warning he hurled the ball toward Mark, and Mark found that instead of giving in to his usual instinct to duck away from the heavy object, he stepped forward, caught it, and immediately shot it back toward the coach with enough force that Collins staggered slightly as it hurtled into his hands.

"Not bad," the coach observed, his right eyebrow arching appreciatively. "Want to try the rope?" He nodded toward a heavy strand of twisted nylon, its length studded with large knots at regular intervals, which was suspended from a heavy hook in the ceiling.

Mark said nothing, but walked over to the rope and gave it an experimental tug. Then, grasping it with both hands, he lifted his weight off the floor. He released his left hand and quickly moved it to the knot above, then repeated the process with his right hand. Without even thinking about it, he automatically bent his body at the hips so that as he moved steadily toward the ceiling his legs were nearly parallel to the floor. He paused at the top for a second, then slapped the ceiling with his right hand. A moment later, on a sudden whim, he released the rope completely, dropping nearly fifteen feet to the floor. His knees bent gracefully and he tumbled to one side, then scrambled back to his feet.

"Careful there," Collins said after whistling admiringly at the maneuver. "If you don't know what you're doing, you can break an ankle that way."

"But I didn't, did I?" Mark replied, grinning.

For the next thirty minutes Collins put Mark through a rigorous set of exercises, but even when he was finished, Mark's breathing was only a little heavier than normal. Though a sheen of sweat showed on his forehead, his shirt was still dry and his muscles felt as if he could have gone on for another hour.

"Definitely not bad," Collins commented when it was over. He signaled Mark to follow him, and went into his office. Flopping down in the chair behind his desk, he eyed Mark speculatively. "Ever thought about going out for football?"

Mark licked his lips nervously. "N-Not until a couple of weeks ago," he said finally. His eyes fixed on the floor a few feet in front of the coach's desk. "I'm kind of small, aren't I?"

Collins wiggled his right hand indifferently. "A lot of guys make up for small size with other things," he observed. "Speed, agility, all kinds of things can make the difference. And there's the basic will to win," he added. "If you have that, it can make up for a lot."

Mark turned the coach's words over in his mind. He knew it was true—knew it if only from the rowing exercises he'd been doing at the sports center, where the sight of other rowers overtaking him had been enough to send adrenaline streaming into his blood, giving him that extra surge of power he needed to catch up.

"I think I'd like to try it," he said finally, and Collins grinned at him, standing up.

"Then I'll see you after school today," he said. "Talk to Toby Miller about a practice uniform."

Mark's eager expression faded. "I'm supposed to go see

Dr. Ames today,'' he began, but Collins silenced him with a gesture.

"It's okay," he said, winking at Mark. "I thought you might want to take a shot at it, so I already fixed it with him. You're rescheduled for later, after practice.''

Mark stared at the coach in surprise, then a slow smile spread across his face. "Hey, thanks," he said. "Thanks a lot. See you later.''

He trotted out to the locker room, stripped off his gym clothes, and hit the showers. As the hot needle spray stung his skin, he felt a sharp surge of joy run through him.

It was going to be great, he thought. He was going to make the team, and his father would finally be proud of him.

And then, unbidden, an image of his mother came into his mind. His joy was suddenly blunted. He could already hear her telling him he was too small for football, that all that would happen would be that he'd get hurt.

Even as he began dressing, the tiny germ of anger toward his mother that had sprouted in the shower was already beginning to grow.

20

Sharon Tanner stared dolefully at the list of Colorado mental hospitals she'd copied at the library on Monday. Since then she'd called every one of them, and yesterday had even driven over to Canon City to inquire after Charlotte LaConner personally. But of course she'd gotten nowhere. Although most of the private hospitals had simply denied that they had a patient named LaConner at all, others had simply refused to answer her questions, citing policies and confidentiality laws.

It was an exercise in futility, and Sharon knew it. Even if Charlotte or Jeff were patients in one of the hospitals she'd called, they might have been admitted under other names, or they might have notations in their records to the effect that no information was to be given out.

And now, on Wednesday afternoon, she was finally ready to face the fact that what she had really been doing was procrastinating, putting off the moment when she would finally have to deal with the mice in the freezer—the one that seemed so normal, the other that was so grotesquely deformed and unnaturally large.

She knew she'd been trying to evade the issue, trying to deny the possibility that the mice had anything to do with the sports center at all. And yet, every time she thought about them, an image of the Silverdale High football team kept coming unbidden into her mind.

Big boys—oversized boys—all of them.

But it wasn't possible, was it? Surely TarrenTech wouldn't allow any kind of experimentation on human subjects, let alone on the children of their own employees? After all, Jerry and Elaine Harris's own son was on the football team.

And he was big, she reminded herself. Much bigger than either of his parents.

Once more she remembered the skinny asthmatic boy who had left San Marcos three years before. Was it really possible that nothing more than a regimen of vitamins and exercise, combined with clean mountain air, had effected such a change in Robb? It sounded too good to be true.

But if something was going on at TarrenTech and at the sports center, it meant that Mark was already involved.

That, of course, was what she'd been avoiding facing up to. She didn't want to believe that the changes in Mark—the changes she'd tried to deny were taking place until Kelly had talked about them this morning—could be anything except the natural changes that occur in every teenage boy.

But the mice kept coming back to haunt her.

She looked at the phone again, reaching out to pick it up, then hesitated. She told herself there was no reason for her to be worried, that she'd done nothing wrong in calling around, trying to locate Charlotte LaConner. And yet several times as she'd talked on the phone during recent days, she'd heard an odd hollowness, as if someone, somewhere, had picked up an extension. Twice she was certain she'd heard faint clicks, as if someone had either come on the line or gotten off it.

Could her telephone be tapped?

My God, she groaned to herself, I'm starting to sound as paranoid as Charlotte LaConner! She gasped out loud at the thought. Hadn't she herself insisted that perhaps Charlotte wasn't paranoid, that maybe something really was going on and that Charlotte had stumbled onto it?

Taking her fears firmly in hand, she picked up the phone and dialed the county hospital. A moment later she recognized Mac MacCallum's friendly voice at the other end of the line.

"D-Dr. MacCallum?" she stammered, still not quite certain what she was going to say. "It's Sharon Tanner—Mark's mother."

"Well, hello," MacCallum said, then his voice took on a note of concern. "What's going on? Mark's all right, isn't he?"

"Yes," Sharon said. Then, even though she knew the doctor couldn't see her, she shook her head. "I mean—well, I guess he's all right. But I was just wondering if I could talk to you about something."

In his office, MacCallum frowned. He could tell from Mrs. Tanner's voice that she was upset, but if there was something wrong with Mark, why had she said he was all right? "What's the problem, Mrs. Tanner?"

Sharon hesitated, and was just about to try to explain her fears when she heard a soft click and the phone took on that odd, hollow quality she'd noticed before. She felt a chill run through her body, and when she spoke again, she knew she sounded nervous. "It—Well, it's not something I feel comfortable discussing on the phone," she said.

MacCallum's frown deepened. What was going on? Had someone come into the room as she spoke? Was the woman afraid her phone was tapped? "I see," he said slowly. "Then perhaps you'd like to come out here," he suggested, glancing at the appointment book that lay open on his desk. "How about four o'clock this afternoon?"

Sharon hesitated a split-second, and tried to keep her voice casual. "That's not very good for me," she countered. "I mean—well, this isn't really a medical matter. It's just something I need some advice about, and . . . well . . ."

MacCallum sat up straight in his chair. When Mark had been in the hospital that night, Sharon Tanner had struck him as a strong woman who knew her own mind and seldom hesitated to speak her thoughts. But now she was floundering around, searching for words, apparently unable to tell him what was on her mind.

She *was* afraid her line was tapped.

And her husband was second in command at TarrenTech.

"Tell you what," he said. "I have a couple of errands to run in the village. If you're going to be down there, maybe we could have a cup of coffee."

Sharon felt almost weak with relief. He'd understood and gone along with her. "As a matter of fact, I do have some shopping to do," she said. "Shall we say half an hour?"

"Sounds good," MacCallum replied. He hung up the phone, sat pensively at the desk for a moment, then headed toward the main doors. As he passed the admissions desk, Susan Aldrich glanced up at him curiously. "Since when do you take the afternoon off?"

MacCallum grinned. "Since that phone call," he told her. "It seems like we might just have a chink in the great wall of security around TarrenTech."

Jerry Harris's private intercom buzzed discreetly and he immediately picked up the receiver that would connect him directly with the security office in the basement. "Harris. What's up?"

"Might be nothing," the voice at the other end replied. "But Mrs. Tanner's been on the phone a lot the last couple of days, trying to find Charlotte LaConner. And now she's set up a meeting with MacCallum."

Harris frowned thoughtfully. "Okay," he said after a few seconds of silence. "I want that meeting monitored, and I want to know what happens right away." Knowing his orders would be obeyed without question, he put the receiver back on its cradle and returned to the file he'd been studying.

It was a complete report of the experimental procedures Martin Ames had implemented in the case of Mark Tanner.

*   *   *

Sharon nearly took the car to the village that afternoon, but changed her mind at the last minute. She knew it was stupid—knew she was once more giving in to the same kind of paranoid thoughts that had made her wonder if her phone were tapped. Still, better to look as if she had nothing more on her mind than a leisurely walk to the store. She pulled the collapsible shopping cart out of the broom closet, struggled with it for a moment before it suddenly expanded in her hands, its wire bottom falling into place, then went to the hall closet and pulled out her parka. Only when she was ready to leave the house did she finally go to the freezer and pick up the small package containing the dead animals she'd brought home from TarrenTech. Her stomach feeling vaguely queasy at the knowledge of what the little package contained, she carefully tucked it into the bottom of her large carryall, then slung the bag itself over her shoulder. At last, awkwardly pulling the little cart behind her, she went out the back door and up the driveway to the street.

It was a chilly afternoon, but the sky was clear, a deep cobalt-blue dome over the valley which made it seem as if Silverdale had been cut off from the rest of the world and was now accessible only to those few people fortunate enough to live here.

Except that every day the perfection of the village had felt more and more claustrophobic to Sharon. Eventually she had come to believe that one way or another, nearly all the people in Silverdale were living lives that were as artificially decorated and as carefully planned as the community that housed them.

She saw a few other women walking in the streets that afternoon, their shopping carts rolling along behind them like so many tiny cabooses. Sharon nodded to the ones she didn't recognize, spoke to the ones she did.

As she walked, she had to force herself not to look back to see if she were being followed.

By the time she got to the village, she was beginning to

feel a bit foolish about the whole thing, but still, the knowledge of what was in her bag—and the changes that had taken
place in Mark—kept her wary. Even as she recognized Mac
MacCallum lounging on one of the benches on the boardwalk
that connected the shops, she hesitated, her eyes scanning the
area for anything suspicious. She chuckled hollowly to herself as she realized ruefully that she wasn't even certain what
she should consider suspicious and what she shouldn't. At
last, striding purposefully, she approached MacCallum.

He stood up as she drew near, his eyes crinkling as he
cocked his head slightly. "Sounds like you've got some kind
of mystery on your hands," he said, his voice dropping so
that, though Sharon could hear him clearly, she doubted that
anyone else in the area would overhear him at all.

"I—I don't know," she stammered. She nodded toward
the small park across the street. Surrounded by the neat white
picket fences that were so prevalent in the village, its gardens
were deserted this afternoon except for a small black and
white dog sniffing around the playground at the north end.
"Why don't we go over there?"

MacCallum nodded his assent and the two of them crossed
the street, then moved into the park itself.

"What's going on?" MacCallum asked. "And you might
start by telling me why you think your phone is tapped."

Sharon flinched. "Was it that obvious?" She couldn't
resist glancing around now, but the park was still empty, and
the few people on the sidewalk seemed oblivious to their
presence. "Well, if it *is* tapped, I suppose I was as obvious
to whoever was listening as I was to you." Then, settling
onto a bench in the center of the park, she began explaining
everything that had been happening, from her worries about
Charlotte LaConner to her ill-defined concerns about Mark.
"I suppose it sounds kind of nutty, doesn't it?" she asked
when she was finished.

Almost to her surprise, MacCallum shook his head. "It
sounds like what you're postulating is some kind of conspiracy, with TarrenTech right smack in the middle of it all."

Sharon bit her lip and nodded. "But that's crazy, isn't it?"

MacCallum took a deep breath. "Maybe it is," he conceded. "But on the other hand, if you're not part of TarrenTech, sometimes this place looks pretty weird." He glanced sharply at Sharon out of the corner of his eye, but her face betrayed no trace of defensiveness. He smiled wryly at her. "Or maybe you don't think it's strange that even in a company town like this, TarrenTech either supports or runs everything. *Everything.* The schools, the town council, the library, even Rocky Mountain High."

"And the hospital?" Sharon asked, her heart suddenly skipping a beat. To her relief, MacCallum shook his head.

"We're county. Completely independent, although even that isn't by TarrenTech's choice. In fact, they offered to buy the hospital from the county a few years back. Claimed they could run it more cheaply and efficiently than the county. Unfortunately for them," he went on, making no attempt to keep his sarcasm and anger toward TarrenTech out of his voice, "all of us aren't quite as thrilled to have TarrenTech here as the company thinks we ought to be, and the county didn't see it quite the company's way. They had the idea that a public hospital should be run by the public, and wouldn't knuckle under to Thornton." His lips curled into a wry grin. "So anyway, if you think there's some kind of conspiracy going on, I won't argue with you. This whole place has always been a little too perfect for my tastes. In fact, I was very happy with it the way it used to be. Anyway, the whole thing smells bad to me." He fell silent for a moment, then went on. "I assume you know all about Ricardo Ramirez?"

Sharon nodded.

"Well, if you ask me, TarrenTech wouldn't have been so antsy to avoid any kind of legal action on Maria's part if they didn't have something to hide. I'm afraid I just don't believe in that much corporate altruism. Which, I have to confess, is one of the reasons I'm here this morning." He looked at her pointedly now. "I'm assuming you know something you haven't told me about yet."

Sharon was silent for a few moments, making up her mind whether to trust him or not. But of course, she had no choice. Finally she nodded, reaching down to pull the small white package out of the bottom of her purse. "I—I found these out at TarrenTech the other day," she said, her voice dropping so low MacCallum could barely hear her. "They were in a box marked for incineration, and when I had a chance, I just—well, I just took them."

She handed the package to MacCallum. He stared at it for a moment, then slowly unwrapped it. A moment later the brilliant glare of the afternoon sun shone on the two dead animals, both of them still frozen solid.

His frown deepening, MacCallum read the tags. "Same litter," he said. "Born May eighth. Their parents were Male Number 61 and Female Number 46."

"That's what I thought," Sharon replied. "But what could the other number mean? The one on the big one?"

MacCallum studied it for a moment. Suddenly he was almost certain he knew. And then, as he thought about Jeff LaConner and Randy Stevens—maybe even Robb Harris?—he felt a wave of nausea rise in his stomach. "Growth hormones," he breathed almost to himself. His eyes, oddly dazed, drifted toward Sharon. "That's what it has to be, doesn't it?" he asked. "They're experimenting on animals with growth hormones." He stared at the larger of the two mice once more. Now its strange deformities seemed to stand out.

The enlarged feet and the long claws.

The heaviness of the bone structure around its eyes, and the distended look to its jaw.

He shook his head, unable to accept the idea that had taken such sudden form in his mind. "You're not thinking they're experimenting on the kids, are you?"

"I don't know what I'm thinking," Sharon said numbly,

but knew in her heart that that was precisely what she had been thinking.

"Look," MacCallum told her. "Let me take these things back to the hospital and run some tests on them. It could be that we're on the wrong track completely. I mean—maybe they're experimenting with some kind of genetic engineering techniques out there. Certainly all kinds of things are possible with that now, and the big one might be nothing more than some kind of mutation. If it is, it won't be too hard to find out—all I have to do is get a lab in Denver to run a DNA comparison on them."

"And if it's not?" Sharon asked, hearing in her mind once again echoes of Blake's assurances that Mark's treatment was nothing more than a vitamin complex of some sort.

"Then we'll take it one step at a time," MacCallum told her. He wished he could tell her not to worry, assure her that nothing as evil as human experimentation could be going on in Silverdale.

But he couldn't.

They parted a few minutes later, MacCallum having carefully rewrapped the two small corpses in their butcher paper and put them into his briefcase.

As soon as they left the square, the man who had been parked in a station wagon half a block away, his presence unnoticed by either Sharon or MacCallum, stepped out of his car and moved across the sidewalk to a pay phone, ignoring the unsecured convenience of the cellular phone mounted in the console next to the driver's seat.

For this call he needed privacy.

MacCallum drove slowly away from the village, only part of his mind involved in negotiating the familiar route from the town out to the hospital half a mile beyond the city limits. He was going over the conversation he'd had with Sharon Tanner once more, examining every bit of it, wishing he could find a way to disagree with her. But he'd known Charlotte LaConner, too, and to him Charlotte had never seemed the sort to harbor paranoid tendencies.

He turned onto the main highway but didn't bother to speed up. There was little traffic on the road, and he was in no hurry. Beside him, resting on the passenger seat, was the briefcase containing the dead mice. As he glanced down at it, he was already speculating on what might have been done to the larger of the two.

He was aware of certain experiments taking place with human growth hormones, aware that since the technology of synthesizing them had been developed, it was beginning to be possible to correct all sorts of genetic deficiencies and glandular imbalances.

And, of course, it was just the sort of thing that the TarrenTech pharmaceutical division might be interested in.

Also, it was just the sort of thing that Martin Ames would be interested in, with his ongoing research in the area of human physical development.

But surely they couldn't have begun experimenting on human beings. That was the sort of thing the Nazis had done back in the Second World War. And this was the end of the century! Even to consider such a thing—

The thought broke off as MacCallum was suddenly distracted by something on the road ahead.

It was a truck, a big semi, and even from here MacCallum could see that it was going far faster than the fifty-mile-an-hour speed limit posted all along the two-lane highway that branched off from the main north-south route to the west.

He frowned. Didn't the guy know there was a lot of open range to the west and he might come across a cow wandering along the road? At the speed the truck was traveling, it would have as little chance of survival as the cow itself.

Instinctively, he pulled to the right, giving the oncoming vehicle plenty of space.

*   *   *

In the cab of the truck, the driver spotted the car ahead—an Audi, dark green. He raised his binoculars and checked the license plate, then glanced in the rearview mirrors. Just as he'd been told, there were no cars behind him.

Nor were there any cars following the Audi, either.

He smiled.

The job was going to be easy.

He pressed harder on the accelerator, and the pitch of the diesel engine under the hood changed slightly. A belch of black smoke rose from the twin exhausts flanking the cab itself, and the speedometer crept up toward the eighty-mile-per-hour mark.

He saw the Audi move slightly away from the center line as its driver attempted to give him more room.

"But not enough, you sorry son of a bitch," the driver muttered to himself.

He was closing fast on the Audi now, only a hundred yards still separating them. He stepped harder on the accelerator, gaining yet a little more extra speed.

Fifty yards now, then twenty-five.

His hands tensed on the steering wheel and his left foot hovered over the brakes, ready to execute the quick maneuver he'd practiced so many times before.

Ten yards.

Mac MacCallum didn't realize what was happening until the last possible instant. He was far to the right of the oncoming lane now, the tires on the right-hand side of the car kicking up a cloud of dust as they touched the hard-packed dirt and gravel of the road's shoulder. The oncoming truck had almost reached him, and its left tires had drifted over the center line. For a moment Mac thought the truck must have lost its brakes and was running wild, but then he realized that the road here was almost level—surely the truck's engine alone would have been enough to slow it down.

Then he heard the scream of tires skidding against pavement, and the truck suddenly slewed toward him, its air horn blasting, the immense mass of its cab hurtling straight at the closed window next to his head.

He wrenched at the wheel and for a split-second felt the tight steering mechanism of the Audi respond, but then the great chrome bumper of the truck smashed into the car.

The window exploded inward and a maelstrom of shattered glass tore into his face, blinding him. The car itself rose into the air, its side all but torn away by the impact, then flipped over onto its back and landed upside down, skidding across the ground for nearly thirty feet before slamming into a large boulder.

The roof had collapsed instantly when the car hit the ground, and now Mac, blood streaming from the lacerations that covered his face, struggled feebly to free himself from the tangled wreckage. The steering wheel was jammed against his chest, and every breath brought a searing agony of pain as his shattered ribs pierced both his lungs and tore at the muscles around his rib cage.

But the car hadn't caught on fire, and he wasn't dead yet.

The driver of the truck brought his vehicle to a skidding stop, all its wheels locked by the massive force he'd applied to the braking system. He scrambled out of the cab, a small air pump clutched in his right hand, its cord already attached to the cigarette lighter on the dash.

Ignoring the car that lay smashed almost beyond recognition a few dozen yards away, he attached the air pump's hose to the stem of the left front tire. Only when he'd made certain that the pump was operating properly did he turn his attention to the ruined Audi and the faint cries for help emanating from its twisted body.

He moved quickly to the car, then paused warily, waiting to see if it was going to burst into flame. A small puddle of gasoline had formed beneath the filling pipe, but nowhere did he see any signs of smoke.

Ignoring the driver's side, he hurried around the car and squatted down, peering inside until he spotted what he was looking for.

A black briefcase—the old-fashioned kind that opened at the top—was wedged between the passenger seat and the collapsed dashboard.

The truck driver reached through the window and quickly worked it loose. He opened it, rifled through it for a moment, then pulled out the small package wrapped in white butcher paper. Satisfied, he shoved the briefcase back into the car and stepped back.

"H-Help . . ." he heard a faint voice mumble. "I can't . . ."

"Sorry, buddy," the truck driver said. "If you're gonna stick your nose in where nobody wants you, you gotta expect some trouble."

Reaching into his pocket, he fished out a battered book of matches. Casually glancing in both directions, and still seeing no traffic approaching, he struck one of the matches and lit a cigarette. Then, stepping back and taking careful aim, he flicked the match into the small puddle forming beneath the gasoline intake, turned and fled.

For a moment the puddle only blazed up, but then the fumes in the tank itself ignited and the muffled roar of the explosion filled the air. As the tank came apart, a glowing fireball rose over the car and the car itself was engulfed in flames.

Inside the car Mac MacCallum, still conscious, saw the orange flames whirl around him and felt the heat of the air as he tried to breathe.

A moment later, as the fire sucked the oxygen out of the air in the car, he felt himself passing out.

The last thing in his mind before he died was Sharon Tanner.

He wondered if they had killed her, too.

*   *   *

The driver stood well away from the truck until the small pump had overinflated the tire to the point where it blew out, then quickly returned the pump to its storage place under the front seat. He glanced only once at the wide black lines his skidding tires had left as he'd slewed the truck into the Audi, already well aware that they were an almost perfect imitation of the marks he'd have left trying to regain control of the big semi after a tire had blown.

Satisfied, he snapped on the C.B. radio mounted on the dash of the truck and tuned it to Channel 9. Only after he'd reported the accident on the emergency band did he at last move back toward the burning car, so that when the police arrived, it would be clearly seen that he was doing his best to rescue the man he'd just killed.

21

"Mom?" Kelly said. When her mother didn't turn around, she repeated the word, louder this time. *"Mom!"* Sharon was sitting at the kitchen table, staring out the window but not really aware of what was happening outside. As had been the case ever since her meeting in the park with Mac MacCallum, she was considering what to do next. She'd already come to one decision: as soon as Mark came home, she would tell him that he was to spend no more time at the sports center.

Blake wouldn't like it—she knew that—and she still wasn't sure what she would tell him when he demanded an explanation. What could she tell him? That she was almost certain the sports center was nothing less than a laboratory using the Silverdale children for experimentation? The least he'd do was laugh at her, and she wouldn't really blame him if he accused her of falling victim to the same kind of paranoia Chuck LaConner insisted had overcome Charlotte.

"Mom!" Kelly said once again, and this time the little girl's voice penetrated Sharon's consciousness. She turned and managed a smile.

"I'm sorry, honey. I was just thinking about something."

Kelly was standing by the back door, her brows knit in a

frown. "When are we going to have dinner?" she demanded. "I'm hungry!"

Sharon glanced up at the clock. It was almost six-thirty, and she realized that she'd been sitting at the table for almost two hours. Hurriedly, she stood and went to the freezer, making a mental inventory of its contents.

"Did Mark come home yet?" she asked.

Kelly shrugged. "I don't know. I didn't see him."

Sharon headed toward the kitchen door to call up the stairwell, then noticed Chivas curled up by the stove, his chin resting on his forepaws, his large eyes staring dolefully up at her. The dog's presence was enough to tell her that her son wasn't in the house—if he had been, Chivas would long ago have disappeared from the kitchen to trail along after Mark, whatever he might be doing.

The front door slammed, and a moment later Mark himself appeared in the kitchen. Chivas instantly scrambled to his feet and skidded across the slick vinyl floor, his tail wagging madly.

"Hey! Get down, you big idiot." Mark pushed the dog aside, his face lit by an oddly triumphant grin that Sharon had never seen before. "Is Dad home yet?"

Sharon shook her head. "And where have you been?" she countered, nodding pointedly toward the clock. "Look what time it is."

Mark's smile faded only slightly. "At the center," he replied. "I didn't get there till almost four."

Sharon frowned, but when she spoke, she tried to keep her voice neutral. "What on earth did you do out there for two hours?" she asked.

Mark shrugged, and idly picked an apple from a basket on the counter. "Just the usual stuff. Marty checked me over and then I did some exercises."

Sharon's lips tightened. "What kind of exercises?" she asked.

Mark's smile faded away. "What does it matter?" he challenged her. "You don't like what I'm doing anyway."

"Can't a mother be curious?" Sharon said lightly, ignoring the faintly contemptuous tone his words had carried.

"Aw, Jeez, Mom," Mark replied, his eyes rolling with impatience. "What do you care what I do out there?"

Now Sharon allowed her tone to harden. "I'm your mother. And is it some kind of big secret? Is something going on out there you don't want me to know about?"

Mark stared at her for a moment, then his mouth twisted into an insolent grin. "Yeah," he said. "Marty's gay, and we're all getting it on together. Is that what you want to hear?"

"Mark!" Sharon exclaimed, her eyes instantly going to Kelly, who was now staring curiously at her brother. "What on earth would make you even think of a thing like that?" she asked before her daughter could get a word in.

Mark shrugged. "I don't know. It just seems like you have this thing about the center, that's all."

"It's not a 'thing,' as you put it," Sharon said tightly. "I just want to know what you were doing, that's all. And if you don't want me to keep asking you questions, you can start giving me some answers."

Mark's eyes flashed with anger now. "All right!" he flared. "If it's so damned important to you, here's what happened. I went out there and stripped down, and they took my pulse and my blood pressure, and my measurements. Okay?" His eyes bored into her, but he didn't give her a chance to say anything. "And then I did twenty minutes on the rowing machine. Okay? And then that was all, and I came home. Is that all right with you?"

Sharon shrank back slightly, dazed by the intensity of the anger in Mark's voice. Then her own temper flared. "Don't speak to me in that tone of voice, young man," she snapped. "And no," she plunged on, suddenly deciding to get it all out right now, "it is *not* all right with me! It doesn't take two hours for the simple examination you keep describing and then twenty minutes on a rowing machine."

Mark's eyes narrowed. Why was she picking on him? He

hadn't done anything. But that's what she was always doing. Always watching him, like he was doing something wrong, and staring at him over meals, as if he was some kind of freak! A tight knot of anger burned in his stomach, and his fists clenched at his sides. "What do you care what I'm doing out there?" he demanded, his voice harsh. "You just want me to quit going out there, don't you? You want me to go back to being a wimp!"

Sharon glared at her son, her whole body trembling. This wasn't what she'd envisioned at all. She'd wanted to sit down with Mark and talk this thing out, explain her worries and listen to his explanations of what was happening to him at Rocky Mountain High. But now they were facing each other down, and Sharon realized that if she backed off, she would lose whatever control she had over her son. "You're right," she said. "I do want you to stop going out there. I don't know what Ames is doing to you, but you're not the same boy you were a month ago. And I don't like what I'm seeing."

"You don't like what you're seeing," Mark mimicked, his voice rising and falling in an abrasive singsong. His vision clouded slightly and he seemed to be seeing his mother through a reddish haze.

A nearly uncontrollable urge to strike out at her rose up from somewhere in the depths of his subconscious, and he took a half step toward her.

At his feet, Chivas growled softly, his hackles rising as his body stiffened. His eyes fastened on Mark, and his tail, held high a moment ago, dropped toward the floor.

"That's it!" Sharon exclaimed. "You can go up to your room and stay there until you've decided to apologize to me!" She paused for a moment, but Mark didn't move. "Did you hear me?" she demanded.

Mark felt a quick surge in the tension within his body. Every one of his muscles seemed to be tingling, and in his mind he heard a tiny voice whispering to him, demanding that he release the pent-up energy inside him.

With a strangled sound rasping in his throat, he took a step forward. But before Mark could move any closer to his mother, Chivas sprang at him. With an angry snarl, his lips drawn back to expose his fangs, the big dog hurled himself at his master's chest. Mark stumbled backward, staggered by the weight of the big retriever. His arms flew up to protect himself, and his hands closed around the dog's throat.

Sharon froze, her eyes wide as she stared at the spectacle before her. Mark's eyes seemed to have glazed over, and his jaw was clenched so tight, the tendons in his neck stood out. His fingers, trembling with fury, tightened around the dog's throat. Chivas, held now a foot above the floor, was struggling to loose himself from his master's grasp.

"Mommy," Kelly cried out. "Mommy, what's Mark doing? Make him stop!"

But there was nothing Sharon could do. It felt as if her feet were rooted to the floor. Still, she reached out toward Mark. "Stop it!" she shouted. "For God's sake, Mark—you're killing him!"

Mark felt his fingers tighten around the dog's throat, and as if from far away he could barely make out a voice calling to him to stop. But his entire concentration was focused on the dog now. He felt it wriggling in his grip, felt its forepaws clawing weakly at his chest. Then, as he continued to squeeze tighter, the clawing stopped and all he felt were a few faltering twitches.

Then nothing.

His vision began to clear. Suddenly he was staring into Chivas's face. The dog's eyes, bulging in their sockets, seemed to be staring at him, and its tongue lolled limply from the side of its slackened jaw.

"Ch-Chivas?" he asked, his voice choking with emotion. His eyes left the dog, then, and fixed on his mother, who was staring at him, her face ashen, her eyes reflecting shock.

In the corner, near the back door, Kelly was huddled on the floor, crying.

Then Mark's tears overflowed as he stared helplessly at

the lifeless body he still clutched in his hands. The strength drained from his fingers, and Chivas slid to the floor, sprawling out almost as if he were only asleep.

"I—I'm sorry," Mark wailed. "I didn't mean it!" Turning away, unable to face his mother or his sister, he shambled out of the kitchen and stumbled up the stairs to his room. He slammed the door behind him, then stood still, leaning his weight against the closed door, his breath coming in rough, choking gasps.

It wasn't possible—he couldn't have killed Chivas. He couldn't have!

But he knew he had.

The dog had attacked him, so he'd killed it.

But that wasn't true, either, not really. Chivas had only been trying to protect his mother.

His mother!

He could remember the rage now, remember the blinding fury that had risen inside him, overwhelming him, driving him on to want to hurl his fist at her, smashing it into her face.

His mother!

It wasn't possible.

Choking back a sob, he stumbled toward his bed, then paused as he caught sight of himself in the mirror on his closet door.

His hair, limp with sweat and matted down against his scalp, framed a face he could barely recognize.

His eyes seemed to have sunk deep within their sockets, peering out suspiciously from beneath the ridges of his brow.

His jaw seemed thicker and his lips were twisted slightly, giving him a sullen look.

"Nooo . . ." he wailed softly. "That's not me. That can't be me."

And suddenly the rage was on him again. His fist clenched, and he pulled his arm back then smashed it into the mirror with all the force he could muster. The mirror shattered, jagged lines flashing out in every direction from the point of impact. "Nooo," he sobbed once again. He staggered back and for a moment was unable to tear his eyes from the distorted image in the broken mirror. But at last he turned away, lurched toward the bed. He tore at the bedclothes, stripping them away with a single furious wrench, then grabbing the thick coverlet with both his hands and ripping it a quarter of its length before throwing it aside.

His eyes, glittering with rage, darted around the room, searching for something else to destroy.

When he finally collapsed on the bed half an hour later, his anger at last spent, the room was a shambles.

Feathers from an exploded pillow covered everything and still floated in the air. His clothes, hurled mindlessly from the closet and the bureau, were scattered over the floor. The clock was smashed, and a lamp, its shade crushed, lay in one corner.

But the rage within him at last was quiet.

The tension in the house was almost palpable. Finally, Sharon threw aside the magazine she'd been holding in her lap, unread, for the last twenty minutes. "We have to talk about this," she said, her eyes fixing on Blake, whom she was certain was no more involved in his television show than she had been in her magazine.

"I'm not sure how we can talk about it, when you won't even let me talk to Mark," he replied. Though his voice was even, there was an edge to it that made Sharon wince.

"You weren't there," she said. "You can't possibly understand what happened."

"He killed Chivas," Blake told her. "He looked like he was going to take a punch at you, and when Chivas went after him, he killed him. Isn't that about it?"

Sharon knew he was right, and yet even as he spoke the words, she wanted to cry out to him that it was something else entirely, that Mark hadn't been himself, that it was as if some furious stranger had taken over Mark's body.

But she'd already tried to explain that to him.

He'd come home from the office a few minutes after Mark had disappeared into his room, listened in shock as Sharon had brokenly explained what had happened, then buried Chivas in the backyard, with Kelly looking on, her body shaking as she tried to control the sobbing that had overcome her when she realized Chivas was dead.

He'd already started up the stairs to deal with Mark when Sharon had stopped him. "Leave him alone," she pleaded. "He's as horrified about what happened as you are."

Blake had stared at her in bewilderment. "He tried to take a swing at you, and killed his own dog, and you say he's horrified? I say he needs a good talking-to, if not a whipping!"

That's when she'd tried to explain what had happened, tried to explain that from the moment Mark had come home that day, there was something different about him, something more than the changes that had been taking place over the last few weeks. "There was a look in his eye," she said. "And when I told him I don't want him going back to Martin Ames, he just went crazy."

Blake had stared at her then. "You told him *what*?" he echoed.

"You heard me," she'd said, her voice dropping, unwilling to have Kelly—who'd gone up to her own room after announcing she didn't want any dinner—overhear what would probably develop into an argument.

She'd been right. It had gone back and forth as she'd prepared dinner, and when finally she and Blake had sat alone at the table in the kitchen, it had continued. Finally Blake pushed his plate aside and tossed his napkin onto the table.

"I don't get it," he said. "You don't have any idea of what Ames is doing, but you're convinced that it's some kind of terrible experimental program that's turning our kids into monsters. And you won't let me discipline my own son, even after what he did this afternoon." He'd stared at her for a moment, and when he spoke again, his voice was uneven. "What the hell do you want me to do, Sharon?"

She had looked up at him pleadingly. "I want you to agree that he won't go back to Ames until we know what's going on out there. And I don't want you to start punishing him for something I'm absolutely certain he didn't intend to do."

Blake had regarded her speculatively for a moment. "And how are we going to do that?" he asked, his voice cool. "Am I supposed to go out there and confront Ames? Tell him you think he's some kind of modern Mengele and demand to see all his medical data? Hell, I wouldn't even understand whatever he might tell me!"

"But you understood enough to let him start medicating Mark, didn't you?" Sharon demanded, her voice bitter.

That's what had set Blake off. "Yes, I did, damn it!" he exploded. "And it hasn't hurt Mark at all. He's in better shape than he's ever been in. I should think you'd be pleased about it."

She'd almost told Blake about the mice then, but had quickly changed her mind. It wasn't so much that she'd stolen them from his own company, but that in his present mood he only would have mocked her further, then demanded to know what she'd done with the mice. And if she told him she'd given them to MacCallum . . .

She shuddered inwardly, remembering his rage a year ago when he discovered a program he'd been about to market had been leaked to a competitor, who'd cloned it—with a few improvements—and then beaten TarrenTech to the marketplace.

Since dinner they'd barely spoken to each other, but the tension of the argument, heightened by Mark's failure to emerge from his room at all, still hung over them.

"All right," she sighed. "We won't talk about it, then. Good night." She stood up and started out of the room, Blake's eyes following her. But it wasn't until she was at the door that he spoke.

"You want me to come with you?" he asked uncertainly.

Sharon turned back to face him. "I never thought I'd hear myself saying this, but if I can't talk to you, I certainly have no desire to sleep with you. Maybe you'd better stay down here tonight."

Blake made no reply at all as she left the den and started up the stairs.

She paused outside Mark's door, as she'd done twice before that evening. As before, she could hear no sounds from within, yet she was certain he wasn't asleep. Indeed, she could almost picture him lying on his back, staring up at the ceiling, his hands folded behind his head. Should she leave him alone, or go in and try to talk to him?

After hesitating, she tapped softly at the door. For several seconds there was no answer. Then she heard Mark's voice. "It's not locked."

She twisted the knob and pushed the door open, gasping at the sight of the wreckage. Clothes, bedding, feathers—the chaos was everywhere. The dresser drawers were scattered around the room, and the lamp still lay in the corner where Mark had flung it. She bit her lip, forcing herself to ignore the damage. "Are you all right?" she asked, her voice gentle. She moved to the bed, where Mark was sprawled facedown on the bare mattress. As she touched his shoulder, he rolled away and lay on his back, looking bleakly up at her.

"I don't know what happened," he said. "It—It was like there was someone else inside me. I didn't want to hit you, Mom. I—I just couldn't help myself."

Sharon's eyes closed for a moment and she felt them sting with hot tears. "It's all right, darling," she said, her voice quavering.

Mark sat up straight and shook off the hand she had once more extended toward him. "It is not!" he said. "It's not all right at all. I killed Chivas, Mom! I killed my own dog!" His own eyes filled with tears then, and he wiped them away with the back of his hand. "What's wrong with me?" he demanded.

Once again Sharon tried to reach out to him, but he

swung his feet off the bed and stood up. As he looked down at her, she saw again a strange light in his eyes—the same dark glow of fury she'd seen in the kitchen earlier. "M-Mark?" she asked. "Mark, what's happening?"

Mark backed away from her. "I—I don't know," he stammered. "It—Mom, it's starting to happen again."

Sharon was on her feet now, too. "What, Mark? What's happening?"

But Mark only shook his head and edged toward the door. "I've got to go, Mom. I've got to get out of here!"

"Mark, wait!" Sharon pleaded, but it was too late. He was already out of the room, then she heard him pounding down the stairs. By the time she got to the top of the stairs herself, he was at the hall closet, rummaging in it for a jacket. He stared up at her briefly, his eyes burning. Then he was gone, the front door slamming behind him.

A moment later Blake emerged from the den, peering up the stairs at his wife. "What the hell's going on around here?" he demanded. "Was that Mark?"

Sharon nodded. "Something's wrong with him, Blake," she said. "When I went in, he was all right for a minute, but then he just went crazy again."

Blake's brow furrowed. "What did you say to him?"

"Nothing!" Sharon exclaimed. "I just wanted to tell him that I wasn't angry at him, to let him know I love him. And he was so unhappy. Blake, you should have seen him! And then all of a sudden . . ." She struggled for a moment, searching for the right words, then gave up. "I can't even describe it," she said. "He said it was like having someone else inside him." She sank to the top stair and buried her face in her hands. "Oh, God, Blake. What's happening to him? I'm so scared. So terribly, terribly scared."

Blake climbed the stairs quickly and took Sharon in his arms. "It's going to be all right, baby," he crooned. "He's just going through a rough period, that's all. And he'll grow out of it. You'll see."

Behind him there was the soft click of a doorknob, then

Kelly was standing in the hall, rubbing her eyes sleepily. She came over and put her arms around her father's neck. "What's wrong with Mark?" she asked. "Is he sick?"

"No," Blake told her, circling her waist with his free arm and drawing her close. "Nothing's wrong with Mark at all, and I don't want you to worry about it."

"B-But he killed Chivas," the little girl whimpered.

This time it was Sharon who responded to their daughter.

"It wasn't Mark, darling," she said. "Whatever happens, I don't want you to think Mark killed Chivas. He wouldn't do that, honey. Not your brother. Not Mark."

"Then who did?" Kelly asked, cocking her head as she tried to puzzle out her mother's words.

"I don't know," Sharon admitted. "But it wasn't Mark!"

Mark hurried through the dark streets, uncertain of where he was going or why. His mind was whirling, trying to sort out what had happened.

Why had the rage swept over him again? He'd been okay when his mother came in. He'd finished crying and was lying there, trying to figure out what had happened.

And his mother had wanted to help him.

She hadn't been mad at him, hadn't yelled at him, hadn't even mentioned the way he'd wrecked his room! All she'd wanted to do was help him.

And then the fury had come over him again. He'd rolled over and looked at her, and all of a sudden the flame inside him had ignited once more and he'd wanted to reach out, put his fingers around her throat, and squeeze and squeeze. . . .

Squeeze like he'd squeezed Chivas, until she stopped talking, stopped breathing, even stopped writhing in his grip.

And he'd have done it, if he'd stayed another minute.

He slowed down and looked around. Across the street was the Harrises' house, and he suddenly knew what he had to do. He glanced up and down the street, then darted

across it, slipping between the houses into the Harrises'
backyard.

The house was dark, as was the house behind it, and the
one next door.

He tapped softly at the window of Linda's room, then a
little harder. From inside he heard a sound, then the curtains
parted a fraction of an inch and Linda peered out, squinting
into the darkness.

"It's me," Mark whispered. "Come out."

"Mark?" Linda asked. She opened the window. "What
are you doing out there?"

"I have to talk to you," Mark whispered. "Please?"

Linda hesitated, but the urgency in his voice made up her
mind. "Just a minute," she said. "I have to get dressed."

A couple of minutes later she slipped out the back door,
holding a finger to her lips as she led him quickly back up the
driveway to the street. "What's wrong?" she asked when
they were safely away from the house.

Mark tried to tell her what had happened, his voice
choking as he recounted how he'd strangled Chivas.

She turned to stare at him. "You killed Chivas?"

Mark nodded mutely, his eyes flooding with tears. "I
didn't want to," he sobbed. "And I didn't want to hurt
Mom, either. But I was going to! I know I was going to!"

At his words, an unbidden image of Jeff LaConner flashed
into Linda's mind, and she remembered the night he had put
his hands on her arms, squeezing her so hard that it hurt.
She'd slapped him, and then he looked surprised, almost as if
he didn't realize what he'd done.

And she was almost certain he'd begun crying as he
turned away from her and ran off into the night.

"Wh-What are you going to do?" Linda asked.

Mark shook his head helplessly.

Linda reached out to take his hand, but Mark pulled away
from her. "D-Don't do that," he said, his voice shaking.
"That's what my mom did. All she did was touch me, and I
almost went crazy!"

Linda withdrew her hand, then met Mark's eyes. "It's like Jeff, isn't it?" she asked. "Like the night he beat you up. You didn't do anything to him, or say anything to him, or anything. He just came after you."

Mark stared at Linda in the darkness.

"M-Maybe it's Dr. Ames," Linda said finally. "Maybe he did something to Jeff, and now he's done something to you."

"But he's helping me," Mark protested. "Hell, I even made the football team this afternoon."

"You what?" Linda asked, staring at him blankly.

"I made the football team," Mark repeated. "I was going to tell my folks tonight, before . . ." His voice trailed off.

"But you don't even like football," Linda protested.

Mark shook his head. "I—I guess maybe I've changed."

A faint glow from a streetlamp down the block barely illuminated Mark's face, but even in the dim light, Linda could now see that Mark had, indeed, changed.

His face looked heavier, and his gentle features seemed to have become harder. His eyes, sunken deep in his sockets, had a wild look to them, and his mouth—the full lips that had always looked so soft—had a harshness about it now.

Once again the image of Jeff LaConner came into her mind.

"I'm going to talk to my father," she said suddenly. "Tomorrow morning I'm going to tell him everything that happened, and he'll know what to do. Okay?"

Jeff looked at Linda uncertainly for a moment, then nodded. "Okay," he said.

They turned and began walking back toward the Harrises'. When they were in front of the house, Mark put his arms around Linda and held her close. "I don't want to hurt you," he murmured, burying his face in her hair. "I don't want to hurt anyone."

"And you won't," Linda told him. "You're not like Jeff, and you won't hurt anyone."

She stepped back then, and for a moment thought she felt

Mark's grip on her tighten. But he abruptly released her and turned away. She almost called out to him, but changed her mind as she remembered Jeff LaConner once more.

She waited until he'd turned the corner and disappeared, then hurried back into the house. Tomorrow, after she told her father what was happening to Mark, everything would be all right.

After all, her father ran TarrenTech, didn't he?

If anyone could help Mark, surely he could.

22

When she woke up the next morning, Sharon thought for a moment that it had all been a bad dream. She would reach out to Blake, as she did every morning, and slip her arms around him for a moment, snuggling close to him before slipping out of bed to begin the day. Mark would already be up, and she would hear Chivas snuffling at his door as she passed it on her way down to the kitchen to put on a pot of coffee.

But then she reached out to Blake, and he wasn't there, and she realized that it hadn't been a dream.

She was exhausted this morning, as if she hadn't slept a wink, but when she finally forced herself to peer groggily at the clock on her nightstand, she saw that she'd not only slept—she'd overslept. It was almost eight o'clock. She started to haul herself out of bed, then flopped back on the pillow, a wave of despair washing over her.

For a few moments last night, after Mark had left, she thought the rift between her and Blake might heal, and for a little while it had, as the two of them waited in the den for their son to come home. Her first instinct had been to call the police, but Blake convinced her to wait, at least for an hour.

"He's not going to get into trouble," he'd told her. "He's just upset. When he calms down, he'll come home."

Of course, Blake had been right—it was a little less than an hour later that they heard the back door open quietly, then close again. Mark had appeared in the hall, and started up the stairs. It wasn't until Blake spoke to him that he'd realized they were both there, sitting in the near darkness of the living room, waiting for him.

He hadn't come in, but had instead remained in the shadows of the hall. His voice strained, he'd apologized once more for what had happened earlier. When Blake asked him where he'd gone, he hesitated for a moment, then shrugged. "Nowhere," he said. "I just walked around for a while, then came home."

He'd gone upstairs, and for a moment neither Blake nor Sharon had spoken. Then Blake uttered the words that started the argument all over again: "You see? He's fine, honey. He just had to be by himself."

It had gone back and forth for almost another hour until Sharon had finally come upstairs again, leaving Blake to sleep in the den, and crawled into bed, her body exhausted but her mind still whirling with conflicting thoughts. At some point she'd drifted into a restless sleep.

Now she got up, slipped into a robe, and went downstairs. The house was quiet, and for a split-second she found herself wondering where Chivas was. She wandered into the kitchen and poured herself a cup of coffee from the pot Blake had left for her, then glanced at the note he'd written. It was a strange note, sounding like nothing so much as a quick report from a husband who had simply decided to let his wife sleep late one morning. He'd fixed the kids breakfast, he had scrawled, and sent them off to school:

P.S. Mark seems fine this morning. He made the football team yesterday! Isn't that great?

Mark seems fine. That was it, after all that had happened yesterday? *Mark seems fine!* She crushed the note into a ball and hurled it across the kitchen. If Mark was so fine, how did Blake account for the condition of his room? She'd glanced into it on her way downstairs this morning, then quickly turned away from the mess, as if by ignoring it, she could pretend the episode had never happened.

She glanced at the clock, wondering if it was too early to call Dr. MacCallum at the hospital, and told herself that it was. If he had anything to report, he'd have called her.

She cleared the dishes off the table where her family had left them—at least *that* was normal—and began scraping the remains into the sink. Automatically, her eyes roamed out to the backyard, falling on the rabbit hutch.

The rabbits, too, looked perfectly normal, huddled together as always in the corner of the cage.

Then she saw a layer of frost still on the ground from last night—even the sky itself looked cold—and she frowned. What were the rabbits doing outside? For the last few days they'd come out only to eat, then scurried back into the warmth of their shelter.

She stopped what she was doing and stared out the window, a dripping plate held immobile in her left hand.

The rabbits weren't moving.

Her hand started to tremble. She quickly put the plate on the sink, pulled her robe tighter, and stepped out the back door into the icy chill of the morning.

The grass crunched under her slippers as she hurried across the lawn to the hutch, and her teeth began to chatter as the cold quickly penetrated her thin robe.

She stared at the rabbits for a moment, then her eyes shifted to their food dish.

It was full, and there was fresh water in the bowl next to the food.

And the rabbits still weren't moving.

They had frozen to death.

But even as the thought came into her mind, she knew it wasn't true. They were not huddled together as they normally were. They were simply piled up in the corner, two of them lying on their backs, the others looking as if they'd been tossed there like so many rags.

With shaking hands she opened the hutch door and reached inside to pick up one of the little creatures.

Its head rolled, dropping back so that it rested along the little animal's spine.

Its neck had been broken.

Numbly, she checked the other four rabbits.

All of them had died the same way.

Unbidden, an image of Chivas came into her mind, a vision of his body suspended limply above the floor with Mark's hands clenched tight around his throat. The rabbit dropped from her hands. A tiny cry erupted from her throat as she turned and stumbled back to the house.

She lowered herself onto one of the kitchen chairs, struggling to regain control of her emotions. Mark couldn't have killed the rabbits—he *couldn't* have! He loved them!

But he'd killed Chivas.

No! she shouted to herself. Something inside him killed Chivas. Something inside him over which he had no control!

She fumbled with the phone book for a moment, then punched the number of the county hospital.

She knew as soon as the voice came on the line at the other end that something was wrong.

"Th-This is Sharon Tanner," she said. "Is Dr. MacCallum available?"

There was a momentary silence, then the voice replied, "Oh, Mrs. Tanner, haven't you heard? Dr. MacCallum—" The voice broke, and Sharon could hear the woman taking a breath. "I'm sorry, Mrs. Tanner," the voice went on. "He's dead. He—He was in an automobile accident yesterday."

Sharon barely heard Susan Aldrich explain what had happened, for in her own mind she could still hear the soft click and the hollow sound that had made her think someone had been listening to her conversation with him yesterday.

Someone *had* been listening, and now Mac MacCallum was dead.

She didn't care what Susan Aldrich had said—she knew that whatever had happened to Andrew MacCallum had been no accident.

Charlotte LaConner knew she was insane.

It was the only possible answer, for only insanity could have explained the nightmare world she was in.

She couldn't move at all.

Her limbs felt heavy, her body immobilized by a lethargy she had never experienced before. The most she could do was roll her head slightly from side to side.

She'd been drifting in and out of sleep, but had long since lost any ability to discern which condition was sleep, which was wakefulness.

Around her the muffled howlings of the nightmares went on, low moans of despair punctuated every now and then by sharp cries of agony, or perhaps fury.

She didn't know which, didn't really care—for by now her spirit was becoming inured to the terrible sounds and her mind had almost given up trying to conjure the reality behind them.

They were worse during sleep, for then the horrible sounds lent hideous life to her dreams. There were shapes attached to them, bizarre creatures that circled her in the darkness, only allowing her faint glimpses of their horrible countenances before retreating back into the blackness, leaving her alone with her dread of what might be coming next.

The creatures were going to kill her sooner or later, of that she was certain. And she could do nothing about it except wait in the cloying darkness for the final moment to come.

But each time the creatures crept close—so close she could smell their fetid breath and hear their rasping between the terrifying bursts of sound—each time she felt them draw near again, and began to pray that at last they would close on her and end the misery in which she lived, they would slink away once more, back into the darkness whence they had come, and Charlotte would sob silently, craving even the release of death if only it would free her from the torturous hell of her life.

Now she was swimming back up into a state of semiconsciousness. It was like being underwater and slowly coming to the realization that if she didn't do something, she would die. Although she often wished for death, in those strange half-rational moments when she felt she could wish at all, she still found herself pulling back at the last moment, fighting down the urge to take a deep breath and feel the cool oblivion of limpid water flooding into her lungs.

She moaned softly and once again moved her head to the side. The darkness seemed at last to be washing away, and then a shaft of light struck her eyes. With a muted yelp she tried to twist away from the pain it brought.

Once again she tried to move her limbs, and again she could not. She lay still for a moment, then slowly became aware of herself.

This time, she knew, she was truly awake. She tried to move her tongue within her mouth, but it felt thick and numb, and her mouth was dry.

A second later she began coughing. As the spasms seized her body, she for the first time felt the restraints that bound her to the bed.

So she truly couldn't move at all.

She wanted to open her eyes now, but even that effort was too much for her to accomplish. At last, as the coughing eased and she felt her breathing return to normal, she managed to force her lids to open a crack.

She was in a room lined with white tile. Overhead, a bright globe of light seemed suspended in midair.

But the sounds of the nightmare continued. And then there was a lull in the din and she heard a voice.

"She's awake, Dr. Ames."

She closed her eyes again, a feeling of hopelessness

overwhelming her. She didn't know how long she lay there then, nor did she care, for even though this time she was certain she was awake, she was equally certain the nightmare was not about to end. Then she heard another voice.

"Charlotte? I know you're awake, Charlotte. Can you speak to me?"

Her eyes flicked open again. The light was softer now. To one side of her she could make out a face.

Marty Ames's face.

She tried to speak, but the words choked on her palate.

"Give her a little water," she heard Ames say. "Not much—just enough to rinse her mouth."

She felt a hand raise her head, then felt the touch of a glass against her lips. She sucked thirstily at the water, sloshing it into the corners of her mouth, then swallowing it as she tried to suck in yet more.

"That's enough," she heard Ames say. Then he was looking down at her once again.

"Wh-Where am I?" Charlotte gasped, barely able to recognize the croaking sound that was her own voice.

"In my clinic," Ames told her. "You had a breakdown, Charlotte. You've been asleep."

"H-How long?"

"A few days," Ames replied. Charlotte groaned softly and closed her eyes again. And then, dimly, she remembered what had happened just before the darkness had settled over her.

"Jeff . . ." she whispered. "Where's Jeff?"

"He's here, too," Ames told her.

Charlotte's features moved slightly, as if she were trying to frown but couldn't find the strength. "Here? But I thought—"

"He's sick, Charlotte," Ames told her. "He's very ill, and we're trying to find a cure for him."

"Sick?" Charlotte echoed. "I thought—" She faltered then, unable to formulate the words that seemed to hover just beyond her grasp. "See him," she breathed. "I want to see him. Please . . ."

For a long time she heard nothing, but the effort to speak was too much for her. Then, once more, she heard Ames's voice. "He's very sick, Charlotte."

Charlotte struggled again, forcing herself to find the right words. "I—I'm his mother," she gasped. "I can help him." She blinked her eyes open again and stared up into Ames's face. "Please," she begged, "let me see him . . . let me help him."

Slowly, a smile spread across Martin Ames's face. "Yes," he said. "I think maybe you can help him. And there isn't really any reason why you shouldn't see him, if you really want to." He disappeared for a moment. When he came back, he was pushing a wheelchair in front of him. He released the restraints from Charlotte's body, then gently helped her off the table. Her entire body felt exhausted from the slight effort required to get into the chair, and though she tried to keep her eyes open, tried to watch as Ames pushed the chair out of the room and into a corridor, the effort was too much. She let her eyes close again. She could feel sleep overtaking her once more. She tried to fight it, tried to concentrate on the words Ames was speaking as they moved slowly through the building. She could only catch snatches of it, though, and her fogged mind couldn't make sense of even the little she heard: ". . . tried to correct the imbalance . . . hormones . . . something . . . out of control . . . have to try something else . . ."

Then his words were drowned out as suddenly the air was filled with the nightmare sounds that had plagued her sleep and her consciousness for so long. But the sounds were clear now, no longer muffled. They pierced the air and swept away the mists that had settled over her mind.

She stiffened in the chair and her eyes came open to see at last the source of the screams that had haunted her.

It was a room very much like the one in which she'd awakened, except that in this room there was a series of cages—large cages, built of heavy-gauge wire mesh supported by iron posts. Most of them were empty.

Two were not.

In one of them a creature huddled in the far corner, its legs drawn up against its massive chest, its head dropped down as it stared out at the world through burning eyes that glinted from beneath a jutting brow. The creature's jaw, hanging slack, exposed a row of massive teeth, and from the depths of its throat an unending series of low moans was rising and falling, as if it were in some kind of unutterable pain.

Its arms were wrapped around its legs, and at the ends of its enormous fingers Charlotte could see the jagged remnants of fingernails that had turned to claws. As she stared at the creature, one of its fingers disappeared into its mouth and it began mindlessly chewing at the claw, all the while still moaning softly to itself.

Charlotte, horrified, had never seen a creature like it. The sight of it both sickened and mesmerized her. Finally she tore her eyes away and, hesitantly, turned to look at the other cage.

A scream rose in her throat, but was choked off by the sudden constriction in her vocal cords as she realized with terrible clarity that she was staring at her own son.

Or at what had once been her son.

Jeff was still barely recognizable as having once been human. Indeed, it was still possible to recognize his blue eyes peering out from their sunken sockets. His face was twisted now, and his jaw had grown heavier. His teeth, protruding from his mouth, had forced themselves out of alignment as they grew, and now he could no longer close his mouth at all.

His shoulders had broadened grotesquely, and at the ends of his arms, which now hung below his knees, his hands had grown into massive clubs out of which sprouted the gnarled, twisted claws that were his fingers.

It was from Jeff's throat that the hideous sounds of rage were boiling forth. As Charlotte watched in paralyzed horror, he hurled himself from one side of the cage to the other, tearing at the mesh until his fingers bled.

Ames pushed the wheelchair closer. Suddenly Jeff caught sight of his mother for the first time. A howl surged up from the depth of his torso as his eyes fixed on her, blazing with uncontrolled fury. As the roar of pure rage resounded through the room, bounding off the tiled walls to assault Charlotte from every direction, Jeff threw himself toward the front of the cage. There was a narrow gap there, a small hatchway through which attendants could slide a bowl of food. Jeff's right arm snaked through the tiny space.

His hand closed around Charlotte's throat, his long fingers completely encircling her neck, the claws that were his fingernails digging deeply into her flesh.

She tried to scream once more, but this time her entire throat was closed by the pressure of Jeff's grip and no sound came out at all.

And then, with a sudden jerk of his wrist, Jeff snapped his mother's neck.

Ames stared at the spectacle before him in silence for a moment, then reached out and pressed a button near the door. Immediately an alarm sounded. A few seconds later three attendants burst into the room, only to stop dead as they saw Charlotte's body, still held tight in Jeff's hands.

"Jesus," one of them whispered. "What the hell—"

"I couldn't stop it," Ames broke in. "She pushed herself toward the cage, and he just grabbed her." Then his voice grew angry. "Don't just stand there like idiots—get the hose!"

Instantly, one of the attendants pulled a fire hose from its rack on the wall, expertly flipping the kinks out of it as another twirled the valve that would release the torrent of water.

It took two of them, gripping the nozzle together, to keep it under control and aim it at Jeff.

The stream of water struck him in the chest, and for a moment he seemed surprised by what had happened. He looked up, bellowing with rage, then released his mother's neck and staggered back a step. Then both his hands closed

on the wire mesh and he braced himself against the force of
the water, screaming mindlessly at his tormentors. While the
first two attendants concentrated on keeping the nozzle trained
on him, the third wrestled Charlotte's body back into the
wheelchair and pushed it quickly out of the room.

Martin Ames followed after the chair. As soon as they
were away from the furious cacophony, he said, "Get her
into dissection immediately. I want her pituitary and adrenal
glands within five minutes—the rest can wait."

His mind already concentrating on how he might use
Charlotte LaConner's organs, he turned away and strode
down the corridor toward the lab.

Sharon had just finished dressing when the chime of the
door bell drifted up the stairs. She hurried down to the small
entry hall, determined to get rid of whoever it was as quickly
as possible. But when she opened the door and saw the ample
figure of Elaine Harris standing on the porch, she hesitated.

"Elaine! My God, it's not even eight-thirty yet. I was just
on my way—" Then her words broke off. What was Elaine
doing here? Before she could ask, Elaine told her.

"I wanted to know if there's anything I can do to help,"
she said, offering Sharon a look of sympathy.

Sharon looked at her in confusion. "I—I'm not sure what
you mean."

"It's all right, Sharon," Elaine went on, stepping inside
the house and closing the door behind her. Her voice dropped
slightly. "Linda told us what happened last night."

"Linda?" Sharon echoed, her confusion growing.

The smile faded from Elaine's face, replaced by a look of
concern. "You mean Mark didn't tell you he came over and
talked to Linda last night?"

Sharon shook her head, her mind numb. What had Mark
told Linda? And what had Linda told her parents?

Within two minutes she knew, and her heart sank. Whatever was going on, she was certain that TarrenTech was behind it, and that meant Jerry Harris, if not Blake, too. In the time since she'd heard about Mac MacCallum's death, she'd begun to wonder if it was possible that even Blake had allowed himself to become involved. She'd wanted to reject the idea, but as she thought about it—thought about his unwillingness to discuss what Ames was doing at the sports center, and his outright hostility when she'd told him she wanted to pull Mark out of the place—she'd begun to wonder.

About Jerry Harris, though, she had no doubts at all.

"Jerry promised to get in touch with Marty Ames this morning," Elaine went on. "I'm sure that whatever's happened to Mark, it isn't anything serious."

"Like nothing 'serious' happened to Jeff LaConner?" Sharon blurted out. She wished she could retrieve the words as a dark look flashed in Elaine's eyes. But a second later Elaine was shaking her head sadly.

"Jeff was never very stable," she said, and Sharon felt a chill as she realized that Elaine was almost parroting what Blake had told her only a couple of days ago. "I suppose he inherited it from Charlotte. But that doesn't have anything to do with Mark, does it?"

Sharon bit her lip, determined not to say anything more to Elaine. "No," she said. "I don't suppose it does."

When she remained silent, Elaine looked uncomfortable, as if the visit hadn't gone quite the way she'd hoped it would. Her eyes darted around the foyer, as if she were looking for something but wasn't sure what, then came back to Sharon. "You were going somewhere," she said, and left the words hanging as if waiting for an explanation.

Sharon's mind raced as she searched for something plausible that wouldn't arouse any suspicions in Elaine. And then she knew what she had to do. "Actually," she said, managing a rueful smile, "I was just about to hike out to TarrenTech to get Blake's car." She glanced up toward the second floor. "I'm afraid most of Mark's room is going to have to go to the dump, and I'm damned if I'll start dragging a bunch of ripped-up bedding through the streets of Silverdale. I'll look like a bag lady!''

For a split-second she was afraid Elaine didn't believe her, but then the other woman smiled. "Tell you what," she said. "Why don't you just walk home with me, and you can borrow my car. I'm not going to need it today."

Sharon breathed a silent sigh of relief and agreed that Elaine's idea certainly beat hiking all the way out to Blake's office. She put on a coat and left the house, not bothering to lock the door.

Aside from the fact that there was no real need to lock doors in Silverdale, Sharon had just made up her mind what she was going to do, and it occurred to her that there was no point in locking a house she had no intention of ever coming back to again.

For as soon as she got Elaine Harris's car, she was going to the high school to pick up Mark, then to the grade school to pick up Kelly.

And then, without telling anyone at all where she was going, she intended to drive away from Silverdale and never come back again.

23

The headache began during first period.

It crept up slowly, and for a while Mark hardly noticed it at all; it was nothing more than a slight throbbing at the base of his skull. But as the hour progressed, the pain inched up the back of his head, and when the first sharp pang struck, Mark flinched, his head coming up and his eyes widening with surprise. The math teacher, Carl Brent, happened to be looking right at Mark when it happened. He paused in his lecture.

"Do you have a question, Mark?"

The flash of pain was already ebbing, and Mark shook his head. Brent frowned, then went back to his lecture.

The next pang was stronger, and as it drove straight into Mark's skull, he bore down on the pencil he was holding until it broke with a sharp snap. Carl Brent's frown deepened and he gazed at Mark uncertainly. The boy's face looked pale. "Is something wrong, Mark?"

Mark hesitated. The pain was easing, but not as quickly as the first quick stab. "I—I just have a headache, that's all," he said. He leaned over to pick up the broken pencil, and as blood rushed into his head, a sickening wave of pain came over him. For a second he thought he might throw up. He straightened up quickly, but already his forehead was beaded with sweat. He wiped it away, then scrunched down in his seat.

He rummaged in his book bag for a pen, and tried to concentrate on the lesson, but then his vision blurred and everything in the room seemed to be tinged with red. And as Carl Brent went on with his lesson in plane geometry, a tiny flame of anger began to burn deep inside of Mark.

The third wave of the headache made Mark's whole body break out in a cold sweat, and suddenly he was afraid he was going to have an attack of diarrhea. He felt dizzy, and finally bent his head forward, as if trying to duck away from the pain.

"I think maybe you'd better go see the nurse, Mark," Carl Brent said. The rest of the class had turned to look at Mark now, but he made no move, and finally Brent spoke again. "Mark, did you hear me?"

Mark swallowed the lump that had risen in his throat, and managed to nod. He stood and took a step up the aisle. Another wave of searing pain slashed through his skull, and he had to put out a hand to steady himself against the wall.

Instantly, Linda Harris rose from her seat and went to him, instinctively glancing at the teacher.

Brent hesitated, then nodded. "Go with him."

"It's okay," Mark mumbled. "I can make it. It's just a headache. It's no big deal." The flame of anger inside him burned brighter.

Brent said nothing, but looked pointedly at Linda, who took Mark's arm.

"Come on," she said.

Mark's eyes met hers, and a pang of sudden fear shot through Linda. Mark's eyes—sunken even deeper than they'd been last night—seemed to bore into her. For a split-second she had a horrible feeling he was going to strike her. Then his eyes cleared and he winced as yet another wave of pain broke over him. Saying nothing, he started once more toward the door, Linda beside him, clutching his left arm to give him a little extra support.

Verna Sherman heard the door to the waiting room of her office open, and called out for whoever was there to come straight into her office. She quickly finished putting a final notation in the file she was updating, then put it to one side as Mark Tanner, leaning heavily on Linda Harris, lurched inside then sagged into one of the chairs, cradling his head in his hands.

Verna felt her stomach tighten as she saw Mark. It wasn't the first time she'd seen that strange look in the eyes of one of the boys. She reached for the phone and punched in the intercom code for Phil Collins's office. As soon as she heard his voice at the other end of the line, she told him to come to her office right away. "It's Mark Tanner," she said. "It looks like we have a problem. He . . . well, he looks just like Randy and Jeff did when they first started getting sick."

She put the phone back on the hook, then stood up and hurried around the desk. She laid a hand on Mark's forehead, but quickly withdrew it as he flinched away from her touch. She picked up one of the thermometers arrayed on the shelf above her sink, automatically swabbing it with cotton soaked in alcohol. "Headache?" she asked.

Mark nodded. Another wave of pain was cresting in his head, and he was unable to speak.

"It just started a few minutes ago, Miss Sherman," Linda told her. "M-Maybe he needs some aspirin." Even as she made the suggestion, Linda was certain that whatever was wrong with Mark, aspirin wasn't going to help. "Is he going to be all right?" she asked anxiously as the nurse tried to slip the thermometer into Mark's mouth.

Instantly, Mark's hand came up and knocked Verna Sherman's away. The thermometer clattered to the floor and rolled beneath the desk. Linda gasped, but Verna waved her away.

"Leave it," she snapped as she reached down to retrieve the thermometer. Then, sensing the lash of her own words, she spoke again, more gently. This wasn't, after all, Linda's fault. "It's all right. I can take care of him now. Just go on back to class."

"But—" Linda started to protest.

Verna shook her head. "I can't take care of both of you," she insisted. "I'm sure Mark will be fine, but not if you and I waste time arguing. All right?"

Linda still hesitated, but as the nurse turned back to Mark, kneeling next to him now and reaching tentatively toward his face, she decided she'd better do as Miss Sherman had told her. As she started out of the office, she heard the nurse speaking to Mark, her voice low, her words carefully enunciated.

"Now, Mark, I'm going to look at your eyes. I'm not going to hurt you. I'm your friend. Do you understand?"

Frowning, Linda turned around in time to see Mark, his eyes once again glowing oddly, staring at the nurse, finally nodding his head so slightly Linda almost missed it. Carefully, almost warily, Linda thought, the nurse reached out and tried to tip Mark's head toward the light.

Once again Mark's hand flashed up, striking the nurse painfully on the wrist.

Linda was about to go back into the inner office when a voice stopped her. "It's all right. I'll take care of this."

Linda, surprised, spun around to see Phil Collins, his breath coming quickly, as if he'd been running, standing just inside the door of the waiting room. Without waiting for her reply, he hustled her out into the hall, firmly closing the door behind her. As Linda started slowly back to her classroom, she heard the inside door close as well.

In Verna Sherman's office Phil Collins took one look at Mark Tanner and picked up the phone. A minute later he was talking to Marty Ames. "It's Tanner," he said. "Christ,

Marty, it looks like Jeff LaConner all over again! What the hell's going on?''

Ames cursed silently. He knew he'd been taking a risk with Mark, but after his conversation with Jerry Harris last week, he'd decided it was worth it. And yesterday, after another call from Harris, he'd doubled Mark's dosage of the growth hormone again, added a steroid compound, and strengthened the subliminal suggestion as well. If the boy turned on his own mother, who could blame anyone but Mark himself? And from what he'd heard already this morning, it apparently had almost worked.

But now . . .

"All right," he said aloud. "Just calm down, Phil. We'd better bring him out here. Just keep talking to him and try to keep him calm. If he *is* going—" He broke off his words, then began again. "If he's having a breakdown, there's a lot of pressure building up inside him, both physical and mental. The van'll be on its way within a couple of minutes."

Collins hung up the phone, then looked once more at Mark. He seemed to have shrunk back in his chair, but his eyes were flicking watchfully between the coach and the nurse, and when Collins moved toward him, his whole body tensed and his hands knotted into tight fists.

"Easy," Collins said. "Take it easy, Mark. We're going to help you. We're going to take you to the doctor, find out what's wrong, and fix it. Okay?"

Mark said nothing, but his head dropped down, hunching low between his shoulders. He flinched as yet another stab of pain shot through his skull. It felt as though his head were going to explode. As the pain spread out through his body, the red haze that fogged his vision deepened, and he squinted his eyes nearly closed in an effort to see.

Then a flicker of movement caught his attention and he instinctively struck out at it. There was a muted cry, then a thump as something hit the wall and fell to the floor.

"Jesus!" Collins swore softly. "You okay?"

Verna Sherman nodded and struggled to her feet, rubbing

the bruise on her shoulder where Mark's fist had struck her. "What's wrong with him?" she asked. "Some of the other boys got sick, but I've never seen anything like this."

She started to move toward Mark once again, then thought better of it and retreated to the chair behind her desk. "Is Dr. Ames coming?"

Collins nodded. "There should be a van here any minute," he told her.

His words seemed to strike a nerve in Mark. He leaped out of the chair and started toward the door. Instantly, Collins threw his own heavy frame toward Mark and his arms snaked around the boy's waist as they both fell to the floor. For a second Collins thought it was going to be all right—Mark was pinned beneath him, and he outweighed the boy by at least fifty pounds. But as Mark lunged upward and to the side, Collins felt himself lose his balance, then Mark wriggled loose from his grip entirely and made another try for the door. Collins reached out, grasped one of Mark's ankles and jerked hard.

Mark dropped heavily, grunting as his left knee struck the floor, then spun around to glower at the coach, his grunt of pain giving way to an animallike snarl as he confronted his attacker. The sheer fury in his eyes made Collins instinctively draw back, and Mark coiled himself to strike out once more.

Suddenly the door opened and three men from Rocky Mountain High pushed their way into the small office. As two of them grabbed Mark, the third one began forcing a straitjacket over Mark's head.

Bellowing with anger, Mark tried to duck away from the heavy canvas garment, but the two attendants holding him were too strong. The armless tube dropped over his torso, pinning his arms to his sides, and one of the men instantly pulled a heavy strap between his legs and buckled it in place while another one adjusted the neck so it couldn't slip down over Mark's shoulders.

"That's it," an attendant said when the straitjacket was firmly secured. "Let's get him out of here." Half carrying

Mark, half dragging him, they escorted him out of the office and into the corridor. They were almost to the main door when the bell signaling the end of the hour clanged loudly and the corridor, empty only a moment before, instantly filled with milling teenagers.

As soon as they saw Mark, swaddled in heavy canvas and supported by two men, they stopped, staring curiously. Just as the attendants were hustling Mark through the front doors, Linda Harris pushed her way through the crowd.

"Mark? Mark!"

Mark had been struggling wildly against his bonds, a series of unintelligible grunts and snarls boiling up from his lungs. But as Linda Harris called his name, he froze for a second, then turned toward her.

His eyes, burning with fury only a second earlier, cleared, and he focused on Linda. For a moment he was silent, then his mouth opened.

"Help me," he pleaded, his voice barely a whisper as his eyes now flooded with tears. "Please help me . . ."

As Linda stared after him in shocked silence, the attendants led Mark to the van, put him inside, and drove away.

Twenty minutes later, driving Elaine Harris's car, Sharon pulled up in front of the school, shut off the engine, hurried up the front steps and into the main hall. She glanced in both directions, then spotted the sign on the door of Malcolm Fraser's office. Her heels clicking loudly on the marble floor, she strode toward the principal's door, then stopped to compose herself before stepping inside. Finally, praying that the fear that still held her in its grip didn't show too clearly on her face, she went in.

Shirley Adams, only back at her desk for a few minutes after helping the rest of the staff herd the students back into their classrooms, looked up from her desk, her expression annoyed. "I'm sorry," she began, "but I don't know—"

Her voice faltered as she realized the person who had just come in wasn't one of the kids. "I beg your pardon," she said. "I thought you were—" She faltered again, then managed a recovery. "May I help you?"

Sharon's breath caught as all her internal alarms sounded a warning. Something was wrong—she knew it as certainly as she knew her own name. She forced herself to produce a friendly smile. "I'm Sharon Tanner," she said. "Mark's mother." She heard the secretary gasp audibly and saw her eyes flick instantly toward the inner office. Every nerve in Sharon's body tingled.

The secretary pressed a button on an intercom. "Mr. Fraser? I think you might want to come out. Mrs. Tanner is here."

There *was* something wrong. Why would the woman have summoned the principal before she had even stated her business? The inner door opened and a balding man of fifty or so years came out, rubbing his hands nervously before offering one of them to Sharon. "Mrs. Tanner," he began, and Sharon was certain his voice was a shade too hearty. "I was just going to call you."

She felt her knees begin to shake. "It's Mark, isn't it?" she demanded. "Something's happened to him."

"Now, just take it easy," Fraser began, but Sharon's eyes only fixed on him furiously.

"Where is he?" she asked, her voice rising dangerously. "What have you done with him?"

Fraser's eyes flicked toward the secretary, and Sharon knew beyond a shadow of a doubt that whatever he was about to tell her would be only a part of the truth. "I'm afraid he got sick this morning," the principal said. The fingers of his right hand were nervously twisting at the wedding band on his left, and he couldn't meet Sharon's eyes as he spoke. "I'm sure it's nothing serious, of course, but we always want to do the best we can for our kids."

Sharon felt a chill in her spine. "I want to know where he is!" she exclaimed. "If you've done something to my son—"

"Mrs. Tanner, please," Fraser begged. "If you'll just calm down, I'll try to explain."

"No!" Sharon stepped toward him. "I will not calm down, and you will tell me immediately exactly what has happened to Mark."

Fraser seemed to wilt before her anger. "The sports center," he said, his voice suddenly weak. "The nurse—and Phil Collins, too—they thought it would be best to send him out to Dr. Ames."

"Dear God," Sharon groaned. Turning away from Fraser, she pushed her way out of the office then broke into a run toward the main doors.

The sports center.

They'd sent him to the sports center, where all this had started.

As she bolted from the building and stumbled across the lawn toward Elaine's car, she prayed she wasn't too late.

Phil Collins stared at Mark Tanner in disbelief. The van was parked in the garage in the rear of the Rocky Mountain High building, and the three attendants were struggling to get Mark out of the vehicle. That brief moment of calm—those few seconds when Mark had stared so piteously at Linda Harris—had long since passed, and now he lashed out with his legs, his torso thrashing madly in the rear of the van. One of his feet caught an attendant on the chin and the man swore loudly, but ignored the ooze of blood that instantly began dripping from the cut on his face. Snatching a coil of rope from the corner of the van, he tied a loop in it, and when Mark again struck out at him with his foot, the attendant was ready. He slipped the loop over Mark's ankle and jerked it tight. Before Mark knew what was happening, the attendant yanked on the rope, pulling him out of the van and dropping him to the ground. Mark's head struck the concrete with a loud crack. He lay stunned for a few seconds, his vision blurred.

The attendant seized the opportunity to throw three more loops of rope around Mark's legs, binding them tightly together, fixing the end of the rope to the buckle of the straitjacket.

"Okay," he said grimly when he was done. "Let's get him inside."

The other two attendants, with Phil Collins helping, picked Mark up and carried him through the same door through which Jeff LaConner had been brought the night the police had carried him down from the hills. Collins gazed curiously at the tile-lined corridor and the light fixtures covered with heavy wire mesh. He'd never been in this part of the building before, and his first fleeting thought was that it looked more like a prison than a clinic.

As they took Mark into a small cubicle and strapped him onto an examining table, Collins heard a high-pitched wail echo from somewhere nearby. He glanced at the attendants, but none of them seemed even to have noticed the strange sound.

A moment later Marty Ames came into the room and went immediately to Mark. Ignoring Collins completely, he set to work. Making certain that Mark's body was strapped securely to the table, he directed the attendants to begin cutting away the straitjacket.

A brilliant overhead light was suddenly switched on. Mark howled with pain as the white glare struck his eyes. He clamped his eyes closed and turned his head, and suddenly Collins could see his face clearly.

It seemed to be changing almost before his eyes.

His forehead had taken on a slope, and his brows jutted out, giving him a simian look. His jaw, too, was enlarged, and when his lips curled back as a snarl of rage rose in his throat, Collins could see the roots of his teeth where they emerged from the gums.

Mark's teeth seemed too large for his jaw, and two of his incisors were already overlapping.

His canines, much longer than the rest of his teeth, had taken on the look of fangs.

The attendants finished cutting away the straitjacket, and now Collins could see Mark's hands.

His fingers, the knuckles swollen into misshapen knots, were working at the straps as he struggled to loosen them, and his thick nails—almost like claws—were scratching at the heavy webbing, leaving rough abrasions on the nylon from which they had been constructed.

"Jesus," Collins breathed. "What's happening to him?"

Ames glanced at him. "He's growing," he snapped. "Isn't it obvious?"

"But yesterday—"

"We stepped up the treatment yesterday," Ames said. "His whole system's gone out of balance, and now it's out of control." He plunged a hypodermic needle into Mark's exposed arm, but even before he could press the plunger home, Mark lunged upward. The strap over his chest parted, and as Mark came to a sitting position, the needle snapped, leaving its end still buried beneath Mark's skin.

"The prods!" Ames commanded, but the order was unnecessary, for already two of the attendants were holding electric cattle prods against Mark and pressing on the buttons that would activate them.

As the shocks entered his body, Mark's muscles went into convulsions and he flopped back to the table. "Again!" Ames demanded, already preparing a second injection. As Mark once more went into a convulsion, Ames slid the second needle home and in the same movement pressed the plunger.

Mark continued to struggle, and Ames administered another shot. Only then did Mark's thrashings against his bonds slacken. As the drugs took hold, he stopped struggling, his jaw working, his eyes glowing with sullen fury. Then, at last, a sigh drifted from him and his eyes closed.

For a few seconds there was silence in the room. It was Phil Collins who finally broke it.

"H-How did it happen?" he asked. "Is he going to be all right?"

Ames, his eyes still fixed on Mark, ignored the first question. "I don't know," he said. "It's going faster with him than with the others. We're trying to figure out how to control it, but—"

Collins stared at him. "The others?" he echoed. "You mean there are more like him?"

Ames turned to gaze contemptuously at the coach. "What the hell did you think happened to the others?" he demanded.

Collins's mind reeled. He'd known there had been problems, known that some of the boys had reacted badly to the pressures of the sports program and had had mental problems.

Problems he'd been assured had been solved.

But of course, he'd wanted to believe the problems had been solved, because he liked what Ames—and TarrenTech—had done for his team. And Ames—as well as everyone at TarrenTech, from Jerry Harris on down—had always assured him that the problems were minor. It was just a matter of stopping the treatment and giving the boys time to recuperate.

And of course he'd never asked what that treatment was. Or what happened to the boys after they left Silverdale.

He hadn't wanted to know.

It had been easier to assume the boys were all right, living with their families in other parts of the country, going on with their lives.

But now, as he stared at Mark Tanner, he had to face what he'd known, deep inside, all along.

"They're still here, aren't they?" he asked, his voice hollow as he heard once again the bestial howl that had echoed through the corridors a few minutes before.

Ames nodded. "Of course they're here," he said.

"B-But you told me they were all right," Collins protested. He was grasping at straws now, trying to justify what he'd allowed himself to do, to become a part of. "You told me you'd just stopped the treatments! You told me they'd be fine!"

"And you believed it," Ames replied, his voice hard. "You believed it because you wanted to believe it. You wanted to believe in magic—in a miracle with no price—but there isn't any such thing! There's only science, and experimentation, and a lot of failure before you find success. And there's always a price, Collins." His voice dropped slightly and a cold smile twisted his lips. "Do you really think the lives of a few boys are too high a price for what TarrenTech and I have given this town?"

Without waiting for an answer, he turned his back on Collins and began issuing orders on what was to be done with Mark Tanner.

24

Sharon could see the Rocky Mountain High campus now. It was only a quarter of a mile ahead, but the large building in the center of the lawns and playing fields was clearly visible, and as she approached it, Sharon found herself wondering how she could ever have thought that it looked like anything but a prison. Now that she was certain that something evil was happening within its rustic-looking walls, the lodge had taken on a forbidding look that sent a chill down her spine.

She slowed the car and turned up the side road that led toward the sprawling grounds of the sports center, telling herself that the eerie feeling she suddenly had of being watched was only a trick of her imagination. Against her will she found herself looking around, examining every tree she passed, searching for signs of a sophisticated security system. And yet she knew her observations were futile, for if, indeed, a system of cameras and alarms guarded the premises, surely it would have been designed to be totally invisible.

She slowed the car even more as she approached the gates, resisting her impulse to turn around and go back to town. But even if she did, what could she say? An image of herself striding into the tiny Silverdale police department came to mind. She could picture the skeptical looks of guarded incredulity on the officers' faces as she tried to tell them she was certain her son had been made the victim of some kind of medical experimentation. At best they would dismiss her as a crank; at worst they'd consider her deranged. And so she drove on, passing through the gates and starting along the drive toward the lodge itself.

Glancing into the rearview mirror, she saw the gates swing slowly closed behind her. For an instant a wave of panic threatened to engulf her. Had she come here only to become a prisoner?

She told herself it was ridiculous, that the situation couldn't be nearly as serious as she was letting herself imagine it. And yet, as she parked Elaine Harris's car in front of the lodge, left the keys dangling in the ignition, and mounted the steps to the wide veranda, she had to fight down the urge to turn and run away.

She touched the front door almost tentatively, only realizing as it started to open that she'd half expected to find it locked. When she stepped into the lobby itself and saw that it was deserted, she felt her senses heighten, her nerves begin to tingle.

Danger.

She sensed danger all around her.

But nothing in the lobby had changed since the last time she'd been here.

The same comfortable sofas and chairs were arranged in groups on the polished hardwood floors, and in the immense hearth, a fire had been laid. A few magazines were scattered on the top of the large burl coffee table that separated two of the sofas. Rocky Mountain High still looked for all the world like the lobby of a resort hotel.

Except that nobody was there.

She walked through the lobby to the dining room, her heels echoing loudly on the bare floor, then turned left and headed toward the suite of offices that belonged to Martin Ames.

The feeling of being watched—of having her every move-ment closely monitored—increased. Twice she found herself glancing back over her shoulder, anticipating seeing someone behind her, moving up close to her, ready to seize her.

But the corridor remained empty, and then she was stand-ing at the closed door to Ames's office. She hesitated a moment, reached out and twisted the knob.

She pushed the door open.

Marjorie Jackson glanced up from the phone. As she recognized Sharon, an expression of surprise came into her eyes. She stopped dialing and dropped the receiver she was holding back in its cradle.

"Well," she exclaimed a little too brightly. "I guess I can stop trying to track you down, can't I?"

It was the last thing Sharon had expected to hear. She stared at Ames's assistant, nonplussed. "Y-You've been trying to reach me?" she asked.

Marge Jackson pursed her lips sympathetically. "You must have already heard about Mark," she said.

Sharon recovered then and nodded tersely. "I want to see him," she said. "And I want to know why he was brought here."

The smile faded from Marjorie Jackson's lips, and her brow creased fretfully. "Oh, dear," she said. "I—I'm not certain you *can* see Mark right now. I believe he's in treat-ment with Dr. Ames. If you'll just let me check—" She reached for the phone again, but Sharon cut her off.

"What kind of treatment?" she demanded. "No one here has any right to treat my son without my permission. The school had no right to send him here, and you have no right to treat him."

Mrs. Jackson seemed stunned by the cold anger in Shar-on's voice. "Mrs. Tanner—I—I'm not sure what to say. Perhaps there's been some mistake."

"The only mistake," Sharon said, her voice harsh, "was my husband letting Mark get involved at all in whatever's going on out here."

"But he's ill, Mrs. Tanner," Ames's assistant began again, licking her lips nervously. "We're just trying to help him."

"Is that what you believe?" Sharon flared. She glared at the woman. "Well, let me tell you that Mark was perfectly fine until he came out here. Now where is he?" Her voice rose and she leaned forward, bracing herself on the assistant's desk. "I want to see my son," she said once more. "And I want to see him this instant! Do you understand me?"

Marge Jackson's demeanor changed. Her look of sympathy congealed into officiousness and she rose to her feet. "I understand that you're upset," she said, her voice stern. "And you have a right to be. If my son were ill, I'd be upset, too. But you do not have the right to storm in here making demands that are impossible to meet. We're trying to help your son—at the request of your husband—and if you will calm down, I'm sure Dr. Ames will be able to explain everything to your satisfaction. But he cannot attend to both you and Mark at the same time, so I would suggest that you make up your mind right now what is more important to you—having your questions answered or having your son cared for?"

Sharon took a step backward. Her tone, as well as her words, had pierced Sharon's armor of indignation. She suddenly felt uncertain of herself. What if she were wrong?

As she stood staring at the assistant, trying to judge the sincerity of the woman's words, the silence that had fallen over the office was broken by a faint scream.

Sharon stiffened.

And then it came again, louder this time.

Like a wild animal howling in the night.

Sharon froze, remembering Kelly's nightmare and the sound she had heard drifting through the early morning darkness as she'd opened her daughter's window.

The sound of an animal howling in the night.

She spun around and strode to the door, her mind made up. She knew Mark was here, knew she had to find him. The sound she'd just heard hadn't come from an animal at all.

It had come from a human being.

Or at least something that had once been a human being.

As she stepped into the corridor, two white-coated attendants appeared on either side of her, seizing her arms.

"No!" She tried to jerk free, but knew she had no chance. Both of them were far larger than she was, and their hands closed tighter, digging into her flesh like bands of iron.

My God, it *is* a prison, she thought as one of the guards gagged her and both of them hustled her along the corridor. It was a prison, and now she was a prisoner.

She knew now that it had indeed been a mistake to come here.

But she also knew it was too late.

Blake Tanner sat staring at the computer terminal in front of him, but his mind refused to focus on the columns of figures that covered the screen. Finally he leaned back, stretched, stood up and walked to the window. He gazed out at the mountains rising to the north and east, their jagged, forbidding peaks covered with snow. In another couple of weeks the skiing season would begin. It had been years since he'd taken the time to go skiing in California, and he was looking forward to it now. In fact, on the coming weekend he might take Mark shopping and get him outfitted for the winter sports ahead.

Mark.

His son had been on his mind all morning. Indeed, he'd gotten little sleep the night before as he'd lain restlessly on the sofa in the den, his head propped up at an awkward angle by the hard pillow that had never been intended to serve as anything more than an armrest. But it was more than the discomfort of the sofa that kept him awake, for despite the stance he'd taken with Sharon, he was beginning to worry about his son, too.

That morning he'd once again gone over the material waiting for him the morning after Mark had been beaten up, when Jerry Harris had first suggested putting his son under Martin Ames's care. And this morning all the data he'd reviewed still looked totally innocuous.

There was a lot of theoretical work, speculating on the relationship between vitamins and hormone production within the human body, and even more data—not all of which Blake had understood—that purported to demonstrate the factual basis of the theorizing. All of it, this morning as well as when he'd first studied it, seemed totally harmless.

Too harmless?

He tried to reject the question but found he couldn't. For if the compounds being administered to Mark were truly as innocuous as the data made them out to be, how could the changes in Mark have taken place so quickly and been so radical?

Nor was it simply a matter of the physical changes—perhaps, if there'd been nothing more, Blake could have accepted them at face value. But the personality changes?

About those Blake wasn't nearly so comfortable, despite the assurances he'd made over and over to Sharon that their son was merely going through the normal vacillations and inconsistencies of adolescence. Indeed, as the night had worn on, he'd begun to wonder whom he'd truly been trying to convince: his wife or himself.

This morning, his eyes heavy with lack of sleep, he'd tried to study Mark as the boy gulped down his orange juice and gobbled a bowl of cold cereal before departing for school, but he still wasn't convinced he'd actually seen anything.

Perhaps, after the argument with Sharon, he'd only imagined that Mark's features looked coarser and his eyes sunken. For a moment he'd thought that Mark's fingers looked oddly oversized, too, but he decided that was ridiculous and dismissed it from his mind.

And yet . . .

The intercom buzzed, rousing him from his thoughts. He turned away from the window, returned to his desk and pressed a key beneath a flashing light. "Tanner."

"It's Jerry, Blake. Can you come over to my office?"

Though the words were innocent enough, there was something in Jerry Harris's voice that made Blake frown. "Problem?" he asked.

There was an empty silence for a moment, then the speaker in the intercom crackled to life again. "You might say that," Harris finally replied. "Just get over here, will you?"

Blake released the switch and saw the light go out. Leaving his computer screen still glowing with the report he'd been staring at all morning, he headed for the door to the corridor, then changed his mind and went toward his secretary's office instead. As he came out of the inner office, Meg Chandler glanced up at him. "Shall I hold your calls or forward them?"

"Hold them, I guess," he said. Then: "Anything going on this morning?"

The young woman shrugged. "Nothing that I know of. Why?"

Now it was Blake who shrugged. "Who knows? Harris just called me and he sounds sort of . . ." He hesitated, searching for the right word. "I don't know—sort of funny."

Meg shook her head. "Don't ask me. One thing that's not in my job description is to know what's going on in Jerry Harris's mind."

"Remind me to revise your job description, then," Blake observed darkly as he left the office to go to the suite next door.

Jerry Harris's secretary waved him directly into the inner office, and when he entered, Harris himself waved him to a chair. His voice dropped as he quickly finished the phone conversation he'd been involved in. When he finally turned to face Blake, his eyes were grave.

"I'm afraid we do have a problem," he said. His eyes met Blake's, and suddenly Blake was certain the problem concerned his son.

"It's Mark, isn't it?" he asked, trying to keep his voice steady.

Harris nodded. "I'm afraid he got sick at school this morning," he said. "He's at the sports center right now, and Marty Ames is taking care of him."

"Sick?" Blake echoed. "But—But he was fine this morning." He glanced at his watch. It was barely ten-thirty. "Christ, I only saw him three hours ago! What's wrong?"

Harris took a deep breath, then stood up and came around his desk. He leaned against it, gazing down at Blake. "I'm afraid something's gone wrong with his treatment," he began.

Blake felt a sudden chill. "I—I'm not sure I understand," he replied.

Harris's hands spread in a gesture of helplessness. "I'm not sure I can explain it to you precisely," he said. "As I told you, Ames is doing experimental work and—"

But Blake didn't let him finish. He was on his feet now, his eyes sparkling angrily. "Now, just a minute, Jerry. You told me that what he was doing was perfectly harmless."

Harris shook his head doggedly. "No, I didn't. I said there was an element of risk to it. Slight, yes, but there."

Blake's jaw tightened. "All right," he said, regaining his composure. "Let's not argue about that right now. What's wrong with Mark, and why were you told even before I was?"

Harris's tongue ran nervously over his lower lip. "I guess Ames thought I should be the one to break it to you."

Blake sank back into his chair, his face ashen. His voice desolate, he whispered, "He—He's dead, isn't he?"

Harris took a deep breath, then let it out slowly. "Not yet," he said, and saw the tension in Blake ease slightly. "But I'm not going to tell you it can't still happen. In fact," he went on, "you're going to have to prepare yourself for that possibility."

Blake stared up at Harris. "No . . ." he breathed. "You told me—"

Harris's voice turned cold. "I told you there was an element of risk involved," he said heavily. "And it was you who signed the releases allowing Ames to treat Mark. Nobody forced you."

The words struck Blake like a series of blows. So Sharon had been right all along that something was wrong with the sports center, that whatever they were doing out there wasn't nearly as harmless as Harris had claimed. "Sharon," he said out loud, "I've got to talk to her."

He started to get to his feet, but Harris stopped him with a gesture. "She's at the sports center now, Blake."

For a split-second Blake felt relieved. At least she was there, at least she already knew. Then he realized that Jerry Harris had spoken in the same icy tones he'd used only a moment ago. Before he could say anything else, Harris continued.

"She's out there trying to make trouble." His eyes fixed on Blake. "When we talked about this, you told me there'd be no trouble from Sharon. You assured me that she'd go along with what we're trying to do here!"

Blake's mind reeled. What the hell was Harris talking about? Was he only worried about the company's project? And then, with terrible clarity, he realized that that was exactly the case. He'd been used, manipulated into allowing TarrenTech to use his own son as a guinea pig. But it wasn't possible. The others—

And then he understood.

"Jeff LaConner," he breathed. "That's what happened to him, too, isn't it?"

Harris offered a single nod. "Chuck knew the risks, and he knew the payoff." As Blake stared mutely at him, his tone softened. "And this doesn't have to be the end of the world for you, either, Blake. The company is prepared to take care of Mark. If he survives, everything will be done for him. And for you and Sharon, and Kelly, too, life can go on. You'll be transferred, of course, and there will be a major promotion, with a pay raise in keeping with"—he hesitated, groping for the right word—"well, let's just say that although your raise can't possibly compensate for"—he hesitated again, then pushed on—"for your loss, I think you'll find that it's surprisingly generous. And, of course, there will be stock options."

Blake gazed at Jerry Harris, hardly able to recognize him. Was this really the man he'd known for more than a decade and had thought of as a friend? Did he really think that any amount of money, any kind of job, could ever begin to assuage the guilt and loss he would suffer for the rest of his life? It was impossible—incredible! And then he realized that Harris was still speaking.

". . . we'll take care of Sharon, too, of course, in the event you aren't able to make her listen to reason. I'd hoped it wouldn't come to this, but—"

Take care of Sharon.

Kill her.

That was what the words meant. The translations were battering at his mind now; all the true meanings of the euphemisms he'd heard from Jerry Harris over the past weeks.

"New compound . . ."

That meant experimental medicine. Hormones? Drugs? *Vitamins! How could he have been so stupid!*

"We can help Mark . . ."

That one was easy: we can change your son into someone else. We can make him whatever you want him to be.

"Of course, there's always a slight element of risk."

Your son might die.

"We'll take care of him."

They'd taken care of Ricardo Ramirez, too, but it hadn't kept the boy alive. And Harris had already told him Mark was going to die.

"We'll take care of Sharon."

We'll kill her. If you can't make her listen to reason, if you can't convince her to keep her mouth shut and be happy with a fancy job for you and unlimited money—for he was quite certain the money would indeed be unlimited—then we'll kill her.

Suddenly it all closed in on Blake, and a cold fury, only made more intense by the knowledge that he was as much responsible for what had happened as anyone else, coursed through him. He rose to his feet, staring at Jerry Harris.

"What the hell do you think I am?" he demanded. "Do you really believe I'll trade my son for a raise and a promotion? Do you really think I'll just stand by and let you kill my wife and son? I thought I knew you, Harris, but I don't know you at all!"

Blake shoved Harris aside, slamming him hard against the desk, then jerked the door open.

In the outer office, waiting for him, were two uniformed guards. Their guns were drawn and trained steadily on him.

"I'm afraid we're not going to be able to let you go anywhere, Mr. Tanner," one of them said.

Mark woke up slowly, his mind rising grudgingly from the black depths of unconsciousness. For a few minutes the disorientation was total, then fragments of memory began to come back to him.

The terrible headache he'd suffered during his first class of the day.

Going to see the nurse, with Linda Harris walking beside him, supporting him when the blinding waves of pain threatened to knock him to the floor.

The rage that built in the nurse's office.

Then the terrible confines of the heavy restraints the three attendants had put him in.

He knew where he was now—they'd brought him to the sports center.

He opened his eyes a crack, and for a second was certain that he must be dreaming, for there was heavy wire mesh all around him, fastened to a framework of iron pipes.

He was in a cage.

His eyes popped wide open then, and he swung himself upright, letting his feet drop to the concrete floor of the small cubicle. He was sitting on a bare iron cot that held no mattress whatsoever, and his muscles felt stiff from the cold of the metal. He was still wearing the clothes he'd put on that morning, but his jeans felt tight, and his shirt, one arm ripped almost completely away from it, had lost most of its buttons.

The upper portion of his left arm felt sore. He rubbed it for a moment before noticing the twin punctures where the two needles had been placed, and the shallow cut where the broken needle had been removed.

His shoes felt too tight, and he bent down, loosened the laces, kicked them off and flexed his toes.

Then he heard a sound.

He glanced around, and for the first time saw the rest of the large room in which he was held captive. There were more cages, lining one entire wall, and in the cage two down from his own he saw a strange creature staring back at him. Its lips, stretched taut over enormous teeth, were working spasmodically, and a strangled sound bubbled ominously from its throat.

Mark frowned. It looked almost like some kind of ape, but it wasn't like any ape he'd ever seen before. Then, as the sound issuing from its throat began to take form, he felt a chill.

"Maaaarg . . ." the creature uttered. Then again, a little clearer this time. "Maaarkhh!"

Mark staggered back. It wasn't possible, and yet as he gazed at the creature and it stood up to reach out to him, its full six-and-a-half feet rising up from the floor where it had been crouching, he realized it was true.

He was staring at what had once been Jeff LaConner.

A scream of horror rose in Mark's throat, but he stifled it before it managed to escape his lips. His mind was working furiously now, and he was remembering more.

The fits of rage.

Like Jeff had had, before they'd finally taken him away that night.

The strange changes he'd seen in his own face just last night.

His hands rose to his face and he traced his features with his fingers. They felt different now. His brow was jutting forward, and his nose seemed to have changed, too. And his jaw . . .

He ran his tongue over the suddenly unfamiliar contours of his teeth. They felt large—too large for his mouth.

Then he looked at his hands.

His fingers, long and thick, seemed to splay out from his enlarged knuckles, and where before his skin had been smooth, tufts of hair were now sprouting on the backs of his hands.

His fingernails, thicker than they should have been, were curving downward, almost like claws.

Panic welled up in him, and again he felt the urge to scream. But again he stifled the urge as his eyes flicked wildly around the room, searching for a means of escape.

That was when he saw what had once been Randy Stevens, no longer in the least recognizable as human, huddled in the corner of one of the cages, chewing obsessively at one finger while his eyes darted aimlessly from one place to another.

Then Mark looked up and saw the television monitor suspended from the ceiling, beyond the confines of his cage.

He recognized the image on the screen at once, and this time an enraged scream rose in his throat before he could contain it.

The image on the screen was that of his mother.

She was sitting on a straight-backed chair, a look of abject terror on her face.

As Mark stared at the image, his maniacal howl rose once more, echoing off the tiles that lined the room, bouncing back at him again and again, then becoming lost in the sounds of his next high-pitched shriek of fury.

The door at the end of the long narrow room flew open and three men hurried in. One of them was unreeling a fire hose and another carried a cattle prod. The third man waited nervously by the door, ready to open the valve as soon as the hose was straightened out.

The first attendant jabbed the cattle prod through the wire mesh of the cage, but before he could trigger it, Mark snatched it from his hands, jerking it into the cage, then shattering it against the side of the cot.

"Get the goddamn water on," he heard the attendant shout. As the hose bulged with the pressurized water of the fire system, Mark hurled himself against the gate.

The mesh bulged out, but held.

Then water spewed from the nozzle, and as the attendant struggled to control it, Mark grasped the wire mesh with both arms and began to shake it, hurling his full weight back and forth. He felt the mesh give slightly, and redoubled his efforts. Finally, as the full force of the jet of water struck him, the mesh gave way, the entire panel covering the cage door coming loose from its frame. Bellowing with rage, Mark threw the mesh aside and plunged through the opening, his hands reaching out to grasp at the nearest attendant. The man screamed as Mark picked him up, his scream cut short as Mark smashed him to the floor. The attendant's head struck the concrete with a crunching noise and immediately a pool of blood began to form around his skull.

The stream of water hit Mark full on the chest then, and he staggered back, his balance momentarily lost. Then, as if spurred on by Mark's own action, Jeff LaConner hurled himself against the door of his cage, too, the force of his greater weight enough to burst the mesh from its stays. The attendant with the hose tried to scream a warning, and for a moment the jet of water strayed from Mark. Instantly, Mark threw himself on the man, his right arm snaking around the attendant's neck, then jerking backward. There was a sharp popping sound from the man's spine and he went limp in Mark's grasp. The third attendant froze, stunned into total inaction by what had happened. An instant later, as he realized his danger and tried to slam the door of the room, Jeff LaConner leaped past Mark, his fingers closing around the man's throat. While Mark watched, Jeff lifted the man off the floor, shaking him like a rag doll, then spun around, slamming the attendant against the hard tiles of the wall. Dropping the man to the floor, Jeff disappeared out of the door to the cage room.

Mark paused for a moment. All his instincts told him to follow Jeff, to escape while he could! But then his eyes caught a glimpse of Randy Stevens and his mind suddenly cleared. He reached down and ripped the key ring loose from the belt on the body at his feet. Working quickly, he shoved one key after another into the last of the locked cages, until one turned and the door swung open. Leaving the keys where they were, Mark scuttled after Jeff LaConner.

In the cage, Randy Stevens gazed blankly at the open door for a few moments, then his eyes focused slightly and he shuffled forward, slowly stepping across the threshold. He paused by the body of the dead attendant for a moment, poking experimentally at the flaccid corpse, then moved on to the man Jeff LaConner had slammed against the wall.

That man lay on the floor, his spine shattered, unable to move anything below his waist. He was moaning softly and his fingers were working spasmodically at the floor as he tried to drag himself toward the door.

Randy studied him curiously for a moment, then reached out and jabbed at the man with one finger.

The man screamed in agony, his face turning pale as the blood drained out of it.

Chuckling insanely, Randy repeated the jab, then repeated it once more. As each jab produced its scream, Randy's giggling increased, as did the pace of his mindless game of torture.

It wasn't until the man fell silent—overcome by his pain to the point where he passed out—that Randy at last lost interest in the hideous sport.

Getting unsteadily to his feet, he shuffled slowly out the door.

His head weaved from side to side as he looked first in one direction, then in the other. Finally, mindlessly, he drifted away down the hall, snuffling softly as he tried to follow the scents of Jeff LaConner and Mark Tanner.

But of course, it had been months since Randy had been capable of putting names to anything, human or otherwise.

For Randy, the transformation from human to beast had long since been completed.

Now, in the manner of the creature he had become, it was time for him to expand his territory.

25

Marty Ames was staring at the split screen of a high-resolution monitor, comparing the genetic structure of a sample of Charlotte LaConner's pituitary gland with that of her son's. Somewhere, he was certain, there was a minute difference, and if he could find that difference, buried somewhere with the DNA of the cells, he might find a clue to the mystery of Jeff's uncontrollable growth. He glanced up irritably when the alarm bell disturbed his concentration. No tests of the security system had been scheduled for that morning, and the sudden interruption of his work was an annoyance he needn't tolerate. He was just reaching for the phone to demand an explanation when one of the monitors on the wall caught his eye.

It displayed an image of the cage room. Ames's eyes widened in shock as he stared at it. The door of one of the cages stood open, and two others were ripped away entirely, their heavy wire mesh tossed aside like so much tissue paper.

One of the attendants was sprawled on his back, his head in the center of a pool of blood, and another lay limply a few feet away. The third, his fingers still clawing spasmodically on the floor, was staring up toward the camera, his expres-

sion an agonized grimace of pure pain. Of the occupants of
the cages, there was no sign at all.

Swearing out loud, Ames punched at the buttons on the
telephone and a moment later heard Marge Jackson, her voice
strained, come onto the line. "They're loose, Dr. Ames."

"I know that, damn it," Ames rasped. "Don't you think
I can see? Where are they?"

"I—I don't know," Marge stammered. "I think they're
still downstairs, but I can't find them on the monitors."

Ames cursed once more. He should have had the cameras
mounted everywhere, leaving not so much as a square foot of
the building unmonitored. But the cages were supposed to be
escape-proof—strong enough to contain practically anything.

"I'll be right there," he said. "Get Harris on the phone
and tell him what's happened. We're going to need help!"

He slammed the phone down and moved quickly to the
laboratory door. It was on the main floor, and there were two
locked doors sealing off the stairwell that led to the security
area in the basement. With any luck, the creatures were
contained in the bowels of the building. Still, he listened at
the door to the lab for a moment, then opened the door a
crack and listened again. But the racket of the alarm bells
effectively drowned out anything else he might have heard,
and finally he pulled the door wide and darted out into the
corridor. He glanced both ways, then hurried down the hall
toward his office. A moment later he found Marjorie Jackson,
her face pale, standing behind his desk, speaking frantically
into the phone. As Ames came in, closing and locking the
door behind him, she finished her call, her hands trembling
so badly that the receiver dropped to the desk when she tried
to hang up.

"Mr. Harris says there are people on the way right now,"
she told him. "They were bringing Mr. Tanner over and—"

Ames cut her off. "What happened?" he demanded.
"How did they get loose?"

Marge Jackson shook her head helplessly. "I—I don't
know. I was just coming back to the office when I heard a

scream, and when I looked at the monitor, they were already gone.'' Almost against her will, her eyes drifted to the TV screen, where the grim image of the cage room was still displayed, and she gasped as the attendant whose spine was crushed made another feeble attempt to drag himself toward the door. ''My God,'' she breathed. ''George is still alive. We've got to help him!'' She started toward the door, but Marty Ames's hand closed on her arm like a vise.

''Are you out of your mind?'' he asked. ''They're still down there!''

Marge's eyes widened. ''But we've got to do *something*.''

Ames's expression set grimly as he watched the screen for a few seconds, then flipped the switch to the other cameras scattered through the building. ''There's nothing we can do for anyone until we get some help.''

Suddenly there was a movement on the screen, and then they could see Jeff LaConner, his eyes darting furtively as he moved slowly along the corridor toward the stairs.

''That door better be locked,'' Ames breathed as Jeff's enormous form filled the screen. He reached out and touched another control, and the camera swiveled around to track Jeff's progress as he moved closer to the stairwell door. As if sensing the eye of the camera watching him, Jeff turned back and for an instant looked directly into the lens.

For a split-second nothing happened, then Jeff's lips curled back, and though neither Ames nor Marjorie Jackson could possibly hear it, both of them shivered involuntarily at the snarl they could see escaping the twisted maw of the creature that Jeff had become. At last Jeff's enormous hand came up, and the camera was blocked by its mass.

The screen went blank, and Ames and his assistant knew Jeff had torn the camera from its bracket.

Jeff stared mutely at the camera in his hands for a moment, crushed it between his palms and dropped its twisted wreckage to the floor. Then he turned to face the closed door a few feet away. He reached out almost tentatively and grasped the knob with his gnarled fingers. He twisted it, and when he found it was locked, a snarl of anger bubbled in his throat. Then he grasped the knob more tightly and jerked hard. Like the camera that had been suspended in a metal bracket only moments before, the knob resisted slightly, then came loose. Hurling it at the wall, Jeff began poking at the mechanism of the door's latch, and after a few seconds it dropped away on the other side.

The latch slid free.

He pulled the door open, swinging it hard. The crash of the metal door against the tile wall of the corridor echoed loudly for a moment, then died away. Jeff, breathing hard, gazed at the stairs for a few seconds, then started up. He came to the top and pushed his way into the carpeted hallway that led past the various offices and on to the dining room.

Rage built inside him as he stared at the open door halfway down the corridor that led to the suite of offices he still remembered as belonging to Dr. Ames.

He could remember Dr. Ames very well.

Other things might have fogged in his mind as his brain had begun to crush itself within the confines of his skull, but an image of Ames still burned brightly.

It was Ames who had done this to him.

Ames, who had pretended to be his friend, pretended to like him.

Ames, who had turned him into the pain-ridden creature he had now become.

It was all Ames's fault, and as he began shuffling along the hall toward the suite of offices, he could smell the man, feel the man's scent filling his nostrils, fueling the fury inside him.

He lurched through the door into the outer office. Grunting, his breath coming in short, heavy rasps, he felt the anger within him building to the breaking point.

Grabbing Marjorie Jackson's desk, he upended it, lifted it

off the floor, and flung it against the wall. The plaster shattered under the impact of the heavy, walnut desk, and behind the plaster there was a snapping sound as the laths themselves broke under the force of the blow.

Then, his eyes glowing beneath the deep ridge of his brows, he moved toward the closed door to the inner office.

"Get back," Marty Ames told Marjorie Jackson. Her face had paled as the crash in the outer office confirmed that the beasts were no longer confined to the basement. She was huddling close to the wall now, and as Ames spoke, she moved around behind the desk itself.

Marty Ames opened the bottom drawer of his desk and pulled out the .38-caliber pistol he'd started keeping there when he first realized that some of the boys might become dangerous. But since he'd bought the gun, there hadn't been a single instance in which he felt he might have to use it, and after the first year he'd even given up the target practice he began the day he made the purchase. Now, as he fumbled with the safety and checked to see if there were bullets in the gun's cylinder, he prayed it was still in working order and that his aim would still be good enough to kill.

He had just slapped the cylinder back into the gun when there was a splintering sound. Then the door of his office, a single slab of solid walnut, was ripped off its hinges, falling across the floor in two immense pieces.

In the doorway, his deformed body hunched over so that his fingertips nearly touched the ground, his heavy jaw hanging slack as saliva dripped from his lower lip, was Jeff LaConner.

Marjorie Jackson screamed out loud as she stared at the inhuman form, but her scream was quickly drowned out by Jeff's own rising bellow of pure fury.

He lunged into the room, his long arms reaching out toward Marty Ames, his fingers already starting to close as he strained to reach his victim's neck.

Ames, his heart pounding, raised the gun and squeezed the trigger, firing point-blank into Jeff's chest.

Jeff staggered, looking down in surprise as a spurt of blood poured forth from the hole in his chest. Then, his eyes flicking once more to Ames, he bellowed and hurled himself forward.

Ames fired the gun again, then again, but on the next shot the weapon jammed. He hurled it aside and ducked the other way as Jeff pitched forward and crashed to the floor.

For an instant Ames was certain Jeff would heave himself to his feet and renew his attack, but when Jeff didn't move, Ames finally reached out with his foot and carefully rolled the body over.

One of Jeff's eyes was gone, and blood was slowly oozing from the pulpy mass of the empty socket. Ames stared at the body for a moment, then grabbed Marge Jackson by the hand and started dragging her from the room.

Outside, one of the TarrenTech station wagons was approaching, speeding up the road toward the main gates.

Randy Stevens shambled slowly through the maze of corridors. His brain had long since ceased to function with any sort of reason, and now he was moving aimlessly, his nostrils catching first one scent, then another. He turned a corner and saw an open door ahead of him. He passed through the door and began climbing the stairs, clumsily heaving his weight upward by grasping at the metal railing with his deformed fingers. He reached the top at last and stumbled out into the hall. He hesitated, his head swinging back and forth as he sniffed at the air. Then he caught a scent that stirred dim memories deep within his brain.

Vague images floated into his consciousness, images of trees and bushes, the river, and the sky above.

His nostrils sucking thirstily at the odors of fresh air, he turned toward the door to the right, where a bright line of sunlight shone beneath a crack. He fumbled with the door, then threw his weight against it. It burst outward.

He stood still, blinking in the glare of the sun as he breathed deeply, his lungs filling up with the first fresh air they'd tasted in more than a year.

In the distance he could make out the shapes of the mountains rising upward toward the sky, and some deep-seated instinct told him that there, in the mountains, he might find safety. He started toward them, his body lumbering on twisted legs, his knuckles dragging along the ground, half supporting him in the strange, loping stride of a great ape.

Then a movement caught his attention. He paused to swing around and stare dumbly at the car coming around the corner of the building.

Blake Tanner sat between two guards in the backseat of the station wagon. In the front, next to the driver, a third guard was twisted half around, his back to the door as he kept his eyes on Blake. For the first few minutes, after the guards had stopped him at the door to Jerry Harris's office, Blake's mind had gone blank with fear. But as the guards had marched him into the garage at the back of the TarrenTech building and hustled him into the station wagon, he had begun thinking again. He'd slumped in his seat, his eyes half closed, trying to give the guards the impression he'd gone into shock. But as the car left the TarrenTech grounds and moved along the highway toward town—never varying from the posted speed limit—then took the road up the valley toward the sports center, Blake began to understand the hopelessness of his situation.

This wasn't like one of the Robert Ludlum books he'd always enjoyed so much, in which a mild-mannered English professor always managed to overcome five highly trained master spies in a dark alley at midnight, emerging unscathed from a cross fire of bullets, with maybe a knife or two thrown in for good measure.

This was reality. And while Blake was in good condition, and felt sure that he could have taken any one of the guards in a one-on-one fight, he was acutely aware that he wouldn't last a minute against all three of them. Nor did he kid himself that they would delay shooting him if he pressed them. There would be none of the convenient delays James Bond always experienced while the villain toyed with him just long enough to give Bond an opportunity, which he always managed to seize.

No, these men intended to kill him, and while they would just as soon wait until they got him to the privacy of Ames's fenced-off compound, he was certain that if he made so much as a single false move, the guard in the front seat would squeeze the trigger of the .45-caliber pistol in his hand.

It wouldn't come from either of the guards at his side—too much risk of the bullet penetrating him and slicing on into the guard on the other side. But if they lost the rear window of the wagon, who would ever care?

The wagon had slowed as it approached the gates, but the driver pressed a button on a control attached to the visor of the car and the gates swung wide, then immediately began closing again as they passed through. The car sped up, veering to the left to head around to the back of the building.

If he was going to have a chance at all, it would be when the car came to a stop and one of the guards at his sides got out. Unless there was a garage inside the building here, as there was at TarrenTech.

"Jesus!" The word exploded from the mouth of the guard behind the wheel, and the man in the passenger seat jumped with surprise, then glared at the driver.

"Goddamn it," he began, but the driver ignored him, slamming on the brakes, and pointing ahead.

"What the hell's going on?" he asked. "What the hell is that?"

Blake sat up straight, peering between the two guards in the front seat.

Twenty yards ahead, standing in the driveway and staring

at the car as if it wasn't certain what it was seeing, was a creature such as Blake had never seen before.

It looked like some kind of strange evolutionary relic, some odd dead-end species that was neither man nor ape. It crouched down on its haunches, its head bobbing back and forth as if it were having difficulty focusing its eyes on the automobile.

The car screeched to a stop, and for a moment, as all five of its occupants stared at the strange half-man half-beast in the driveway, there was dead silence. As the driver started to speak, they heard a shout from the building. Seconds later Marty Ames burst out of one of the side doors, Marjorie Jackson right behind him. The creature in the road swung around, its eyes fixing on Ames. Suddenly it rose to its full height, a howl of fury bursting from its throat.

"Christ," the driver breathed. "It's going for Ames!"

He jammed the emergency brake on, then jerked at the seat belt with one hand as he shoved the front door open with the other. Then he was out of the car, his gun already out of its holster. Dropping to his knee, he grasped the pistol with both hands, braced it against the hood of the car, and squeezed the trigger.

The creature hesitated as the searing-hot bullet sliced through the flesh of its thigh, and then bellowed once more. For a split-second it couldn't seem to make up its mind which way to turn, then it headed toward Ames once more.

"Shoot it!" Ames shouted. "For Christ's sake, kill it!"

Marjorie Jackson had run in the other direction at the creature's approach, and managed to flee around the building. Ames was alone now, pressed against the building. Watching Randy Stevens charging toward him, he recognized the same fury in Randy's eyes that he'd seen only moments ago in Jeff LaConner's. He wanted to run, wanted to turn away and flee back into the building, but his legs refused to obey the commands of his brain, and he stood where he was, frozen in panic.

Another shot rang out, and Randy hesitated again, staggering to the left. He dropped to the ground and his head swung around as if looking for some unseen assailant that was jabbing at him with an invisible weapon.

All the guards were out of the car now, and Blake saw his opportunity. He scrambled out of the backseat on the side away from the building and broke into a sprint, hurling himself toward the fence that surrounded the property.

It wasn't much, but it was a chance. If he could scramble over the fence while the guards were still occupied with the nightmarish creature in the yard, perhaps he could get away.

Two more shots rang out, but Blake ignored them, concentrating on the fence, his legs pumping. He was only thirty yards from it now, then twenty.

Another shot rang out, and this time he saw a puff of dirt and grass rise up ahead of him and to the right. One of the guards was shooting at him now, and he dodged to the left, then ducked back to the right. When he was still five yards from the fence, another bullet struck the earth ahead of him and he dodged away once more.

Then he was at the fence and he threw himself at it, leaping as high up as he could, his fingers closing on the heavy mesh only a foot or so below the top.

The two thousand volts with which the fence was charged blazed through his body, convulsing his muscles, frying his brain in an instant. His fingers, frozen in place by the sheer power of the shock, clung to the fence, holding his dead body suspended nearly three feet above the ground.

A third bullet sliced into Randy Stevens, burying itself in his left lung, and he felt a stab of searing heat in his chest. He turned away from Ames now, every rational remnant of his mind focusing on escape.

He gazed once more toward the mountains, and broke into an uneven lope. His right leg was crippled, and every step sent spasms of pain shooting through his body, but he ignored it, plunging on toward the distant hills and the refuge he sensed in them.

Another bullet slammed into his body, then another, and finally he toppled forward, pitching face first into the ground, then dragging himself along, his left arm now as powerless as his right leg. But he wouldn't stop—couldn't—for some deep instinct for survival drove him on. He was near the fence now, and as yet another bullet slashed into him, he reached out toward it, stretching himself almost beyond his own limits.

The fifth bullet struck him in the head, exploding in his brain just as his fingers touched the fence and his body recoiled with the sudden jolt of electricity.

The mountains were still far away, but it didn't matter, for after a year locked in a cage in the basement of the sports center, Randy Stevens had at last found a final refuge.

Mark had searched the basement carefully, and finally found a room that held a control panel for the security system. He'd heard Randy Stevens scuffling around outside the closed door to the room he was in once, but had ignored the sounds, concentrating on fiddling with the switches and knobs on the control panel until suddenly one of the monitors flashed with the image of his mother. He'd glanced at the label on the switch—TREATMENT ROOM B—then looked once more at the picture on the monitor. His mother turned around and looked up at the camera. Immediately, the familiar anger rose in Mark. He turned away from the monitor and hurried from the room.

He was at the foot of the stairwell when he heard the sounds of gunfire from outside. He hurried up the stairs, then paused as he saw the open door to the outside. An instinct inside him urged him to make a dash for the freedom beyond the door, to escape from the building while he could, but he forced the urge aside. Instead he hurried to the door, closed it and threw the bolt that would lock it, then turned back, loping quickly along the corridor toward the dining room and the gymnasium beyond.

As he passed Ames's suite, he glanced inside. Beyond the wreckage of Marge Jackson's office he could see the crumpled form of Jeff LaConner lying in a pool of blood on the floor. He froze for a second, then rushed on.

He pushed his way into the gym and dashed across it to a small room on the other side.

There was a placard riveted to the door: TREATMENT ROOM B.

He crashed his weight against the door, and it burst inward.

He froze where he was and stared into the room.

Sharon, still strapped to the metal table, raised her head as the door burst open, her eyes falling on Mark.

His facial distortion had worsened, the supraorbital ridge over his eyes now jutting outward so that his eyes themselves had almost disappeared within the depths of their sockets. His jaw seemed far too heavy for his face and hung slightly open, and he held his overlong arms akimbo. As she stared at him, an anguished wail escaped his lips. Sharon stifled a scream. "Mark," she gasped. "Help me." She struggled against the heavy nylon straps, but they held firm, pinning her to the table.

Mark stared at her face, and the familiar rage welled up in him again. But she hadn't done anything to him—he had no reason to be angry at her.

And then, vaguely, a memory stirred.

A memory of being on the rowing machine and feeling a growing anger toward the images of his opponents. It was part of the treatment—he knew that now. They'd been giving him some kind of drug, a drug that induced anger, releasing extra stores of emotional energy from deep within his body.

A drug that made him furious, and made him desperate to win.

But yesterday—could it really have been only yesterday?—there had been other images, too. He could remember the flickering in the picture, could remember his anger shifting, focusing itself on his mother.

It was what they had wanted, and it had worked.

It was the sight of his mother's face that triggered the irrational rage, nothing more.

"Don't look at me!" he shouted. "Just don't look at me!"

Sharon hesitated, but something inside her told her to obey Mark without question. She let her head flop back onto the table, and her eyes fixed on the ceiling overhead. In the distance, dimly, muffled by the building, she could hear the sound of gunfire.

"What's happening?" she asked in a frightened whisper as she felt Mark's fingers working at the straps, jerking them loose. "What are they doing?"

"Killing us," Mark replied.

He jerked the last strap free, then turned away as Sharon sat up and rubbed at her numb legs.

"They want me to kill you," Mark told her. "That's what happened last night. I wasn't mad at you, Mom. They— They did something to me. If I look at you, I just go nuts!"

Sharon felt a sob rise in her throat and forced herself not to give in to it. Not yet—not now.

Now she could think of only one thing—getting herself and her son away from this place.

"Where are we?" she demanded. She swung her legs off the table and tested them against her weight. They threatened to buckle beneath her, but she steadied them with the sheer force of willpower.

"The—The gym," Mark stammered. "Behind the dining room."

"Come on," Sharon told him. She started to face him then, but remembered his words just in time. "Just follow me. I won't turn around unless you tell me to." Without waiting for Mark to reply, she ran out the door and across the gym toward the dining room.

Her heart was thumping and she was certain that at any second the attendants would appear, blocking her way, but when she burst into the dining room, she found it empty.

With Mark behind her, she ran through to the lobby and the front door beyond, praying that Elaine Harris's car was still parked in front of the building.

She hesitated at the front door, gazing fearfully through its heavy glass.

The car was still where she'd left it. In the yard there was a strange silence now. She took a deep breath, then threw the door open.

"Get in the backseat," she called over her shoulder to Mark. "Just get in and stay down."

She jerked the driver's door open and scrambled into the car, her fingers fumbling for the keys before she'd even slammed the door behind her. She heard the back door slam as she twisted the key, then uttered a silent oath as the starter ground but the engine failed to catch. Then, as her eyes flooded with tears of frustration, the engine roared to life. She released the brake and jammed the transmission into gear.

She pressed her foot to the floorboard, and the tires screamed as the station wagon shot forward, slewed around, then straightened. She ignored the driveway, heading straight across the front lawn toward the gates, coming back onto the roadway when she was still fifty yards from the fence.

She glanced at the rearview mirror, and behind her she could see Martin Ames, his hand waving wildly as he tried to get the guards' attention. But they were all huddled around a nearly shapeless mass on the ground near the fence, and by the time they looked up, she had almost reached the gates.

The car was moving at forty miles an hour when it struck the gates, and only at the last second, when she was certain the car wouldn't hit the stanchions to either side, did she duck her head down to protect herself if the windshield gave way.

She felt the impact as the car smashed into the metal. It lost some of its speed, then the gates gave way and the car once more sped up.

The windshield had held, and Sharon looked up again. Her foot was still jammed against the floorboard and the speedometer was going up rapidly now.

She braked as she came to the main road, then veered to the right, toward the mountains, and smashed her foot on the accelerator once more.

The car, with Mark crouched low in the backseat, raced away from Silverdale into the foothills of the Rockies.

26

Dick Kennally stood with his back to the window, staring out through the big picture window of Rocky Mountain High's dining room toward the mountains that rose majestically to the east. There was silence in the room, and he could feel the eyes of the three people behind him, feel them watching him, waiting for him to say something.

His eyes left the mountains and scanned the broad lawns and playing fields within the confines of the fence surrounding the property. It looked serene and peaceful, and there was, truly, no sign left of the carnage he'd seen when he arrived at the sports center two hours earlier. He'd been stunned at the sight that greeted him: Blake Tanner's body, still suspended from the fence, his dead fingers locked in the mesh, his body hanging limp, a pool of blood spreading beneath his feet.

A hundred yards farther down the fence another body, this one crumpled on the ground, riddled with bullets, but no more dead than Tanner himself. Ames had told him that the ruined remains had once been Randy Stevens, and as a wave of nausea threatened to overwhelm him, Kennally had rejected the statement as impossible. Whatever it was on the ground, surely it had never been human.

But then he had seen Jeff LaConner, and slowly the full truth of what had been going on within the confines of the sports center had begun to sink in.

For the better part of an hour he'd put his emotions on hold and gone about the technical business of dealing with the mess. Photographs had been taken—photographs he was now certain would be destroyed—and the bodies had been removed to a room in the basement—the basement he hadn't known was there, with its isolation room and cages, its stark white-tiled walls and hard iron cots. The four guards from TarrenTech had done the work, for even in his initial shock, Kennally had instinctively known better than to call in his own men. The driveway and lawns had been hosed down—even the fence itself had been washed—so that now as he looked out the window, no traces remained of the carnage that had taken place.

And he had no doubt that the same thing would happen within Ames's office. By tomorrow morning the rooms would be repainted, the carpet and door would be replaced, and Marjorie Jackson's desk—or an exact duplicate of it—would once more be standing in the outer office, with Marjorie herself again guarding the privacy of her employer.

Outside, on the road leading up into the mountains, a roadblock had been set up by a team of TarrenTech security men. It was a mile away, around a bend, invisible to anyone coming from the town, but it was unlikely anyone would be driving that direction today. The road led only to a ski area seven miles away, and there was no reason for anyone to go up there for another two or three weeks at least.

But if Sharon Tanner tried to come down again, the roadblock would bar her way. Not that she would come down—Kennally was certain of that. No, he and a team of TarrenTech men would have to go after her, and hunt her—and her son—down.

Hunt them down like animals.

And then it would be over.

Jerry Harris had already explained it to him. There would

be another accident, but this time it would take place far from Silverdale. There were plenty of witnesses to what had happened at the school that morning—half the student body had seen Mark being taken away in restraints.

The story was simple. His parents had decided to take him to the state facility in Canon City, but as they drove through the mountains, an accident had occurred. Blake had somehow lost control of the car on the winding mountain road—perhaps it had even been Mark's fault, perhaps the boy had suddenly gone into one of the sudden rages that had been plaguing him yesterday, and attacked his father. But the point was, the car had gone out of control, plunged off the road and dropped into one of the deep canyons below, where it had burst into flames.

There would even be bodies—burned beyond recognition, perhaps—but still, bodies that could be buried right here in Silverdale. Eulogies would be spoken and tears shed.

And then life would go on as before.

If Dick Kennally agreed to go along with the plan.

Harris had explained the alternative, and even now, as he gazed out at the peaceful autumn afternoon, it made Kennally shudder.

If what had been happening in Silverdale got out, the whole town would be ruined. For nearly all of them, one way or another, had let themselves be involved in the TarrenTech project that was based at Rocky Mountain High. Perhaps not actively involved, perhaps not even consciously involved, but still culpable. For some of them—and Dick Kennally knew beyond a shadow of a doubt that he was one of them—the involvement had been active. It had been he himself who had delivered Jeff LaConner to Marty Ames that night a few weeks ago; he who over the years had let himself begin taking more and more of his orders directly from Jerry Harris.

It had been he himself who filed a report on the death of Andrew MacCallum that left no possibility of any findings other than the "accidental" verdict the coroner had reported only a few hours ago.

Phil Collins had been actively involved too, cooperating with Ames and Harris at every turn, doing what was asked of him to keep the program supplied with subjects. Perhaps he didn't know exactly what was going on, but surely he must have known that what Ames was producing couldn't come from exercise and diet alone. So Collins, too, was directly culpable.

Kennally even now couldn't begin to count how many people had been involved over the years, how many of the boys who'd played on the Silverdale teams had had their bodies altered and reformed by Martin Ames's biological alchemy.

Dozens, certainly.

And the whole town—in blissful ignorance—had gone unquestioningly along, for the project had brought them prosperity and fame.

Even the major college athletic scouts came to Silverdale every year now, eager to take their pick of the oversized, hard-playing Silverdale boys, the boys who had grown up in the fresh air and healthy climate of the Rocky Mountains.

And in Martin Ames's laboratory.

If it got out, TarrenTech would be ruined, of course, along with Silverdale.

How many of them would wind up in prison? How many of them would even survive if it were ever revealed that they had been experimenting with human lives?

The name of Silverdale would still be famous, but Dick Kennally shuddered as he realized what that fame would now mean.

And none of them would ever be able to put it behind them.

"There really isn't any choice, is there?" he heard Jerry Harris asking.

Finally he turned around and faced them. Jerry Harris and Marty Ames were staring at him, their eyes hard.

Even Marjorie Jackson, her face pale, her hands clasped nervously together in her lap, was watching him expectantly.

Finally, he came to his inevitable decision.

"All right," he said. "But what about the little girl? Kelly, isn't that her name?"

Suddenly the tension in the room broke. Marge Jackson, sighing with relief, stood up and went to a large coffee urn that sat on a sideboard, poured herself a cup, then poured another for her boss.

"She'll be taken care of, of course," Harris said. "Lord knows, none of this was her fault." He glanced sharply at Kennally. "What about your men?" he asked.

Kennally shook his head. "We'll keep them out of it entirely. No one but Collins and I should ever know exactly what happened out here." His eyes met Harris's. "So I'm going to need some of your men for the search party."

Harris nodded abruptly. "How many?"

Kennally shrugged. "No more than half a dozen. I'll use Mitzi to track them, but I don't expect they'll get far." His eyes wandered to the mountains again. "Fact is, I'll bet they're just sitting up there in your wife's car, waiting for us."

The decision at last made, he rubbed his hands together briskly, eager to get started. The sooner it was over, the sooner he could begin trying to forget it had ever happened.

Kelly Tanner had been fidgeting all day long, squirming in her seat, barely listening to her teacher. She wasn't sure what was wrong, but as the day stretched on and the clock didn't seem to move at all, she got more and more nervous, until she felt as though she might jump out of her skin. But the last bell finally rang and she slithered out of her seat, scurrying toward the door to be the first one out. Erica Mason, who Kelly had already decided was going to be her best friend, caught up with her in the hallway.

"Want to come over to my house?" she asked. "My mom said we could make cookies this afternoon if we wanted to."

Kelly shook her head. "I think I better go home."

Erica's expression crumpled in disappointment, but then she brightened. "Maybe I'll come with you," she offered. "Maybe your mom will let us make cookies."

But Kelly shook her head.

Something was wrong at home, but she didn't know exactly what it was. All she knew was that something was wrong with Mark and that her parents had been fighting about it most of last night. And then her mother hadn't even come down for breakfast in the morning, which only happened when she was sick.

But her father hadn't said her mother was sick—in fact, he'd hardly said anything at all. But he'd kept looking at Mark, and Mark had gone off to school earlier than usual, and he'd hardly said a word, either.

And all day she'd had one of the feelings she got sometimes.

It wasn't anything she could identify very clearly—just a funny feeling in the pit of her stomach, and an idea that something was going to happen.

And whenever she had that feeling, she had one of her fidgety days. But she'd never had a fidgety day as bad as today. "I just have to go home," she mumbled. "There's some stuff I have to do." Turning away, she left Erica standing in the hall and hurried out into the schoolyard. She stopped to pull on her jacket, then slung her book bag over her shoulder and started home.

Fifteen minutes later she turned onto Telluride Drive and saw her house halfway down the block, on the other side of the street.

She stopped walking and stared at it.

Though it looked just the same as it always did, there was something different about it this afternoon.

Even from here it looked sort of empty.

Moving more slowly, the strange queasy feeling in the pit of her stomach getting worse every second, she continued toward the house, then stopped again when she was directly across the street from it.

Suddenly she wished she'd gone over to Erica's after all, or let Erica come home with her. Standing on the sidewalk, staring at the house, she had a lonely feeling.

But that was dumb, she told herself. She wasn't a baby, and she'd come home lots of times to find nobody home. And there would always be a note, stuck to the refrigerator door with a magnet, telling her where her mother was and what time she'd be home.

But of course, before, Chivas would always be there, and he was lots of company for her.

Today, Chivas wouldn't be there.

Tears flooded her eyes, but she resolutely wiped them away with the sleeve of her coat. Finally she trudged on across the street and up the walk to the front door.

Her feeling that the house was empty was even stronger now. She started to reach into her pocket for her door key, then a tiny voice in her mind told her to try the door.

It was unlocked. She frowned and pushed it open.

Usually when the door was unlocked it meant her mom was home.

But today the house still had that funny empty feel to it.

"M-Mom?" she called out as she stepped into the foyer, leaving the door standing open behind her. "It's me! Is anybody home?"

Her voice echoed back to her, and when there was no reply, her vague feelings of worry closed in on her. If there wasn't anybody home, how come the door was unlocked?

She told herself that nobody in Silverdale ever locked their doors, but she still knew that her family always did.

She went to the kitchen and dumped her book bag on the table, then searched the refrigerator for a note.

There was none.

Her first impulse was to call her father at work and ask him where her mother was, but she decided not to. She was only supposed to call her father if it was a real emergency, like the house was on fire, or someone was sick, or something like that.

Just because her mother hadn't left her a note didn't mean anything was really wrong.

She opened the refrigerator, her eyes scanning its contents as she tried to decide if she wanted to eat something, then closed it as she realized she wasn't hungry at all.

Pursing her lips, she went to the back door, parted the curtains and looked out into the backyard.

And for the first time she saw that something *was* wrong.

The door to the rabbit hutch was standing wide open, but inside she could see the rabbits all squinched up together.

That was strange, because whenever they had a chance, the rabbits always tried to escape from their cage, slipping through the door whenever anybody opened it.

She remembered Chivas again, and a chill ran through her.

She shivered as she opened the back door and stepped out once more into the chilly afternoon. She zipped the jacket all the way up to her chin, but it did no good, for as she reluctantly crossed the lawn toward the rabbit hutch, her whole body seemed to turn cold.

Kelly was standing silently, tears running down her face as she stared at the limp corpses of the rabbits, when she felt a hand touch her shoulder.

She jumped with the unexpectedness of the touch, then looked up, expecting to see her mother. When she recognized Elaine Harris and saw the look of strain on her face, she knew that something was, after all, terribly wrong.

"I'm afraid there's something I have to tell you, Kelly," Elaine said, gently leading the little girl back toward the house. Kelly moved stoically, her feet feeling leaden, certain she already knew what Mrs. Harris was going to tell her.

She listened silently as Elaine Harris slowly explained that her parents and her brother were dead. Her eyes, wide and unblinking, fixed on Elaine, and she struggled to control the tears that threatened to overwhelm her.

"It was a terrible accident," Elaine finished, repeating the words her husband had spoken to her only a little while ago, words that she had no reason to doubt. She slipped her arms around Kelly and tried to hold her close, but the little girl's body felt stiff. "We don't know what happened, and I'm not sure we'll ever find out. But your mommy and daddy were trying to help your brother. He—Well, he was sick, and they were taking him to the hospital."

Finally a sob shook Kelly's body and she slumped against Elaine.

Elaine said nothing for a while, but simply held Kelly close, her own eyes flooding with tears as she felt the child's acceptance of what had happened. "It's going to be all right," she assured Kelly. "Your Uncle Jerry and I are going to take care of you, and you'll never have to worry about anything."

She held Kelly for another moment, then gently disentangled herself from the little girl and started leading her out of the house. "Let's go now," she said softly. "We'll go over to our house and come back and get your things later. All right?"

Kelly, her mind numb, nodded mutely as Elaine took her through the house and out the front door. But then she paused, tugging at Elaine's hand until Elaine stopped walking.

Kelly turned and looked back at the house.

She knew deep in her heart that she was never going to see her family again.

The image of the house began to swim crazily as tears flooded her eyes. Then, once more, she turned away.

Sharon was breathing hard and her whole body had turned into a mass of aching muscles, but still she trudged onward. Ahead of her on the trail, Mark seemed to be tireless, striding ahead, pausing every now and then to wait for her to catch up. But even when she could go no farther and had to sit down for a few minutes to catch her breath, he'd kept moving, hurrying back down the trail or moving off it entirely, always searching for a spot that would give him a view of the valley. Each time he found such a spot, he would stand and stare like a frightened animal, his eyes searching the terrain below, looking for signs of the hunters they both knew must be coming after them.

When they'd arrived abruptly at the end of the road several hours ago, where there was nothing but a large parking lot at the base of a ski lift, Sharon's heart had sunk. She should have gone the other way, sped through Silverdale and headed down the valley. Now they were trapped. For a moment she was tempted to turn around, but Mark seemed to read her mind.

"We can't go back," he told her. "They'll block the road and we'll never get through."

"Well, we can't stay here, either," Sharon replied, but Mark was already out of the car, staring up at the mountains.

"Up there," he said at last. "We'll have to hike out."

He began rummaging in the back of the station wagon, but the only thing he found that would be of any use at all was a worn blanket that looked as if it hadn't been used for anything but spreading on the ground for picnics over the past dozen years. Worn and thin, and filled with fragments of grass and leaves, it would offer little protection against the cold of the night, but it was better than nothing. With the blanket tucked under Mark's arm, they had set off.

For the first few miles they moved quickly, but as they climbed steadily upward, Sharon began to tire.

Mark, on the other hand, felt his body quickly begin to respond to the exercise. His legs seemed to take on a rhythmic stride of their own, and as he climbed the steep trail, his body began to sweat as his system struggled to keep his body temperature in equilibrium. Finally he felt the last remnants of the headache fade away, and he kept moving, breathing deeply. When his mother eventually called out to him that she had to rest, he turned back to face her without thinking.

For a moment, as he caught sight of her face, the now-familiar anger built inside him, but he fought it, forcing it back down, repeating to himself over and over again that it wasn't real, that it was only something Ames had induced in him, a Pavlovian response like a dog salivating at the sound of a bell. Finally, as the afternoon wore on, he found that he was able to control the rage completely.

It was still there, smoldering within him, but he was no longer afraid that at any moment he was going to strike out at his mother, close his strong fingers around her throat and begin squeezing.

The sun was setting when he spotted the search party. He wasn't certain how many of them there were, but they were moving swiftly, climbing the trail he and Sharon were following, and for a moment he wondered how they could be so certain they were following the right path.

Then he caught a glimpse of the dog—a big shepherd—straining at a heavy leash as it pressed forward, its nose close to the ground.

"Oh, God," Sharon moaned when he told her about the dog. "What are we going to do?"

"Keep going," Mark replied, his voice grim. "We're not just going to sit down and give up."

And so they'd gone on.

Darkness closed around them, and with the night came a cold breeze, slicing through their clothes to chill their skin. Sharon felt herself shiver as the wind cut through her thin jacket, but Mark, his legs still moving with an apparently endless energy, barely seemed to notice it. And then, as the dusk turned into pitch-black night, Sharon stumbled, a sharp pain shooting up her leg as her ankle twisted.

She yelped out loud and sank to the ground, rubbing gingerly at her injured joint. "Mark?" she called out. "Mark!"

He turned back, then hurried down the trail and squatted beside her. Taking her ankle gently in his large fingers, he tried to massage it. Sharon winced, partly with pain, partly from the sight of his deformed hands and the strange feel of his rough skin against her flesh. At last, with Mark supporting her, she got to her feet and tested her weight on her throbbing leg.

She was able to walk, but she was limping badly now.

Saying nothing, Mark moved next to her and slipped his arm around her, then started walking up the trail again, half supporting her, half carrying her.

After an hour Sharon could go no farther.

They were on a hillside, and the trail wound through a maze of enormous boulders. Mark left Sharon where she was and moved forward a few yards, scouting the area. Finally he found a boulder that was deeply undercut, with another, smaller rock sitting a few feet from it. Between the two rocks there was enough space for the two of them to sit for a few minutes, and the rocks themselves would provide them with at least a small amount of shelter from the wind. But even as he led Sharon to it, he knew the boulders couldn't protect them from the dog that was tracking them.

And the dog would bring the men with it.

"We can't get away, can we?" Sharon finally said after they'd been sitting for several minutes. The blanket was wrapped around her shoulders, and her injured leg was stretched out straight in front of her. She felt like crying, but wouldn't give in to the urge.

"I—I don't know," Mark replied after a few more moments. "Unless I can figure out a way to kill the dog."

He said it so matter-of-factly that Sharon shuddered. But then she remembered the carnage she'd seen in the yard of the sports center, and steeled herself against the weakness of her own emotions. So Mark had once killed a dog and would do it again? So what? Compared to what Ames had done . . .

"How?" she asked. "How could you do it?"

Mark shook his head. "I can't, unless they let it go. But they won't let it go."

They sat silently then. After a while they began to hear the baying of the dog as it climbed the trail below. At first it was nothing more than a faint sound in the distance, but it grew steadily closer.

Even as the fear built inside her, Sharon couldn't bring herself to get up, couldn't force her body to respond to the need to get away.

Mark, as if understanding, sat next to her, apparently resigned to whatever might happen next.

The dog was close now, barking, and they could even hear the voices of the men shouting to each other and see the flickering beams of flashlights as they tried to light the trail ahead. Then, as if sensing it was closing on its prey, the dog fell silent.

A moment later a man's voice blared through the darkness, amplified by a bullhorn.

"It's all right, Mrs. Tanner. It's the State Patrol. It's all over. You can come down."

Sharon froze. Was it really possible? But how?

And then the voice came again.

"We're here to help you, Mrs. Tanner. Your husband called us this afternoon when they wouldn't let him speak to you at the sports center. It's over, Mrs. Tanner. We have them all."

Blake! Blake had finally believed her and called the State Patrol! Almost crying out with relief, she struggled to her feet, but Mark's hand closed on her wrist.

"They're lying, Mom," he whispered. "It's just a trick!"

"No!" Sharon whimpered. "It's all right—we're going to be all right!" She couldn't see Mark's face at all in the darkness, but she felt his hand tighten on her wrist. She spoke again, struggling to keep her voice calm. "Mark, what if it is a trick? We can't get away. I don't think I can take more than a few more steps. So let me go out, darling. Please? If it isn't a trick, we're all right. And if it is, well—" Her voice caught for a moment, then she went on. "If it is a trick, you'll have time to get away from them by yourself. If you don't have to carry me, they won't be able to catch up with you." She paused, and could almost feel his indecision. "Please?" she breathed.

Slowly, she felt Mark's grip on her wrist ease, but then he pulled her close.

"I love you, Mom," he whispered. "No matter what happens, I love you."

She kissed him then, her lips brushing against his distorted mouth, her fingers tracing the rough line of his swollen brow. "I love you, too," she whispered. Then, her ankle threatening to give way beneath her, she stepped out into the trail.

"I—I'm here," she called out, and instantly the night was filled with lights, all of them trained on her. She took a step forward.

And then the guns began to sound.

The night exploded with shots, and Sharon's body crumpled, dead before it even hit the ground.

Bullets ricocheted off the boulders, screaming like angry hornets as they flew through the night.

The sounds of the shots echoed and reechoed through the mountains, but even as they began to die away, Mark dashed from the shelter behind the boulder, slithered through a narrow gap between two others, and began scrambling up the mountainside, threading his way between some of the rocks, clawing his way over others.

"Turn the dog loose!" he heard a voice shout behind him. "Let her go, damn it!"

Then the night was filled once more with the barking of the dog as it hurled itself after him, ignoring his scent now, easily following the sounds he made as he scrabbled up the mountainside. The men were coming, too, doing their best to keep up, but they weren't nearly as fast as either Mark or the dog, and within less than a minute he was well ahead of them.

Suddenly there was a furious snarl behind him, and Mark whirled around just as the huge shepherd threw itself at him.

He caught it in midair, grasping it by the throat, holding its snapping jaws well away from his face.

This time he didn't waste time strangling it to death, for this time he knew exactly what he was doing.

It was either kill the dog or let the dog kill him.

His fingers tightened on the animal's throat, then he raised it over his head, slamming its body down onto one of the rocks.

There was a sharp cracking sound as the dog's back broke over the rock, and it went limp. Dropping it instantly, he turned and darted away once more into the safety of the darkness.

Without the dog, he knew the men had no hope even of following him, let alone of catching up with him.

He breathed deeply of the night air and his lungs filled with scents he'd never experienced before, all the subtle odors the human nose can never respond to but which lead an animal through the night.

Then he was out of the maze of boulders, finding himself on a gentle slope of grass-covered earth dotted with pine trees and clumps of aspen. He ran through the night then, his powerful legs once more taking on the easy rhythm that he felt could carry him forever.

He began moving up the mountain, upward into the vast reaches of forests and meadows where he could almost smell the rarefied scent of true freedom that only a wild animal ever knows. . . .

27

It had been nearly two weeks since the funeral at which they'd buried her family. Every morning since then, when she'd awakened, totally disoriented, in the unfamiliar surroundings of the small bedroom next to Linda's that the Harrises had moved her into the day her family had died, Kelly Tanner felt the dampness on her pillow and knew she'd been crying. But this morning—a Saturday—Kelly knew where she was from the moment she came awake.

And the pillowcase was dry, which meant she hadn't been crying that night at all. Or at least not enough to get the pillow wet.

She lay in her bed for a few minutes, listening to the sounds of the Harrises's house. It wasn't really much different from the way her own house had sounded in the morning, and if she closed her eyes and concentrated very hard, she could almost imagine that nothing had changed, that she was back in her own room in the house on Telluride Drive.

The shower going on would mean that her father was already up, and the clatter of pans in the kitchen meant that her mother was making pancakes. She could even imagine that the thumpings from down the hall were coming from

Mark's room; that he was doing the exercises he'd started a month ago.

But it wasn't Mark, and it wasn't her mother and father. It was just the Harrises, and even though she knew they were trying to be very nice to her, she always had a niggling feeling at the back of her mind that they didn't really care about her, that they thought they had to be nice to her because she was an orphan now.

An orphan.

She turned the word over in her mind, kept examining it, until suddenly it had no meaning at all. It was a game she played sometimes with herself—taking the simplest word and repeating it over and over and over, until instead of meaning something, it wasn't anything but a sound.

For the first time that morning she was able to think about the funeral without crying. She didn't know whether it had been like other funerals, because she'd never been to one before. There hadn't been very many people there, and it hadn't taken very long, and as she sat in the front pew of the little church, listening to a man she'd never seen before talking about her family—and she knew he'd never even met her family, so how could he talk about them?—she tried to convince herself that it really was her father and mother and brother in the three coffins lined up in front of the altar.

But the tops of the coffins were closed, and nobody had let her see the bodies at all, and it had been hard for her to accept that any of it was real. In fact, when she'd heard the door open at one point, she looked back, almost expecting to see Mark walking down the aisle toward her. But it hadn't been Mark at all. It had just been another stranger, so she turned back and faced the front again. And then, when they'd gone out to the little cemetery behind the church, she had the strangest feeling as they put Mark's coffin into the grave.

He's not in there!

The thought had come into her mind out of nowhere. She tried to tell herself that it was dumb—that if Mark wasn't in the coffin, they wouldn't be burying it.

But the thought stayed with her. Several times since the funeral—she wasn't sure how many—she'd come awake in the middle of the night, the memory of a dream fresh in her mind.

It was like she was in the grave, too, and Mark was with her, and they were both pounding on the sides of the coffin, but nobody could hear them. They knew they were buried and that they weren't going to be able to get free, but they weren't dead.

She remembered crying those nights.

The other nights she must have had other dreams that had made her cry, but she didn't remember them.

Only the one of Mark, struggling to get them both out of the terrible prison of the coffin. When she awakened from the dream and found she wasn't in the coffin at all, she'd known that Mark wasn't, either.

Tears threatened to overcome her, and she put the thought out of her mind, determined not to start crying again. She got out of bed and dressed, pulling a clean pair of jeans out of the bottom drawer of the dresser they'd brought over from the house on Telluride Drive. Then she put on one of Mark's old flannel shirts and pulled a sweater over that.

She liked the feel of Mark's shirt against her skin, even though it was much too big for her; and even though it had been washed last week, she imagined she could still smell Mark in the shirt. When she wore it, she felt close to him.

It was as she left her room that she decided what she was going to do that morning.

Today, she would go and visit her parents.

The Harrises were already at the breakfast table when Kelly came out and silently took her place next to Linda. Mrs. Harris, whom she still hadn't managed to call Aunt Elaine—even though Mrs. Harris had told her she ought to—was looking at her. She finally managed a polite smile.

"Did you sleep all right, Kelly?"

She nodded, then her gaze returned to the stack of pancakes on the plate. She really wasn't very hungry, but she remembered her mother telling her that it wasn't polite not to eat whatever was put in front of you.

She began forking the heavy cakes into her mouth.

Twenty minutes later, when her plate was empty, Kelly looked up shyly. "May I be excused?" she asked.

"Of course," Elaine Harris told her.

She scuttled out of her chair and went back to her room, where she dug in the bottom drawer of her dresser until she found the little bank she had kept her allowance in for as long as she could remember.

She pried the bottom of the little brass box open and pulled out five dollars. She wasn't certain how much flowers cost, but it seemed like five dollars should be enough. She hid the bank away again, pulled on her jacket, then walked quietly to the front door. She'd just pulled it open when she heard a voice behind her.

"Where are you going, Kelly?"

It was Linda, and Kelly looked shyly up at her. "The— The cemetery," she admitted, and felt herself blush. "I just wanted to go visit my family."

Linda smiled at her. "Can I go with you?"

Kelly hesitated, then bobbed her head. "All right."

Half an hour later they walked into the little graveyard behind the church and slowly approached the three graves that were lined up next to each other, a single wide slab of marble marking the spot. In Kelly's hand were two red roses. At the flower shop, when she'd bought them, Linda had asked if she didn't want three, but Kelly had shaken her head, and Linda, frowning thoughtfully, had said nothing. Now, as they stood in front of the graves, Linda watched as Kelly carefully placed one of the roses on her mother's grave and the other on her father's. Only when the little girl finally straightened up did Linda speak.

"Why didn't you get one for Mark?" she asked.

Kelly was silent for several seconds, then her brows knit thoughtfully. "B-Because he's not here," she said, her voice barely audible.

Linda felt her heart skip a beat and her breath catch in her throat. "Not here?" she echoed.

Kelly shook her head.

"He's not dead," she said. Her eyes drifted toward the mountains to the east. "I think he's up there," she said. "I think he's up there, and he's going to come back someday." Her eyes met Linda's, and there was a pleading quality to them that made Linda want to cry. "If he were really dead, I'd know it, wouldn't I? I mean, wouldn't I feel it, like I do about Mom and Dad?"

Linda slowly nodded.

"But I don't," Kelly said. "I just feel like Mark isn't dead at all."

Now it was Linda who was silent for a few moments. Finally, she reached out and took Kelly's hand.

"I know," she said as they slowly walked out of the cemetery. "I feel the same way." She smiled at Kelly again, and winked. "But we won't tell anybody, will we? It'll just be our own little secret."

Kelly said nothing, but squeezed Linda's hand.

Now she didn't feel quite so alone in the world.

"But what if he's not dead?" Phil Collins asked. He was in Marty Ames's private quarters in the sports center, and though a fire blazed cheerfully on the hearth, its warmth had done nothing to dispel the chill Collins felt every time he glanced out the enormous picture window that faced the mountains. The thought that Mark Tanner might still be alive up there somewhere had haunted him from the moment Jerry Harris's men had given up the search two days after Mark's disappearance. But now Marty Ames looked at him scornfully, and Collins felt the sting of the doctor's open contempt.

"How many times do I have to explain it?" Ames said, his voice taking on the condescending tone he might have used on a child. "He was already dying when he escaped. Every system in his body had gone out of balance—his growth hormones, adrenal gland, the works. You saw what he was like when we brought him out here. He was already half crazy. The only way we were able to keep him under control at all was with heavy doses of barbiturates."

"Which didn't work," Collins reminded him, his voice bitter.

"All right, I'll admit we shouldn't have lost him," Ames replied. "But the fact is we did, and the fact is also that he's dead! Christ, Collins—he was sick, he was going crazy, and he didn't know anything about survival in the first place. You really think he could have survived up there?"

He nodded toward the mountains, and as if to underscore his words, a gust of wind howled outside, rattling the shutters and making the pine trees bend.

"I suppose not," Collins reluctantly agreed. Each day was getting shorter than the one before. Though it was only six o'clock, it was already dark outside. But the mountains, he knew, were covered with snow now, and this morning he'd seen a few early skiers heading up the valley toward the lift, intent on being the first to hit the slopes that year.

What Ames had told him made sense. "But I still wish we knew for sure."

"We never will," Ames told him, rising to his feet in an obvious gesture of dismissal.

Collins drained the last of a double shot of bourbon from the glass in his hand, then heaved himself out of his chair and walked to the door, where his thick, plaid hunting jacket hung from a brass hook on the wall. Shrugging himself into it, he eyed Ames warily. "What about the rest of the boys?" he asked. "How are they looking?"

Ames offered him a wintry smile. "If you mean are any of them getting sick, the answer is no," he said coolly. "If you mean are any more of them *going* to get sick, obviously

I can't tell you. That's what experiments are all about, you know: finding out what will happen.'' He held the door open for Collins, and as the coach left the apartment on the second floor and headed for the staircase, Ames spoke once more, his voice edged with sarcasm. "Sure you're not afraid to walk home alone in the dark, Collins? You never know what might come out of the hills, do you?''

Collins ignored him, walking heavily down the broad staircase and leaving the lodge. He walked quickly toward the main gate, where men were now posted twenty-four hours a day, and nodded to the guard as he passed through. As he moved down the driveway toward the main road for the half-mile walk back to his home on the eastern fringes of the town, he found his pace quickening and suddenly wished he'd brought his car instead of deciding that the hike would be good for him.

Five minutes after Collins left his office, Marty Ames glanced at his watch, winced at the lateness of the hour, then shrugged indifferently: If Jerry Harris didn't want to wait for him, that was his problem. After all, Ames was in the driver's seat now, at least as far as TarrenTech was concerned. They'd covered up so much, allowed themselves to become so deeply entangled in Ames's research, that they would never be able to extricate themselves. From now on, Jerry Harris—and Ted Thornton, too—would do exactly as Marty Ames told them.

As he left the building and slid behind the wheel of one of the station wagons with ROCKY MOUNTAIN HIGH emblazoned on its side, he smiled to himself. He was, indeed, the man who knew too much, and it was his own knowledge—his own brilliance—that made his position within TarrenTech impregnable.

He pulled through the gates, raising only a single finger from the steering wheel as an acknowledgment of the guard's presence, then stepped on the accelerator, his whole body responding to the surge of power from the car's engine. The car was still gaining speed as it passed Phil Collins a minute later. Ames, if he noticed the coach at all, didn't bother even to wave to him, let alone offer him a lift.

Ten minutes later he was on the west side of Silverdale, speeding toward the TarrenTech building. His mind was only partly concentrating on the road, for most of his attention was focused, as always, on his research. A new family was arriving in Silverdale next week, and the medical records for their son had been placed on Ames's desk only that morning. Already his mind was at work on the boy's treatment and how he might avoid the failures he had experienced with Mark Tanner, Jeff LaConner, and Randy Stevens.

When the headlights of the station wagon first picked up the oddly hulking shape that stood frozen in the middle of the road a hundred yards ahead, Ames didn't even see it.

And when he did see it a couple of seconds later, his first thought was that it must be a deer, for all he could truly see in the glare of the headlights was the bright glow of a pair of eyes shining out from the dark shape.

Large, animal eyes.

Then, as the car sped closer, Ames realized that it was not a deer in the road at all. It was another sort of creature entirely.

A creature of his own creation.

He gasped as he stared at Mark Tanner.

It wasn't possible—the boy should have been dead by now—should have been dead at least a week ago! Ames's hands froze on the wheel as he stared, transfixed, at the creature that now seemed to be hypnotized by the glare of the lights.

The car was only a few yards away from Mark when Ames suddenly realized that the boy wasn't going to move out of the path of the speeding vehicle, that he was only going to stare dumbly into the headlights until the car overtook him, and crushed him.

Ames was going to kill his own creation.

At the last second, he knew he couldn't do it.

He jerked his right foot off the accelerator and smashed it down on the brake, at the same time twisting the wheel violently to the right.

The tires screeched angrily as they lost their traction on the pavement, and the station wagon slewed off the road, shooting across the shallow ditch beyond the shoulder only to smash head-on into a boulder on the other side.

Marty Ames experienced an odd sensation of detached surprise as the frame of the station wagon crumpled beneath the force of the impact, and the engine block moved back, jamming the steering wheel and the twisted wreckage of the dashboard into Ames's chest. At the same moment that the wheel crushed his chest, his head flew forward, snapping his neck and shattering the windshield.

He was dead even before the brief moment of surprise had faded away.

Mark Tanner gazed curiously at the wreckage of the car, then crouched low to the ground. His eyes—the wary, canny eyes of an animal—remained fixed on the ruins of the station wagon as he crept close. He paused a few feet away, sniffing cautiously at the air, then reached out and touched the twisted metal of the driver's door, which was attached to the body of the car by only a single broken hinge.

The metal felt cold to his touch. He moved his finger away and touched the neck of the man inside the car.

Though the man's face was covered with blood and totally unrecognizable, Mark knew who he was.

For a moment he had an urge to wrench Martin Ames loose from the wreckage and tear his body limb from limb, leaving the remains wherever they fell.

But then the urge passed, and he turned away, silently disappearing into the night.

*   *   *

The wind was rising now, and Phil Collins tugged his jacket collar up around his neck, hunching his shoulders, resisting the urge to turn around and look up toward the mountains that rose around him.

He came to the corner of Aspen Street and turned right. He paused then, and his skin crawled with the uneasy sensation that he was being watched.

Now he did turn around, shading his eyes against the glare of the streetlamp that glowed overhead, but seeing nothing in the inky darkness; only a silent blackness that seemed to close in around him, a suffocating, strangely malignant stillness.

He told himself he was imagining things, but once more his pace quickened.

His house was dark as he approached it, and he had a fleeting moment of uncertainty as he tried to remember if he'd turned the porch light on or not. But of course he hadn't—it had still been broad daylight when he'd left the place a couple of hours before. He took the steps to the front porch in two quick bounds, then reached up to the ledge under the eaves for the key that he always left there.

A moment later he stepped through the front door and groped for the wall switch. The overhead light came on, washing the shadows from the living room.

Collins hesitated.

Something was wrong. His big German shepherd, who was invariably waiting for him by the door, was nowhere to be seen.

"Sparks?" he called out. "Where are you, boy?"

He heard a quick bark, followed by an eager whimpering, but the dog still didn't appear. Frowning deeply and with an odd prickling sensation running over the back of his neck, Collins moved through the living room into the small kitchen.

Sparks was crouched down by the door to the cellar, his muzzle pressed to the crack between the door and the floor.

He looked up as Collins came into the room and his tail wagged, but then he went back to his eager snuffling of the gap below the door.

Collins's frown deepened. There couldn't be anyone down there. He'd trained Sparks as a watchdog himself, and he knew the animal wouldn't let anyone into the house without his permission. He'd even had some complaints from the neighbors about the dog's fierceness; complaints he'd totally ignored.

"What is it, boy?" he asked. "What's wrong?"

The animal got to his feet, his tail wagging, and scratched eagerly at the closed door.

"Okay," Collins said, pulling the door open. "Go on down and get it, whatever it is."

The dog dashed down the steep flight of stairs and disappeared into the darkness.

Collins waited for a moment, listening. He could hear the shepherd whimpering eagerly, but there were no other sounds. Finally he reached for the light switch by the door and flipped it.

Nothing happened.

Cursing softly, Collins rummaged in the top drawer by the kitchen sink and found a flashlight. Its batteries were weak, but it glowed dimly when he pressed the switch. From another drawer he took a large butcher knife.

With the light held firmly in his left hand and the knife in his right, he started down the stairs.

When he came to the bottom, he stood in the darkness for a moment, listening. He could still hear Sparks, off to the right, making the eager whimpering noises that always emerged from his throat when Collins scratched him behind the ears.

But why?

There was no one there—there couldn't be.

He played the light in the direction of the sounds and suddenly froze. Reflected in the light, glowing strangely, were a pair of eyes.

Not the eyes of an animal.

But not the eyes of a human being, either.

They were something else, something Phil Collins had never seen before. And as he stared at them an icy finger of terror moved slowly down his spine.

He took a step forward, his fingers tightening on the knife. He knew he had to strike first, plunge the knife into the creature in the basement before it could attack him.

He had to kill it while it was still blinded by the glare of the flashlight.

Then, without warning, there was a sudden howl and Sparks lunged out of the darkness toward him. The knife clattered to the floor as Collins dropped it in shocked surprise. He raised his arms to fend off the animal, but it was too late.

Spark's jaws closed on his throat, and he felt razor-sharp teeth ripping into his flesh, felt his windpipe puncture, then felt a warm sticky gush as the animal's fangs ripped into his jugular vein. He sank to his knees. A scream rose in his throat as he groped wildly for the knife, but it was already too late, for his vocal cords had collapsed under the dog's furious attack and the knife was far out of his reach. He dropped sideways, sprawling, to the floor, then rolled over, facedown on the concrete.

Sparks, snarling furiously, tore at the fallen body, ripping away large pieces of flesh and tossing them aside, then leaping to the attack once more.

At last a strange guttural voice spoke in the darkness, and it was over. The dog stopped its attack, whimpered once, then turned and trotted up the stairs.

Mark Tanner waited a moment, then stepped over the body of the football coach and started up the stairs himself.

Sparks was waiting for him by the back door.

Together the two of them slipped out into the night, moving silently through the darkness, away from the village and up into the foothills above the valley.

* * *

Mark had no idea what time it was when he reached the cave ten miles away from the valley. He'd lost all sense of time days ago and was now aware only of daytime and nighttime.

He slept in the daytime, curled up at the back of the cave he'd discovered on his third day in the mountains, always having carefully banked his small fire—the fire he never allowed to go entirely out—so that it would still have a few coals left when he awakened just before sunset and began preparing for the night's hunting.

His eyes had changed quickly, and now the glare of sunlight nearly blinded him. But at night his large pupils gathered in every trace of light and he could see clearly; watch the owls and bats flitting through the darkness, see the other creatures of the night as they crept about in the constant search for food.

He was one of the hunters now, too, and though he had survived those first few days on little more than water from the streams and a few fungi he'd risked sampling, he was quickly shifting over to a carnivorous diet.

He'd captured his first rabbit on the fourth day, but it had been crippled—nearly dead when he'd stumbled upon it. Nevertheless, he skinned it clumsily with a broken knife he'd scavenged from an empty campground, then cooked it on a skewer over the fire he'd spent hours trying to light the day before, when he first discovered the cave. For a while he'd been afraid someone would see the smoke of the fire and come looking for him, but he never let the flame burn too high, and the smoke was nothing more than a faint wisp that quickly dispersed in the constant breezes of the mountains.

Almost every night he'd found himself drawn back to the hills overlooking Silverdale. Tonight he'd known he was going down into the village itself almost as soon as he left the cave. It hadn't taken him long to make the trip, for his body had hardened and he could move tirelessly all night long.

He'd stopped twice on the way to the little valley where the town lay, the first time for only a few minutes. He'd heard a sound in the brush and paused, listening. But when he heard it again, he knew it was only the rustling of a mouse and went on.

A few miles later he'd smelled a rabbit and stopped instantly, his nostrils sniffing the wind eagerly. He located the rabbit after a few minutes, nibbling at a small patch of dried grass beneath a clump of aspens. He stalked it carefully and patiently, keeping himself downwind of the creature, moving silently until he was only a few yards from it.

When he finally pounced, the rabbit had no time even to react. It had simply paused in its eating, its ears pricking up before Mark's hands had closed around its throat, killing it with a fast twist that snapped its neck.

He tucked the rabbit under the piece of rope he'd found somewhere and now used as a belt, then gone on. Mark was almost certain the creatures he killed felt nothing at all, just as he was certain Martin Ames had felt nothing when his car had hurtled off the road a little while ago.

It had been odd, watching the car race toward him, and knowing that he wasn't going to move out of its path. It had been a strange experience, staring into the headlights, blinded by them, for the first time truly feeling like the wild animal he had become.

And when he'd paused for a moment to gaze at the body of Martin Ames, he'd realized once again just how much he'd changed. For as he stared at the body of the man who had taken his very life from him, he'd felt nothing.

No rage, and no remorse.

And yet he knew, even then, that although part of him was now truly feral, there was another part of him that was still human and always would be.

When he'd come within sight of the village, he sat for a while, oblivious of the cold, staring down into the town. He knew there were things he needed, some things he hadn't been able to scavenge in the campgrounds, or even in the dump he'd discovered forty miles away, on the edges of another village.

He might have stolen from anywhere, but he knew he wouldn't. It was Silverdale that had made him what he had become, so it would be Silverdale that supplied him with what he needed.

And only certain people in Silverdale.

He'd known Collins's house was empty from the moment he'd seen it. All his instincts told him that it would be safe for him to go inside. Even when the dog had begun barking before he'd managed to force the back door open, he hadn't been afraid.

His instincts told him the dog wouldn't hurt him.

And he'd been right, for as the door had finally given way under the strength of his arms, the barking stopped abruptly, and the dog's head had lowered. Then the dog came forward, sniffing curiously, and finally licked tentatively at his hand.

Mark had spoken to it in the strange guttural half-language that was all his deformed jaw allowed him now, then reached down to pet him. As his hand touched the animal's fur and he whispered softly to it, the dog had become his.

He'd gone quickly through the house, taking only the things he needed most—a pair of heavy denim pants and a thick flannel shirt from the closet in the bedroom.

In the cellar he found a set of camping pans and a Swiss army knife.

He'd been about to leave when he heard the front door open, and he moved swiftly up the stairs to close the cellar door. He would wait until the house was silent, then slip away.

But the dog had unwittingly betrayed him, and then, when he recognized the voice of the man who came down the stairs a few minutes later, he'd felt a pang of fear, a pang the dog understood.

He had let the dog kill Collins—he knew that. He could have stopped him, but he hadn't.

After it was all over, he found that the last of the rage that had plagued him was gone, and that at least a part of what had been done to him was over. There was no more anger left in him. Still, as he loped back to the cave with the dog trotting along beside him, he knew that he would return to Silverdale one more time that night.

But not yet.

Not until the darkest hour of the night, when the moon was low, and the people of the village were asleep.

Kelly wasn't certain what woke her. One moment she had been sound asleep, and the next wide awake, sitting up in bed, her senses tingling with anticipation.

Mark.

He was here, somewhere very close to her.

She slipped out of bed, crept to the window, and peered out into the blackness beyond.

The moon was low, almost ready to disappear behind the mountain ridges, and deep shadows lay across the Harrises' backyard. Although she could see nothing, she could still sense that there was something outside in the night.

She backed away from the window, then slipped through the door of her room and let herself into Linda's room next door.

Linda, too, was wide awake.

"He's here," Kelly whispered. She moved across the room to Linda's window and moved the curtain aside. A moment later Linda, pulling a robe around her shoulders, joined her, and together they gazed out into the darkness that shrouded the house. It was as if a shadow had slipped over the fence—a presence so silent, so nearly formless that for a moment neither of them was sure she had seen it at all. And then, very suddenly, a face appeared at the window.

Though it was an ugly face, a twisted, grotesque mask that was barely human anymore, neither Linda nor Kelly flinched or turned away.

For it was Mark's face, and from beneath his lowering brows, it was Mark's own gentle eyes that looked out at them.

His hand came up and gently touched the windowpane, and Linda knew immediately what he wanted.

She unlocked the window and slid it silently upward.

For a long moment nothing happened at all, and then, his gnarled, misshapen fingers trembling, Mark reached out and touched Linda's cheek.

The fingers of his other hand gently brushed a lock of hair away from Kelly's brow.

He leaned forward and slipped his arms around them, pressing the two girls close to his chest.

A slight sound, almost like a sob, rose in his throat.

Then he released them and turned away, disappearing into the night as silently and as swiftly as he'd come.

Kelly and Linda stayed where they were for a long time, neither of them saying a word. Finally, Linda slid the window closed again and gently guided Kelly back to bed.

"Will he come back again?" Kelly asked as Linda tucked her in.

Linda bent down and kissed the little girl on the brow.

"Of course he will," she said. "He'll always come back, because he'll always love us."

Kelly gazed up at her, her brows knit into a worried frown. "But will we always love him?" she asked.

Linda was silent for a moment, then nodded.

"Why would we stop loving him?" she asked. "It doesn't matter what he looks like, or what's happened to him. He's still Mark, and inside he isn't any different than he ever was."

That night, for the first time since the funeral, both Linda Harris and Kelly Tanner slept soundly, undisturbed by dreams.

For on a hillside, far up in the mountains above the town, Mark Tanner sat alone, watching over them.

About the Author

In 1977 *Suffer the Children*, John Saul's first novel of psychological and supernatural suspense, became an immediate phenomenon, leaping onto national best-seller lists and selling more than one million copies. Each year since has seen the publication of a new novel of horror—among them *The God Project*, *Nathaniel*, *Brainchild*, and, most recently, *The Unloved*—each a million-copy-plus *New York Times* best-seller. The publication of *Creature* marks his twelfth consecutive best-seller. John Saul lives in Seattle, Washington, where he is at work on his next novel.

ENTER THE TERRIFYING
WORLD OF
JOHN SAUL

A scream shatters the peaceful night of a sleepy town, a mysterious stranger awakens to seek vengeance. . . . Once again, with expert, chillingly demonic skill, John Saul draws the reader into his world of utter fear. The author of twelve novels of psychological and supernatural suspense—all million copy *New York Times* bestsellers—John Saul is unequaled in his power to weave the haunted past and the troubled present into a web of pure, cold terror.

THE GOD PROJECT

Something is happening to the children of Eastbury, Massachusetts . . . something that strikes at the heart of every parent's darkest fears. For Sally Montgomery, the grief over the sudden death of her infant daughter is only the beginning. For Lucy Corliss, her son Randy is her life. Then one day, Randy doesn't come home. And the terror begins . . .

A horn honked, pulling Randy out of his reverie, and he realized he was alone on the block. He looked at the watch his father had given him for his ninth birthday. It was nearly eight thirty. If he didn't hurry, he was going to be late for school. Then he heard a voice calling to him.

"Randy! Randy Corliss!"

A blue car, a car he didn't recognize, was standing by the curb. A woman was smiling at him from the driver's seat. He approached the car hesitantly, clutching his lunch box.

"Hi, Randy," the woman said.

"Who are you?" Randy stood back from the car, remembering his mother's warnings about never talking to strangers.

"My name's Miss Bowen. Louise Bowen. I came to get you."

"Get me?" Randy asked. "Why?"

"For your father," the woman said. Randy's heart beat faster. His father? His father had sent this woman? Was it really going to happen, finally? "He wanted me to pick you up at home," he heard the woman say, "but I was late. I'm sorry."

"That's all right," Randy said. He moved closer to the car. "Are you taking me to Daddy's house?"

The woman reached across and pushed the passenger door open. "In a little while," she promised. "Get in."

Randy knew he shouldn't get in the car, knew he should turn around and run to the nearest house, looking for help. It was things like this—strangers offering to give you a ride—that his mother had talked to him about ever since he was a little boy.

But this was different. This was a friend of his father's. She had to be, because she seemed to know all about his plans to go live with his father, and his father's plans to take him away from his mother. Besides, it was always men his mother warned him about, never women. He looked at the woman once more. Her brown eyes were twinkling at him, and her smile made him feel like she was sharing an adventure with him. He made up his mind and got into the car, pulling the door closed behind him. The car moved away from the curb.

"Where are we going?" Randy asked.

Louise Bowen glanced over at the boy sitting expectantly on the seat beside her. He was every bit as attractive as the pictures she had been shown, his eyes almost green, with dark, wavy hair framing his pugnacious, snub-nosed face. His body was sturdy, and though she was a stranger to him, he didn't seem to be the least bit frightened of her. Instinctively, Louise liked Randy Corliss.

"We're going to your new school."

Randy frowned. New school? If he was going to a new school, why wasn't his father taking him? The woman seemed to hear him, even though he hadn't spoken out loud.

"You'll see your father very soon. But for a few days, until he gets everything worked out with your mother, you'll be staying at the school. You'll like it there," she promised. "It's a special school, just for little boys like you, and you'll have lots of new friends. Doesn't that sound exciting?"

Randy nodded uncertainly, no longer sure he should have gotten in the car. Still, when he thought about it, it made sense. His father had told him there would be lots of problems when the time came for him to move away from his mother's. And his father had told him he would be going to a new school. And today was the day.

Randy settled down in the seat and glanced out the window. They were heading out of Eastbury on the road toward Langston. That was where his father lived, so everything was all right.

Except that it didn't quite *feel* all right. Deep inside, Randy had a strange sense of something being very wrong.

For two very different families haunted by very similar fears, THE GOD PROJECT has only just begun to work its lethal conspiracy of silence and fear. And for the reader, John Saul has produced a mind-numbing tale of evil unchecked.

NATHANIEL

Prairie Bend: brilliant summers amid golden fields, killing winters of razorlike cold. A peaceful, neighborly village, darkened by legends of death . . . legends of Nathaniel. Some residents say he is simply a folk tale, others swear he is a terrifying spirit. And soon—very soon—some will come to believe that Nathaniel lives . . .

Shivering, Michael set himself a destination now and began walking along the edges of the pastures, the woods on his right, climbing each fence as he came to it. Sooner than he would have expected, the woods curved away to the right, following the course of the river as it deviated from its southeastern flow to curl around the village. Ahead of him he could see the scattered twinkling lights of Prairie Bend. For a moment, he considered going into the village, but then, as he looked off to the southeast, he changed his mind, for there, seeming almost to glow in the moonlight, was the hulking shape of Findley's barn.

That, Michael knew, was where he was going.

He cut diagonally across the field, then darted across the deserted highway and into another field. He moved quickly now, feeling exposed in the emptiness with the full moon shining down on him. Ten minutes later he had crossed the field and come once more to the highway, this time as it emerged from the village. Across the street, he could see Ben Findley's driveway and, at its end, the little house, and the barn.

He considered trying to go down the driveway and around the house, but quickly abandoned the idea. A light showed dimly from behind a curtained window, and he had a sudden vision of old man Findley, his gun cradled in his arms, standing in silhouette at the front door.

Staying on the north side of the road, he continued moving eastward until he came abreast of his own driveway. He waited a few minutes, wondering whether perhaps he shouldn't go back to his grandparents'. In the end, though, he crossed the road and started down the drive to the abandoned house that was about to become his home. As he came into the overgrown yard, he stopped to stare at the house. Even had he not known that it was empty, he could have sensed that it was. In contrast to the other houses he had passed that night, which all seemed to radiate life from within, this house—his house—gave off only a sense of loneliness that made Michael shiver again in the night and hurry quickly past it.

His progress slowed as he plunged into the weed-choked pastures that lay between the house and the river, but he was determined to stay away from the fence separating Findley's property from their own until the old man's barn could conceal him from the same man's prying eyes. It wasn't until he was near the river that he finally felt safe enough to slip between the strands of barbed wire that fenced off the Findley property and begin doubling back toward the barn that had become his goal.

He could feel it now, feel the strange sense of familiarity he had felt that afternoon, only it was stronger here, pulling him forward through the night. He didn't try to resist it, though there was something vaguely frightening about it. Frightening but exciting. There was a sense of discovery, almost a sense of memory. And his headache, the throbbing pain that had been with him all evening, was gone.

He came up to the barn and paused. There should be a door just around the corner, a door with a bar on it. He didn't understand how he knew it was there, for he'd never seen that side of the barn, but he *knew*. He started toward the corner of the barn, his steps sure, the uncertainty he'd felt a few minutes ago erased.

Around the corner, just as he knew it would be, he found the door, held securely shut by a heavy wooden beam resting in a pair of wrought-iron brackets. Without hesitation, Michael lifted the bar out of its brackets and propped it carefully against the wall. As he pulled the door open, no squeaking hinges betrayed his presence. Though the barn was nearly pitch dark inside, it wasn't the kind of eerie darkness the woods by the river had held, at least not for Michael. For Michael, it was an inviting darkness.

He stepped into the barn.

He waited, half expectantly, as the darkness seeped into him, enveloping him within its folds. And then something reached out of the darkness and touched him.

Nathaniel's call to Michael Hall, who has just lost his father in a tragic accident, draws the boy further into the barn and under his spell. There—and beyond—Michael will faithfully follow Nathaniel's voice to the edge of terror.

BRAINCHILD

One hundred years ago in La Paloma a terrible deed was done, and a cry for vengeance pierced the night. Now, that evil still lives, and that vengeance waits . . . waits for Alex Lonsdale, one of the most popular boys in La Paloma. Because horrible things can happen—even to nice kids like Alex. . . .

Alex jockeyed the Mustang around Bob Carey's Porsche, then put it in drive and gunned the engine. The rear wheels spun on the loose gravel for a moment, then caught, and the car shot forward, down the Evanses' driveway and into Hacienda Drive.

Alex wasn't sure how long Lisa had been walking—it seemed as though it had taken him forever to get dressed and search the house. She could be almost home by now.

He pressed the accelerator, and the car picked up speed. He hugged the wall of the ravine on the first curve, but the car fishtailed slightly, and he had to steer into the skid to regain control. Then he hit a straight stretch and pushed his speed up to seventy. Coming up fast was an S curve that was posted at thirty miles an hour, but he knew they always left a big margin for safety. He slowed to sixty as he started into the first turn.

And then he saw her.

She was standing on the side of the road, her green dress glowing brightly in his headlights, staring at him with terrified eyes.

Or did he just imagine that? Was he already that close to her?

Time suddenly slowed down, and he slammed his foot on the brake.

Too late. He was going to hit her.

It would have been all right if she'd been on the inside of the curve. He'd have swept around her, and she'd have been safe. But now he was skidding right toward her . . .

Turn into it. He had to turn into it!

Taking his foot off the brake, he steered to the right, and suddenly felt the tires grab the pavement.

Lisa was only a few yards away.

And beyond Lisa, almost lost in the darkness, something else.

A face, old and wrinkled, framed with white hair. And the eyes in the face were glaring at him with an intensity he could almost feel.

It was the face that finally made him lose all control of the car.

An ancient, weathered face, a face filled with an unspeakable loathing, looming in the darkness.

At the last possible moment, he wrenched the wheel to the left, and the Mustang responded, slewing around Lisa, charging across the pavement, leading for the ditch and the wall of the ravine beyond.

Straighten it out!

He spun the wheel the other way.

Too far.

The car burst through the guardrail and hurtled over the edge of the ravine.

"Lisaaaa . . ."

Now Alex needs a miracle and thanks to a brilliant doctor, Alex comes back from the brink of death. He seems the same, but in his heart there is a coldness. And if his friends and family could see inside his brain, they would be terrified. . . .

HELLFIRE

Pity the dead . . . one hundred years ago eleven innocent lives were taken in a fire that raged through the mill. That day the iron doors slammed shut—forever. Now, the powerful Sturgiss family of the sleepy town of Westover, Massachusetts is about to unlock those doors to the past. Now comes the time to pray for the living.

The silence of the building seemed to gather around her, and slowly Beth felt the beginnings of fear.

And then she began to feel something else.

Once again, she felt that strange certainty that the mill was not empty.

"D-Daddy?" she called softly, stepping through the door. "Are you here?"

She felt a slight trickle of sweat begin to slide down her spine, and fought a sudden trembling in her knees.

Then, as she listened to the silence, she heard something.

A rustling sound, from up above.

Beth froze, her heart pounding.

And then she heard it again.

She looked up.

With a sudden burst of flapping wings, a pigeon took off from one of the rafters, circled, then soared out through a gap between the boards over one of the windows.

Beth stood still, waiting for her heartbeat to calm. As she looked around, her eyes fixed on the top of a stairwell at the far end of the building.

He was downstairs. That's why he hasn't heard her. He was down in the basement.

Resolutely, she started across the vast emptiness of the building. As she reached the middle of the floor, she felt suddenly exposed, and had an urge to run.

But there was nothing to be afraid of. There was nothing in the mill except herself, and some birds.

And downstairs, her father.

After what seemed like an eternity, she reached the top of the stairs, and peered uncertainly into the darkness below.

Her own shadow preceded her down the steep flight of steps, and only a little spilled over the staircase to illuminate the nearer parts of the vast basement.

"Daddy?" Beth whispered. But the sound was so quiet, even she could barely hear it.

And then there was something else, coming on the heels of her own voice.

Another sound, fainter than the one her own voice had made, coming from below.

Something was moving in the darkness.

Once again Beth's heart began to pound, but she remained where she was, forcing back the panic that threatened to overcome her.

Finally, when she heard nothing more, she moved slowly down the steps, until she could place a foot on the basement floor.

She listened, and after a moment, as the darkness began closing in on her, the sound repeated itself.

Panic surged through her. All her instincts told her to run, to flee back up the stairs and out into the daylight. But when she tried to move, her legs refused to obey her, and she remained where she was, paralyzed.

Once again the sound came. This time, though it was almost inaudible, Beth thought she recognized a word.

"Beeetthh . . ."

Her name. It was as if someone had called her name.

"D-Daddy?" she whispered again. "Daddy, is that you?"

There was another silence, and Beth strained once more to see into the darkness surrounding her.

In the distance, barely visible, she thought she could see a flickering of light.

And then she froze, her voice strangling as the sound came again, like a winter wind sighing in the trees.

"Aaaammmyyyy . . ."

Beth gazed fearfully into the blackness for several long seconds. Then, when the sound was not repeated, her panic began to subside. At last she was able to speak again, though her voice still trembled. "Is someone there?"

In the far distance, the light flickered again, and she heard something else.

Footsteps, approaching out of the darkness.

The seconds crept by, and the light bobbed nearer.

And once more, the whispering voice, barely audible, danced around her.

"Aaaammmyy . . ."

For Beth Rogers, the voice seems like a nightmare, yet not even a little girl's fears can imagine the unearthly fury that awaits her in the old, deserted mill. Soon all of Westover will be prey to the forces of darkness that wait beyond those padlocked doors.

THE UNWANTED

Cassie Winslow, lonely and frightened, has come to False Harbor, Cape Cod to live with her father—whom she barely knows—and his family. For Cassie, the strange, unsettling dreams that come to her suddenly are merely the beginning . . . for very soon, Cassie will come to know the terrifying powers that are her gift.

Cassie awoke in the blackness of the hours before dawn, her heart thumping, her skin damp with a cold sweat that made her shiver. For a moment she didn't know where she was. Then, as she listened to the unfamiliar sound of surf pounding in the distance, the dream began to fade away, and she remembered where she was.

She was in False Harbor, and this was where she lived now. In the room next to her, her stepsister was asleep, and down the hall her father was in bed with her stepmother.

Then why did she feel so alone?

It was the dream, of course.

It had come to her again in the night. Again she had seen the strange woman who should have been her mother but was not.

Again, as Cassie watched in horror, the car burst into flames, and Cassie, vaguely aware that she was in a dream, had expected to wake up, as she had each time the nightmare had come to her.

This time, though she wanted to turn and run, she stood where she was, watching the car burn.

This time there had been no laughter shrieking from the woman's lips, no sound of screams, no noise at all. The flames had risen from the car in an eerie silence, and then, just as Cassie was about to turn away, the stranger had suddenly emerged from the car.

Clad in black, the figure had stood perfectly still, untouched by the flames that raged around her. Slowly, she raised one hand. Her lips moved and a single word drifted over the crowded freeway, came directly to Cassie's ears over the faceless mass of people streaming by in their cars.

"Cassandra . . ."

The word hung in the air for a moment. Then the woman

turned, and as soundlessly as she had emerged, stepped back into the flames.

Instinctively Cassie had started toward her, wanting to pull her back from the flames, wanting to save her.

The silence of the dream was shattered then by the blaring of a horn and the screaming of tires skidding on pavement.

Cassie looked up just in time to see a truck bearing down on her, the enormous grill of its radiator only inches from her face.

As the truck smashed into her she woke up, her own scream of terror choked in her throat.

Her heartbeat began to slow, and her shivering stopped. Now the room seemed to close in on her, and she found it hard to breathe. Slipping out of bed, she crossed to the window at the far end of the narrow room and lifted it open. As she was about to go back to bed, a movement in the darkness outside caught her eye.

She looked down into the cemetery on the other side of the back fence. At first she saw nothing. Then she sensed the movement again, and a dark figure came into view. Clad in black, perfectly silent, a woman stood in the shadows cast by the headstones.

Time seemed to suspend itself.

And then the figure raised one hand. Once more Cassie heard a single word drift almost inaudibly above the pounding of the surf from the beach a few blocks away.

"Cassandra . . ."

Cassie remained where she was, her eyes closed as she strained to recapture the sound of her name, but now there was only the pulsing drone of the surf. And when she reopened her eyes a few seconds later and looked once more into the graveyard, she saw nothing.

The strange figure that had stepped out of the shadows was gone.

She went back to her bed and pulled the covers close around her. For a long time she lay still, wondering if perhaps she'd only imagined it all.

Perhaps she hadn't even left the bed, and had only dreamed that she'd seen the woman in the graveyard.

But the woman in the graveyard had been the woman in her dream. But she didn't really exist.

Did she?

Cassie's dreams will alienate her from the other kids, as will her strange bond with crazy old Miranda Sikes—for both feel unwanted. And in the village of False Harbor, nothing will ever be the same as John Saul spins his supernatural spell.

THE UNLOVED

The splendid isolation of a picturesque island off the South Carolina coast seems like paradise, but for Kevin Devereaux—who returns with his family to help care for his aged and ailing mother, Helena—homecoming will mean a frightening descent into his darkest nightmares . . .

"Why are you here?" he heard her demand. "You know I don't want you here!"

He tried to think, tried to remember where he was. He looked around furtively, hoping the woman wouldn't see his eyes flickering about as if he might be searching for a means to escape.

The room around him looked strange—unfinished—the rough wood of its framing exposed under the tattered remains of crumbling tarpaper. He'd been in this place before—he knew that now. Still, he didn't know where the room was, or what it might be.

But he knew the woman was angry with him again, and in the deepest recesses of his mind, he knew what was going to happen next.

The woman was going to kill him.

He wanted to cry out for help, but when he opened his mouth, no scream emerged. His throat constricted, cutting off his breath, and he knew if he couldn't fight the panic growing within him, he would strangle on his own fear.

The woman took a step toward him, and he cowered, huddling back against the wall. A slick sheen of icy sweat chilled his back, then he felt cold droplets creeping down his arms. A shiver passed over him, and a small whimper escaped his lips.

His sister.

Maybe his sister would come and rescue him.

But she was gone—something had happened to her, and he was alone now.

Alone with his mother.

He looked fearfully up.

She seemed to tower above him, her skirt held back as if she were afraid it might brush against him and be soiled. Her hands were hidden in the folds of the skirt, but he knew what they held.

The axe. The axe she would kill him with.

He could see it then—its curved blades glinting in the light from the doorway, its long wooden handle clutched in his mother's hands. She wasn't speaking to him now, only staring at him. But she didn't need to speak, for he knew what she wanted, knew what she'd always wanted.

"Love me," he whispered, his voice so tremulous that he could hear the words wither away as quickly as they left his lips. "Please love me . . ."

His mother didn't hear. She never heard, no matter how many times he begged her, no matter how often he tried to tell her he was sorry for what he'd done. He would apologize for anything—he knew that. If only she would hear him, he'd tell her whatever she wanted to hear. But even as he tried once more, he knew she wasn't hearing, didn't want to hear.

She only wanted to be rid of him.

The axe began to move now, rising above him, quivering slightly, as if the blade itself could anticipate the splitting of his skull, the crushing of his bones as they gave way beneath the weapon's weight. He could see the steel begin its slow descent, and time seemed to stand still.

He had to do something—had to move away, had to ward off the blow. He tried to raise his arms, but even the air around him seemed thick and unyielding now, and the blade was moving much faster than he was.

Then the axe crashed into his skull, and suddenly nothing made sense anymore. Everything had turned upside down.

It was his mother who cowered on the floor, gazing fearfully up at him as he brought the blade slashing down upon her.

It was he who felt the small jar of resistance as the axe struck her skull, then moved on, splitting her head like a melon. A haze of red rose up before him, and he felt fragments of her brains splatter against his face.

He opened his mouth and, finally, screamed—

The horror is a dream, only a dream. Or so Kevin thinks. Until Helena, suddenly, horribly, dies inside the locked nursery. And now there is no escape, as tortured spirits from the sinister past rise up to tell the true terror of the unloved.

CREATURE

A terrible secret lurks beneath the wholesome surface of Silverdale, Colorado, where well-behaved students make their parents and teachers proud, and the football team never—ever—loses. But soon, some of the parents in Silverdale will begin to uncover the unimaginable secret that can turn a loving child murderous . . .

"It's two in the morning, Chuck. And Jeff isn't home yet."

Chuck groaned. "And for that you woke me up? Jeez, Char, when I was his age, I was out all night half the time."

"Maybe you were," Charlotte replied tightly. "And maybe your parents didn't care. But I do, and I'm about to call the police."

At that, Chuck came completely awake. "What the hell do you want to do a thing like that for?" he demanded, switching on the light and staring at Charlotte as if he thought she'd lost her mind.

"Because I'm worried about him," Charlotte flared, concern for her son overcoming her fear of her husband's tongue. "Because I don't like what's been happening with him and I don't like the way he's been acting. And I certainly don't like not knowing where he is at night!"

Clutching the robe protectively to her throat, she turned and hurried out of the bedroom. She was already downstairs when Chuck, shoving his own arms into the sleeves of an ancient woolen robe he'd insisted on keeping despite its frayed edges and honeycomb of moth holes, caught up with her.

"Now just hold on," he said, taking the phone from her hands and putting it back on the small desk in the den. "I'm not going to have you getting Jeff into trouble with the police just because you want to mother-hen him."

"Mother-hen him!" Charlotte repeated. "For God's sake, Chuck! He's only seventeen years old! And it's the middle of the night, and there's nowhere in Silverdale he could be! Everything's closed. So unless he's already in trouble, where is he?"

"Maybe he stayed overnight with a friend," Chuck began, but Charlotte shook her head.

"He hasn't done that since he was a little boy. And if he had, he would have called." Even as she uttered the words, she knew she didn't believe them. A year ago—a few months ago; even a few weeks ago—she would have trusted Jeff to keep her informed of where he was and what he was doing. But now? She didn't know.

Nor could she explain her worries to Chuck, since he insisted on believing there was nothing wrong; that Jeff was simply growing up and testing his wings.

As she was searching for the right words, the words to express her fears without further rousing her husband's anger, the front door opened and Jeff came in.

He'd already closed the door behind him and started up the stairs when he caught sight of his parents standing in the den in their bathrobes, their eyes fixed on him. He gazed at them stupidly for a second, almost as if he didn't recognize them, and for a split-second Charlotte thought he looked stoned.

"Jeff?" she said. Then, when he seemed to pay no attention to her, she called out again, louder this time. "Jeff!"

His eyes hooded, her son turned to gaze at her. "What?" he asked, his voice taking on the same sullen tone that had become so familiar to her lately.

"I want an explanation," Charlotte went on. "It's after two A.M., and I want to know where you've been."

"Out," Jeff said, and started to turn away.

"Stop right there, young man!" Charlotte commanded. She marched into the foyer and stood at the bottom of the stairs, then reached out and switched on the chandelier that hung in the stairwell. A bright flood of light bathed Jeff's face, and Charlotte gasped. His face was streaked with dirt, and on his cheeks there were smears of blood. There were black circles under Jeff's eyes—as if he hadn't slept in days—and he was breathing hard, his chest heaving as he panted.

Then he lifted his right hand to his mouth, and before he began sucking on his wounds, Charlotte could see that the skin was torn away from his knuckles.

"My God," she breathed, her anger suddenly draining away. "Jeff, what's happened to you?"

His eyes narrowed. "Nothing," he mumbled, and once more started to mount the stairs.

"Nothing?" Charlotte repeated. She turned to Chuck, now standing in the door to the den, his eyes, too, fixed on their son. "Chuck, look at him. Just look at him!"

"You'd better tell us what happened, son," Chuck said. "If you're in some kind of trouble—"

Jeff whirled to face them, his eyes now blazing with the same anger that had frightened Linda Harris earlier that evening. "I don't know what's wrong!" he shouted. "Linda broke up with me tonight, okay? And it pissed me off! Okay? So I tried to smash up a tree and I went for a walk. *Okay?* Is that okay with you, Mom?"

"Jeff—" Charlotte began, shrinking away from her son's sudden fury. "I didn't mean . . . we only wanted to—"

But it was too late.

"Can't you just leave me alone?" Jeff shouted.

He came off the bottom of the stairs, towering over the much smaller form of his mother. Then, with an abrupt movement, he reached out and roughly shoved Charlotte aside, as if swatting a fly. She felt a sharp pain in her shoulder as her body struck the wall, and then she collapsed to the floor. For a split-second Jeff stared blankly at his mother, as if he was puzzled about what had happened to her, and then, an anguished wail boiling up from somewhere deep within him, he turned and slammed out the front door.

Secret rituals masked in science . . . hidden cellars where steel cages gleam coldly against the dark . . . a cry of unfathomable rage and pain . . . In Silverdale no one is safe from . . . Creature.

John Saul is "a writer with the touch for raising gooseflesh," says the *Detroit News,* **and bestseller after bestseller has proved over and over his mastery for storytelling and his genius at creating heart-stopping suspense. Enter his chilling world, and prepare to realize your own hidden fears . . .**

Available wherever Bantam paperbacks are sold!

(And now, turn the page for an exciting preview of John Saul's new masterpiece of terror, SECOND CHILD.)

*An isolated enclave on the coast of Maine
provides the eerie backdrop
to this terrifying tale . . .*

SECOND CHILD
by John Saul

Secret Cove. Here, ruggedly beautiful and remote, bordered by dark woods and deserted beaches, a postcard-perfect village harbors the mansions of the wealthy—families who have summered in splendid seclusion at Secret Cove for generations.

Secret Cove. Here, one hundred years ago, on the night of the annual August Moon Ball, a shy and lovely servant girl committed a single, unspeakable act of violence. An act so shocking its legacy lives still in Secret Cove.

And now, long after the horror of that night has faded to shuddery legend, a tale whispered by children around summer campfires, an unholy terror is about to be reborn. Now, in Secret Cove, one family is about to feel the icy hand of supernatural fear . . . as Melissa Holloway, shy and troubled and just thirteen years old, comes to know the blood-drenched secret that waits behind a locked attic door. . . .

When Polly MacIver awoke just before dawn that morning, she had not the slightest presentiment that she was about to die. As her mind swam lazily in the ebbing tide of sleep, she found herself giggling silently at the memory of the dream that had just roused her. It had been Thanksgiving Day in the dream, and the house was filled with people. Some of them were familiar to her. Tom was sprawled out on the floor, his big frame stretched in front of the fireplace as he studied a chessboard on which Teri had apparently trapped his queen. Teri herself was sitting cross-legged on the carpet, grinning impudently at her father's predicament. There were others scattered around the living room—more, indeed, than Polly would have thought the room could hold. But the dream had had a logic of its own, and it hadn't seemed to matter how many people, strange and familiar, had come in—the room seemed magically to expand for them. It was a happy occasion filled with good cheer until Polly had gone to the kitchen to inspect the dinner. [There, disaster awaited her.] She must have turned the oven too high, for curls of smoke were drifting up from the corners of the door. But as she bent over to open the oven door, she was not concerned, for exactly the same thing had happened too many times before. For Polly, cooking was an art she had never come close to mastering. She opened the door and, sure enough, thick smoke poured out into the kitchen, engulfing her, then rolling on through the small dining room and into the living room, where the coughing of her guests and the impatient yowl of her daughter finally jarred her awake.

The memory of the dream began to fade from her mind, and Polly stretched languidly, then rolled over to snuggle against the warmth of Tom's body. Outside, a summer storm was building, and just as she was about to drift back into sleep, a bolt of lightning slashed through the faint grayness of dawn, instantly followed by a thunderclap that jerked her fully awake. She sat straight up in bed, gasping in shock at the sharp retort.

Instantly, she was seized by a fit of coughing as smoke filled her lungs.

Her eyes widened with sudden fear. The smoke was real, not a vestige of the dream.

A split second later she heard the crackling of flames.

Throwing the covers back, Polly grabbed her husband's shoulder and shook him violently. "Tom! Tom!"

With what seemed like agonizing slowness, Tom rolled over, moaned, then reached out to her. She twisted away from him, fumbling for the lamp on her nightstand before she found the switch.

Nothing happened.

"Tom!" she screamed, her voice rising with the panic building inside her. "Wake up! The house is on fire!"

Tom came awake, instantly rising and shoving his arms into the sleeves of his bathrobe.

Polly, wearing nothing but her thin nylon negligee, ran to the door and grasped the knob, only to jerk her hand reflexively away from its searing heat. "Teri!" she moaned, her voice breaking as she spoke her daughter's name. "Oh, God, Tom. We have to get Teri out."

But Tom was already pushing her aside. Wrapped in one of the wool blankets from the bed, he covered the brass doorknob with one of its corners before trying to turn it. Finally he pulled the door open an inch.

Smoke poured through the gap, a penetrating cloud of searing fog that reached toward them with angry fingers, clutching at them, trying to draw them into its suffocating grasp.

Buried in the formless body of smoke was the glowing soul of the fire itself. Polly instinctively shrank away from the monster that had engulfed her home, and when Tom spoke to her, his shouted words seemed to echo dimly from afar.

"I'll get Teri. Go out the window!"

Frozen with terror, Polly saw the door open wider; a split second later her husband disappeared into the maw of the beast that had invaded her home.

The door slammed shut.

Polly wanted to go after him, to follow Tom into the fire, to hold onto him as they went after her daughter. Without thinking, she moved toward the door, but then his words resounded in her mind.

"Go out the window!"

A helpless moan strangling in her throat, she dragged herself across the room to the window and pulled it open. She breathed the fresh air outside, then looked down.

Fifteen feet below her lay the concrete driveway that connected the street in front to the garage behind the house. There was no ledge, no tree, not even a drainpipe to hang onto. If she jumped, surely she would break her legs.

She shrank back from the window and turned to the door once

more. She had started across the smoke-filled room when her foot touched something soft.

The bedspread, lying in a heap at the foot of the bed. She snatched it up, wrapping it around her body, then, like Tom a few minutes earlier, used one of its corners to protect her fingers from the searing heat of the door. Drawing her breath in slowly, filtering the smoke through the thick padding of the spread, she filled her lungs with air.

At last, battling with the fear that threatened to overwhelm her, she pulled the door open.

The fire in the hall, instantly sucking in the fresh air from the open window, rose up in front of her, its crackle building into a vicious roar.

Time seemed to slow down, each second dragging itself out for an eternity.

Flames reached out to her, and Polly was helpless to pull herself away as panic clasped her in its paralyzing grip. She felt the burning heat against her face, even felt the blisters begin to form wherever her skin was exposed.

She heard a strange, soft sound, like the sizzling of oil in a hot skillet, and instinctively reached up to touch her hair.

Her hair was gone, devoured by the hungry fire, and she stared blankly for a moment at the ashy residue on her fingertips. What had been a thick mass of dark blond hair only a moment ago was now only an oddly greasy smudge on the blistered skin of her hand.

Her mind began closing down, rejecting what she saw, denying the searing heat that all but overwhelmed her.

She staggered backward, the bedspread tangling around her feet as if it had joined forces with the fire to destroy her.

Faintly, as if in the distance somewhere impossibly far beyond the confines of the house, she heard Tom's voice, calling out to Teri.

She heard vague thumpings, as if he might be pounding on a door somewhere.

Then nothing.

Nothing but the hiss and chatter of the flames, dancing before her, hypnotizing her.

Backing away, stumbling and tripping, she retreated from the fury of the fire.

She bumped into something, something hard and ungiving, and though her eyes remained fixed on the inferno that was already invading the bedroom, her hand groped behind her.

And felt nothing.

Panic seized her again, for suddenly the familiar space of the bedroom seemed to vanish, leaving her alone with the consuming flames.

Slowly, her mind assembling information piece by piece, she realized that she had reached the open window.

Whimpering, she sat down on the ledge and began to swing her legs through the gap between the sill and the open casement; her right leg first, then her left.

At last she was able to turn her back on the fire. Gripping the window frame, she stared out into the faintly graying dawn for a moment, then let her gaze shift downward toward the concrete below.

She steeled herself, and clinging to the bedspread, let herself slip over the ledge.

Just as she began to drop away from the window, the corner of the bedspread still inside the room caught on something. Polly felt the pull, found herself unreasonably speculating on what might have snagged it.

The handle of the radiator?

A stray nail that had worked loose from the floor molding?

Falling! Suddenly she was upside down, slipping out of the shroud of the bedspread.

Her fingers grasped at the material; it slipped away as if coated with oil.

She dropped toward the concrete headfirst, only beginning to raise her arms to break her fall as her skull crashed against the driveway.

She felt nothing; no pain at all.

There was only a momentary sense of surprise, and a small cracking sound from within her neck as her vertebrae shattered and crushed her spinal cord.

It had been no more than three minutes since she had awakened, laughing quietly, from her dream.

Now the quiet laughter was over, and Polly MacIver was dead.

Teri MacIver stood rooted on the lawn in front of the house, her right hand clutching at the lapels of her thin terry-cloth bathrobe with all the modesty of her nearly fifteen years. Her eyes were fixed on the blaze that now engulfed the small two-story house that had been her home for the last ten years. It was an old house, built fifty years earlier when San Fernando had still been a small farming town in the California valley of the same name. Built entirely of wood, the house had baked in the sun for half a century, its wood slowly turning into tinder, and tonight, when the fire had started, the flames had raced through the rooms with a speed that stunned

Teri. It was as if one moment the house had been whole; the next it had been swallowed by flames.

Teri was only vaguely aware of what was going on around her. In the distance, a siren wailed, growing steadily louder, but Teri barely heard it. Her mind was filled with the roar of the fire, and the crackling of the siding as it curled back upon itself and began to fall away from the framework of the house, venting the interior to the fresh air that only fed the raging flames.

Her parents.

Where were they? Had they gotten out? Forcing her eyes away from the oddly hypnotic inferno, she glanced around. Down the block, someone was running toward her, but the figure was no more than a shadow in the breaking dawn.

Voices began to penetrate her consciousness then, people shouting to each other, asking each other what had happened.

Then, over the roar of the fire and the babble of voices, she heard a scream. It came from the house, seemingly unmuffled by the already crumbling walls. The sharp sound released Teri from her paralysis, and she ran around to the driveway, her eyes wide as she stared up to the second floor and her parents' bedroom.

She saw her mother, a dark silhouette against the glow of the fire. She was wrapped in something—a blanket, perhaps, or the bedspread. Teri watched as her mother's legs came over the windowsill, and a second later she saw her jump . . . then turn in the air as the bedspread tightened around her legs.

Her mother seemed to hang for a moment, suspended in midair. A scream built in Teri's throat, only to be cut off a second later as her mother slid free from the swaddles and plunged headfirst to the driveway below.

Had she heard the sound as her mother's head struck the concrete, or did she imagine it?

Teri began running then, but her feet were mired in mud, it seemed to take forever before she reached the spot where her mother lay crumpled and still on the driveway, one arm flung out as if reaching out to her daughter, as if even in death she were grasping for life.

"M-Mom?" Teri stammered, her hand falling away from her robe to tentatively touch her mother. Then her voice rose to an anguished wail. *"M-o-m!"*

There was no response, and as Teri became aware of someone running up the sidewalk, she threw herself on Polly's body, cradling her mother's head in her lap, stroking the blistered cheek of the woman who only a few hours ago had stroked her own before kissing her good night. "No," she whimpered, her eyes flooding with tears. "Oh, no. Please, God, don't let Mommy die." But even as she uttered the words, Teri already knew somewhere deep inside her that it was too late, that her mother was already gone.

She felt gentle hands on her shoulders and slowly looked up to see Lucy Barrow, from across the street. "She's dead." Teri's voice broke as she spoke the words. The admission seemed to release a tide of emotion that had been locked inside her. Covering her face with her hands, she began to sob, her body shaking.

Lucy, her own mind all but numbed by the sight of Polly Mac-Iver's seared and broken body, pulled Teri to her feet and began leading her back down the driveway. "Your father . . ." she said. "Where's your father? Did he get out?"

Teri's hands dropped away from her face. For a moment her shocked eyes flickered with puzzlement. She started to speak, but before the words emerged from her mouth there was a sharp crack, followed instantly by a crash.

Lucy Barrow grasped Teri's arm tightly, pulling her down the driveway as the roof of the house collapsed into the fire and the flames shot up into the brightening sky.

Three fire trucks clogged the street in front of the MacIvers' house, and a tangle of hoses snaked along the sidewalk to the hydrant on the corner. An ambulance had taken Polly's body away more than an hour before, but as more and more neighbors arrived to gape in dazed horror at the smoldering ruins of the house, others would point with macabre fascination to the spot where Teri's mother had plunged to her death. The newcomers would stare at the driveway for a few seconds, visualizing the corpse and imagining with a shudder, the panic Polly must have felt as she died.

Did she know, at least, that her daughter had survived the fire?

No, of course not.

Heads shook sadly; tongues clucked with sympathy. Then the attention of the crowd shifted back to the smoking wreckage. Most of the beams still stood, and parts of the second floor had held intact even when the roof collapsed. Now, as sunlight cast the ruins into sharp relief, the house looked like a desiccated blackened skeleton.

Teri, who had spent the last two hours sitting mutely in the Barrows' living room, unable to pull her eyes away from the spectacle of the fire, finally emerged onto the porch. Next to her, Lucy Barrow hovered protectively, her voice trembling as she tried to convince Teri to go back inside.

"I can't," whispered Teri. "I have to find my father. He—He's—" Her voice broke off, but her eyes returned to the ruins across the street.

Lucy Barrow unconsciously bit her lip in a vain attempt to take some of Teri's pain onto herself. "He might have gotten out," she ventured, her quavering voice belying her words.

Teri said nothing, but started once more across the street, still clad in the bathrobe she'd worn when she escaped the inferno. An eerie silence fell over the block, the murmurs of the bystanders dying away as she moved steadily through the crowd, which parted silently to let her pass.

At last Teri came to the front yard of what had been her home. She stood still staring at the charred wood of the house's framework and the blackened bricks of its still-standing chimney. She took a tentative step toward the remains of the front porch, then felt a firm hand on her arm.

"You can't go in there, miss."

Teri's breath caught, but she turned to look into the kindly gray eyes of one of the firemen. "M-My father—" she began.

"We're going in now," the fireman said. "If he's in there, we'll find him."

Without a word, Teri watched as two firefighters, clad in heavily padded overcoats, their hands protected by thick gloves, worked their way carefully into the wreckage. The front door had been chopped away, and inside, the base of the stairway was clearly visible. The men started up, testing each step before trusting it to hold their weight. After what seemed an eternity, they finally reached the second floor. They moved through the house, visible first through one window, then another. From one of the rooms an entire wall, along with most of the floor, had burned away. As the firemen gingerly moved from beam to beam, they appeared to be balanced on some kind of blackened scaffolding. At last they moved out of Teri's sight as they carefully worked their way toward her room at the back of the house.

Ten minutes later the fireman with the kind, gray eyes emerged from the front door and approached Teri, who stood waiting, her eyes fixed on him.

"I'm sorry," he said, his voice made gruff by the memory of the charred remains of Tom MacIver which he had found in front of the still-closed door to Teri's bedroom at the back of the house. "He was trying to get you out. He didn't know you'd already gotten away." His large hand rested reassuringly on Teri's shoulder for a moment, but then he turned away and began issuing the orders for Tom MacIver's body to be removed from the ruins.

Teri stood where she was for a few more seconds. Her eyes remained fixed on the house as if she were still uncertain of the truth of what she had just been told. Finally Lucy Barrow's voice penetrated her thoughts.